ANGEL WALK

ANGEL WALK

KATHERINE GOVIER

Little, Brown and Company (Canada) Limited
Boston • New York • Toronto • London

Hardcover edition first published by
Little, Brown and Company (Canada) Limited in 1996.

Canadian Cataloguing in Publication Data

Govier, Katherine, 1948 –
Angel Walk

ISBN 0–316–31906-6 (bound)
ISBN 0–316–31048-9 (pbk.)

I. Title.

PS8563.0875A54 1996   C813'.54   C96–931303-9
PR9199.3.G68A54 1996

Cover Design: SARAH PERKINS

Cover Photos: CANADIAN DEPARTMENT OF NATIONAL DEFENCE
(NEGATIVE NO. PL14357)

Interior Design and Page Composition: JOSEPH GISINI
OF ANDREW SMITH GRAPHICS, INC.

Printed and bound in Canada
by BEST BOOK MANUFACTURERS INC.

LITTLE, BROWN AND COMPANY (CANADA) LIMITED
148 YORKVILLE AVENUE,
TORONTO, ON, CANADA, M5R 1C2

10 9 8 7 6 5 4 3 2 1

For my parents,
for my children,
and for John.

Chapter One

CHRISTOPHER "TYKE" DITCHBURN TIPTOED PAST THE PIANO draped with a Spanish shawl and over the spare hand-woven rug, intending to switch on the lamp. Seated in the darkness in a Mission-style chair was his mother. Erect, she was just visible, staring fixedly into the winter garden. Corinne Ditchburn, the photographer. He saw her that way, as a woman with a name, a title even. He always had, even as a boy. At the sight of her, he was suffused with admiration, rage and the half-humorous indulgence that had replaced his long-ago hurt.

The lampshade, made of tiny gold glass beads, was from the island of Murano in the shallow sea basin off Venice. She had brought it home from the war; he didn't know the story. It hung over the long pine table, which had belonged to her mother, Eliza, and had been fashioned in Parry Sound by her grandfather. The carpenter grandfather, a fearsome bearded Irish Protestant, had also left a tool chest where Cory's papers and letters were jealously guarded against her son's intrusion. On the wall, framed and covered by glass, was a woman's kimono exquisitely patterned with lilies, another war memento the meaning of which he did not understand. The house, the garden, her few treasures would be his one day, although until now he'd had little hope she would divulge the private self they sheltered.

"Tyke?" Her voice was deep and dry. "I know you're there. No use trying to surprise me."

He reached the lamp and pulled the chain; a cone of amber light fell over her. Her hair waved back from her forehead thick and white, short as a man's; her long neck was lined and her hands lay motionless in her lap. Her eyes were grey and steady, though her sight was blurred now — old age had done that. Her sharp tongue, however, was unchecked.

"I wasn't." He'd never succeeded in putting anything past her, though she never stopped suspecting him.

Getting her agreement to have the Retrospective go ahead was a minor miracle. For years, she claimed that any summing up of her life's work would mean she'd never work again. "They'll think they've nailed me down." After she stopped saying it would kill her, after she admitted that in fact she wanted an exhibition, she began to cavil about who would do it. She had refused poor Professors Sullivan and Moore, though they had published critical essays about her work for the last decade, and were responsible, in part, for her current high standing. "None of those brown-nosing scoundrels," she said, including all academics and most art dealers, save her own ever-loyal Miss del Zotto.

Then a certain Maida Kirk, the Curator of Photography at the Royal Ontario Museum of Art, put in a request and got lucky.

"She's agreed. I guess your timing is right," Tyke had said bemusedly over the telephone. "She keeps promising to die."

Maida Kirk had nipped her victory shout at its root. She was a gentle soul, Tyke knew, pot-bellied and unpretty, but when she spoke he heard a new proprietorial tone. "Now that she's agreed, she can't go and die on us." Not on the Royal Ontario Museum of Art. He began to see his mother's point.

"The catch is..." said Tyke.

The catch was that Miss Ditchburn insisted on working with him, her son. "Oh. Well," said Maida Kirk, pondering.

"Perhaps she thinks I'll be easy to handle," he apologized. As he had proven to be for most of his fifty-five years.

"I wasn't trying to sneak up." He repeated, treading more noisily on the hardwood and putting out a hand. The old woman, lean and hard and forbidding in every way, even in the line of her arm as she reached for him, seemed to scour him with her unclouded grey eyes. He never knew if she really saw him.

So here it is, Cory thought. At the end of her life her son had come to record her confession. And in cahoots with the Flounder. Amazing how that curator Maida whatsit looks like a flounder. Flounder: Now there's a fish for you. A bottom feeder, normal until it's adult and then all of a sudden it turns over and starts swimming on its side along the bottom. It goes flat as paper and one eye even migrates so both can look. She ate one alive in Yokohama. It was impaled on spikes at either end and the sides sliced. So tender with green mustard.

She smiled inadvertently. If she could stomach a live flounder, she could stomach anything. Now all she had to stomach was herself, since she'd decided to do this thing. She had refused for a long time. She said no whenever they were interested in her because of Albert Bloom. When all they wanted was pictures of war, she said no, because that was fifty years ago and it isn't what she did now. But this time she said yes. Vanity wins out in the end. Vanity and the need to —

She sought the words. *To justify herself.* No. Words were not her medium. Not justify. Not explain. *See.* The need to *see* it all, one more time.

FIGURE 1

Photographer unknown

Corinne Ditchburn

Parry Sound, Ontario, taken on the North Road
in front of the elementary school,
between 1935 and 1938
Collection of Christopher Ditchburn, Toronto

Corinne Ditchburn as a young woman teaching school is rendered here by a friend? colleague? relative? Only a narrow track, the square schoolhouse and a few clapboard houses form a background. Squinting in the sun, burdened with an armload of primers, she is less than willing to be captured on film. Nor does she appear to be one of those teachers on whose skirts the children hang;

she has a cool, assessing eye, and a tilt of her head that indicates she is detained here for only the briefest of moments. She is speaking, her mouth in motion. Given her subsequent career, one might be tempted to interpret her words as cautionary: Is she telling the photographer how to compose the shot? Her hair is cropped and lifted by the wind, her face open and boyish, her expression ready.

TYKE PULLED THE CORDS TO LOWER THE BLINDS, LEVOLOR blinds. They could be left in place, the angle adjusted by twirling a plastic dropper, but she insisted on yanking them up to the very top of the windows. Before she could complain, he spoke.

"The photographs have arrived from del Zotto," he said. "I've got them all in boxes here. We'll have a look through."

While she watched, he began to clear the long single-plank pine table. He pulled on a pair of soft white cotton gloves. They made his hands cartoony, the hands of a Mickey Mouse. Or sinister, the hands of someone performing an autopsy, thought Cory.

The big white hands opened the top portfolio and, with eerie delicacy, removed the first cardboard folder. He opened it and lifted the thin veiling paper that lay over the print.

"I've sorted all the prints and all the negatives starting with the thirties. But I'd like you to look at them, just to be sure they're what we think they are. Can you see in this light?"

It depended on her mood. She was like the deaf man who won't answer when spoken to but hears a whisper across the room.

"I haven't looked at those in forty years."

He returned to her side and this time, when she caught his arm, there was warmth between them. He led her to a chair and slid the large exhibition print toward her. "Here's what it says," he said, reading. "Epiphany fire in Chelsea, 1937. Can you tell me about it?"

Cory put her long, tendon-striped forearms on the table. Under the light, her face pulled up close to the photograph, she scanned its surface, side to side, up and down — as if she were a beam of light, searching, as if she could sense what lay on the paper by exposing her face to it.

She laughed, a sudden bark. "Oh my god, there's Aunt Eunice in her hat. The huge one is Valentine. Gone to wherever now."

"Do you remember when you took this?"

"Of course. It was the fire. That first day I arrived in London."

Chapter Two

"SO THIS IS HOW ROBERT'S GIRL TURNED OUT?"

Aunt Eunice was tall, with a wide brow and unsentimental grey eyes. The wave of white hair that crested about them was so much like Cory's father's that Cory stared. A maid dressed in black and white was visible through the small bevelled panes of the French door. Further behind stood a man, heavier, possessive.

"This is how," said Cory. She was nearly as tall as her aunt and her shoulders were broader. She had the wide clear brow but her face was triangular, narrowing to a sensitive mouth and pointed chin.

There was no smile.

"A Ditchburn through and through. Just as I'd heard," said the older woman. They held each other's gaze.

The man pushed through the door. His waistcoat was chained across the front. His hand strayed across the stretched fabric.

"Who, may I ask, is Robert?"

"Robert was my brother, you'll recall, Harry."

"What does that make her to you?" asked Harry, attempting to stare Cory down.

"A niece, I should say," said Aunt Eunice dryly, pointing at Cory's valise. "Take this, will you, Leary?"

The maid, awaiting this command to dart forward, picked up the bag with a furtive grin at the young stranger. Cory swayed, as if to step in, watching her aunt.

"I'm warning you — don't get used to my hospitality. I'm only going to keep you here a few nights, and then you'll be on your own."

Cory was through the French doors now and into the main hall. To her right another pair of doors opened: A drawing room, where a coal fire brightened the grate.

"Come in, come in," said Eunice impatiently. "We won't bite."

The candles leapt upward in their wall sconces. Little repeat flames were reflected all over the room, in polished brass and silver. Aunt Eunice was a widow. Her husband had been rich, a financier; she had met him in Toronto but his business had taken them to London. She looked Cory up and down.

"I saw you once, when I visited Parry Sound. You were only little. I doubt you remember. I never went back. Your Uncle Charles," Eunice said, "didn't hold much with relations. He said they always wanted something from him, and most of the time they did."

The tea scalded Cory's mouth.

"Remember the advice Robinson Crusoe's father gave him when he set out? 'The middle station in life is the happiest. Don't aspire to go up, or down, if you can have the middle,'" said Eunice.

"The rich see the worst in people," agreed Harry, patting his waistcoat.

"I wouldn't know."

Cory set down her immense green cup on its gold saucer. The surfaces in London were slippery, the conversations too. A brass rhinoceros in a corner of the room winked at her with a jewelled eye.

"Tell me, what do you think of London?" Harry had not been introduced, but it didn't seem to bother him.

"It's laid out funny. All the streets are crooked."

"*Laid out*?" he snorted. "My dear, London was never laid out at all. London *grew*. From footpaths. And cart tracks. Roman roads. Ride the buses, that's what you must do."

"I intend to," said Cory. "After I find a room." Because she could not hold it back any longer, she spoke directly to the unknown but so familiar woman. "I won't impose. You've given me enough."

Aunt Eunice frowned. "I please myself. I want to do something for my brother's child. It's nothing personal. There are people I'd like you to meet. You sketch, I believe."

"Not any more."

"Your father used to send me your drawings. One I liked was of a wedding party on a railway cart. I kept that one."

"I have a camera now," said Cory.

"Why a camera?"

Cory couldn't tell whether Aunt Eunice was actually interested, or just pretending.

"It's drawing with light."

"What do you draw, with light?"

"Rocks. And animals." Cory saw by Eunice's face she'd caught her interest. "If you let an animal alone, he lets you alone. If he's dangerous, you know. People are unpredictable."

Aunt Eunice laughed. "Ditchburns speak plainly. It's our worst habit, don't you agree?"

Harry smiled back at her. "I withhold judgment, darling," he said.

"You may be right about people, Corinne, but before you renounce the species altogether, perhaps you'd care to meet a few more of us. You might make something of the opportunity."

The round dining table with its white cloth glowed like a giant mushroom in the dark, wood-panelled room. The silver chandelier had been lit; a serving man with a pole hoisted it up to its hook. The guests clustered in the drawing room around the harpsichord. It was, said Harry, a very good one, made by a man who'd since lost his reputation.

"Ah-ah-ah. Does that make him disreputable?" joked the solicitor.

"Not at all," smiled Harry. "He simply makes bad harpsichords. He deliberately lowered the quality of his product, once it gained general acceptance."

"He could have had a lot more fun becoming disreputable," said a very fat man, Valentine Castlerosse, whom they called Count.

The actress pulled at the sides of her black satin cocktail gown. It was bias-cut, put together with half a dozen trapezoidal pieces of material, so that it fit intricately and intimately over her pelvis bones. Cory recognized the style from copies: Eliza, her mother, had struggled over just such patterns in her front room, for her Parry Sound customers. She'd have made Cory one, but Cory wouldn't take it. She wore a serviceable navy wool, which hung loose around her waist.

At the table Cory watched her aunt, imagining that she was eating porridge in Parry Sound instead of lamb with mint sauce in Chelsea. Her father had regarded eating as an anti-social activity and always sat with his napkin tucked under his chin, never looking up. That hermit fisherman and this imperious imperial grande dame were brother and sister. What connected them? Blood and memory, she supposed. But with her spectacles and her powdered face, it was impossible to tell how powerfully they surged in Eunice.

The solicitor was offering his assessment of colonials and refugees who came to London. "Ah-ah-ah the Indians will never hurt you. Maybe a little fraud, that's all. The Africans who first came here were great people; yes, religious, family people. But aaah now, these Jews from Europe, they are *trouble.* Artists and intellectuals to begin with —"

"I should think we're honoured to receive the thinking people from Germany —" said the actress.

"Oh, no, no, no," continued the solicitor, "you don't understand. These are the *dregs*, the dregs; otherwise Hitler would want to keep them himself, wouldn't he?"

The mirrors on the facing wall made Cory confront her own face. Pale, and shaped like a trowel, its only hint of mirth was the small thrusting chin with its dimple. Her short brown hair and pale eyelashes all but disappeared in the candlelight. As she tried to follow the conversation, her face blurred and twisted this way and that in the glass, like a fish trapped in shallow water.

"The game is up," said one thin man dolefully. "The game is up, that's all I have to say. New year or not. We can't go on as we have."

"Your Lord Beaverbrook's gone and said the poor ought to spend more and that if they did, they'd become richer. He said *he* was spending more. And I can tell you, it's true. His Christmas decorations are more extravagant than ever this season. He had pine trees flown in from the Miramichi, and the champagne —"

"Dear Max," said Aunt Eunice. "He's often right about these matters. It's only that his phrases are too definite for the English. He lacks —"

"— polish?"

"An element of hypocrisy, I should say. Decorum. You know it's all you English really care about."

"I think what he wrote was truly shocking, *truly*," insisted the actress.

"Do you?" asked Valentine. "But he only said society hostesses ought to give more parties, and that ladies ought to buy more pretty frocks." He bestowed on her a charming smile. "Of course, you've got such a pretty one already."

"You never ought to have let him out of Canada, Eunice," said the solicitor.

"Oh, we didn't let him out, we *chased* him out — didn't we, Cory?" said Eunice. "Back in the early days, Cory's father, my brother Robert, had dealings with Mr. Aitken."

"You don't say," said someone. Heads rotated to reassess Cory.

"So what do you know of our Max Aitken, then?" murmured Valentine in Cory's ear.

"He was a blue-sky drummer." It was what her father always said.

The bloated face looked inexplicably pleased. "How marvellous. Did you hear that? He was a blue-sky drummer?"

"Of course he was," said Aunt Eunice, faintly miffed. "Everyone knows that. Commercial traveller. Regular sort of thing. He sold intangibles. Ideas, I suppose you could say. Insurance policies. Money schemes."

"Extraordinary," said the vicar. "When you think of where he is now. But then I suppose this is what the new world is all about, that very peculiar — I suppose it's rare enough — but that very disturbing, I think you'd have to say, way people have of straying from their origins, of getting up into the ranks where, of course, they are completely out of place."

Valentine beamed at Cory, his waxy face ashine. "Say it again, my dear. Blue. Sky. Drummer. Oh, you've just done me the most terrific favour."

"This man is the most notorious gossip in London,"

said Eunice. "He is also the very shadow of Lord Beaverbrook and responsible, I should think, for that man's image in the press — that is, the press other than his own newspaper. You've just given him a fine little arrow which he will use to puncture his benefactor's ego."

Cory felt the world shrink a little. They used to decry Max Aitken in her mother's house in Parry Sound, too. Aitken was the demon who ruined Robert, took his money and lost it, so that the poor man saw nothing for it but to go back to those miserable bits of rock along the water and fish with the Indians. Or so Eliza and her family used to say: In fact, Robert Ditchburn had never considered himself ruined at all. Only happily released from a world of buying and selling dreams, to a world of living them.

"Ah-ah-ah, getting back to the point, unpropertied people ought to save," the solicitor went on. "It's a skill, by means of which they can gain a few advantages for their children."

"The Tories may repudiate him now but they'll come round to his view soon enough. They always do. They'll come around and the worst of it is they won't even know they've come around, they'll think it was all their idea anyway."

"He's for the little man, he always was —"

"What nonsense, Valentine. All the little men were always getting ruined by his manoeuvres."

"You're right of course, Eunice," conceded the Count. "You always are." But there was more at stake, suddenly. He quaffed his glass of wine. He raised his voice.

"You see, a man has many parts. And while he has never stinted to squash a few who got in his way, Beaverbrook, in power, *is* for the little man. He is because he was a little man and in his heart he still loves the little man. But in the flesh — that being at the end of the day in control of his being — he is in favour of spending because he does not want the parties to end. He wants to woo those ladies in their pretty dresses. He wants to make love to them! He wants to hire more secretaries so that he can make them run when he shouts, and make love to them too, after they cry. He wants life, and as much of it as he can get."

There was a palpable tension. Foreheads furrowed; serviettes were folded.

"Life!" cried the Count. "Do you know what that means?" The tomato aspic trembled in its crystal bowl.

"Valentine! Do behave!" said Eunice.

There was silence. Cory sipped her water; the hairs on her neck stood up.

"Well you may be right, Viscount," said the vicar, draining the last drops of his own wine. "But if you are it only proves one thing, and that is that the man is not a Conservative and never was."

At last Valentine laughed, and the black lines of his eyebrows wiggled like worms in his loose flesh. Just then maids entered with a wobbly layered trifle and a great round of Stilton cheese. The diners took turns digging into its soft centre with a long-handled silver spoon. When at last they rose, overfed and longing for coffee in the drawing room, Eunice announced other plans.

"Don't settle in, people; we must go out to light the fire!"

By the door she donned a three-cornered hat, which made her look like an actor in a Venetian carnival; all the guests pulled Wellington boots out of bags they had deposited with Leary. Thus shod, full-stomached and grumbling under their breath, they marched into the darkness. Eunice led, carrying a candle, which pressed the night back from her face.

"It's wet," she warned.

The ground squished underfoot.

"Did you know that under this part of Chelsea there's a secret lake?" asked the vicar.

"Sometimes it's not so secret."

"I shudder to think of the churchyard," he giggled. "The corpses must be floating!"

They sloshed their way toward a fifteen-foot pyramid of dry Christmas trees; bits of tinsel still hung on the brown needles. Someone threw kerosene, and the vicar lit a match. After three tries, flames erupted amidst the needles and ate their way steadily into the pyre. In minutes, accompanied by a great crash, the orange blaze rippled up through the dry needles to the sky.

The actress gave a little cry and retreated, covering her cheeks from the heat. But Cory stayed close. She felt it mark her face, like a brand.

FIGURE 2

Corinne Ditchburn

**Epiphany Fire in Chelsea,
London 1937**

January 6, 1937
Chelsea
Gelatin silver, 34 x 23 cm

*Fitting, that the first image from Corinne's time in Britain
is one of burning. The figures are dwarfed by the flames
but apparently drawn to them with a fervour matching
that of the fire itself. Even here in Ditchburn's early work
she pits humans against elemental disaster of their own
making, portraying them nonetheless in a communal,
even celebratory ritual.*

⁂

OH MY. THAT FIRE. HOW IT THRILLED HER! ALL FIRES. AS A KID,
playing hooky on the island with her Dad, burning garbage
in old oil drums. The deadwood bonfires they used to have
on the shore in fall, their orange flames feasting on inky air.
The rocks beneath the coals would crack, and it sounded
like gunshots: All the kids screamed and ran.

Perhaps she was an incendiary. She was in love with
explosions too. Those savage summer storms out in the Bay,
the lightning's silent eruption into that huge web across the
sky. Take a breath, it's praying time: one steamboat, two
steamboats, three steamboats. Then: crash of thunder.

When she discovered the camera, its little explosion
captivated her. You held the flashgun up beside your head

like a torch. You pressed the shutter, the bulb lit and the world at your feet became for a split second your lighted object.

At first the landscape was not damaged by these explosions: It had only been borrowed from, reproduced. Yes, for that fraction of a second when the flash went off, she was blinded. But *she* set the explosion, she owned it. Afterward, before her was the same landscape, unaltered, except as it would alter normally, the sun having sunk a little lower into the horizon, the bicycle having rolled out of view.

Chapter Three

CORY HIKED THE CITY STREETS UNTIL HER LEGS FELT ABOUT TO splinter, and then jumped on the spiral stairs at the back of a double-decker bus. She sat above the driver and gazed downward as the blunt nose of the bus pushed between bicycles, horse carriages and barrows. Her camera warmed the palm of her right hand, heavy, slim, with rounded ends and beautiful steel fittings. Her most prized possession, it was a 1932 Leica "minicam." She loved the way the name was written on top, in rounded cursive, the tail of the L extended to underline the word as if a careful schoolteacher had done it. It was her father's last purchase. He'd hardly used it before he died; the leather case was smoothed to her hand. Her fingers automatically sought and found the shutter, had memorized the settings. Looking out the bus window, she ran the tips of her forefingers over the crosshatching on the dials, lifted the film advance lever. Then she snapped the cover closed and let it slide on its leather strap around her side and under her arm where it was lost in the folds of her coat.

At Oxford Street she jumped off to see the rag and bone man with his sack. Waiting at the traffic light, she watched a coal lorry drop its load through the basement window of a house on Harley Street. She walked beside the scummy waters of railway canals and in grassy parks where gaunt-cheeked women stalked with sniffing hounds. Tea and toast was all she ate between morning and dark. When she arrived back at the house in Chelsea after walking home along the Embankment from the Houses of Parliament, she was too tired to eat Leary's dinner. Eunice saluted her through the glass doors. Cory was barely aware; she had cast herself into London. The city would be hers. But how? Where was she to fit into this gigantic circus?

"She'll find you a place with some young-uns," Leary whispered, pouring Cory another cup of tea. "You wait, she'll have a plan. It's not like her to proceed without a plan. She's just waiting to see if you're up to it."

Aunt Eunice towered over him by a good six inches, but Lord Beaverbrook was not cowed. He rose on his toes, rocked back once and waited.

They were in Selfridge's party room. Aunt Eunice had taken Cory there, Cory in the ghastly blue frock.

"My brother Robert's girl," said Eunice, pushing her forward. "I told you I'd bring her. Involve her in your doings. For the sake of an old friend."

"Robert Ditchburn!" Lord Beaverbrook seized Cory's tightly proffered hand. "Now there was a fool. Rather paddle a canoe than make money. But he'll die happy. Perhaps it's me who's the fool." He smiled, the grin so wide his lower jaw appeared about to disengage, like a ventriloquist's dummy's.

"He did die," said Cory.

"Oh, my god, don't tell me," said Beaverbrook. His voice carried the hard a's of his Maritime origin, and also its lilt. His skin was as crumpled as a paper bag. His eyes were quick, eager. They scaled her like a knife's edge scales a fish, so that the markings on her flesh must show.

Valentine Castlerosse hove into sight. "It's my favourite Canadian girl!" He drew her away and lay a finger alongside his nose, affecting discretion. "This is where the old man offers you the job of a lifetime, at a lowly wage. But you'll rise like the phoenix."

At that moment a woman with jet-black hair took Max's elbow, and he was gone.

"It depends what you want from the old man," Valentine continued. It made no difference if his subject were present or not. "Generally, he'll give women cash, and save his advice on the market for men. A mistress can get six thousand a year and a cottage."

Cory said nothing.

"I see I'm shocking you. Mind you, you seem to invite it. But you really must have a think about this man, since you've got a connection. He's terribly rich and powerful. Of course, in all the real ways he's failed. I'm talking about the ways which count. You see, everyone reads his papers but they don't pay the slightest attention to what he says in them. Newspapers! They're wrapping fish the next day. Whereas you strike me as someone with higher ambitions."

Cory cocked her head.

"He's generous to the people he loves, but he can never tell for sure if they love him for himself or for the donations."

"You've appointed yourself my guide, I think."

"Yes. You're safe with me: The devil loves his own."

Even so, he wandered off, leaving Cory alone.

When people came near she couldn't think of what to say, so she took to stalking the edges of the room, as if in search of some lost friend or article. The guests left, one after another, putting out their faces for kisses. Cory had found Eunice when Max Aitken caught up to her.

"So, my dear." He put his hands deep into the pockets of his pants, then jerked his fingers sideways so the fabric flared. "I have an idea. We can help each other."

"We can?"

"You want to meet artists."

"My *aunt* wants —" she began.

"No, wait. I have one for you. He's a rather famous artist, fallen on hard times. I took pity on him. I offered him a lot of money to do some portraits. Myself, a few of my friends. He had them sit for him, for an hour or two. He took photographs. Then he disappeared. No money. No portraits. He's refusing to turn them over.

"This artist has no telephone. He hides in something called the Stable Cottage at Ford Manor in Surrey. Why don't you go by and bring back the portraits? Eunice will lend you her motorcar — I assume you can drive? All you Canadian girls are useful that way. See if you can get me my pictures."

"What's the artist's name?" she said.

"Albert Bloom."

Valentine examined his pointed patent shoes. Absently, he rose on his toes and swivelled his heels twice to the side, as if he were about to dance the Charleston. His round torso remained still. Then he looked up. "You're making mischief, Max."

"What's the matter with Albert Bloom?"

As it happened, Cory had seen a painting by Albert Bloom in a gallery on Maddox Street. A woman in a doorway, her back to the viewer, was replacing her blouse, her face half turned, wearing an ambiguous look of injury and achievement. The painting made Cory stop. It cut into her composure, startled her somewhere deep. And it was filled with the light, that orange London twilight she loved.

It wasn't only the woman, and the dark figure at the door. It wasn't only their story. It was the candour, the coarseness of the painter's imagination. It reminded her of that word the solicitor used at Aunt Eunice's Epiphany dinner. *Dregs.* Real people, raw emotions. The life polite London did not want to see.

At a petrol station Cory paid a shilling four pence for a gallon, and was offered a handful of fresh eggs. She asked directions to Ford Manor. She couldn't understand the young man's Surrey speech, and had to trust her sense of direction. But the country was claustrophobic, the roads sunken, with the hedges high above them. Every mile or two there was a crossing, with signposts like a clutch of hands pointing all ways. A trio of cyclists with sheaves of bluebells over their back wheels crowded the road, and, further on, herds of fat sheep were scolded along by yapping dogs. Spring had come. She felt euphoric.

Near Dormansland the road dropped even further; tree roots bulged out of the banks on either side. The flat green fields were above the roof of Aunt Eunice's car. At last she saw the little pub called the Plough. Not far beyond it was the open gate to Ford Manor.

At the top of the hill the road veered hard to the right. Ahead stood a fine large house of dove-coloured stone, with several wings and a sweeping view down over the fields. Left, and beyond, was a pond. Bluebells lay in scattered glory under stands of willow and chestnut trees. The low brick buildings through the entranceway to the courtyard must be the outbuildings attached to the estate. One would be the Stable Cottage where Albert lived.

Cory stopped the car and climbed out. She tucked the camera under her elbow and stepped away from the car into deep grey mud, which bulged over the sides of her shoe. When she tried to lift her foot, the mud sucked the shoe from her heel. She made for grass and, hoping she was not being watched, took off one shoe at a time and wiped the sides on the turf.

FIGURE 3

Corinne Ditchburn

**Greenhouse at Stable Cottage,
Ford Manor**

April, 1937
Surrey, England
Full frame enlargement from original negative, 1993

This realistic image seems to have emerged from a dream — broken glass, crumbling garden tools and a creeping ivy that overtakes all. The man's hand on the door frame, almost camouflaged in the peeling paint, is a threat or a deliverance.

ॐ

LUMINOUS GREEN MOSS COATED THE BARK OF THE TREES. THE greenhouse ahead sagged as if the glass had not broken but melted; it too glowed with phosphorescent rot. She was drawn to the glass house, her camera in front of her. The old door was propped half open. She wondered what the light was like inside.

It was as if she'd dived underwater on a dark day. The greenish refracted light came from all sides, a lighter glow from above. From a pile of garden implements, she picked up a trowel and pushed it into one of the waist-high beds. The handle broke off.

Vines were everywhere, forcing their way inside and out again, knitting the broken pieces of glass together. The air was musty and sun-warmed. Feeling trapped, Cory began to back out. On the clammy bricks, her feet seemed to have merged with each other, or with the fog. They were far away and out of her control. It was like the dream where you had to run, but couldn't.

She was suddenly conscious of being watched, of an intense, fey presence. She reached out and grabbed the door frame. As she did, she nearly touched the other hand.

It was a thin hand, liver-spotted, with tobacco stains around fingertips and paint stains elsewhere. It was an old man's hand: White hairs sprang from the knuckles. Now she did scream, but only a peep came out of her mouth.

"Good day, miss," he said, tipping his hat. "Are you looking for something?"

He was whiskered, and wore a wide-brimmed black hat. He was not much taller than she was but deep in the chest. He stepped lightly into the greenhouse. There was grace in his carriage, but a threat in the way he held his upper body, and something half mad in the set of his face. His eyes were large, sad and deep.

"Birds," she breathed.

"Birds? Surely not." He put his hand out to guide her back through the door. She withdrew from his touch, but went ahead of him, guilty as a child. "A bird would be mad to get in here. You can see. He'd never get out alive, now would he?"

He had a beautiful voice, textured and courteous and slightly raw. He spoke with the smooth vowels Cory had already come to recognize as educated.

"There are the rooks, of course, you know. You're not from these parts, are you? Irish perhaps, but no, I'd have to hear you speak more before I said where you were from. Rooks," he repeated. "You see? All black with a grey patch over the lower part of the face, like a knight's mask. They're building now, in the chimney. They did last year, but something made them change their minds before they had their family. I suppose they knew I was watching."

He scanned the sky over the back of the greenhouse, where the trees marked a drop off to a flat place, the edge of what must have been the old kitchen garden. "Down there, you can see great tits and a skylark. There is a collared turtle dove. Now that makes a lovely homey chuck, you must know it. And those big black and white birds, they are bad. Very very bad — magpies. They eat the eggs out of other birds' nests."

His eyes were dark blue or black, it was difficult to say; they took the colour from his hat brim. They were enlivened by patches of light, reflection of the glass and the sun, which had just emerged from the bank of cloud that had hidden it all day. His face was layered, too, younger underneath than it was on the surface, thickened by years of hard living, but moved by strong feelings. He was Albert Bloom and he was as advertised: a drinker, a scoundrel, a genius.

"Now," he said to her very gently, taking her by the arm, "suppose you come along inside and let Liss give you a cup of tea and tell us what brought you. I know it wasn't the birds."

There were stairs up, and the banister was painted white.

Climbing, you entered the flat's one large room head first. In all four directions were dormer windows. They let in the suddenly dazzling light: The clouds had gone. Under the slant ceilings, the tables were covered with long cloths printed with blossoms and shells. A pair of dark reed chairs was drawn up before the windows, which looked out past Ford Manor down the rolling hill marked with huge old oaks and hedgerows. She could see through an open door to the kitchen in which there was a healthy confusion of onions and cabbage, and fresh-cut lilacs. On the other side was a step up to a narrow passage: the studio?

And Liss. Liss made no impression that day. She was only a peaceful, all-seeing presence. She had no face or figure and no voice either; she carried a cane. She was just there, and he knew it and Cory knew it. His wife was there and her judgment was to hang over them always.

"She'll want tea," said Liss.

"She hasn't said who sent her," said Albert.

They spoke of her in the third person, cutting her out, at the same time making her the centre of their considerable concentration.

"I've come to collect the portraits for Lord Beaverbrook," she said. Although she told the truth, it didn't feel like the truth.

"How very enterprising of Mr. Aitken."

Albert walked around her in a circle.

"Did you know I met him in the war? He came out to the front in a taxi. He's a coward, you know. He becomes quite ill when there's to be a battle."

"You were in the war?" He must be very old.

"I was a war artist."

"Sit! Sit!" commanded Liss.

Cory sat down and got a view down the passage to the studio; she saw the scatter of magazines and the dust and smelled the paint.

"I can't stay long," she said lamely. "I have an appointment this evening."

"She cannot lie!" said one of them to the other. "Isn't she marvellous! Without guile!"

Albert paced, stopping in front of a painting. "Edward Burra," he said. It was a fruity domestic interior of a particularly jolly English sort.

"Colourful," Cory said.

"Yes — rather too much so."

Mondrian, Kokoscha, Wyndham Lewis, Brancusi, Klee, Paul Nash and Francis Bacon. Albert stopped before each and every one and asked her opinion. When she pronounced it both of them smiled and nodded, terribly pleased. Cory thought — I've done something right, I've acquitted myself well.

Albert's entire body reacted with pleasure when Cory spoke. By contrast, Liss was still, her small hands folded over the knob of the cane she held in front of her waist. Cory knew somehow they were childless. They had art, that was the product. It was a shocking novelty: two adults, thinking and feeling together, no chores, no children. Just people in rooms, neither working nor praying, but talking animatedly of art, letting the night draw closer.

There was the fire, the cushions, the tea Liss carried out, set like a picnic on a low table. There was sliced ham and pickle, cheese and bread and mango chutney served on blue plates, and the tea came in cups and saucers with red poppies painted on them. In fact, flowers had been painted everywhere. It was obvious they were Liss's flowers; they were jolly and clung, like a fine net that had been cast over the flat, petals and stamens and long, serrated leaves. The trim around the windows was lacquered blue, a frame for the greenery outside. Now those blue rectangles disappeared into the sky, which grew darker by the moment, and as it did the room opened outward to join a vast country silence, which Cory had not imagined England to possess.

"Aside from this ridiculous errand for Lord Beaverbrook, what do you want?" asked Albert.

To be an artist, to live like you, to be with you.

No, she didn't say that. But she knew it. It was the first time she'd known it, the first time she'd said even to herself what had brought her from Canada to England, from London to here. How do I become an artist? Can I be one and be a woman too?

Being a woman seemed to Cory no particular prize. It was a licence to work hard and die inside rather than outside. She already knew that if her womanhood got in her way, she could surmount it, disguise it, defeat it. If amputation were necessary, she was prepared for the most savage alteration to her person. It would be nothing more than taking a new country. Her angular white body would not give her away.

That was before she knew Albert.

"Stay the night," he pressed. "And I shall give you the portrait."

"And you must tell us everything about yourself," Liss said, and the smile spread evenly across her face. She was not calm, Cory thought, she was *calmed*, like one sedated by suffering, a nun or a saint.

What could she tell them? She was Corinne Ditchburn, twenty-seven, of Pointe au Baril, Ontario, a place of rocky islands and what you call Red Indians and forests, many of which have been razed for lumber. If you went, you'd say there was nothing there. No history, not like here. But there was. Indians had used the water route for thousands of years. Samuel de Champlain travelled south in his canoe from the French River to collect furs from the friendly Huron Indians on the sandy beaches at the southern end of *la mer douce.* The missionaries who followed were burned alive, and the Huron fled back north, trying in vain to escape their enemies, the Iroquois. But the Iroquois caught up with them and bashed their heads on the white rocks of Head Island, near her home.

But almost no sign of this was left, only a shard of pottery or perhaps a bent silver spoon caught in a cleft in a rock. Grander signs of civilization, like your manor house here, were never attempted, nor would they have lasted. Oh no, it was a trackless expanse of scalped rock, the skull of the earth, the oldest land and the youngest state. The rock shows up in bizarre stripes, salmon, white, black, crystalline, like the frozen entrails of the earth.

Virgin territory, and likely to remain so. You couldn't get there if you wanted to: The water was treacherous at the best of times and closed over by ice seven months a year. A hundred years ago the Ditchburns came from County Armagh — Irish, as Albert had picked out — and homesteaded five hundred acres on the shore in Carling, a place now called Nobel because they make explosives. Cory was the third generation. They said her grandfather had killed a priest in the old country and escaped by hiding in a culvert: Who knew?

Last on the immigrants' minds was the waterfront, but her father loved the jagged, useless shore. He went west and ended up with a job selling insurance in Calgary with Max Aitken. Max was sharper with the dollar, and her Dad never liked to be far from water anyway. Her mother realized too late she'd picked a man with no prospects. She opened a dress shop in Parry Sound called Parisian Fashions. Her husband drowned in the big storm of '32. By then Cory was teaching school, but when school was out she went to his island and took up where he left off, all but the drinking. Then Aunt Eunice wrote the letter and said she should come to London; it was her gift.

She stopped talking, self-conscious suddenly. You could never tell how the English took you. She brushed the cup with the cuff of her sleeve. Tea slid over the edge and made a yellow pool on the cloth. They didn't comment on her tale, and there was silence.

"The portrait. You promised."

He rose without a word and beckoned her. They had to bend, she just a little less than he, to get through the cramped corridor that led to the studio. Once in the room, Cory stood. The air was cold from open windows on either side. The space was dominated by his easel; a canvas with a half-finished painting stood on it, another of his retreating, suffering women. "Are they all like that?" she said, and he laughed.

"I feel I know you," he said.

Another huge canvas leaned against the back wall, painted red and marked out in squares. A mass of sketches lay on the floor. Beside the easel was a small round table, which he used as a palette. Before she could stop herself, she picked up one of the brushes, to feel it between her fingers. He was hard on his tools. The bristles splayed out at right angles. It was all there, all that would later mean *him* to Cory: the smell of paint, of cigars; the feel of those old stuffed horsehair chairs covered with Liss's embroidered shawls; on the mantle the collection of glass ornaments and theatre bills, dusty and curling in the humidity. An oak coat rack bore his black cape, a walking stick and an umbrella.

She mused; all these were portents. She could feel them.

Albert stood bandy-legged in front of the portrait of Beaverbrook.

"I don't owe him anything, do you understand? He did not *buy* the portraits. He gave me money to paint. He said that he had a great deal of money. As I at this time had comparatively little it would give him pleasure. Then, later, came the requests. Paint this friend, and that, one of himself to present to the Canadians. I know your Mr. Aitken."

"Not mine —"

"— A dark character. Great intellect, much mischief. Him I can paint. But not the rest. Bankers. Philanthropists. I'm no organ grinder's monkey. I am only interested in people in whom I am interested, do you understand? But since our Mister Aitken has been creative enough to send you, I will give him the portrait of himself. He should be grateful."

"Thank you," said Cory. "Now I must go."

She would have left then. But there was the issue of how to transport the canvas. It had to be strapped to the side of the car, and they couldn't do that until morning. Liss folded Cory's hand between her two. In the end she agreed to stay. The three of them discussed this carefully. Cory's heart raced and her breath refused to go in and out on time, and her flesh burned when Albert came within two feet of her. It grew dark and the cuckoos called in the fields. Finally, Albert and Liss took their respective stick and cane and went for their evening walk.

In the morning there were noises in the kitchen. A clatter of crockery, cupboard doors being shut. Cory lay on the studio sofa under a rough quilt made of small, pale triangles, all in the same mint green. Someone stole in with a tea tray. She pretended to doze when his steps came to the side of her couch. When she heard him leave, she dressed under the covers.

From the window, she saw the rook on his chimney perch, the other birds pecking at the bricks. Two glass milk bottles with foil caps were at the doorstep. In the dawn's brightness the postman toiled on his bicycle, red sacks of mail at either side of the back wheel. Her handbag sat on the chair, her coat was thrown across the seat nearby. Now! She could escape. At the door she stopped. She looked down at the mat and saw his boots.

"Good morning, Cory."

There were moth holes in the front of his cardigan. His cheeks were rosy. He had been out already, walking. She dropped her chin, blushing furiously.

"I want to leave," she said. It felt like a plunge into intimacy. It felt as if he understood.

"Are we not kind?" His voice was rough.

"Too kind."

"That's nonsense," he said. Then, in a considered way, as if he were totting up points for and against, he added, "You are so young."

"I don't know what you mean," said Cory stoutly. Her heart raced.

He reached out and put his arms around her, drew her toward him in an embrace. His lips grazed her eyelids.

"We will be friends. The three of us. Excellent friends. I can see it all ahead of me; our friendship will carry me to my grave."

They stood together in the circle of his arms. She could feel the heat of his chest, radiating. It seemed to reach into her own heart. Friends. But a squirrel ran along the eaves of the dormer and stopped, up on its hind legs, its teeth and tiny front paws trembling with what looked like mirth.

"You see," he said, "even the squirrel is laughing at me."

Tyke had never heard this before. He reeled a little, inside, under so much information. Softy, he replaced the photograph and pulled the white gloves from his hand.

"I don't believe I've ever seen Albert's portrait of Max," he said evenly.

"You have," said his mother. "It was there, in Fredericton. When we went. Max eventually gave it to the Beaverbrook Art Gallery in his old home town."

"I don't remember," said Tyke. Because he hadn't known how it had come about. "Well did he like it? Did Max like his portrait?"

Cory laughed. "Max? Oh, Max stood in front of it with his chin pushed forward, and said, 'Why didn't he get me smiling?'"

The portrait had been done from a photograph, but Albert had anticipated the photograph; his painting caught Beaverbrook the second before the shutter closed. Caught the slant of misery that came down on him like the swipe of a hand as he was preparing a face.

"What do you think?" he'd say to any socialite who came in the door. "Albert Bloom painted my portrait." When they said they liked it he shook his head, no you don't; and when they said they didn't like it he pronounced them philistines.

None of this diminished his pleasure in her heist. She was the star, not Albert.

"Look at that, she's done it," he crowed to his new secretary, a young man he'd met working as a bellhop in the Ritz Carlton in Montreal and would in a short time make Literary Editor of the *Express*. Beaverbrook believed in the fulfillment of dreams, his own and other people's. "Drove home with it tied to the side of the car — how about that?"

She was his pet for at least a week, at the end of which he turned to her and said, "Well, Miss Ditchburn, you've proven yourself. How would you like to work for the *Express*?"

"Thank you very much," she said, "but I don't think so."

This annoyed him. "Why not?"

"Because it's not what I want. It won't give me what I want."

"Nonsense. I can give you anything you want." Exactly those words.

"No, you can't. Not when what I want is to be an artist."

His laugh was only a face he made while he contemplated getting even. "Oh, you too? You may be a photographer," he said, "but that's not the same."

Valentine was eavesdropping. "Ah, independence!" he laughed. "We rather like it. But it won't last," he said. "In the end the self-sufficient ones disappoint us most."

Cory knew right off she wouldn't ask Beaverbrook for

money or for a job on the *Express*. The way she saw it was this. He had all the money in the world. On his payroll, she'd be just one more joe-girl. If you took the job you said, OK, money is what this game is about. But then the game would be over because if it was about chips, he always had more. He won and she lost.

Oh it wasn't that calculated. Maybe later, she said to him. Of course later she did ask. But by then she disbelieved what people said about him. Even his friends stood in tight semicircles at his parties, drinking his champagne, saying he traded in souls. Corrupted people, preyed on their weaknesses, got them hooked on his money. She doubted he could be blamed for it all. At first her instincts were all she had to go on. She knew that money was cheap to him. And jobs. It seemed as if there was only one thing he hated to give, and that was nothing. So nothing was what she took.

"He'll never trust you after this," said Valentine. "Because you don't behave like the rest of them. He's got the uneasy sense you're doing business but he doesn't know what business."

That was how it began, with Beaverbrook and Cory. She wondered, sometimes, if she'd been someone else, would he have tried harder? If she'd been one of those bright young men he'd discovered driving taxi? Or one of those sirens he had affairs with? But she was only the daughter of an old friend who was dead. Being dead made a big impression on him. He was terrified of being dead. You can't do deals with the dead.

Chapter Four

People in rooms, drinking and talking and making it a calling, all in the middle of a perfectly good day. The beer made ideas ferment in the brain. The fire's lick warmed shoulders and cheeks; you felt lucky compared to passersby with their hurried, worried faces.

❧

TWO O'CLOCK IN THE AFTERNOON AT THE DUKE OF WELLINGton: Domino players sat in columns of smoke. In the corner by the window, Albert's opinion was sought around the table. It made him magnanimous.

"Seen the new issue of *New Verse*, Albert? What do you think of the Auden poem?"

"We can't all be great artists — and there's always room for a middling one."

Mostly the other men laughed, though from time to

time someone would disagree. Then, Albert's tongue grew sharper, his elbows dug into the table top, the skin on his cheeks took on a waxy shine in the weak light.

The talk swirled around: Albert decrying the Surrealists, someone insisting that the English never knew how to paint until the French came over to show them, others shouting down this obsession with France as being too Bloomsbury. Cory listened and watched as the waning sun struck one pale, blasted cheek after another. Sometimes her eye retreated from the greedy mouths closing over the lips of the pint glasses, and she saw herself among these people as if from outside the window.

She knew what Eliza would say. Talking and drinking all day long: It went against God and nature, and very likely would come to no good. Who was this man who called himself artist but practised an art suspiciously close to idleness? A deadbeat. A man who would do this would fail on his land claim, be a burden on his neighbours, let his children go hungry and then come asking for handouts.

The poets and artists were kind enough but Cory could not speak, even to answer the smallest question: "How do you manage to get on with that curmudgeon?" and a friendly jerk of the head at Albert. She made up answers in her head. When they spoke of arresting a moment, she knew the camera could do it better. She had ideas but not the words to say them, not the quickness of these people with their curved and splendid sentences, their carefully rounded tones from schools the names of which she was yet to recognize. They threw their language like a net over her, weighted at the edges. She felt dumb as a circus animal.

Once she tried to explain working from nature.

"Nature?" said one of the men. "Frightfully Georgian, isn't it? This is the machine age."

"But machines come from nature, they imitate nature, don't they? Look at the camera, it's only the same as an eye, a mechanical eye."

Another time she tried to describe her "naked earth" but eyes began to cloud and stray as she spoke. Still, when the crew shuffled for the door after the bell rang for closing they said if one could get past the accent she wasn't a bad girl; they were beginning to see why Albert had her around.

Albert and Liss were back in London, and Cory was his assistant. How did it come about? On this point she was vague. She remembered the first meeting, at the Stable Cottage, so well; she remembered later, their afternoons in his studio on Gloucester Avenue. But in between? How did they get from "We mustn't" to "We must"? Cory did not know.

There were many things she did not know about her own life, about her behaviour. At first she was all fear. She did not know how she overcame her fears, not just of acting, but of getting, or saying, or being, what she wanted. Even when she dared once, the fear did not go away. Afterward she could not imagine how she had navigated the narrow paths, survived the slappings down. Once was not enough: Ten times was not enough. Each time she had to dare again.

The "apprenticeship" had been Albert's idea, of that she was certain. She was hired to take photographs. He was working on a series of London moments in which there was an echo of the past. He told her how he worked. He scorned the photograph, in general.

"It gives you too much detail. Clutters the image, clutters the mind. Do you know how one paints from real life? Of course you don't. I shall tell you."

She stood behind him as he sat at his easel in the twilight: It was always twilight in that room. He watched himself paint, and she did too, the wet trail of the brush over the thick ridges of colour. The smell of turpentine hung in the damp air — and the smell of his cooled, forgotten cup of tea. She was always conscious of his barrel chest, and the beautiful voice, the phrases turned so elegantly she felt his conversation gave her entry to a world of golden thoughts.

"Locate your subject. Wrought-iron gateway, man descending an alley beside the cemetery, whatever. You get in a taxicab and have the driver go by. Just once. Seize the image and memorize it. *Etch* it in your mind. Keep driving. Of course, if you are an amateur you can knock on the window and ask the driver to go slowly."

He was joking, of course. But no.

"Photography is very bad, bad for the mind, for the eye. It does too much of the work."

"Then why did you hire me?"

"Because," he said, "I have so little time and so much to paint. I'm too old to be corrupted and I know what I am doing. So I can send you out to capture my scenes. You shall be my vulgar man on the street. I shall test you. To see if you can see what I want you to see. Besides," he added, "you are magnificent and you make my heart glad."

Cory drank in the sweet with the sour.

"I am the rag and bone man of the art world," Albert went on, in his rolling, mellifluous voice. "Look at this. I like this print. I am very fond of this print. There is something in it, some nuance, no one can do this any more —"

It was a Degas, or it had been. A woman with a parasol, poised on a pathway, dogs racing ahead, she deliberating whether to go forward or back. He had copied it.

"Do you see? I've squared it up, and then painted one just like it, you see? Squared it up, and then painted it in monochrome. After it dried I rubbed it down with linseed oil and a silk rag. To soften everything. Now I simply add the colour. Touching her, as if I am a god giving her lips and cheeks and hair and waist."

"But it's not new, what you've done," she protested.

He whirled to where she stood in the shadows. "New? But nothing is new. Everything has been done by the masters." He joined arrogance with humility with wonder: She laughed out of the sheer pleasure of being his audience.

Albert was different, in London, in winter. With his pallid skin and hands that trembled in the cold, he looked more fragile than the man she'd met in the rotting greenhouse.

But he was quick in the city, he knew the back streets, the steep stairs of the underground. He had an instinct for tunnels and tracks. For Cory, there was London above ground, and tunnels below; she could see no connection between the two. But Albert would say, we'll take the eastern staircase, we'll go this way and come out closer to Longacre, or Trafalgar, or Regent's Park.

Albert taught her London, but the Stooks brothers taught her photography.

She met the Stooks through the bird man in Oxford Street. He sold shivering hunched parrots, their feathers fluffed and their tropical colours drained by contrast with the purple satin necks and chests in the jewellery shop window. The parrots came from Brazil; he'd bought them from a bloke who got them off a boat at London dock.

"I don't know what you might be doing with that picture, do I, taking it off to the coppers. Or is it the RSPCA?"

But as one street vendor to another he let her profit by him. She kept smiling and snapping: It attracted notice, she told him, and he had to sell those parrots, didn't he? In the gaudy reflections from the shop window, he was striped, like the bird itself, although in a cage of his own. And when the camera jammed, he said, "Eh, love, you after knowing where to get that camera fixed?"

She took the Northern Line to Camden Town and got out on the High Street. A grizzled man with stumps for fingers sat in a brick alcove in the tube station. A family of gypsies with baleful regard hawked lavender sprigs. One of them had a bad eye, which rolled up.

"Buy it," hissed the thin man. "If you don't she'll put the evil eye on you."

So she bought it, and thought to send it in a letter, because the dry sweet smell reminded her again of Eliza, and the little shop of ladies' clothes, the niceties that she fought so hard to install in Parry Sound. Eliza would die before she'd write first. "It's the feckless Ditchburn coming out in you again," she said, when Cory quit her teaching job to go to London. "Some bad habits you can learn and others just come naturally." Her tiny mouth closed and she pulled disapproval down over her face like a spotted veil.

Cory walked north in a wind full of cinders. Her legs were wrapped in flying sheets of newspaper. "Is there a shop called Stooks here?"

"Stooks!" said a newsagent. "You'll never find it unless you know." He told her to look underneath a railway pass, and in the bottom of a car repair barn, with a very fine car out front belonging to Mr. Stooks.

"Oh," she said, disappointed. "Is it a grand place, then?"

"Wait till you see!"

The overpass was lined with narrow terraces with mean windows hung with tattered lace curtains. At the bottom was a bottle-green Jaguar parked at the kerb. The door with the sign Stooks Electrical did not push open, but like a barn door could be slid, with difficulty, to one side. Cory looked in on a wasteland of metal cabinets, barrels, chopping blocks, disused wireless sets, tubing and packing crates. Closer examination revealed narrow pathways winding their way at odd angles into the piled stores. With even closer examination she saw, in a little glass cabin, two identical white-haired men at desks. The telephone rang as she stepped in.

"Stooks!" said one of the men, snatching up the receiver. The other stood and gazed in astonishment at Cory.

"Are you open to the public?" she faltered.

"That depends on what public you are."

The second man put down the telephone and picked up a dish and spoon from the desk. He rose.

"Gooseberry fool," he said, holding it out toward her. "Would you care to try some? It's excellent." The two of them stood side by side, taking her in.

"Gooseberries," she said. "They grow down by the river off Mill Lake, at home. They make a nice pie, but sour."

They continued to examine her.

"Colonial lady," said one to the other. He edged his way between the bales of wire toward her.

"Wonder how she found us?"

"Wonder what she wants."

She produced the jammed Leica. One of them took it, frowned at it. The other watched.

"Wait! There's film in it."

"We'll develop that," he said.

When she made her way again under the railway overpass, along the street of saggy curtains and through the mad collection of mechanical refuse to their office, the Stooks brothers rose to greet her.

"Colonial lady!"

They liked her shot of the gypsies waving her camera away, an angry blur with one face turning. "You had a choice here: Either he's in focus and everyone else is fuzzy, or you crop it like that," said George, putting the edge of his hand beside the face.

He deferred to Harry on technical matters.

"Now look at this negative — see the way the shadow of that tree falls across the man's face? — if we darken it down, you'll lose him, but you'll get all manner of lines from that branch against the wall. So what do you want us to do?" Harry gazed up at Cory.

"It's about the wall, it's not about him."

"So darker."

"You only have a Leica?" said his brother. "You mean to be a serious photographer? You must have another camera. Wait, George, you remember that Speed Graphic we had back here somewhere?" He took a turn off the pathway and disappeared behind some crates. "It came in with those neon tubes we got last fall? George?"

"It's in the third drawer of the metal cabinet, where the fuses are on top," called George without turning his face from Cory.

"You must have a very good mental filing system," said Cory.

"Hah!" said George.

Harry emerged with the large box camera in his hands.

George spoke first. "You'll like this Speed Graphic, if we rebuild it. They call them 'Old Reliable.' All the best press photographers use it. This one has a Graflex back so it will take a rollfilm holder. It's a bit battered; the box is more than twenty years old. It can give you more detail, you see, but you've got to get close up. The timing is tricky with the flash, so you'll have to work on that. You can't snap in any old light like you do now, but it has a reflex system so you can see exactly what you're taking." He hung the heavy box around her neck. "See? Hands free! And the box is strong enough that you can use it as a seat — or even a weapon, if you want."

On the third visit they presented her with the rebuilt Speed Graphic. When she offered money they were annoyed and disappeared behind their packing crates. On another visit they produced an enlarger they'd built from bits and pieces.

"You want to do this yourself," he said. "Pull your own prints."

"I don't have room."

"Living?" said Harry. "She's living in Camden? Where?"

"I'm not living anywhere," said Cory, and it felt true. Aunt Eunice had found her a place with one of her friend's daughters, a "working girl." It was in Albany Street. There were army barracks facing, and the roar of lorries in the night was so intense it seemed they were about to drive right through the front wall and into her dreams.

"Have we got a place, George?" said Harry. "Think where."

"Only that garden flat at the bottom of Primrose Hill. Fitzroy. Not such a good area for a young lady."

"Oh yes it is," cried Cory.

So the Stooks became her landlords. It was a small two rooms, dark, with the kitchen in front, looking into the window well and the street.

Albert paid her five pounds a week, a good sum. Her rent was one pound a fortnight and Albert's house was in England's Lane, only a ten-minute walk away.

With the Stooks's enlarger Cory developed prints in her kitchen at night. It wasn't easy to get a blackout, because directly in front was a lamp post whose yellow pool of light fell down the well to her window. Sometimes when she lifted the blind, Albert's butterfly shadow was there, the wide wings of his cape flapping and the old bowler hat set back on his head. Ready to go walking, to show her the moon in the ponds at Hampstead Heath or the streets where Jack the Ripper walked, or the high point on Highgate Hill from which he had once watched Crystal Palace Burn. Like Cory, he loved a good fire.

They'd walk without talking, he pacing in a plumb-line from the height of Primrose Hill down, down, sometimes as far as St. Paul's, with his face turned upward, as if he could drink the air, with Cory keeping up. Without warning he would stop, turn, take her shoulders under his hands. His eyes would fill with the most piteous emotion and he would try to speak. But words would frustrate him and he'd shake himself and begin to stride again.

"I had a dream," said Cory one tea-time as they sat in the darkening Gloucester Avenue studio. She met his eyes.

"Tell me about your dream, then." He reached toward her and with surprising force twisted the cup out of her hand.

"It was here, in the studio. We were in this house, but it was not this house." She felt she could say anything to him. "There was a white ceramic bowl. A mortar and pestle. There was powder in the bowl, and I wanted it very much. I put a finger in. It was a colour that can't be made. Dye, I think. I wanted it to run through my veins. I knew if I got it I would be doomed. You were beside me. You disapproved."

Having said it aloud she knew the dream was about being his lover. She was not embarrassed.

Albert put down her teacup. He looked through the wooden frame of the window down the hill toward Camden Town. "You see," he said. "That's perfect. She's had a perfect, straightforward, Canadian dream."

"You said to me, 'no, Cory, you mustn't. If you do that it will never end. It will be a disaster for' — and you named someone, or more than one, I don't know who —"

"But you see, Cory, that's just it, isn't it? I was exactly right, in your dream." He took a step toward her, and this time in a kindly way, like a father, he set his hands on her shoulders and planted a kiss of renunciation on her forehead.

This way, the better part of a year passed. Cory had work, she roamed the city with her camera, either for Albert or for herself: Sometimes his mission and hers ran together. "I'm teaching you to see," he repeated, as he took her pictures and slashed them across with his black pen. Humbly, she listened because she admired him so and he was right. But for praise, she had to go to the Stooks. Together they peered at her prints.

"Eye, she's got an eye!" George would say. "Look, Harry."

If they were particularly excited by one of her shots, one of them would clap her awkwardly on the back. "You are the real thing, colonial lady. You make all the right decisions. Anyone can press the shutter, you know, but only an artist can see."

"Take a lot of shots, take the whole roll," George Stooks said to her one day. "If it's something you want, it's worth it. No use taking one or two and hoping. Go all the way with it."

Cory was happier than she had ever been. There was London's orange sky before dusk and London of night when the lamp posts dropped their tents of yellow onto the wet paving stones of the Hampstead walkways, and the trees were blacker than blotters against the sky. There was Albert, the sheer power of his being, focussed on her. And Liss, like an easier mother. She walked to tea in Albert and Liss's house in England's Lane. She'd be greeted, a house-width away, by the sound of the gramophone with Brahms or Beethoven circling, scratching out into the evening air.

The house would be dark except for the kitchen, which was warm and full of yeast smells and the steam of a lamb stew, the windows open to wet-slick leaves bobbing in the night air. Liss seated with her needlework flowing off her lap, as if she had woven herself into immobility in the centre of this work of art which was her life.

"Liss?" Cory would say, leaning in the door on which no one ever knocked: Liss was neither alone nor in company. She was there, a setting. "Can I come in?" Liss would reach for the cane she always used but didn't seem to need. She would lean on it to get up from her chair, her unfashionable long skirt tangling in her legs.

"Cory. You've come!" As if she had been invited: She never was. "How marvellous. And I was just longing for a cup of tea."

She would put down her work. This work Liss did was never obvious until she put it down. But the flora collected: There were pansy screens and poppy cups on tables clad in embroidered shawls, like the cats that lay on chair-backs.

Liss put the kettle on the cooker. The fabric of her sleeves pulled tight against the flesh of her upper arms. "How did you like *Hedda Gabler*? Albert never tells me — I don't think he listens to the plays, really."

Cory fingered the bluebell salt cellar, the yellow-painted jam jar. She peered deep into the sepia photographs that lined the kitchen wall: Albert and Liss and strangely dressed others in the south of France. She thought of Hedda and her father's firearms. Albert charming the actresses after, Cory with the Speed Graphic fixing them in their eventual retreat in regretful poses he later painted.

They had arrived just before the curtain. Albert pushed his way through the crowd with his stick, and heads rotated. People knew who he was, or thought they did. He had a decadent distinction, an elegance and authority the better for its raggedness.

"Follow me, Cory, we've got to get down to the stalls," he commanded, over heads, pressing deep into an especially resistant pocket of ticket-holders. An exhibitionist, he always broadcast his voice in crowds. She followed, ignoring the annoyed stares directed her way.

"Pardon me, excuse me, I'm sorry, you won't mind if I just go through here, I'm with that gentleman..."

She managed to arrive at their seats only a minute or two after he had arranged himself, majestically, on his outspread cloak. Tripping over feet in the aisle she sat herself with her suitcase of flashbulbs under her knees, her Leica in her lap and the Speed Graphic close to her foot where she could feel it in the dark. As the rows and circles of little red-shaded lights went down around the semicircular edge of the balcony, and overhead on the front of the boxes, Cory sank down in her seat. She sank into the play too; watching how language filled the actors, how one by one they swelled, and then shrank into shadow.

The teapot arrived, swallowed in its swan-shaped cosy. What to tell Liss?

"The people reminded me — despite the fact that they were grand, and much richer — they reminded me of Canadians. Small-town people."

"How's that?" asked Liss, arranging the painted porcelain cups on saucers. Her face was as smooth as ever, perpetually steamed from the stove.

"Feeling such torments but speaking so plainly. Fearing God and neighbours."

"Your parents are like that?"

"They were supposed to be. But neither of them could manage. They couldn't maintain the rules, though they never actually rejected them, either. They just got angry, or drowned, or just — *lived on.* Living's a duty, like everything else."

The tea in her cup was scalding hot, clear. Though the English drank it clouded with milk, Cory liked to see through to the bottom of the cup.

"Was the star as marvellous as all that?"

Liss spoke so carefully, her smile was so firm, so like a true smile, that only seconds after she had heard the words did Cory actually hear the light sarcasm — *really as marvellous as all that.* So she did mind! She was so fixed here in her home, surrounded with Albert's canvases, one hardly noticed she never went out.

"Why don't you ask Albert to take you?"

"I used to go with him. I used to —" here Liss laughed modestly "— take photographs."

Cory flushed red.

"You didn't know?"

Outside on the street a door banged, a delivery van perhaps, and there was the shrill cry of a child who'd hurt himself.

"I didn't know you took photographs."

"Oh, not like you," said Liss and the smile was deeper now, more sincere. Her forehead bulged slightly over her brows, as if the flesh were forced down by an invisible wimple that kept it smooth above. She laughed and began to pick up the tea things. "Not like you, not at all."

Cory looked at the photographs on the shelf.

"Those are mine," said Liss softly.

A pebbly beach in the Riviera. Four people all in long black coats, the women with their hats pulled down over their ears. Albert and another woman, and this strange couple, their friends. All rather stiff. Liss had captured an unease: What do we do, here we are on holiday, on the edge of our lives? It was perhaps ten years ago.

"You do everything well, Liss. You are magnificent."

"I used to block in his pictures too, even paint the backgrounds. In the event, it was too much work for me. I wanted to do my own work you see. And he needed someone — new. Don't worry," said Liss. "Albert has come to use his assistant in a different way these days. You're helping me, as well as helping him. And he needs me. For other things."

"Really, you ought to come to the theatre with us one night."

"The cats," said Liss shortly. "We can't leave the cats alone, can we?"

So it was Albert and Cory who went one afternoon to Wembley, where, under a pale unexpected sun, the greyhounds slunk to the track in numbered jackets of green and red. When the mechanical rabbit on its boom flew over the dogs' heads they leapt, all blurred to one, into their race.

"Take pictures, Cory! I count on you to be my eyes!" Albert forgot himself in the crowd, waving money from the back of the ticket queue as the bets closed.

On the way home he leaned across her on the train. "The camera is good if you make it your servant, never your master." Nearly asleep, he touched her. "What a wealth of consolation there is in the line of your cheek." She sat wondering.

But he was with Liss.

Thursday nights Heraldo opened up his studio and everybody came, bearing bottles of Hungarian wine and copies of little yellow booklets from the Left Wing Book Club. The smoke billowed up, and the guests clustered around the little nodes of greatness in their midst, like earth around a root ball. Heraldo would pull out the long leaves of his dining table, clear it of empty bottles and ashtrays and spread out a roll of wallpaper, printed side down.

The game was to draw a giant isthmus leading to open sea. Everyone drew a section; islands, narrow channels between rocks, coastlines of hostile nations, pirate ships. Albert always pencilled in the Sirens, in different guises each time, on a point of land waving from the trees, or lying in the surf like porpoises.

They all had a moment to memorize the map; then it would begin. This particular night Heraldo first tied the silk kerchief over a young poet's eyes. The poet took his chalk in hand and tried to get down the passage without running afoul of any of the hazards.

The poets were generally useless. This one was no different. After his chalk line ran out of the harbour and into the first bay he landed in the Slough of Despond. The painters were better, but none was as good as Albert, the king of the seafaring game.

While the rest had paced around the table, moving their lips to memorize the shape, Albert had fixed it with one quick glance, turned his back and strode over to the fireplace, where he gazed down at the coals with deep unconcern.

When, inevitably, his only possible rival crashed into a giant rock, Albert submitted to the blindfold. Nimbly he reached across to the starting point, put the tip of his chalk on the page and drew, slowly, without halting, the only possible route past the lighthouse, the shoals, the sirens, the sandbars, Atlantis, the sea monsters and the volcano, to the open water.

During all this Liss had been invisible. But at the point of his victory, she stepped from some corner to untie her husband's blindfold. Her fingers tugging at the knot, she stood so close behind him the mass of her body seemed to merge with his. His face obscured, she took the praise, the round of clapping, with calm and silent nod. He never said, "How did I do?" but later, Cory saw how, thinking himself unobserved, he inspected his line.

She had only watched, for weeks. But now it caused

more notice for her not to play than to play. Cory took chalk in hand. She had watched a long time, studied the shape of shore after shore. Tonight with her eyes shut she could see the isthmus clearly. She was afraid to beat Albert, mostly because she felt bound, with Liss, to uphold him. But she couldn't help it. She navigated without disaster. The room was quiet, until Albert stepped toward her from the fireplace, put a hand on either temple and kissed her forehead.

"Did I not teach her well?"

At Heraldo's she met the German communists. They'd been in a place called Dachau, a jail, or a work camp, that Hitler had built outside of Munich. He built it for his enemies, they said, and he used the men he'd imprisoned as subjects in experiments. Brothers, they'd been artists in Germany, but they wouldn't paint again. They were missing three fingers each, on their right hands, but they felt lucky to have got away alive. Hearing them, Cory made up her mind.

If this war they all spoke of truly happened, she would get to Dachau and help to put an end to it.

Chapter Five

*This photograph was reproduced in the Times of London,
the only photograph Corinne Ditchburn ever published
there. It was used as a publicity shot for Albert Bloom's
1938 art showing, and was captioned as follows:*

*Mr. Albert Bloom and his wife, Liss. An exhibition of
his paintings is being held at the artist's studio, Gloucester Avenue. He declined an opportunity to tidy the room
before the photograph, preferring to leave his things
undisturbed...*

❧

CORY STUMBLED INTO THE CONFRONTATION ON THE DUSTY
wooden staircase to the studio: She stood in the gaslight
at the landing. She could hear the dealer shouting,
something about canvases not returned, commissions
waiting, new work being "thin," "owing a great deal to

nineteenth-century masters." She rounded a corner and saw Albert roar from the top step: "You know nothing, nothing, of what you speak. You're a money changer, that's all you are, that's all you ever were!"

Mr. Lefevre stamped past her, black-faced. Cory nodded stupidly, afraid. Would this mean the end of her work there?

They had tea, in the peace that came after an explosion.

"We shall do the show ourselves, Cory. That's all. It's very simple, really. I shall retrieve my paintings from his gallery. We'll have a private viewing here. The audience comes to see me, not him, not Lefevre. They're vultures, all the dealers, trying to make their fortunes out of artists. What keeps me going is that I know one day, they'll be gone. My work will remain. I will remain."

To prepare for the showing, Liss and Cory cleaned out the studio. They pushed the tattered stuffed chairs to the wall, lifted the drop sheets that covered stacks of canvases, relieved the walls of the Van Gogh reproductions, fashion illustrations and photographs that usually covered them. They painted the ceiling and tied back the heavy curtains in swoops. Albert refused to move as much as a shred of tobacco or a postcard off his desk. "Let them see how an artist runs his life," he said.

The evening arrived. Cory climbed the three flights of stairs as usual, but now she heard a crowd above. The tied-back curtains let great wedges of unaccustomed light push across the floor. Even the ceilings, water-stained before, now awash in white, seemed to float overhead like some lofty cloud. Albert's enormous, disturbing canvases took the walls away. The only landscape was his solid women, his shadowy men, their glimpsed domestic dramas.

Here was the actress playing Hedda Gabler. There were the sulky greyhounds, the gamblers at the window. The domino players in the pub. But he was the one exposed, not London, not its denizens. It was Albert, in his sensuous regard even for a wine glass, Albert in all the women, women looking back over their shoulders; over and over the same pose, women seductive, withdrawing, sullied, erotic.

The young boy who was somebody's son circled offering drinks. Liss entered, her brow cramped. If her eyes had not been Liss's eyes, they'd have been bitter. Cory leaned briefly into her arms and out, the better to see her face. The noise of the party blasted between them.

"He's disappeared."

"How can he have?" Of course he's disappeared, thought Cory. His presence would be redundant.

"He's just gone off. Tuesday at noon. He hasn't been seen since. You haven't seen him." The last was a question, not a statement.

"No."

"I'm afraid of him, Cory," said Liss. Her grip on Cory's arm was painful. "He struck me. And you see, I can't fight back. Do you understand?"

Someone from the Illustrated London News was there, taking photographs. A man with a banana nose and a spotted tie peered at each canvas narrowly, as if to discover if it were a fake, and finally made for the door, muttering sourly. The pictures were not a success. They were not festive. The colours were muddy. They threatened, loomed. They made you uncomfortable. They did not show society. The only fan was a bald man whose face appeared to have been boiled, who liked the portrait of the woman buying a ticket to the Daily Double.

"Isn't she lovely? Vile, but lovely," he mused. "Do you suppose she came here to pose for him?"

A trio of women cruised the walls. "He's so un-English, don't you think? Yes, German I believe. Born there, at any rate."

"We English don't understand depth. It is all surface, English painting. *They* understand it. It's just that what they paint is so bloody awful, that's why he doesn't fit in."

For Cory each canvas was confirmation of their intimacy, of the world she and Albert shared apart from the rest of the world. She felt wild: jealous, offended, shocked at what was revealed, at least to her. Until now she hadn't known how obviously he would use her photographs, how loudly they spoke in his voice, as well as hers. She stood, frightened for him, wanting him. Oceans of feeling sloshed up against each canvas; the floor of the studio seemed to be disappearing under a rising tide. She wanted the paintings to give way to his voice, the walls to the smoke and perspiration smell of his jacket. She wanted the coarse, hoarse, damaged throat to open and his rich words to pour over her.

A dozen times, she explained his absence. Valentine was particularly curious. He looked down at Cory's face, and his eyebrows burrowed into the fat of his forehead. Nerves, with the show, she said. Can't face the critics and so on. His not being necessary, the paintings were so strong. Enemies coming out of the woodwork, that too, not suffering fools gladly, wasn't it better he *hadn't* shown up?

"How very interesting, Miss Ditchburn," said Valentine, and raised his hat before moving off. The talk was like surface electricity, shorting and fizzing out. Then suddenly the public went, crowding through the doorway all at the same time. The pub group dropped into armchairs to do the post-mortem.

"Max had the time of his life."

"He was pinching bottoms."

"Just wait and see. He'll ring up the critic on the *Express* and tell them what to say —"

"Albert sent his regrets."

Laughter all around and then the guilty swing of the eyes to the corners: Where was he? Where was Liss? What was happening?

Cory had gone home and was half out of her clothes when she heard the pounding. She went to the window well and lifted a corner of the curtain. There he was, standing in the honeyed circle of lamp light. Leaning, not standing, not with his usual aplomb. She snatched a quilt and ran up the few steps to throw open the door. When she saw him, she backed down again. He had become another being altogether.

"Albert?"

He loomed over her, dirty, his beard knotted, reeking of drink. A tooth was missing in the front and he looked morose. Then, as his eyes connected with hers, he was taken with wild elation; he looked as if his cape might become wings.

He flew down toward her, arms out. Eliza's voice shrieked in her head: He's a drunken bum, this is what he is.

He embraced her and then, excited to the point where it seemed he hadn't seen her, pushed past her through the door. "My darling! I hate it all. And I shan't agree to sell one thing. But I would have liked to see it with you," he said, grandly. He turned and fell back against her chest, a lead weight.

He smelled and his weight made her stagger.

"Albert — where have you been? Why?"

"Nobody cares about the why of it," she had heard him say to her, how long ago? "It's boring. They only want the how of it." She took him in, his condition.

"But Albert, why?" she said again.

His elation vanished instantly. He sat in the armchair with his elbows on his knees. "You're angry. My wife is angry." His look said that all this world of art had nothing to do with him; he was used up, garbage. The money people and the talk people and the measuring people had taken over, all the vultures, as he called them.

Cory stood. Thunderstruck, helpless. Saying nothing.

Albert moaned. His face was in his hands.

That sound brought her back. I know about this, she thought. I can talk to drunks. My father was one, after all. He got messy and roared. She hated to talk to him then. But if she had known that those were the only conversations she was going to get, that he'd be dead and gone too, too soon, she'd have listened. There was freedom in it, too. Drunks never remember a thing.

She sat opposite him. He smiled slowly, as if she were a friendly vision. He tried to speak. "I am very pleased," he began. He shook his head and let it drop again. He lifted his head, eager, and his lips moved, and his eyes searched her face in jerks, eyes to lips, lips to eyes, he tried to formulate a sentence and then he lapsed again. She took charge of him. She could be other than his student now, his errand girl. Gravity shifted; constellations would move.

"Albert, you seem very tired. Would you like me to take you home?"

His eyes came to focus on her face. He smiled. "Yes," he said. "I'd like that."

He hesitated before he took the first step. She thought perhaps he might fall, and took his arm. He stopped and jerked it away. Angry, he located her face with his red eyes.

"I am in love with you," he said.

She saw the yawning vault of the stairs. There was some mistake. She took his arm again.

"Nonsense. You're drunk and you're in love with your wife."

Albert was watching her face. Disgusted by what he saw there — ignorance? innocence? hypocrisy? — he wrested himself free. "You don't know, do you?" Saliva flew.

She stared. "He struck me," Liss had said. "I can't fight back."

"No," she said, "I didn't know."

As he pulled away from her, his arm caught the side of her head. "Oh well," he said savagely, "it's only a year of my fucking life!" He flung himself up the stairs and through the door.

She dropped the quilt that covered her slip and pulled on her coat. She reached the street in time to see him weave down Fitzroy, the gusty sound of his voice coming back to her. She caught up and steered him down to the corner of Regent's Park Road. She hailed a taxi and got him in it. They pulled up in England's Lane just as Liss was alighting from some car.

Albert cursed and turned out his pockets. They had no money to pay for the taxi. Liss arrived with her pocketbook.

"Come, Albert," Liss called like an efficient nanny. She did not appear to take Cory in, but marched up the walk without a backward glance. Her cane tapped the pavement sharply. Albert lingered. He put his hands on either side of Cory's head, trying to force her mouth to his.

"I love you. But regrettably, you have no brain. Cow!"

She put up an elbow and knocked him away.

Liss was at the door, and through it. As she vanished inward the cat tiptoed out into the night, its tail silhouetted against the white hallway behind, a question mark.

Cory pushed Albert violently through the gate. She saw his back fill up the space in the midst of the arch, his arms by his ears as if they had been boxed. Then he listed up the path.

Cory ran. Ran silently over the cobblestones of England's Lane toward the dark slope of Primrose Hill. You could see St. Paul's in daylight; even now, an orange haze floated over the lights of the City. I didn't know, she wept to herself. But what about the dream? Hadn't they played with fire? And what about the squirrel who laughed at the idea of their friendship that first day they met? And the blossom-spangled day last spring when she urged him to come to the park? He had hung on the iron gate and would not leave home. It was too big a concession, he would not abandon whatever it was he would have had to abandon — safety, perhaps. He stood balky by the gate with a bemused half smile and said, "No, Cory go away, Cory go away!"

What had she wanted? Only to speak. To be with him. To be in his life, in his focus. In the magic circle that came of his eyes and hers, his words and her flesh. When they were with people the others interrupted, put up their baffles to intercept the deeper communication she felt belonged to them.

Still, what had she wanted? Not this, she promised herself. Not to take away from Liss. Only to see him, to speak with him. To know what he knew. To hear his voice in her ear. Only that Albert should recognize her. That he should put into words what he recognized in her, why he had taken her up. But that he love her? Was this her game? She ran and she knew.

And so, was it love? Albert felt it, too. How slow she was. But not stupid. Just inexperienced. And that could be remedied. Wild exhilaration filled her and she ran, faster now, downhill toward home.

She waited all the next day for a knock, a message. It was a day that seemed never to have dawned, cold and silent. She sealed the light cracks around her doors and windows with the long, stuffed snakes of fabric Liss had made her, and spent hours in the dark developing prints. At five o'clock she went out for a cup of tea in the fish and chip shop. The sky was a deep purple and clouds enveloped the hill. That woman in the tall green rubber boots with the two hounds who seemed to define the park came striding across. Cory went to a telephone box in Regent's Park Road.

Liss answered. Albert was in bed. The doctor had been in. She sounded terrible.

"You should sit down and have a good cry," said Cory.

"Do you know what? I have no one to cry to."

Cory was startled, her ideas overturned yet again. What about all the friends, the poets, the artists?

"I can't let them see."

In the phone box Cory grew older by the minute. "Shall I come?" How quickly she'd been promoted from the lowly Canadian apprentice to the only one Liss could cry to.

"Please."

The sun emerged, belatedly, from the murk. There was a bronze wash on the new-leafed trees as the row of lamp lights hastened Cory up the hill. The grass was dark. She felt in love with the soft layers of London town; it was so deep you could put your arm in up to the elbow. The door was unlocked, as always. Liss came to meet her with a face scored with tears. Albert was a shape in the chair behind, in the sitting room.

"Shall I get Cory a bottle of wine?" His voice ricocheted forward, stronger than his presence.

"No," said Cory. "A cup of tea."

But there was no teapot.

"It's in the garden," muttered Liss. But in the garden were only the fragments of the pot.

"Never mind, the clay's good for the flowers." Liss poured water from the kettle over tea leaves scattered in the bottom of a saucepan. She had to use a soup ladle to pour the tea.

"Deft, what?" Albert had come near. Cory's stomach was tight.

"Deft."

They sat around the table. Liss drew deep shuddering breaths and curled her hands around her teacup.

"We sat in the garden yesterday," Liss said. "It was cold and Albert said, you're in love with the artist you wish I was and I'm in love with Cory. That's when the teapot got smashed."

They all smiled. Cory stirred her tea.

"Nonsense, Liss, he's in love with you."

They drank a little tea. "Are you going to cry?"

"Not now that you're here. I don't need to." She had on

her bright, nun's smile. "That was very odd, wasn't it, the opening?"

"What sold?"

"Three. The dogs. Hedda. The ship at London dock."

Albert and Liss fell silent. Their need of Cory swelled and rose like a genie from the teacups. Help us. Put us back together. See us as we wish to be, as you wish us to be. But they were old and broken. It hurt Cory: It seemed unfair. This was how it all became possible, the betrayal. They were helpless. They invited her in. And she was trained, she'd watched them, she knew all about them. She drank her tea and backed out the door, leaving them there.

She felt superhuman. She could do what she wished now. She ran down to the end of the road to get a taxi. She felt perfectly calm, as if she had been given permission. At home in her bed, she slept all night.

The next day she telephoned. Albert answered immediately.

"Heelo?" he said, peremptorily, with a tone of, we're involved in a great many important things here, would you mind getting down to it?

He sounded sober. The composure was convincing.

"Albert, it's Cory." She kept her voice free of implication. Nothing had happened, perhaps.

"Yes, Cory." A hint of tenderness, did he remember? A chink of light? He wasn't making it easy, but he was making it possible.

"You said something to me the other night. It took me by surprise. I'm afraid I was rude to you."

"Oh yes?" He laughed. Drunks never remembered what they said. Or did they?

"I want you to know, I respect and like you very much, Albert."

His breath went in, like a saw through wood.

"Could we get together," he asked, "go for a walk? I shall come by and collect you tomorrow at one."

She heard the muffled slam of a taxi door, steps down to her door, his knock. When she saw him there — his black suede hat with the broad brim, his white hair, depleted pale visage, burning eyes — she thought, my god, how battered he is, and then, but how familiar, how like my life. And how did she look? Did they make a pair? Cory with her angles, her awkward long legs, her level and challenging gaze, her London pallor making her eyes a darker, disturbing blue?

He smelled of smoke. His jacket was stained. He did not smile. It was all very uncomfortable, until they were on the path to the rose garden. It was a maze-like path, trimmed and tamed and geometric, like something from Alice in Wonderland. A sculpted nature, neither of theirs. For their walk, the heavy grey weight had flown out to sea, and the sky was a delft blue. The magnolia tree bore buds on what had been leafless boughs. It seemed too early for so opulent a flower to blossom.

"So you really didn't know?" They linked arms, walked leaning holding each other.

"I didn't realize."

"It's impossible, of course," he said. "But I'm awfully glad you rang anyway."

A flock of schoolchildren in blue pleated skirts and small flat straw hats stood at the edge of the park waiting to cross the road: innocence arrested. He grasped her hand to run back between the cars. At her flat they scrambled down the staircase and drew in beside the door where the rain did not hit. They embraced. They were the same height.

"I suppose we'll have to stop being friends, Liss and you and I..."

"No. We can't."

They embraced, pressing together along the indentations of their bodies. Cory's mind emptied; she heard him in fits and starts, his voice interrupted by rushes of blood to her ears and head.

"Perhaps a trip — to look at some pictures..."

"No, that's impossible," Cory heard herself say. "If something happened — if we just fell upon each other — in London, she might not mind so terribly. But to practise a complicated deception, to plan it, that's unforgivable."

"You're absolutely right." He was kissing her lips. Plucking at the buttons of her coat, and she at his. Her voice shook and as she spoke she thought: Who is it? A rapacious creature in me.

He stopped, panting. "It's nearly three. I must be at the studio. A dealer —"

"Dealer? You hate dealers."

"This one's different."

Slowly she regained her balance. "All right, leave."

Released from immediate consequences, they reached for bare skin under the layers of clothes.

"But come back tonight," she commanded. "That is, if you can get your wife to sleep." Cory heard the hint of scorn, *your wife*. She groaned. This was Liss they were talking about. Gleeful, limp with shame, she collapsed into him. "You see how quickly we become wicked."

Putting his hat over the thinning spot — now she had touched it, touched the parchment skin, and it was moist, not crumbly as she had expected — he drew away. "Not tonight. We'll go away together. To the Lake District."

He was leaving. "What was that you said? About how quickly we become wicked?"

Chapter Six

FIGURE 6

Corinne Ditchburn

Tree Root, The Lake District

October, 1938
England
Gelatin silver, 23 x 36 cm
Developed by the photographer

This image of whorls of wood grain around a tree root where it bulges above ground anticipates Ditchburn's later sensual landscapes of her native Ontario. The observed natural world becomes a projection of hidden emotional life. But the photographer here is reaching out to a new country, England, and has caught in it the struggle between ancient and new, between comfort and strangeness.

ॐ

THE LANDSCAPE WAS ETCHED WITH RAGGEDY FIR TREES AND A few isolated stands of pine. A bleached, bulbous tree root protruded from the bank above the path, at waist level. Cory stopped to examine it. It was a laughing face, stretched as a monkey's, lips drawn back, chin long and forward, an empty eye socket. Cory put her hands all over it, the curves, the fork of it. The rush of creek water carried away Albert's voice as he toiled upward, waving his stick at a green-spotted crag. Behind him on the path, she stopped to lean on a wall.

Fells, thought Cory, raising her camera, are what exactly? Those pleats that run down the hillsides, purple when the crease is in shadow? Or the valley itself, the narrow runs at the bottom?

The walls were the best part, moss covered, made of slabs of charcoal slate piled flat like books. The houses, too, were built this way, and the fences around the houses, sometimes with upright oval stones for gateposts.

Without the stone walls the lakes could have been anywhere, man-sized miniatures you could walk around. Even the rocks were infrequent enough to be named. England: a knowable, measurable, tamed place. She leaned back on a flat rock and closed her eyes. Albert named the Crags: Skiddaw, Langdale Pikes, Great Gable.

Take a wall, she said, gasping out her words as she tried to catch Albert. Or at least how to get past it. There are various ways. A staircase, with extra large stones stuck in it at expedient points. A wagon wheel grafted in, hinged, with a catch. Then there were those walls with ladders built over them, like a tripod. *Stile*, that was called.

The hillsides were rusted with the dried curl of dead ferns. The trees were turning but there was still green amongst the yellow. The trapped sky itself boiled up as if from a pot, white and cumulus clouds around the edges but clearing overhead, to a veiled blue.

"We'll stop ahead," called Albert. "After we take the first turning to Burley Crag." He remained resolutely pointed uphill, turning at his thick waist to order her onward.

"I've stopped here," muttered Cory.

"You'll be sorry. It's going to be much, much more beautiful from the top!"

He held the wooden gate as she went through and easily laid his arm across her shoulder.

"I thought you Canadian girls did nothing but ice skate and swim. I thought you'd be racing ahead of me straight uphill." But he took out a cigarette.

A pair of climbers in britches and bare calves passed them, their heavy woollen socks rolled above their ankles, their hair frizzed around their cheeks. "Hullo." "Hullo." At the top the rocks were all upright, the strata had been turned on their ends, like headstones or canvases piled one against the other. The walls curved over and between them, disappearing, marking some grazing line for sheep many centuries gone. Down at the bottom of the dale she could see sheep being driven, small white burrs on the green, hear the yapping of the dog, which was a black streak, circling them from one side then the other. Then came the farmer. Cory sat on a rock. It was embroidered with lime-coloured lichen; around it, heather put its purple spikes upward and little clumps of grass, like brassy porcupines, caught the sun. Where he pointed, over and down the hills, a finger of lake was visible.

He threw back his head and laughed. His voice entered her.

"Surprised by joy," he said, "impatient as the wind, I turned to share the transport but with whom?"

"With whom?"

"Surprised by joy," he said again. "Wordsworth."

"Of course."

She didn't know if he was joking, mocking Wordsworth, or her. "This place is too much like what it's cocked up to be," said Cory. "I keep thinking I'm in some kind of fantastic imitation." They toiled upward.

"Well it is an imitation, in fact," said Albert. "All used up. So well-trod we can't see it new. No one ought to walk here at all until Wordsworth is gone, lost, forgotten. He's ruined it, you see. Everything has been said. In the same way, everything has been painted. Pity me. This is what I have to work with. Agh! Whereas you — over there in Canada you have it all new."

They lay on their backs beside the path, nearly at the top.

"England is soft."

"I call it petrified," said Albert. "A gentle outpouring long ago, it was. Now it's all bottled up and dead."

"Poor Albert," said Cory. "But soft is good, in a way. Canada is hard. No one leaves any print."

The flock of sheep, the dog and the farmer came toward them on the edge of the hill. Cory began to get out of the way.

"Don't move," said Albert.

They lay in the path of the oncoming flock, the little fragile-looking legs and hooves, the untidy tangle of grey matted hair on the underbodies. The sheep split around their bodies and continued on, with their white faces, their shaggy sides. The dog barked and ran away. In the valley the dry-stone walls and slate cottages went into shadow.

They made it to the top. She sat on the crag and pulled at grasses at her feet. She wanted to be there only, without thinking.

"I asked the taxi man if he knew of a good bed and breakfast in Borrowdale, but unfortunately he didn't. Not in this area exactly."

"We'll go down to the centre of town. Try the hotel, shall we?"

She didn't dare look at him. Months had passed since his opening, since he'd been that drunk. Months of grappling in doorways and long denials. Now they had come away together.

They lost the path on the way down, lost it on a slope of skree, and began to run, sliding on the loose rock, laughing.

Separated from Albert, Cory came to a stand of pine. She wandered into it. The trees were sixty feet tall and close together, each with one perfectly upright trunk. The lowest branches were over her head, catching each other to make a web. The ground was khaki coloured, paved with dead needles in which nothing grew. She walked in the dark, occasional shafts of light coming down on her. She began to run from tree to tree between the knives of light and shadow.

"Cory?"

She put her face cautiously around a tree trunk and saw

him. Detachedly. He was a bald man, deep-chested. His hair flew out above his ears under the Spanish-style hat. A trickster. At this distance she couldn't see the candour of his eyes.

"Cory! Come, I've found a beautiful mushroom."

She ran to another tree.

"It will be tea-time when we get down. You'll not get your scones!"

"Find me," she whispered, but not loud enough for him to hear. It was no longer a question of what kind of a woman she was, what kind of man he. All those moralities were too simple, they were for fools who didn't understand life. She leaned against the tree trunk. She could hear him walking. She closed her eyes and knew she would do anything.

"Hah! There you are!" His big hands came out toward her, they set down on her shoulders. In the midst of her scream his lips landed on hers.

"Come see the mushrooms," he said, gently.

"They're not. They're toadstools."

"No, they're the very best. Come see, the colour. Here —" he picked one of a clump of inverted, twisted brown fluted shapes, and held it to her nose. "Chanterelles, you see. They smell like apricots."

"I know chanterelles. These are not," she said, but he did not like to be disagreed with. "Shall we pick them?" she said, preferring to be poisoned than to offend.

He kicked at the little clump, savagely, and it disintegrated. "No, they're too old." He pulled away from her. She caught his arm and then he pulled her with force against the trunk of a tree and kissed her, hard. The thrill ran riot up and down her body.

Now the path was truly gone. Perhaps no one had ever walked in this forest. They came to its edge. "The edge of the forest," whispered Cory. Like in a fairy tale. There was no edge to the forests she knew, at home. These forests must have been what the brothers Grimm had known. She understood the limits of Europe, then. The edges were known.

They came to a wall. She climbed halfway up it so she could see over: There was their path, and the stile, somehow magically before them. Albert was put out; it went against his dignity to climb a wall. It became necessary for him then to ask her to take pictures of the cliff, the tombstone rocks, the sheep in the valley.

"Somewhere in the world," he said, "financiers are leaping out of windows, and Hitler's men are on the march, but not here."

"Not here," said Cory.

The hotel was ancient, sunken and grey. They roused a ginger-haired young man. After several minutes poring over an enormous ledger he agreed to let them have two rooms, dinner and breakfast. They carried their rucksacks along the hall and parted; Albert across the cobbled courtyard to the annex, and she along the hall to a room on the front.

The bed was narrow but the linen was thick and white. The wall paper was foxed with damp. The cupboard was a corner with a cloth strung across it, the wash basin the size of a cereal bowl.

Cory pulled aside the much-washed chintz curtain and looked into the street of Rosthwaite. Shadows leapt out from the base of the walls as the last walkers, jackets tied around their waists, made for a fire, and tea. She looked from the window to the mirror and saw that she looked the same as the other walkers, pink and wholesome with exercise. She did not feel wholesome. She took off her boots and rubbed her feet and calves. She removed her shirt and washed under her arms. Her nipples stood dark and hard. She put on a white shirt and trousers.

She found Albert in an armchair, his chin resting on his chest, his eyes vacant. He reached for her hand as she came to sit beside him, touched it and then withdrew. Something had made him cast down, the papers beside his chair on the floor.

"It's the humiliation of England you're seeing, Cory. Can you imagine we used to run the world?"

They looked in silence at the gatherings, a family, a trio of school boys, a young couple self-conscious in their togetherness.

"It's very difficult you know. Ten years ago I'd have laughed myself silly at anyone agreeing to paint for these bastards, your friends. Laughed. *My* friends would have fallen about the floor. Now they're bloody impressed. You see it's all about money, isn't it?"

"Why do you call them my friends?"

The tea and a plate piled with scones arrived. Cory poured, not looking at him, letting his words run into her from the side. She thought sometimes she'd fallen in love with a voice. His voice was elegant, ranging from histrionic to intimate, a voice in which anything could be said. Talking to Albert made her aware of what she didn't say to anyone else, all that she never had anyone to speak to about.

"Work I'd have been very insulted even to be asked to do, now I'm desperately grateful for, do you see?"

He raised his hand heavily and took the tea she offered. "You don't see. How could you possibly see? Over there in the new world you are so rich, you can't know how it is to debase oneself this way, simply because the money will pay for the coal or the taxes or buy an electric heating system for your wife who suffers from the cold." He paused, then rumbled on.

"Liss now, with her decorations. She'll do well. You'll see. She'll do very well indeed. And ten years ago it was the other way around. I was on top, and she was just a little thing, not serious, not at all serious."

"I'm not rich."

"But you will be. You are one of the natural ones who rise to the top, wherever you are. Whereas I am a sort of lost generation. Before the war, who would have thought it? That everything we had learned, everything at which we excelled, would be worthless. Worthless!"

She said nothing.

"You see, I wanted my gifts to be recognized. A terrible mistake that, to want something too much — even if it is the most wonderful thing in the world. I'm telling you something very important, Cory. You must not want too much. Everyone wants an electric washer in their home, you see. The politics of peace," he said. "It's what we're living in. That's why we've come to this. There's only one way it can end. Then your like will be everywhere."

"Albert."

"We're going to have to live through another one of those wars."

He stared at her as if she made him curious. Cory thought with a kind of shock that, according to herself right now, a war was of amazingly little moment. Through the window she felt the last daylight pouring over her skin, her neck, her shirt.

First potato and leek soup, then steak and kidney pie with a thick crust and a lot of gravy. A waitress with a lank black plait and wide hips put huge tin bowls of carrots, mashed potatoes and boiled cabbage at each table; the guests ate with no pretense of delicacy. Pudding was half a canned peach with meringue and whipped cream on top. Finally, a tray of cheese and water biscuits and a tall glass of celery stalks appeared on the sideboard.

In the lounge, with coffee, the young marrieds brought out a game of draughts and commenced to play, the wife following the husband's instructions. The others began to chat: How far had they gone that day? were there too many dogs on the paths? was the lack of rain not amazing?

Albert lit a cigarette and asked for two brandies.

Cory took a searing gulp of it and felt it open her throat. This was where they parted, he to his room, she to hers. He stopped at the staircase and groaned.

"What is it, Albert?"

"Your breast," he said, allowing the back of his hand to brush it. They faced each other, narrowly out of sight of the men in the bar. He put his hand on the back of her head and pressed her mouth against his, as if turning a doorknob, half a turn this way, half a turn that. The shock went up the front of her legs, down her arms.

He pushed her back against the wall, put his other hand against her waist. He was stronger even than she knew. He thumped her up against himself, hard, released her, and then ground into her again. Her hips turned away from him, one leg bent and pulled in, across her other leg, protecting herself, but he took a finger and drew a line straight down from her waist over the closing of her trousers. Her brain emptied.

"I am soon going to take you to bed," said Albert, and pulled himself away from her.

Cory stood in the hallway. "When?" Then, for the sake of propriety, she went back to sit in the lounge.

"But I'm boring you," piped the thin-lipped man with red cheeks. He was explaining some technicality regarding Derwent water, and the arrival of the swans, their length of stay. Cory shook her head.

"Not at all." In her mind's eye she could see Albert

across the courtyard in his room, moving heavily, arranging his pocketbook, taking off his watch. Time passed with maddening slowness.

"You can only jump in one direction," said the young husband plaintively. "I'll let you win but I won't let you cheat."

"You'll be lettin' her do both before you've been married a year," pronounced someone in dour tones.

Cory picked up a copy of "Cumbria and Its Environs" from the stack of papers on the corner table. The coal fire was low but the room was very warm. She turned the pages of an article about Sara Coleridge. "I'm very tired," she murmured aloud. The man with the thin lips grunted, not fooled. The married couple smiled in a conspiratorial way. Was it so obvious? Did they feel it? Did the whole room feel what passed between Albert and her?

In her tiny sink Cory washed. Wrapped in a cardigan, she crossed the hall to the communal bathroom. Then she let herself back into her room; the brass lock on the door was very heavy, and made almost no sound. The floor was cold.

The bed was warmer, the blankets heavy. But she lay in a tight knot under it all. Her feet were like ice. She climbed out of bed and put on her thick hiking socks, then lay chattering under the smooth whiteness and stared at the door where the doorknob would soon, she imagined, turn. What if he comes? What if he doesn't? She recalled the path, the scattering of yellow leaves over the blades of green, the particular thick texture of that wet-stained bark. Albert's rough hands overwhelmed the memory, his coarse red beard and the tender paleness on the top of his head.

She wondered if she was, technically, a virgin. There had been poor Judd. Probably he had had too much to drink. Or else he wasn't capable. She had no way of determining; it was the first and only time. "You know Cor darling I have greatest regard for you," he had mumbled as he undressed in the dark. "Nothing that follows should take that away from you."

What followed was not much, actually. Moaning, grasping, smearing of flesh, but either he wasn't hard, or he was too small, because though he squirmed and pressed, he made no entry. It had been a disaster, although afterward she laughed at the way they'd tried to stuff the flaccid thing in her. She'd had no inclination to try it again.

She thought that she would never sleep, yet it was from sleep and nowhere else she was pulled, in one long hoist, by his voice.

"*Coreee!*"

The whisper came from outside the window. She jumped out of bed, parted the flowered curtains and looked out on the sleeping village. He stood in the middle of the street, his cap in his hand, his coat open, his feet loose in his unlaced boots. She pressed her cheek against the glass until he saw her. He pointed to the back door of the hotel and she nodded.

Cardigan over the droop of her flower-sprigged flannel gown, she twisted the latch, expert as a thief, opened the door without a sound and crept down the back stairs to the courtyard door.

He wasn't there. Cold seized her, it ran up her bare legs.

"Oh, damn him," she said to herself. "What on earth kind of game is he playing now?" A half-awake fury seized her. What was she doing with this madman, freezing to death in the middle of the night?

"Albert," she whispered. "You idiot!"

Sock feet on the wet cobblestones, she skated across the courtyard and around the corner of the sagging hotel, into the street.

He was sitting on a water trough, his hand on the spigot. "There you are!" he boomed. He looked at her nightgown, the thick socks bulging around her ankles. He put back his great head and laughed. "My seductress has come!"

"Are you going to laugh at me?" Her voice, soft as she could make it, seemed to echo in indignation against the stones: "at me, at me?"

Albert roared again. "I adore the way you speak, you're so *simple*." He calmed then. "Shall we walk a little?"

"I have no shoes —"

He took her hand, lightly as if they were to perform a minuet. They paraded the street of Rosthwaite, his great loose boots dragging on the stones until he took them off and danced sock-footed, a big man released for the moment from gravity.

"It's not even dark."

"The moonlight gets mixed with the mist, that's why."

They looked for the moon but it didn't show, it was merely a pregnant white cloud over the steeple. The wet leaves of rhododendron and azalea bushes were slick below the absorbent black of tree trunks, the dappled grey of the stone houses. Perhaps everyone in town was asleep. Perhaps they were not, but were watching from behind dark windows.

"You're mad."

"No, you are."

They walked to the edge of the common and then suddenly the ground began to crumble under their feet and they were in the bushy grass at the edge of it. They heard the stream long before they saw it, water over stones.

"Albert, I'm cold."

He was looking into the water. "You're cold? I'm not."

"You're all dressed."

He turned to her suddenly, wrapping his arms around her and drawing her into the warmth of his chest.

"Of course you're cold, my darling. Here I am standing, thinking my own thoughts and forgetting you. You who has made me this happy. I am so very, very pleased," he said.

It was warm inside the cave of his great arms and chest. His beard covered half her face, and the twining of his wrists behind her back tipped her chest up to his. Now he pressed his face down to her breastbone and moaned.

"Oh Cor*ee*, Cor*ee*." He let go of her hands and began to massage her back, feeling her wing bones. He rolled his forehead back and forth across her chest like a great ball.

He was moaning softly and moving his feet, like some giant cat readying himself for a kill. She watched, for a second, the top of his head, freckled, with a few strands of hair over it. The pounding had begun in her again; her body undulated.

"Let's find a tree," he whispered hoarsely. "Any tree." But he was not talking to her, he was talking to himself. "Cor*ee*, be my eyes. Where the hell's a tree in this bloody tree-rotten hole?" He staggered a little, pushing her backward. "You're not a virgin, I trust."

"I'm very, very cold," she said.

"I'll keep you warm. Here, here's a tree."

She could feel the bark against her back. Now his hands slid under the sweater to her breasts and reached down to pull up the nightgown.

"Oh all this time, how bloody long it's been, Cory dear, and you didn't even know, you didn't know —"

There was no history to this moment. It was a revelation, and nothing could have made her speak as he spoke, in sentences, reasoning.

"If I had — all last year if I had told you, if I had said, what would you have done? But it's better I didn't, yes, it is —"

His words were all mixed up with her sweater and her exposed flesh. Head above his, Cory searched out the pale stones that marked the path to the hotel door, standing ajar as she had left it. She would concentrate all her will on getting there. He put his hands under her and lifted. Up against the tree, she wrapped her legs around his waist, holding him with her knees, the soles of her feet against the back of his thighs.

"Oh, stop," he said, "stay like that, just a moment. You limpid white thing —"

"I wish you wouldn't insult me," she complained.

"Oh, such innocence, it is too terrible, you are too dreadful a thing, what can I do with you?" he groaned and thrust himself against her again. A knot in the bark pressed into her spine. Her skin was scraping raw somewhere, she couldn't tell where, and the breath was coming in and out of her in sobs.

"Let me memorize you," he said, "like that. Oh, the outrage." He held her at arms' length but it was tenderness in his eyes, a tender assessment of a new equal, or so she thought. He bent to kiss her.

She pressed her hand to his mouth.

"Please, Albert. Wait, wait, Albert —" She pushed him off and got her feet to the ground. Then she began to run for sheer joy. "Come on, we'll go in." Joy and the power of knowing he'd run after her. At last they were inside, and the door shut on them, and she lay down with him in fiery heat for one solemn moment before they acted, and reduced all that had gone before to rubble.

Chapter Seven

This man is hemmed in by his possessions, books, paintings, photographs: Even the spiders have conspired to weave his prized items to the mantles, the tables and the door frames of his house. The collector and his collectibles appear, in fact, to be choking each other out. Ditchburn never wavered in her disdain for the art market.

છે

IT WAS THE NEXT DAY, AND IT WAS RAINING. THEY WOKE UP together to a world persuasively like the one they had left. But of course it was not the same. Ever. First Albert felt closed in by the lakes. He began to talk about his old friend who lived near York. By noon he was convinced he had to see Wally. They called the taxi to drive them to Keswick, where there was a train. The driver was called Septimus Boyd.

"Do you know what it means?" he asked Cory.

"I suppose it means you're the seventh son," said Cory.

He looked at her with new respect. "The Roman emperor was Septimus," he said. "I suppose it's in me blood." And then after a pause for her recognition of just whose taxi she was in, "Have you been in Borrowdale before?" he asked over his shoulder into the back seat.

"No, she has not," said Albert.

"At least now I know what fells are." Cory spoke up.

"Now you are a fellen woman."

Septimus seemed not to have heard.

The fog was in for good now; it would never lift. Still there were these too-bright greens and yellows, the red of dried blood. She lay back on the seat. She wondered why they had to see Wally.

"Wally thinks I'm lucky. Wally thinks I am charmed, to be still alive."

"What will he think about me?"

"Whatever he thinks will be fine."

It was a luxury to let the landscape go by, beaded by the drops on the windowpane, a general seeping.

"Tears are redundant, my darling."

The station had high, empty ceilings and metal rafters. Its red brick steamed in the mist. The Ladies was outside on the platform. The chain unleashed a gush of water from the tank overhead. Shivering in her rain cape, she stood a distance away from Albert, looking down the track. She thought of the fire last night in the lounge, the faces so rosy, the climbers who had "caught the sun." "A lot

of dogs on the path this year, don't you think?" they said
to one another. "How far did you go?"

Now it was over and done, the night gone and the bed
with its white sheets damp and tangled and left behind.
Back with all those needlepoint signs. Please no Boots
or Backpacks in the Lounge. Please do not Neglect to
Leave Your Key. The hundred thousand pin-prick admo-
nition: What a place they'd chosen for such manifest bad
behaviour!

"Albert, I love you," she had said. "Oh, never stop, never
leave me, never." The words had escaped her throat in a
gasp. It was as if they had been lodged there forever.
Accepting fate was such a childish pleasure.

At the information window, they asked how they could
get to York. The clerk's face was full and white, his eyes
small behind rimless glasses.

"The 10:40 for London. You'll want to get off at
Preston."

From the train window the great bare green hills rose and
drained off backward. Cory sat with her back to London,
facing where they'd been. The hills went by the windows,
and the running streams, and the stationary cows, and the
wheeled carts on the road, farmers staring after them.

Scattered pale-front houses gave back a momentary
sun. A sudden stream under the windows reflected the
narrow, crossed tree trunks in its shallows. Cory wanted
to reach out the window and grasp something to hold herself still.

"We ought to have a child," Albert said calmly.

"A child?" She was astonished.

"It's what people do. One always wants a child when one is in love."

"One?"

"That's the Cambridge first person. A child by us would have the most amazing qualities. Think of it! Your *competence*, that terrifying colonial practicality. Your robust psyche. We Europeans like to destroy. You have not reached that stage in your evolution. It's your charm, my dear, you mustn't *mind* my saying it."

Her hands had fled over his body, taking it and pressing and holding him. She had unbuttoned his shirt. The white curls came out the bottom. He had made curious sobbing sounds. "Am I cold? Are my fingers cold?"

"No, no, not cold," he said. And sobbed more.

"Why didn't you tell me from the beginning?" he asked, after. "That you loved me too?"

"It seemed so halfway. And sordid, somehow. With Liss. I thought, if it can't be right, then I don't want it at all."

"You're like me," he said. "I am so pleased. I too would prefer to have nothing than to have some poor approximation."

At Preston the Tea Shop on the platform had yellow walls and sky-blue trim. Flat skylights in the ceiling let in a watery sun. The wooden tables had red plastic cloths over them, a tiny vase with a dried flower stood on each. Behind the counter the woman's hair was streaked with grey. She did not look up as they came to her counter; she was busy adding hot water to a large metal pot. Then she dug out a handful of tea and tossed it in. She took a wooden spoon to drown the leaves. Albert gave the order.

"Eggs and ham. Peas and chips. No bread and butter, dear. Two teas."

Without a word, the woman jabbed at the tea leaves savagely with her spoon.

Albert brooded with his elbows on the tablecloth. From the kitchen came the sound of a wireless. It was a Gershwin song: "No, no they can't take that away from me." A man's voice sang along, lustily, from the invisible backroom kitchen. Male travellers perched on their stools.

"You from Preston?" said one, staring at Cory.

Albert gave him a fierce look but this man had seen greater impediments. His eyes did not move from Cory, her face, her ankles with their ruff of rolled sock under the skirt.

"You from London, then?"

Cory shook her head.

"Did you come up here for a visit, then? Looking for work, are you?"

Albert was eating his way through the pile of chips, steadily. She wanted him to come to her defence, but he did not. The man with the wild eyes and unkempt hair, the closely buttoned vest inadequate for the cold, the coddled cup of tea at his chest, sat on his stool frankly absorbing every inch of her.

"Do you think you might stay on, then?"

The woman behind the counter spoke up. "The York train will come in on this platform."

The wild singing from the kitchen stopped. A man with a face grey as dust emerged carrying another plate. "That's if it comes," he said merrily, a merriment all out of proportion with the circumstances. "And if it doesn't, you'll walk."

Cory and Albert laughed.

"It's no good laughing about it. Sometimes it don't. Like last night," he said. But they did not want to hear about last night.

The stranger had not taken his eyes off Cory. "I'm from London," he said. "Came up here. I had a job."

Albert stood, pushing his fingers across the embossed plastic surface of the tablecloth.

"I'll pay now, dear," said Albert.

"I'm very sorry about 'im," said the waitress as she counted out Albert's change. "'E comes 'ere every day. 'E's a bit not right, you know. 'E does that. All the time askin' questions, 'e sometimes gets very personal. Where do you live, that way. I have to stop 'im, when it's young girls. 'E used to have a job at the zoo, you see. Bit by a camel 'e was and then they laid 'im off."

"Extraordinary," said Albert.

"'E tries all the time for other jobs. Comes in 'ere and tells me. And it's every time the same thing: 'E's got it already, soon as 'e's been in to see 'em. I have to say to 'im, there's ever so many others trying for the job too."

The sun poured a torrent of its yellow down through the ceiling, illuminating the cook, the waitress and everything they touched. They were hallowed by it, even Albert in his black hat. The red Kit-Kat sign flashed wickedly. The music poured from the kitchen again and the man who was bitten by the camel went by the window on the platform, looking in at them. Cory stood up. Her knees buckled. The cook and the waitress smiled brilliantly as Albert collected his change. The room was in relief as never before and she did not know how to stop it breaking over her. She thought, I never want to be without this again.

"There's ever so many of 'em now," said the woman. "I get 'em in 'ere every day."

Albert was standing by the counter. His flat hat was beautiful, his face thin and peaked under it. A far-gone raffish look had descended on him with the sun, a reminder of something he had been twenty, thirty years ago. *Before she was born.* Coarse grey hairs sprang from the knuckles of his fingers. "We ought to have a child," he'd said.

"Thank you, dear," he said to the kind woman. He knew to call them dear.

"That'll be your train now, flowers," said the cook.

"You're off, then."

"Goodbye!"

The two grey people who were not old stood side by side behind the counter and waved them off. It was like leaving home. Albert opened the train car door and handed her suitcase in.

On the way to Wally's they sat side by side, facing forward, leaning back. Cory was almost asleep. Albert was bleeding words; he had been from the start. Now it was about the Great War.

"Someone said I lost my nerve and I suppose I did. But it was more than that. When I discovered how easy it was to die I didn't want to anymore."

Cory lay her head on his shoulder. She wanted to know what was going to happen, but as there was no knowing, it was fine to listen to his voice.

The taxi dropped them in front of the gate of a huge stone house. In Canada, if you had such a house you'd be rich; if you were rich you would not be mad, and drunk, and sitting in the dark with a few candles in a cold kitchen about to eat a lone egg and a bit of fish for supper, your rooms impassable for the stacks of canvases in every corner.

"We're about to eat dinner," said the woman with the lank black hair and a whine in her voice. "He likes to eat very late." She did not invite them in. The taxi had disappeared into the night.

It was nearly midnight. Albert smiled gently and pushed Cory in front of him through the door. He began to remove his coat.

The woman had a battered look; only hunger for this long-delayed dinner gave her the nerve to resist Albert's slow and deliberate progress into the house. He took pity on her.

"Tell him Albert's here."

"Albert?" she said. Her mouth began to gape. "I think I've heard him mention Albert —" and she turned and flew up the tall steep staircase. Albert continued to remove his things.

"Prepare yourself. No one comes to see Wally any more. He's so bad now I'm the only one still speaking to him."

Steps pounded on the floor above their heads.

"Albert?"

Feet in curled-up leather shoes were visible at the top of the stairs.

"Wally?"

"Al-bert!"

"Hah!" said Albert.

They embraced in mid-stairs.

"You old dog, you!" Slapping each other's backs and embracing, the two men struggled together up to the landing. Wally was gaunt, with ruined teeth and great long fingers black under the nails.

"I love this man, I love him!" Wally opened his shirt. "My heart. It's pounding. See it pounding. Put your hand there." And he seized Albert's hand and put it on his bare chest. To the woman, he said, "He never comes here, Babe, never, that's why I'm so fuckin' happy."

"I only thought, we were about to eat —" whined Babe.

"Hey, Albert, how have you been, Albert, my old friend. Hey what have you got here? Look at me, will ya?"

They had their shirts open, both of them, comparing the hair on their chests.

"You've gone all white man, but look at my crop. It took me fifty years to grow that crop, man! Look at my heart pounding. Look at it pound."

"I suppose I'll have to turn down the dinner," Babe remarked mournfully.

"You do that, Babe." Seeing Cory for the first time, Wally whistled. "Hey, you, man, you are some devil — you never tell me anything, you never come to see me and now — who is it?"

"A friend of mine. She takes photographs."

They all sat at the cluttered table. Wally shaved a nugget of hashish into a pile of tobacco and rolled a cigarette, talking rapidly all the time in an oblique way.

"I love this man, truly. And he never comes to see Wally, never never. So why tonight, you drive up in the friggin' rain, why tonight Albert? You came to see your old friend. Say, I remember, you like photographs?"

Albert's eyes were full of sorrow. The collector was rummaging through the stacks against the wall. His bony back showed in the cold room, his skin a bluish grey, as if embalmer's fluid, not blood, ran in his veins. "Let me show you this one. It's a thousand pounder. Where is it, where is it, has that deformed cow lost it?— no, here you are baby, right here, here you are baby —"

He pulled a yellowed envelope out of the pile and brought it to the table.

"Clear that off, will you?" he said to Cory.

Cory began to push the ashtrays and the teacups to the other end of the table.

"Can't you speak then? Talk to me. You don't like photographs?"

"I *take* photographs —" she got out.

Wally froze. He struck an exaggerated guarding pose. "Oh —oh," he shrieked. "She's not from Albion's shores. She's got this totally fucked up tongue. Say more. Where are you from?"

"She's Swedish," said Albert.

Wally leaned across the table over the surface of the yellowed photograph. "Look at this. Just fuckin' look. It's a thousand pounder, Albert, you wanna know where I got it?" His long fingers wove over the surface. It was a photograph of the sphinx and the pyramids. You could see the individual grains of sand. "You know when this was taken? Eighteen fuckin' fifty-seven, that's when it was taken. Guy called Frith. He developed it right there too, in a tent in the fuckin' desert."

Cory looked at the photograph. It was beautiful.

"You wanna know how I got this, Albert? My friend called me up see. Some bloke brought it in to his shop, said he thought he might be interested, old photographs, from the uncle who died, some story. My friend gives him fifteen quid and calls me in the pub."

"You're still allowed in that pub, then?" said Albert.

Wally waved a long thin hand. "Says I think I've got something you might like. Photographs, Frith, eighteen fuckin' fifty-seven. And I say how much did you pay? And he says fifteen quid. So I offers him five hundred. Now I'm gonna sell it for a thousand."

Wally pressed the long fingers of his other hand into the table.

"You fuckin' believe me, don't you Albert?" Now the

finger was pressing into Albert's chest. "I could have got it from my friend for a hundred, you see? But I don't do that to people."

"Who's buying?"

"People with money, you fucker. You think there's nobody with money out there? Somebody from New Yaark, that's who. Going to lay down his precious dollars for this." He looked at Cory. "Swedish babe? Are you equipped with a brain?" His ravaged instincts caught something between them. Cory bridled.

"Wally insults everyone," Albert said. "Even his oldest friends. Let's go to bed."

"Albert, you're lucky, you always were. How come you're not dead — that's what I want to know?"

They followed Babe through the house. Room after room was choked with boxes, stacks of books, rolled canvases. The parlour had a beautiful carved-marble mantle, and a gilded wooden chandelier hanging from the ceiling. Dust was thick over everything. Albert and Cory walked hand in hand down the hall to the open door that Babe had sullenly indicated. The room was small and surprisingly cosy. The wallpaper was green with winding vines. The bed was covered with two big puffy comforters, and it smelled of damp.

"Wally is one of the ruined people of England," said Albert, with respect. "You should understand about him. It could be me one day, you see? That's why I brought you here. Periodically I have to see him. He was one of the most beautiful young men in London, not so many years ago."

"What happened?" Albert didn't answer. It must have been one of her stupid questions. Cory sat wearily on the bed and began to unlace her shoes.

"It's the lowest kind of people, the very bottom ones, who are the most interesting. Remember that."

They lay on the bed. The huge house was absolutely still; there was only the black night and silence, the silence of the dead, volumes on dusty volumes, canvases stacked on canvases. They undressed each other without haste. Albert's body was hard, full and surprisingly light. He praised her, opened her, examined her. There was no greed and no goal, or this was the goal, to be touching and tasting and bearing the weight of one another.

Drawn up into the fold of his chest, Cory slept. In the night she felt him waken. He turned on the light and began to roll a cigarette. He had a knife, that same knife; she heard the scraping sound, the knife they cut the hash with. He got up and went out of the room. When he came back he had a cup of tea. He wore his sweater and pants. He sat on the edge of the bed. She raised herself on her elbows.

"Do you want some tea?"

She drank a little from the cup, and watched as he smoked the cigarette. "It's the middle of the night."

"Any other night we can sleep. It's only tonight we can be together."

That was when she understood they were going back.

In the morning Wally was gone. Babe was gone. Cory stood before the long window looking at the weeping, bedraggled garden. The wireless was on: an andante from a Mozart piano concerto. The leaves lay like golden paws on the lawn.

Albert walked out in the garden wearing giant rubber boots which half swallowed his legs. Through the window she saw him leaning on a fence post, staring off past the outbuildings. He was doing what he did most intensely: seeing. Like the pianist taking the music into his body, he was seized by his vision. She tried to guess what his eye had chosen. Perhaps the dip in the fields — a small collapse, through which the stream ran, and the swell of the far field beyond it, that row of unpruned apple trees, the graceful brick curve of the bridge.

She was in the land of decay. The house was overflowing with antiques, its mantles and floors slowly greying over with dust. It was a mad collection of the disowned, the disused, the elegantly disintegrating — and Wally, a March hare amongst his collection. The andante continued. Albert's mood filled her. She let herself cry. There were stockbrokers leaping out of buildings, he said; Hitler was on the march. No one could find a job and hoarders lived behind locked doors. But Albert was not Wally. Why had he brought her here?

Cory felt she was watching the wasting of life, the vast profligacy of it, a throw-away glory. Someone's fingers travelled the piano keys, sounding them with sure intimacy, and through the radio, some trick of electricity brought the sounds here. Albert moved amongst the overgrown plants with that ruined grace.

The final notes rose from the wireless. Silence followed.

Then a loud, static-ridden soundtrack shattered it.

"*If you would like to hear more of this music, you can take your coupon from —*"

"Agh! No!" Cory clapped her hands on her ears and jumped out of her chair. She ran to the wireless set.

"*— you may save fivepence by sending your coupon to —*" Cory seized the wireless set and felt for the off button. It was gone. She yanked the plug. "Bloody English!" She was shaking. And life lurched into motion again.

She photographed the cobwebs that attached piles of leather bound volumes to the marble mantles, and the room you could not enter for the pictures in frames that clogged the doorway. Albert came in exultant. He made himself a cup of tea and followed her.

"There is a red band at the back of the field. And a cow out there with the face of a Renaissance Madonna. Everything becomes so strange," he said. "You see we have been put in touch with the strangeness of things. One begins to understand even the surrealists."

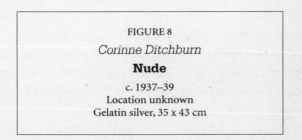

FIGURE 8

Corinne Ditchburn

Nude

c. 1937–39
Location unknown
Gelatin silver, 35 x 43 cm

We can see the photographer had difficulty fitting her subject into a frame, as if he simply overwhelmed it. In the end she captured only the stretch of body from head to hip as he sat in the chair with his chin in his hands, giving us this most interesting torso. That the man is truncated, squashed by the rectangle of the photograph, increases his dominance. She let him fill the frame, great portions of him selected as if by hazard.

❧

ALBERT DID NOT OBLIGE THE CAMERA. SHE HAD TO SPEAK TO him all the while, flattering him, telling him how grand he was — preposterous for his age. She commented on the great patch of chest hair, the rib cage like a bellows, the surprisingly narrow pelvis, taut with musculature, his penis long and shy at the back of that other dark cluster of hair.

In York they went to the Minster. Seen from the pavement, its monster peaks troubled the low, mute skies. The inside was full of racing drafts. Monks or choristers walked through in single file, their long skirts fishtailing at their feet. Albert stared a long time at the memorial to war dead.

They strolled arm-in-arm down the Shambles and stood to watch a pink-faced butcher, the efficient way he slapped the meat on his chill tiles. Sawdust sifted over the toes of his shoes. They kissed in the Merchant's Guild rooms, which were so old that the floors tilted like the deck of a ship.

"These are the guys who started it all. All that buying and selling overseas. The empire builders. Opening up colonies, like your country."

Underneath were the rooms where goods had been stored against sale. Empty now, they had nonetheless an air of riches, of exotic produce, of potential.

"Greed," said Albert, "is so easy to tap in the human. Take your friend, for instance. That's how he controls people, with his money, by tapping their greed. And very sensible of him, too."

"Why do you go on calling Beaverbrook my friend?" said Cory.

"I hear when he meets a woman he admires the first thing he does is send her five hundred pounds and tells her to buy a new dress."

Cory said she did not believe it. "Anyway, what if he did? It's a mark of regard." It annoyed her that she should have to defend Beaverbrook. "Why shouldn't he be allowed to give away money without seeming a cretin?"

"Because it's never without strings."

"You took his money," said Cory.

He went silent.

"Ah, but you see," he finally said, "it used to be possible to do what one did best, what one believed in, and to make a decent, even a respectable living. It is no longer possible, no longer possible at all. One becomes a kind of sponger and even a thief. And by the way, this is a perfectly valid and even laudable position. Integrity of art warrants this loss of another more worldly ethic. Taking Beaverbrook's money was quite justified. It was he who was at fault, expecting that he could buy my art with it."

They strolled out of the Merchant's Guild into a street

of old book-shops, hesitated over whether to go left or right. The sun was declining fast; it was time to go to the station. They walked around a long curve but got no nearer. Cory stopped a man driving a horse cart and asked for directions, all the while Albert standing on the kerb expounding.

"It is not in the nature of art to co-exist with these adventurers, these adroit financiers whose presence you can still feel in this city," he was saying. They stepped into a shop to buy apples and Lancashire cheese, and a loaf of black bread. Cory paid.

Chapter Eight

Albert Bloom is ahead, his hand on the gate, the photographer is in the middle, and Liss, the artist's wife, is on the other side. Arm in arm, they appear at first look to be a family going on an outing. A closer look reveals their roles: artist, acolyte and wife. This was a happy moment for all three in the classic triangle: an older man, his wife, the young woman between them.

⁂

TYKE SNOOPED WHILE HIS MOTHER TOOK HER AFTERNOON NAP. He went through the old tool chest. He had known these photographs were there, but he had not searched them out. He had respected, until now, his mother's privacy.

But, he thought, the old have no need for their secrets, in any case. Crimes committed are in the past. Slights, shames, all fade with age; they become poignant, evocative, or quaint; they reveal something of their time, matters closed off, made innocent by the passage of years. Or so he will tell her when she takes him to task.

Long ago, when he was twenty, Tyke went on a search for his father. He knew only what Cory had allowed him to know, and so in anger and great need he had gone to whatever sources he could find: the dusty libraries of newspapers, art galleries, hat boxes containing letters tied up with fishing line. He was ruthless and efficient, he discovered much and spoke of it never. Then the need passed, like a fever. He hardly recalled the furies that had seized him.

Now he was not searching for his father. He was searching for his mother. After all, he was in charge of the Retrospective. These documents had significance in the overall scheme of her work. They were no longer simply secrets.

He was disappointed because all he found, to begin with, were photographs of himself. There was nothing new to be discovered in a photograph of himself as a boy, or so he thought. Then he found something else. It was framed in porcelain, painted all over with tiny pansies of yellow and purple. In the fading snapshot were three people, three adults. Albert. Liss. His mother. He smiled. It was what he wanted, what he had been missing. It wasn't much of a photograph, but it was the key to the story. A retrospective had to have narrative, didn't it? Cory argued that she hadn't given him the right to put her life together, only her photographs. But, in doing the one, he had of necessity to do the other.

In the photograph, the three of them were coming down the walk to some wide English street. The house from which they had emerged was set back, deep, rhododendron-rimmed, in all its brick propriety. Albert was ahead, his hand on the gate, gazing at Cory, Cory in the middle and Liss on the other side, her arm linked with Cory's. They were all smiling in the broad light of day.

The figures were posed, all three, as if they were stepping out to play themselves in a pageant, as if they must create an effect: They must all project Albert's genius, Liss's intelligent devotion, Cory's youth and good fortune to share this moment with them.

Tyke wondered who took the snapshot. If the photographer's task was to unmask, to un-masque, as Cory has always told him, then he or she had succeeded. The subjects were caught enjoying the image they projected. They seemed to take a deep breath before they entered the street, and like dancers between beats they revealed the dance, the entire dance, in their stopped gesture.

Each photograph was an interpretation, but Tyke imagined that this time the unknown snapshot artist had told the truth: This is exactly how it was. The happy threesome: Albert, Cory, Liss. An older man and his wife and the young woman between them. Albert saw Cory in the light of his wife's presence. Cory saw Albert in the light of his wife's adoration. Liss saw all but her own pain.

Tyke believed he understands. Liss was the prism that made Cory possible for Albert, and Albert possible for Cory. She eliminated the danger. While Liss was there, Albert might have a young lover but not be at risk of losing all. While Liss was there, Cory might dodge the old man's fury, his filth: They were his wife's problems. Because both women were there, Albert was magnified by double devotion. The fact of Cory's palpable desire for her husband must have raised Albert's value to Liss, making him worth the trouble.

This was the message Tyke took from the photograph. Rightly or wrongly, it was a message he found no one to contradict. Tyke felt, holding this snapshot, that he approached the creation of his own character. It was here he began, in the chemistry of these three, two of whom remained unknown to him. Albert and Liss: He had known only their absence in his life. It was as if he lived in a room with an open side, no closing wall. How, he wondered, had his absence felt to them, to his father and his father's wife? He was the child, the grandchild, they never had, not Cory. He stared at his young mother, between them in the snapshot. He wondered: Was it because she could not give up her place between them that he had never known them? Had she usurped his place, taken a love that was rightly his, for herself?

But no. He banished this disloyal thought. It was Cory who gave him life, after all. Albert and Liss had denied him from the start, had they not? It was to Cory he owed it all.

And now his mother had given him this, the threading together of her captured moments. There was a power in it.

I am doomed to be on train journeys in a state of shock, thought Cory. She lay back on the seat facing south this time, her arm wrapped inside Albert's, who sat tight along her side.

In the dark the train hooted on its parabola, throwing them both up against the cold black window. Albert had finally tired himself with talk and slumped, spent, beside her. "Homeward," he said, patting her leg. "Home." He had not mentioned Liss once; now they would see her in a matter of hours.

"I can't do it," said Cory.

"You have done it." There was complacency in his voice.

"We have done it," she corrected.

"We must learn to live with it. We must plan to be alone together. We'll arrange outings. I am certain Liss won't even notice."

"At least she goes to bed early at night." She heard her voice and it shamed her. "Look at how we've become criminals," she said wonderingly.

"Crimes of this nature put you in touch with the whole human race."

As if to prove him right, a little man entered their car. He had an enormous face, and tiny, twisted legs; he walked on crutches, lurching with the jolts of the train. He wormed himself onto the seat ahead, sideways, looking over the back at them.

"I am on a journey to see my sister in Leeds."

Albert offered him some cheese. He shook his head.

"She left her children. Run off with a married man, she did."

The man seemed to know that their politeness made it impossible to look away, which they would have done, had he been made normally.

"She's all I've got," he said. "Go to her twice a year I do, this time of year and spring. And I've been doing that 's long as I lived in York. Now she expects me to change my plans."

Albert shook his head in sympathy.

"You're staring," whispered Cory.

"I like to look at them. They like it, too. No one ever does, you see."

The little man preened himself on the seat, pulling the hairs back behind his ears, smoothing his mustache.

"I'm old fashioned," he said. "I don't hold with these modern ways."

The conductor entered the car. "We are travelling at a reduced rate of speed due to an abnormality in the braking system. This is the six forty for London King's Cross."

"That's excellent," said Albert, tightening his hold on her. "The only reason we ever have to part is if the train stops. As long as the train runs, no matter how slowly, we stay on, though we may never arrive at our destination."

"I should leave London," she said, miserably.

"Nonsense. You will stay, my dearest. You will stay and be my eyes."

She shut her eyes then. She was very, very tired.

"Have you a wristwatch?" asked the little man.

"No need to know the time; you're on a train. Knowing it won't get you there any faster, will it?" said Albert.

"No," said the little man.

Little stations went by, solitary, each lit by one small bulb under the sign that gave its name. At each of them, the train stopped, and a passenger opened the doors and stepped out into the cold, turned, and gave them that last, fatal glance of people leaving light for dark.

The train pulled into King's Cross. It was two hours late. "I don't want to cry, Albert. Stop me."

"How shall I stop you?"

"Tell me about the tea shop, Albert. I want the tea shop."

They gathered their small bags, and walked through the exit, passing their tickets to an uninterested guard. In the queue for taxis, she examined the ground.

"It was all blue and yellow," he said, "with red cloths on the table. The waitress had a square, good face. And a shaft of light came in through the skylight."

"Yes, yes."

"And there was a man there who had been bitten by a camel."

She laughed.

"He had been bitten by a camel and he'd been laid off and he never got his job back again and he will forever hunt for work and stare at pretty women. That's better," he said. "That's better if we end off laughing, isn't it?"

The taxi drew up at their feet.

"Take us to 114 England's Lane," said Albert. "It's too late for you to go back to your place. You must come to us. Liss would be furious if I let you go home."

Cory woke on the couch to the sounds of Liss in the kitchen. Before long, there were soft steps at her side and a large white cup was set down. The heavy sweet morning odour made her lift her head.

"I brought your tea," said Liss. "I thought you'd want to be up soon. It's eleven o'clock."

Cory struggled to her elbows. She could not remember whether it was Tuesday or Wednesday, and she was afraid to ask Liss, who had drawn a chair up beside her, for fear of contradicting some little lie that Albert had told.

"You must have been very tired when you got in," said Liss. "You've left the slides in your hair."

"So I have." Guiltily, Cory removed them. Albert had watched her get into her nightdress, which he much admired, and then had tucked her under the quilts in silence, tucked her up like a baby and then climbed in with her: They made love. After, at some point, he rose and tip-toed out.

Liss had her needlepoint. Cory sipped the hot tea. What a marvel is the privacy of one's mind, she thought. *One's.* An Albert word. It was amazing to her that her secret was not being screamed aloud in this room, that the images she conjured were not visible to Liss.

"I was worried about you. I thought he would run you ragged."

"Huh!" said Cory. "I don't know how you stand it."

Liss smiled. "He needs someone like me. Someone very calm indeed. He needs a sedative, really. That's why he smokes so much hash, that's why he drinks. He's very high strung." She looked up. "But you know this already."

"I don't know how married women manage, I really don't."

"We like to look after someone, most of us," said Liss. "And of course we get a good deal in return. It is not an act of *utter* selflessness to marry a man like Albert. Although..." she said, and smiled.

Cory's emotions were keeling wildly. The thought of his tender ministrations the night before made her eyes cloud, but as soon as they did she tipped violently to Liss's side. Imagine his doing that in his own house! With his wife sleeping soundly beyond the door. Albert was a demon, amoral. She loved Liss; she hated her husband for cheating on this wonderful woman.

"It's strange, isn't it?" continued Liss serenely. "All the strongest, most independent women don't marry. They suppose they will not have to put up with these intrusions into their being. But then they have affairs with married men, and they haven't any choices at all, not really."

Cory felt slapped.

"A woman like that has no choice about when she sees him, or for how long. She is completely under his control. Controlled by his situation."

Liss gazed unblinking at her sewing. The needle went in and out and around, the thread lay bright pink in the hoop. "Why do you suppose a woman would do that?"

"I suppose because she can make her compromises singly and on the spot," said Cory. Disagree though she might, betray her though she had, she felt entitled to Liss's wisdom, to her ear. What had happened with Albert had happened, it was over, far away. The conversation felt quite abstract.

"Just because she's agreed to something once doesn't mean she has to again. There is no institution around it, do you see what I mean? So a single woman *is* more free than a married one, whatever relation she enters into." Cory warmed to this thought. "If you're single, there is no appendage, no man hanging on your side like a giant tuber, you know, no *husband*. At least you can call your life your own."

"I might call my life many things," said Liss. "But I don't suppose I ever wanted to call it my own. It never occurred to me that calling my life my own would be a good thing."

Cory felt Liss was being very stern with her, very unkind. Liss's husband, after all, had brought all this about. Liss ought to be able to keep him under control. She put down her tea cup with a loud clatter.

Liss took the tea cup. "I'll get you more," she said. "It's still fresh." She walked away from Cory, so that her voice came softly, bouncing off the other wall. "Sometimes I forget how very young you are, Cory."

"So have you memorized it?" said Albert tenderly in her ear.

"Memorized what?"

"The shape of our adventure."

"I don't know what the shape is."

"Neat and somehow literary, if you're not careful."

"I didn't think it was finished."

"No indeed, I am certain it is not finished. It may never be."

"But I do know some of the figures in it. One is an artist."

"I think there are two artists in it."

"No. One is the painter and the other is the subject."

"Perhaps we are both the subject, and someone else is painting it," said Albert rather wildly. "We are caught in it." Then he barked his raw laugh.

"But who would be painting it?" she said. This was their game. "I can't imagine anyone but you."

"Not the French. So arranged, so composed. I think one of the Dutch, or maybe the Flemish. Let's see. Van Dyke, yes that's who. It's one of those jokes, where the artist shows his hand in the mirror on the wall."

"Admit it, Albert. *You* are painting this."

"I sincerely hope not," he said. "I'd rather have your clarity, I should think. Yes it might well be one of your photographs. But no, they're too cold, aren't they?"

He pulled away to roll a cigarette.

"Tell me, who are the recurring figures?"

"The woman who is the wife of Christ. The addled collector. The man bitten by a camel. The dwarf on the train."

"Not at all promising."

So it went, until their two-day adventure was contained, made flat, normal. It was better, after all, to have something than nothing.

Cory took a narrow flute of champagne from the silver tray. They were all there, in the sun-streaked reception room, impeccably dressed in pastels, as if they had been there forever, and would never be dislodged. The first person she recognized was Valentine Castlerosse, the Count. His cabbage-leaf ear tipped down toward her while his eye was cocked the other direction, trying to catch some tidbit for his gossip column. A few hairs broke from the smooth backward combing and a narrow greased lock fell over his brow.

"My dear Miss Ditchburn, how lovely to see you," he said. "Now tell me, where do you stand on peace?"

Chamberlain had just emerged the hero from the talks at Munich. He'd been in the papers quoting Shakespeare: "From this nettle danger we pluck the flower safety."

"We can hardly help wanting it now, but perhaps we'll be sorry in five years that we haven't stopped Hitler," she ventured.

Castlerosse roared. "Don't say that around our host, will you. It won't be popular, not at all. He says there'll be no war."

But talk of war was in the streets, an apocalypse averted, with any luck, for a time. There had been celebration for a few days since Chamberlain arrived home. But now, with Prague gone, the shame set in. Shopkeepers went into ten minutes of philosophy while taking her money, and on the bus a total stranger was likely to point out the sandbags alongside Bloomsbury houses. Some of the poets were setting up a fund for Czech artists. Albert uttered dark conjectures on what would happen to the Jews.

"So has old Bloom taught you anything yet?"

She took a sip. Valentine appeared to be a mind reader. "You've said nothing."

"If I had anything to say, what makes you think I'd say it to you?"

"You wouldn't be able to resist," he said, gleefully.

She searched the room for some less treacherous face, but there was none.

"Valentine, haven't you managed to get yourself thrown out of here yet?"

"He can't afford to throw me out. He needs me, Cory, everyone needs me. I and my humble little notes are the only thing that can really write him and his crowd into history." He leaned over her, twisting his mammoth torso away from the shorter figure of Lord Beaverbrook, who was holding the centre of the room. "They practise the black art. Haven't you noticed? They cast no shadow."

"What is the black art?"

"Journalism," he said. "You'll see. It corrupts. Absolutely."

"Why do you suppose he tolerates you?" said Cory, chilled. "Why do we all?"

"Haven't you discovered yet? Ultimately, men want to *become* the news more than they want to control it. The ego triumphs over the superego. Do you know Freud? Fascinating. You must read him." Castlerosse tried another tack. "Has Mr. Bloom figured it out yet, that Beaverbrook thinks the Jews are leading us to war, with their noise about what's happening in Germany?"

"I don't know what he thinks," said Cory. "He's like you. He takes Max's kindnesses and then rebukes him, always behind his back."

Castlerosse bowed slightly toward her. "Touché, my dear. You have a stern and moralistic side. I noticed it the moment we met. It quite becomes you."

Cory moved further into the room. Valentine called after her.

"Has Albert finished my portrait yet?"

She knew where it stood on a shelf behind a dozen others that he had abandoned.

"Not yet, I'm afraid," she said.

Beaverbrook's firm hand closed around hers.

"It is Miss Ditchburn," he said.

"Hello, Max," she said loudly.

"I can't hear women's voices," he'd once complained to her. But he could finish a sentence for some hapless kibitzer across the room when he had a mind to.

Max Aitken's face was unreasonably lined; the skin seemed twice the area of what it had to cover. It was like a chamois leather mask; it should stretch out, when wet, to a great sheet. Behind him, his wedding picture was on the mantle: Max Aitken when he was simply Max Aitken, not The Lord, with his young wife who had not survived the transition. His countenance had been smooth, bland, as a youth, a man whom history held apart, waiting to write on. Now it was a crumpled parchment. She had the odd ambition to touch it, to stretch it out to its original shape and read its text.

He held her hand a trifle long.

"It is Miss Ditchburn indeed," she said, "fresh from the Lake District."

"What were you doing up there?" he said. "Where are all the photographs of London? I want to see them. Every time we put a photograph in the newspaper we sell ten times as many copies, did you know?"

He passed by, and left her standing in the clump of people. Beaverbrook's circle was diminished, and those who were here looked as if they were merely waiting, despite their leader's brave words, "there will be no war." They might have been rich but they had a sadness about them. Their trips to Vienna, to Palm Springs, were now postponed. The postman was held up, the young were going off in uniform, the country houses were to be invaded by schoolchildren. Last week's evacuation had been postponed, but for how long? Could they live on cabbages and potatoes, like the common people, and wait for the casualty lists, again? Insupportable. Still, why didn't they leave, make their own way?

A Dr. Strasser, who came from Berlin, appeared and would not be dissuaded from darkly importuning Valentine. "Make no mistake! You cannot satisfy this man until he has all of Europe. And there must be someplace for the

Jews to run. It is not enough, to take a few in England.
Many, many, many must escape. Your Mr. Beaverbrook, he
must accept not only the pretty women!"

"I suggest you tell him that."

The doctor set off across the room. Cory didn't understand the reference to pretty women until she saw, behind
him, a slight young woman with a gamin face, a narrow
waist and a nervous air. An expensive silk frock hung
loosely on her figure. Her thin fingers moved obsessively,
stroking the exotic fabric, but her hands drooped at her
sides, as if she were helpless.

"This is Mimi," said Valentine, his finger alongside his
nose. "Have you met before? Mimi, this is Cory, the photographer Max was telling you about. She retrieved his
portrait from the scoundrel artist." He grinned mischie-
vously at Cory, who did not rise to the bait to defend
Albert.

Mimi reached out with a nervous hand. "How do you
do?" she said. "Mr. Aitken has bought me this dress, do
you think it is pretty? You know he rescued me."

The woman was so fey her very existence seemed an
appeal for sympathy.

"You'll make several ladies here jealous if you boast of
your frocks from Max," Valentine coached her. "Isn't that
right, Cory?"

"I wouldn't know."

Valentine inclined his head. "Lord Beaverbrook and I
met Mimi several years ago. It was in Juan les Pins, I
believe, was it not, where Max was indulging his notorious

love of the sun? *Il fait le lizard, n'est-ce pas?*" Mimi nodded with pathetic eagerness. "But I didn't think of him as rescuing you. And at the time he was quite busy rescuing me from the casino where I had rather overspent my limit."

"I was singing in the cabaret," said Mimi. "And we spent a day taking a ride in the hills, did we not? I was to stay here in London for six months but it must be longer, it simply must," she said. "Now I am working, I am translating the German news for Max. It is very important work."

Cory found herself alone with Mimi. The wild eyes hooked hers and would not let her escape. The fingers caught her sleeve. "You are a photographer and you have much power," Mimi pressed.

"Not at all. I have no position."

"I must tell you things I know. What my friends have told me. People must understand. You will come with me to the garden."

Her sleeve still caught between those nervous, scissoring fingers, Cory followed Mimi to the garden. It was five o'clock and the low rays of the sun were on the grass of Green Park, just beyond the wall. People had the lawn chairs out, their low scoop of canvas holding the bulge of unseen bodies. Nearer the wall, two women lay on their opened trench coats, basking.

"Do you know," Mimi began, "do you understand what is happening? I'm sorry, but we refugees feel we must talk, talk, all the time to earn the right to be free of it. When Hitler comes to power he builds a prison for his enemies, a jail. It is outside of Munich, where the train stops. A camp which is also a prison."

"Dachau," said Cory. It was strange that she should hear of it again, she thought.

"It is where he keeps now all his enemies, the communists, the gypsies, maybe the Jews. Especially the Jews. And there are doctors too, who make terrible experiments. I hear of a man from whom they have subtracted his parts, you see. Do you take my meaning? So that he can never have children."

"No," said Cory. "Yes. I have heard of this place." She watched the women on the lawn. The sun chose that moment to withdraw from their faces. First one, then the other, sat up, brushed her skirt, stood and lifted the coat. Holding it out by one hand, the first woman shook the coat, gently hitting it to dislodge the blades of grass that had stuck. With a sad finality she moved.

Sometimes we recognize a last moment. From now on it will be winter, or war, or simply that one will not rest again until this cloud that has been introduced, this chill that bears down on us, is gone. Cory always counted that her war began then, as she and Mimi saw the two women pick themselves up from a last bask in the sun, no longer to *faire le lizard*, as Valentine said, and Mimi began to talk.

"You know already the name of this camp," said Mimi. "You must tell whom you can. Tell them it is called Dachau, and there Hitler is keeping many Jews. He is making inhuman experiments. He takes a man and plunges him into ice water to see how long he can live. And if he is alive when they take him out, they put him back in again."

"I don't understand why you tell me, or what you think I can do," said Cory. "You must tell Max. Tell people who can do something. I can do nothing."

Mimi gave her bird cry again. "But no! I tell them and they do not believe. Everybody believes the photograph. You are a woman, like me you are alone, you can do as you like, is that not correct? You will believe me. You have the most power because you are free."

Cory pulled her hand away. "I won't forget what you told me, Mimi," she said.

Mimi flung herself at Cory: The pointed fingers pressed into the flesh at the back of Cory's shoulders, and there were little sobs. Cory winced. She looked over the wall and saw the women retreating from the park.

Chapter Nine

FIGURE 10

Corinne Ditchburn

Aunt Eunice at Home

1939
Chelsea, London
Gelatin silver, 23 x 36 cm
Developed by the photographer

One of the best of the early portraits, this image of a marvellously dignified elderly woman seated in her garden on the eve of the outbreak of the Second World War captures the sadness and fear as well as the pride of that moment in history. Note the plate with crumbs on it and the bird flitting out of the left hand corner of the frame.

❧

ALBERT TOOK HER LARGE PRINTS, PUT THEM UP ON HIS EASEL and squared them off. Then he repeated the squaring on his canvas, afterward blocking in the lines of his subject.

"An artist gets all his inspiration from other arts. It must be second-hand. I can't work from nature, not at all, it's too bald, too face-on, it obliterates itself with a banal directness. What I get from your photographs is false perspective, you see. It's precisely because you are an amateur that you have such luck with these views, don't you see?"

She stood behind and watched him.

"With the photograph, something's not right, and yet we recognize this is how we see as well, that our eyes are constantly telling little lies because of the way light hits surfaces, that even as we see and interpret these lies as truth, we understand *this is not how it should be.* Do you understand me?"

"Shall I put on the kettle?" A generous, calm exhaustion enveloped Cory. She had photographed, had gone home to her flat to process the film, and had come back here, all by tube. They had made love, and he had slept but she had not.

"Photography is inferior to art of course, always will be, because it is mechanical —"

"You've said art is made in the brain, so what does it matter?" she said, a testy note in her voice.

"That *is* where it's made, and not in your viewfinder," he said, astringently. "Photography exists in relation *to*, not on its own merits! Only artists understand how to use it, as I do. You see, the camera can document. I can find it in my memory, which I am losing, alas, along with the rest of my faculties." He made a playful pass at her breasts, turning the nipple between thumb and forefinger as if it were the knob on a wireless. "But better than that, a photograph stops the movement. I've become interested in this freezing quality. It brings your subject to earth, takes out the bubbles, you know, makes it *flat* —"

She moved away.

"You mustn't be insulted, remember I told you. If you take offence you'll never learn."

"Yes, Albert." She was simply too tired to argue.

She buried her head in his shoulder. Opened the buttons of his shirt. Found a home there where she could learn from the slow ticking of his heart, rather than the buzz of his tongue.

"You mustn't work me too hard, darling," he whispered thickly. "You know I'm an old man. Probably when we made love today it was the very last time in my life. I should be quite unable to complain if it were so —"

"But *I'd* complain."

"You are young. You'll have other men. I can't satisfy you. It is always my fate, you see. I awaken a taste, as I did in the public, but then I am incapacitated. I cannot fulfill it. I shall not live long enough."

"I do wish you'd stop going on about dying."

She got his heart pounding and his cock standing up hard under the coarse flannel of his trousers. She sat on him, her lower body bare, while above, the jumper and pearls, a gift from Aunt Eunice, were still in place.

"You'll kill me," he said, his words muffled by her breasts as his lips went back and forth, from nipple to nipple, licking, sucking. They had grown, her breasts, since he'd been her lover.

It was nearly Christmas, 1938. Albert and Cory sat in the studio at night, by the window. London swept by, ever in motion, its black streets gleaming. Beneath the window, they could catch hurried footsteps, a called good night from the arched doorway of a restaurant, the honk and squeal of a motorcar stopping in the rain. They were alone at the window. The power and the glory of London, its hugeness and its numbers, left them cast ashore like this, in the lamp's yellow circle. All else was sucked into the tide, became a flood that passed them — the shops, the grocers, the friends in pubs.

The chess board sat on the small round table between them, its white and black pieces carved of ivory and ebony.

"My father taught me to play," said Albert. He had a glass of spirits in one hand, but the level did not go down. For once his hands were still; he did not smoke or tear at his nails. The intensity of his thoughts was enough, for now.

"In Heidelberg?"

"At his old family home in the Black Forest," said Albert. "Do you know Heidelberg? Of course not, you haven't been anywhere. And now you won't go anywhere. Europe is closing down. You shall never see it."

"Don't be silly, Albert, of course I shall." She had become frightened of what she called his apocalyptic moods.

"Do you know what the Germans really want?"

"To conquer Europe. But Hitler is mad," said Cory.

"Hitler is mad? I suppose. But then, the madman can be wiser than the rest of us. Hitler is logical. It is we, the British, who behave as if mad."

He picked up his knight and placed it in front of her

bishop. "Do you know what Hitler wants? I understand the Germans. It is a small country. And not an island, like this. He wants *lebensraum*. Living space. They feel they are too crowded within their borders. They want farmland, they want to grow food, to find water and forests. This is something foreign to you. Over there you have too much space, too many fields to farm, and trees to cut."

Cory slid her queen off into the corner.

"But here, in our world, there is no space without an owner. And so, when you want *lebensraum*," he said, deftly knocking her bishop off the board with his bishop, "what must you do? You must displace someone. You must take from them. You must fight."

Cory watched her bishop join the growing line of captured pieces.

"I always lose this game," she said.

"That's because you play with your heart," he said. "Always the one who is playing with his heart will lose to the one who is playing with his head. You see, here, on this board tonight, I am Germany and you are Britain. Do you see what Britain has done? Backed away. Tried to find peace. Do you understand that since 1933 we have tried only to enjoy ourselves? To be comfortable? To have the new refrigerator and the motorcar? And we see, with one eye, that Germany is restless, that it is moving. And we hope, we permit, we even suggest. Go that way! You want living space? Take this pawn. Take that knight. It is only on the east, away from me. I am content here. I do not want to engage. But now — aha — now we feel angry. We have paid too high a price. And the land-eating German is still hungry."

Cory stared at the board. "I can't move," she said.

"Of course you can move," he said, laughing. "But you are Britain, remember? It is too late to think straight. Any move you make now would have been better long ago. Any move you make now can only put you deeper into danger."

Cory had been in London two years now. She had been Albert's lover for half that time. She had learned to look at Liss, and speak to her with the same frankness, the same daughter-like affection as before. She and Albert trooped freely around the city — to the theatres, the street markets, the sleaze shops of Soho. She took photographs as studies for his paintings, paintings that remained unfinished, sketched-in lines, drawn and quartered, blocked out, in various stages of execution, all around his studio. She drank Albert's vision like wine, and was drunk on it. She had learned to see what he would see before he saw it, or perhaps instead of his seeing it. Because more and more now he talked, he fretted, he wrote, and did not paint.

Afternoons in the studio they spent wrapped in the scratchy wool blankets on his daybed.

His nicotine- and paint-stained hands moved over her, squeezing, kneading, probing, his beautiful voice carrying on in her ear.

"Open your legs. Don't move. Now that, just there, isn't that marvellous? Don't close your legs, I told you."

Even there, she was the pupil. His hard finger in her pubic bush, drawing down the moisture, or, with thumb and forefinger, rolling her nipple like a bead. Until finally, too wet and too hot to contain only herself, she caught him between her knees, searched out the root of his spine with her two hands, and forced his hard cock inside her. Then, tethered and struggling, neither one the master, keeping on until he became lost as she had been in the beginning, hooting in his loneliness like a train pounding down the track, she held him off, her hands on the cage of his pelvis. She turned herself, and used him from behind, had him riding her bottom.

Their heavy blankets, military-issue grey wool, smelled of tobacco and must and bodies. When she tried to take them out for washing, Albert fought. So they lived with the blankets' odour. She would remember the rough weave against her bare skin, their wild comfort. She never felt so naked as when she ducked out from under them into the cold damp air of the studio.

Albert had become leaner over their year together, which pleased him, but not her. His belly had shrunk. His skin slipped over the layer beneath, was loose on his bones, divided itself from his flesh like the skin of a chicken no longer fresh in the icebox.

To him, all of this was a prelude to death. Often he rolled away from her and took out his cigarette papers. "That just may have been the last time for me. I'm old, you see. The last time I make love before I die." It was his tribute to her.

The more insistent he became, the more radiant Cory grew, cast in the light of his redemption. It gave her so much power that she thought, at times, of giving him up. Would it not be easy, she imagined, in this glut, to find this sort of love again? Was it not common as grass? A natural state? Oh, the conceit of it, of being so well mated. No one else understood. His roughness to her, his belligerence, the way he criticized her work, they were all as nothing. Or as their opposite, rather, gifts. She knew that she was loved beyond reason.

She was without defences when he came near. Even the odour of his old leather coat made her breath come short. Yet despite all this, she imagined that she was not transparent, that *they* were not. That she was opaque, her mind a private space with impenetrable walls. Liss, beloved though she was, had no place there. Liss, Cory believed, did not know. Making love was a fever, it was a sickness. They plotted for weekends away, for weeks alone in a farmhouse in Provence. But they never took one, not after that first. They remained tied to home, to Liss, to the smell of paint and turpentine, to the horns and fumes of London outside the studio window.

They leaned over the wireless at tea-time on April 1, 1939. Chamberlain had just announced the reversal of his appeasement policy. They were motionless. Liss spoke, the embroidery fallen from her hands. "It's about time."

"No, no, it's too little, and it's too late," Albert intoned, gloomily, stirring his tea with the handle of a knife. "You'll see, you'll see, this will bring us war without question, without question."

"But, Albert, you've been complaining all along about how we abandoned Czechoslovakia —"

"Just because one course of action fails, that doesn't mean reversing it six years later will succeed."

Cory watched Liss pucker her lips and silence herself in frustration. Trying to please him, trying to guess what he would think, and endorse it before he did, seeking approval. She felt pity for Albert's wife, and disgust for her lover.

"What have you put in these sandwiches by the way?"

"It's fish paste, dear, that's all —"

Albert spat eloquently into his butter plate.

"I like it," said Cory, swallowing one whole.

Albert gazed gloomily into his white bread and then lay it down, untouched, on his saucer. "War, we shall have war, and then will you women be content? They'll march all the men out again, murder them rank by rank, and you'll be here alone running the show. You'll like that, won't you? And I too shall go, disappear into the trenches with my easel and my charcoal."

"Perhaps you'll be excused this time, Albert," said Liss with mild irony. "Being the age you are and all."

"The woman goads me forth!" he bellowed, and slammed the table.

"Now you've got him signing up and we haven't even gone to war," said Cory, appeaser herself.

"But we shall, my sweet, we shall."

They sat in silence for the few moments in which their tea was hot.

"Liss and I will get out of London, we'll go back to Surrey, to the Stable Cottage. I'm too old for this," he said, "I've done war, it was enough in my life, I don't need it now." Then he uttered his next cruelty.

"You should leave, Cory, and go to Canada. You'd be safe there."

But she couldn't think of going. Not yet. Though she felt sick at heart.

Cory and Liss sat alone at night. Liss was making blackout curtains. She told Cory that someone, a friend of hers, had left her husband and children, and had run off with a student.

"I judge her," said Cory, quoting the little man on the train from York who judged his sister. It was a secret pleasure, a shameful little trick on Liss to use the words she and Albert had heard together from the dwarf on the train; to invoke the taste and smell and mood of that moment without naming it.

"Oh, you mustn't," said Liss. "You really mustn't. It's love, you see. She didn't really have a choice. She was under a compulsion."

"Nonsense," said Cory. "People grow up. They are responsible. They do not get carried away and forget their duties." She spoke in Eliza's voice. She could hear its measured hymn-singing cadence, its flat, nasal, Ontario quality. Duty.

As Liss lifted her needle, the black fabric fell over her knees, down her legs, obliterating the floral print. Cory thought of the needlepoint admonitions in the Rosthwaite hotel. Please Leave your Boots on the Mat. Please be Considerate of the other Guests. Please do not Neglect to Leave Your Key. All the tiny little stitches, the soft and sharp together. The pattern was inescapable.

Cory began to cry.

Cory loped down Fitzroy Avenue and cut against the traffic of Regent's Park Road into the Park.

A far-off bellow from the zoo meant meal-time. The lion was on his last days. As soon as talk of war had become serious, the papers announced that the poisonous snakes and dangerous animals there would be killed, in case a bomb might set them free. Her legs consumed the Boardwalk. She passed the strange little monument put up by the "certain Parsee gentleman" who felt such gratitude to the people of England. She wondered about the Parsee gentleman: What was he grateful for? She too loved England. What had it given him, what had it given her?

Relief, she thought. A relief map. It showed the change of levels, an increase in depth, a coming out. I am always coming out of one country and into another. The country of the past and the country of the present; the country within and the country without. As the sharpness of the new place loses focus, becomes a known, I feel at home. But then, I do not see. I do not feel. A further remove is called for. And she felt it: Already, she was withdrawing from London. Already its lettering, its layers took on the sharpness of regret. She was leaving, leaving.

From Oxford Circus she took a bus. In Chelsea, the brick houses, removed from the street, were stained with wet. In the newsagent on the corner a tiny woman with a wart on her chin sat on a three-legged stool writing laboriously in a ledger under a giant-sized thermometer with a sign saying "Stephen Inks For All Temperatures."

Courage! exhorted the sign on the pub. COOL CLEAR COURAGE. Through the pub window, Cory could see the domino players at their table, with a white pit bull terrier looking on. She passed the bookmakers — *Book Within: Clacton. Colchester. Dovercourt. Eastbourne. Exeter.* At the corner a milk cart stood, the man in his blue hat gleaming white as his bottles.

Eunice sat on a wrought-iron bench in the corner of her garden, in a pale dress, her solitude amplified by the peonies, which, in the wet, were slowly turning to wavy shavings on the lawn. Harry was off somewhere, in America, and she was glad of it, she said. He'd become a bother, trying to tell her what to do.

"I'm going home, Aunt Eunice. When the war comes."

"That doesn't sound like you, Cory. You'll miss a great adventure."

"I don't think I can stay much longer."

"Are you thinking of your mother?"

They never spoke of Eliza. Aunt Eunice was reaching for straws. Her face betrayed not a tremor, but Cory could tell from her even more than usually elaborate composure that the older woman's feelings were at risk.

"It's not the war. It's not my mother. There's a reason."

Eunice smiled grandly. "Ah, a reason, do you say."

A yellow bird flitted amongst the leaves of the rhododendron. They both watched it until curiosity got Eunice, as Cory had known it would.

"What kind of reason would you be referring to?"

There were patches of sunlight on the low pointed black-green ivy leaves, shaped like little arrowheads, which edged across the garden step. The French doors were open to the library. Papers were spread on the footstool in front of Eunice's chair. Never, never again this place. It seemed like such a terrible lot to give up. The air was slow against Cory's face; the sound of the church bell ringing from the next street over was slow; her lips seemed to be moving slowly.

"The reason is that I'm pregnant."

A gap opened in the garden, a fault line, a crater.

"I'm shocked, Cory," Eunice returned swiftly. The two taut lines of muscle that supported her prominent chin drew up once, convulsively. Not a muscle in her face moved. She trained her drop-dead Ditchburn gaze over Cory's face until Cory flushed. Prepare for the worst. "I suppose you think that's rather original."

Cory did not answer.

"Or perhaps you imagine you're being daring?"

Cory was prepared to be pitied; she was prepared to be scolded. She was not prepared to be mocked.

"I hadn't really thought anything — I just am, that's all."

Aunt Eunice pushed down on her knees and rose to her full six feet.

"Well if that's all it is, get unpregnant then."

Now Cory determined she would not cringe. She stood as well, and came nearly to Eunice's height.

"Now you're the one who's shocking me."

"It can be arranged."

"I'm well aware of that." Cory stared back firmly into her eyes. Allowed herself a plea. "This child will be family, after all." She longed for Eunice to ask who the father was, but of course she wouldn't. Nor would Cory tell. It had often been said: Ditchburns were too proud for their own good.

Eunice only stared with greater intensity into Cory's face. "I *choose* my family."

"Why did you never have children?" Cory whispered. "Why, Aunt Eunice?"

The sun went behind a cloud. The colours drained from the garden; England began to vanish before her eyes. Everything good had been swallowed by this. Eunice looked away, back through the windows into her library. The books, the papers. Leary, her cook and companion. It was her life, and now she was reclaiming it, cutting Cory adrift for this crime.

"My husband didn't want children," said Aunt Eunice. "As you know, he thought family meant trouble. At one time I resented it. Perhaps, however, he was right."

Cory flushed with the accusation. She was family: She would not be trouble. She felt the heaviness in the pit of her stomach that had already become companionship. From the moment she knew it was there she had not questioned this baby. To bear him went against all she'd been raised to be, but not to bear him would have gone against all she was. Her penance was to accept the insult, but insult dissolved when it met her, like a handful of dust thrown against a shaft of light. She was thinking of the irregular pattern of the stones, the diamonds and tear shapes made by the deep-etched lines in the tree bark.

"May I ask what you intend to do?"

"I'll go back to the island. The people —" she had to stop speaking. What would Eunice understand of the people? "I can live there on very little money."

"It's a shame," said Eunice. "I heard today they're taking all the manuscripts and papers from the British Museum and having them photographed, in case the museum is hit. You'd be paid well for that."

Cory wondered if this were an invitation, if Aunt Eunice could possibly mean that Cory might stay, even while having a child.

"But it won't do," said Eunice, sadly. "It won't do, and I am let down by you. Of course, everyone lets you down in the end. I don't know why I should have thought you'd be any different." She paused. "Now I've made you cry," she said, not without satisfaction.

"When I can, I'll pay you back what you've given me. I loved being here. I'm grateful, I truly am."

They began to walk into the house. Their separate reflections loomed in the glass door; divided into frames by the panels of glass. Stiffly, Eunice reached over and took Cory's arm. "I wouldn't think of taking money back."

When they parted neither would bend to embrace, but Cory, whose eyes were brimming, felt that she must reassure her aunt. "Don't worry," she found herself saying. "It isn't over. I'll see you again, won't I?"

Chapter Ten

CORY CAME AWAKE IN THE LAST MOMENTS OF THE TORONTO winter's short afternoon; she'd slept through lunch-time. Her pelvis had been rocked by some spasm, some recollection. Passion, that old dog that barked at her door now only in dream. Nagging her: Had it been a misspent life, after all? Perhaps she ought to have been, as Albert suggested, an anatomist of the senses. "You should be making love for a living," he told her once. And later, when she refused him: "I can't understand why you've given it up."

The sun came through the January clouds, exposing one by one the naked limbs of the birch, the lilac, the flowering crab. Sudden beauty was the best kind, sudden and brief. It ambushed the barricades, twisted the heart. The sun came through at the end of the day in London, too. That was its final joke, after you'd dashed from awning to awning all day, dodging the points of umbrellas, rain slopping down on you in buckets.

"London's like that," Albert would say. "The end of things is best here. The end of summer, the end of the year. The end of a life. Don't you agree?"

"There you go, getting all valedictory again," she'd say.

"Just as well I can enjoy it. There's no denying when you're there, my dear."

She still heard his voice. There had been silences, one as long as a decade, but they were temporary and when he returned to mock and flatter, cajole and excoriate her, she welcomed him. Lately she heard him often, speaking from some vantage point of memory or geography, somewhere in her life where she had wandered, unconscious herself of what she'd find there. Tonight Albert seemed to be in her hallway, somewhere between the sun-room at the back and the three doors off to the right, which led to bedroom, kitchen, dining room. Cory walked the length of it, pursuing his ghost, feeling the life come back to her legs.

She'd always been stringy; age hadn't changed that. She'd walked thousands of miles, in war zones, in airports, lugging cameras. Now she put in her miles inside this house, and in the garden where she could feel the walls. Some days with Tyke guiding her she went down to the ridiculous little park with the metal deer sculptures, where the roar of Bloor and Yonge streets cut through the trees.

On her third trip up the hall, she understood that Albert was gone, for today, blotted out by these complaining joints. But he would be back. The cultivated, gravelly voice, its slight drawl, the never-absent hint of venom in the orotone phrases. He would be back.

In the sun-room, she leaned over the pine tool chest that her grandfather, Eliza's father, had made. A pretty fair carpenter, he worked on the ships at Parry Sound, caught rheumatoid arthritis and died at forty-four. Once the box had been filled with hand-made planes, but she'd given those to Tyke. Now the chest held boxes of photographs and letters, boxes that she hadn't published, hadn't shown to del Zotto, Barr, hadn't even shown to Tyke. They were private. Her unguarded thoughts, her secrets, her unvarnished feelings.

The one she sought today was a shot of Tyke on the rocks in front of the Manitou Hotel, the day she came home from Europe. She kneeled. Her knees were swollen; they crackled. She'd carried a man piggyback once, off some killing ground; there'd been a crunching then in the knee joints and her knees had never been the same.

She knew where the photograph was, in which book; she dragged the book to the light. Was that it? That shape might be a boy. The rest she knew to be the pattern of a fish net lying over striped rock. But her memory image — her son's shy joy, his little torso bursting with heart, his face a dish of pure sun — was now only light and shadow.

He was so beautiful that day, she cried, his little body so taut and tender, his sunburnt skin with its white boy-hairs. His shoulders were strong for his age and rounded. She'd seen statues like him, in Italy. But they had been wrapped in sacking against the bombs.

She moved down the hallway to the front room to get the right light to see the photograph. Yes, it was Tyke. The sun had loved him, it followed him, lasted in his eyes, in his laugh, on his shoulders, after it had gone from the water and the rocks. This beautiful, bright boy, she thought, was I ever his keeper?

And where did it come from, his spirit? Sometimes she

almost remembered her own small body that responsive and snug to hold around the knees. How she ran over rocks and threw herself headlong into water. She remembered her quickness by contrast, by how slowly adults thought, how they talked querulously on, forgetting everything important. Perhaps she had been like Tyke then, so sure. And someone had gazed on her with rapture and surpassing love.

Her father, perhaps. But where was his testimony? In his last minutes in the cold grasping water, had he grieved for his sun-blessed girl? Was it he who condemned her to love old men? She at least had her proof for Tyke, testimony for judge and jury when she was called to task for the errors of her life, in this photograph. See how much I loved you, see it even in photographs from which the critics say I excised all emotion.

She once valued pattern above all. It was what they said made her photography "masculine," "modern." She used emulsions to denude the objects she photographed of personal meaning, to scour out the particulars, to turn chairs, trappings, even humans into lines, geometry, darkness, light. There was a strange disconnection of her emotions between the passion to raise the camera and take the shot, and the calculation of the development process. The darkroom was a battleground for control on which she always won.

She won the battles, but had she, as they said, lost the war?

What war was that, Miss Ditchburn? The voice now

was Orestes Hrudy, censor for the Canadian Forces in London. Her old sparring partner. Orest of the pointed, bald pate, and black eye patch.

What war? Well, the fight to keep your head above water. The enemy being yourself, the spurious emotions, panic and desire for oblivion that blotted out reason, and the means to control your camera. The war we all wage against dissolution. And now this blindness.

"Don't you think it's interesting, what life has done to me?" she challenged Tyke, only yesterday.

"*Interesting*? Not the word I'd use, Mother. See how you distance yourself? Even from your own tragedy?"

"*Tragedy*?" She laughed it off. But it *was* interesting that age should attack her eyes. She tried to regard it as a gift, nothing more than a narrowing down of her sight. Part of the process. She reduced people, yes. What artist didn't, to make a statement? This is not Tyke, she said to him when he protested her depictions; this is a photograph of Tyke. Not the you you'd choose to be. But an occasion for my *saying* you, for what I say about you.

"What gives you the right..." he would begin.

"Nobody gave me anything. I took it." And she could count on herself to take it again. But this was what Tyke hated, what Albert called the "callous, rampaging entrepreneur in her." What Max said made her a practitioner of the black art.

She made her way back to the pine chest, and stowed the picture in its book. She turned a page. Here was another photograph no one had seen. Tyke on his tenth birthday. Nine had been the best year of his life, he had announced solemnly. Life would never be so good again. He had been unable to explain how he knew this, but he had been absolutely certain, and nothing Cory saw of him afterward contradicted his theory.

There he stood, a two-digitter, as the men at the Hotel teased him, facing the camera in a thin T-shirt and cut-off shorts, but naked really, his collarbone visible, sharply curved like the jawbone of a fish, his eye sockets hollow, a wild animation in his smile, a feverish happiness damp-ened, there in the eyes, by early wisdom. Something had happened in the time she'd been home with him: several years by then. He had understood, because she was home, that she had indeed been gone, that she had abandoned him those years before.

Those sad, wise children: She'd seen a few, most of them in war zones, but there were others. You met them in New York or Toronto as well, at an ordinary school, saw them currying cows at the Winter Fair or playing on the beach, a little apart, with their haunted expressions. And your heart broke if you let it. She didn't take their pho-tographs, not ever after this, because of the fear of what she would catch in their faces. Something of this pain.

Later Tyke refused to let her photograph him. Said she was stealing his life, he did. She hadn't understood.

But now he was stealing hers.

Retrospective! And what about Lot's wife? she asked herself. There was a poem Eliza used to quote: one of her aphorisms from Pope.

"In vain the Sage, with Retrospective Eye, would from the apparent What conclude the Why."

Tyke laughed: "Mother, for an exhibitionist, you're awfully secretive."

Secretive? She'd had to be. If she let go of all the connections that she was holding secretly, if she gave them to someone, she would be his creature. She was like the wild mink, instinctively independent. Condemned to that.

And to what had she condemned Tyke?

She saw that day again, the day she came home from the war. Tyke running at her as hard as he could, and from three paces back taking a flying leap into her arms, Tyke astonished to see her, yet not at all, because he had believed all along she would come back and he had waited. Such a light of faith in his eyes! When he landed in her arms, his legs wrapping her waist, it was as if she had sucked his weight from the air: She was so glad of it.

She wanted to find that leaping-up boy again. She wanted to tell him she was sorry, she wished she hadn't left him. (Yet she had to leave him: She would not be who she was if she hadn't left him. How to puzzle that out? Her necessity? His secondariness? Perhaps this was why Cory was alone: She'd never been able to work out who came first.) Was it because she left him then, that he couldn't leave her now? Somehow she hadn't understood that his life, too, had its imperatives, that when she left him time passed for him as well, that he couldn't stand still and wait for wars and assignments and dates with whatever destiny. Was his life the less because hers had been the more? It seemed too simple.

And indeed he did not wait but grew, instead, into this angry man who sold her photographs and kept her books and dealt with the taxes. This man who knew more about her work than she did, who had rejected war, and went on to reject women. He could not allow them to have power because his mother had too much (or so she explained his gayness — she knew no other way).

Could she catch him off guard, surprise him again, as she'd done that day? He'd run up the rocks as he did then, and she would fling the cameras on the dock, hold out her arms and call, "Tyke!"

Max always said he knew she was a true journalist because she had perfect timing: If the cathedral wall were going to fall, she would be walking toward it with the sun behind her; if the ship was torpedoed, she was on the deck loaded with film. But a journalist's ideal timing was a disaster for life at large. She, Cory, had always missed people's finest hours. Her son's in childhood, her father's in death. And Albert. She had missed the best of Albert. She didn't meet him until he was old, cunning and rough, nearly broken, a victim of himself and time.

Chapter Eleven

Dearest Coree —

At the last minute I couldn't let you go. I raced up to see if I was too late and saw the back of your head still on shore. I reached her side, but it was not you, only another, utterly dissimilar person whose same brown felt hat, soft as a hound's nose, was jammed over a furious brow. And my heart was broken. In despair I turned and it was then I saw your ankles and your narrow shoes at the very top of the ramp, disappearing.

Somehow I got myself into a cab, hurtled through the Park and over the canal bridge. I saw Primrose Hill from your angle and for the first time understood what you'd said. It does look like a woman's breast when she is lying on her back. Corinne, darling, you have eroticized acres and acres of North London. By the time I was deposited like a sack on the kerb before the house I was weeping.

I thought — you can't possibly be going. It's not so. Your ship will be turned back by German warships ploughing up the Thames, you will call. That beetling taxi on Rosslyn Hill even now carries you back.

> *But no, I climbed the stairs to the house and the loss set in like a terrible mourning. It is too dim to see, and colder. Just this instant the fire is burning in the studio grate and Liss is bringing up the tea. Where are you? I feel as if I've known you for twenty years. How is it possible that you have taken yourself off?*

Maddened, feeling caught out, Cory flushed red. Abruptly she folded the translucent onionskin. It felt alive. His handwriting looked like him, a man in a cape, poking his umbrella forward, swinging it in an arc sideways, monopolizing the pavement.

She slid the pages back into the envelope and the envelope into the pocket of her shorts, pulling her shirt down over it, so it wouldn't get wet. How is it possible, indeed? Again he had said nothing. Absolutely nothing about the pregnancy. For one second, she was on the train again, travelling from the Lake District to Preston, past the draining landscape and the cows with stricken faces. "We ought to have a child," he'd said. "It's what people do."

When she told him she was pregnant, he had said she must do as she wished. Then he refused to speak of it again, other than to say if she must have it, it was hers alone. Children mean pain, he said. I'm too old. I am not ready for birth. I am preparing for death. But you said, she sobbed. Everybody feels that when they're in love. You're so innocent, he railed, so literal. Will it never end, your lack of sense? They quarrelled so violently that he vowed he would never ever speak of the purported child, as he called it, again. He dared her to leave, and she did.

Now he wrote. He spoke of war approaching. Petrol rationed, but sugar available. Children sent to Ford Manor House. Liss making more blackout curtains. London's empty streets. Never a mention of the coming baby.

From the top of the hotel's verandah steps, Cory looked over the bay with its rocky islands and the zigzag line of trees. But she did not see it. From the light, crumpled paper in her fingers and the cadence of Albert's words came a powerful waft of London. The close dark at the end of a wet day, the shadow of Primrose Hill as the sun left it, the lamp posts rimming the edge of the park, the squeal of taxi brakes at the corner.

Oh God, she missed it. She missed Albert. She could almost smell his tobacco, the damp tweed of his jacket. She narrowed her eyes and he was with her; they had climbed out of the taxi at the foot of Fitzroy Avenue, they were leaning together in the rain, under one umbrella, as they walked up toward her flat. The street was very wide; it had been the entrance to Fitzroy's estate. Fitzroy was the bastard of the king, and he had built his house here.

"A bastard is a bastard," Aunt Eunice had said, in her most Methodist voice. And she turned her back. "If your Bohemian friends have taught you to be so open-minded, then why are you going back to Canada to have it?"

That Ditchburn logic overrode all feeling: Why take this thing *there*, where it will be exactly what you say it is not

— a scandal, an unacceptable breach in the code? It was the question Cory could not answer. The problem was not, in her mind, that she, the mother to be, Cory, was unmarried, but that *he*, the father to be, *was* married, married to her friend. She just wanted to go home.

The taxiboat pulled up at the dock, bringing new guests from Pointe au Baril Station. Tourists had increased in the years of her absence. These ones were Americans.

First out was a huge man, with black hair slicked down and parted far on one side. He wore stiff new khaki shorts belted high over his protruding stomach, and glaring white runners.

"Hey, don't take that! That's ma booze!"

A boat hop, likely a Pamajong kid, had taken his case and was now fearfully handing it back.

"C'mon out, you gang. Take a look. This'll set your eyes jingling, what did I tell you?" Out of the boat tripped an overgrown boy and girl and a woman too young to be their mother, clutching a fluffy white dog to her breast.

"Lawrence, you told me this was the most beautiful place in the world," wailed the little woman with the dog.

"It is," he tossed over his shoulder at her, "but it takes getting used to."

The kid began lifting the bags while the three others stood looking up the rock, taking stock of the place. The big man set off toward the hotel. When he came to Cory he stopped and tipped his hat. She gave him her worst scowl. He beamed and marched onward. Cory pulled the brim of the Panama hat she'd bought in Portobello Road further down over her eyes, and stepped off the verandah.

At the end of the dock she bent and swung easily into her canoe, both hands on the gunwales the way she'd been taught when she was three or four. She untied and pushed off, then dug the paddle in deep, feeling the twinge between her shoulder blades. Ernest threw her painter into the canoe as she pulled away.

"Got your mail, Cory Ditchburn?" he said as she drew away. It was a typical conversational gambit around here: Say nothing until the person is departing, and then you're not in danger of getting into anything prolonged. "Good news or bad?"

She arranged her facial muscles to approximate some locally known expression: "Well, yes and no," she said.

He smiled: That was the right answer. "Head right on home, you hear, looks like we're in for a bit of weather."

But she was already talking to Albert.

Darling —

I am breathless with rage at your audacious refusal to know what is going on. I am going to have your baby! Don't you care?

No, you don't. You are a monster. I'll never ever forgive you. No. That's not true. I said I'd take this on myself and I will. We shall be just as before. I promised. And it's true. It's not only rage that has me puffing. I am breathless too from the transports of seeming to hear your voice. Oh why are you so far away, or rather, why did I leave?

Whole conversations come back to me. Like this one:

— So have you memorized it? The shape of our adventure?

— I don't know what the shape is.

— Neat and somehow literary, if you're not careful.

— One of us is the painter, and the other is the subject.

— I didn't think it was finished.

— Indeed, I'm certain it is not finished. It may never be. It may see me to my grave.

The water was almost flat; only the surface raised into tiny hard ridges to portend this storm Ernest warned of. She took pleasure from the straight line of her journey, a straight line she maintained with the deep draw, then the J-twist as she pulled the paddle out of the water behind.

There were three rocks in the mouth of the bay. Heading between the two on the right, she skimmed over a shallow channel. The water was low this year. She saw a giant turtle drifting just under the surface, its medallion revealed briefly before the angle of the sun obliterated it, leaving the mud-bottomed channel opaque again. Lily pads whose shade turned the water black flapped up in the breeze. She shot forward. Now the water was deep again, a chasm beneath her. As she passed beyond the shelter of an outer island, the wind hit; she had to pull harder on the paddle. Just here she came in sight of home.

Safe Harbour was a small island, under two acres, smaller still when the water was high, exposed on the southwest to the open water of Georgian Bay, and several hundred miles of inland sea stretching across to the far shore of Lake Huron. But the inner side from which she approached was a U-shaped natural harbour, steep-sided and narrow at the mouth. Boaters, fishermen, natives had all found refuge here when they were caught in high winds crossing the open channel.

From this side, she could barely see the shack under the huge old pines. The trees were larger on the island now than on the mainland: These little sprits of land were too much trouble for the otherwise omnivorous loggers. It was unpainted board and batten with wooden shingles. Most of one side was the fireplace wall, made of oddly matched rounded stones, built in "step and fetch it" style by her father's old guide and friend, Pierre Pamajong. The small screened porch was on the front; the dock was at the back, protected from the wind and waves by the rocky island itself.

She landed the canoe and pulled it up. She climbed the granite incline, past the shed containing the gasoline-motored pump, past the lozenge-shaped propane tank. Here was her little bit of forest, the pines, a few stands of cedar trees, blueberry and juniper bushes, a drying carpet of emerald moss. A path zigzagged up the shaded, uneven rocky terrain passing the corner of the cabin and around to the open side. It was utterly different: The pink rock had been scoured by waves to marble smoothness. Above the waterline it was stippled with lime and orange lichen. The light was stronger here, too, whiter, pouring in from the west.

The west wind hit. Rolling black clouds were coming in fast. The trees suddenly dipped, exaggerating their accustomed wind-driven posture. Dodging up the two cedar steps, she let the screen door bang behind her. She crossed the porch and opened the cottage door.

Inside it was dark. The little windows were rectangular breaks in the walls where the intense daylight flared like lanterns in a cave. It smelt of wood stove, breakfast coffee, (faintly) of yesterday's fish dinner, and overwhelmingly of the sharp disturbance of photographic fluid. She saw one of Liss's patterned rugs, the blue and yellow pottery bowls that had been a goodbye present, and her breath stopped.

Oh why did I leave, Albert? At least today I could have seen you, working in your studio with that silly old smock you put over your shirt, at least I could have made us both a cup of tea and we could have pulled the stuffed chairs up to the window and peered out in the rain, listened to the hiss of London traffic.

She had seen that last attempt to stop her, that bearded, round face with the devastated eyes combing the faces for hers. But her anger made her see him as a stranger. Albert was old! Albert was mad! Even in a crowd of jostling travellers something marked him as outside the normal. The over-careful way he set his feet on the ground, as if he, and only he, knew that it might heave and buckle under him. She turned her back. Albert was dangerous. Anyway, Albert belonged to Liss.

For that moment she was paying, still, with longing. What if she had let him catch her? She'd have given in to whatever he wanted, and she'd still be there. But now she was here. Alone. At Safe Harbour. With her cameras, a baby in her stomach and a grievous emptiness in her heart.

The first rain clattered against the windows. She forced herself into motion. She would cook herself some tinned bacon, throw together a tomato sandwich with mustard pickles, take a beer out of the icebox and watch the storm blow in. All she could do was concoct letters to him in her mind, full of sentiments she was too proud to write.

She chewed and swallowed the sandwich without hunger. She ate not for herself but for the baby. She had not gained a lot; she was four and a half months now, and still no one knew.

Darling—

"My body is a memory," you said once. Well, it's a memory to me now too. I remember your full rounded belly, and your thighs indented at the side where the muscles ran long. A great crescent scar you have above your left knee. The uncircumcised cock, long, when somehow I had expected less. This

is the secret of you, Albert, the more you take away, the more there is!

Albert, did you predict this? Is this why you talked about dying? This awful pain and longing, wanting you and not being with you and not knowing if I can ever be with you? I feel I have taken some disastrous step over the edge, that I can never go back, and as I struggle here in midair you, whose natural milieu it is, look at me disapproving saying, tch tch, it was not good for me and I should not have done it.

But here I am in Safe Harbour. I fall into my old place. Robert Ditchburn's odd daughter with her camera. I'm convincing, as if I were the same as before I left. No one notices the difference. Only I know I'm someone else, someone all tangled up with you and elsewhere. That they could reach right through me and out the screen door into the mosquito-loud twilight.

Maybe this is all we could take without drowning, you said. But I want to go under. It is too painful up here treading air with trappings — camera, negatives, Panama hat, patterned rug, blue and yellow painted bowls — what I got away with, these trappings bought with slaughtered passion.

Oh, Albert. Could it be worse? You were my teacher. You're old. You drink and you're married and your wife is my friend. You don't want the child.

Yes, it could be worse. You could not exist. It could never have happened.

Cory stood in the open door of the Manitou dining room. The need for human company had driven her here. The need to still within herself that voice that went on speaking to Albert. It was Saturday; she had forgotten. The huge raftered room was full of laughing family groups.

She looked over her shoulder. It was not too late to escape. Except that the American voice like a boat horn sounded in her ear; it was the man she'd seen on the dock.

"Hey you, young lady. Y'all going to join us? You owe it to me after the way you nearly ran me off the front steps there."

The big American, now plaid-shirted, leapt from his chair with strange buoyancy. His hair was parted on the right and pasted across his forehead; it was shoe polish black, and his eyes were a washy blue behind the metal frames of his glasses. His hand, which held hers now, was beefy and soft.

"I'm Lawrence Barr." He dragged her to his table. "And this is my daughter, Ruthie, my son Gerald, my secretary Miss del Zotto. We're all up here from New York. You're a local, I hear."

"You don't have enough fish down there?" asked Cory without a trace of a smile.

"I think she is," said Miss del Zotto, as if Cory could not speak English. "Part of their charm is that they don't want anyone finding out about their little piece of heaven here."

"That so?" said Lawrence Barr. "Well, we heard about it from one of our artists. We run a gallery there in New York."

As Cory's hostility began, slowly, to abate, she noted that Miss del Zotto's long fingernails didn't look very useful for stenography. Without the white dog, however, she had a saner aspect. A woman in her late twenties, perhaps, having an adventure? A governess for the overgrown children *cum* a trusted bookkeeper? Her hair was frizzed and her face pinched, but in her eyes there was intelligence and more than a hint of humour.

"My secretary is fond of wildlife," said Lawrence Barr.

Ruthie and Gerald snickered, casting evil looks at one another.

Minty Pamajong set down a big platter bearing a bass, with piles of fried onion and lemon, and parsleyed potatoes. She grinned at Cory, showing the gap between her front teeth. Her father, Peter, and Cory's father drowned together in '32. Marge Pamajong was left with six kids; the youngest was Minty, so called because she used to crawl around behind the kitchen door in the mint patch in her diapers. They were all handsome, hawk-nosed, wry creatures and they had been Cory's best friends.

Deftly Lawrence drew his knife down the centre of the barred side of the fish and lifted the flesh off the bone.

"Did you catch this? By your smile, I thought you invented it, instead of just tricking it to bite a hook," Cory said.

Lawrence Barr laughed affably. The fillets went out to

his sneering children. "What island is your family's then?"

Cory waved her hand behind her. "Out there." There were ten thousand islands out there. It took a newcomer years to find where he was, once he got out of this channel. "And it's only me now."

"Husband signed up, did he?"

Cory said nothing.

"Your folks don't come up any more?"

"My mother never did."

"And your Dad?"

There was no end to his impudence. And he couldn't be silenced by shame, for she tried staring him down with a look that would fell any Englishman. But Lawrence Barr assumed she was only tardy in replying, and busied himself applying ketchup to his potatoes.

"Dead," she said finally.

Lawrence Barr looked up. "Now that's a crying shame. Young lady ought not to be up here alone without someone lookin' out for her."

Cory sucked in her breath.

Oh Albert, you'd have loved the people I had dinner with; he was your idea of the future, with his blunt acquisitive nature, his stupid kindness. It was a good face, overlaid with far too much flesh, with those big American teeth which tell of a childhood full of milk and red meat, yet there was an intelligence under the lines of his brow, around his somewhat recessed eyes struggling against stupefaction

*under the burden of good living. The woman with
him was much more acute, and watching everyone
at every minute, but so urban it made me laugh.
They say they run an art gallery.*

She attempted to quell the epistolary voice. It had become
an addiction. They stood up to take coffee on the verandah.

"Can I interest you in bridge?"

"I never learned how to play and I don't want to now,"
said Cory.

"She might prefer ping-pong," said his daughter.

"I'm going home," said Cory.

"You okay in that canoe?"

Cory brushed away his concern with a hand.

"I wonder," said Miss del Zotto, delicately, in Cory's ear.
"If you would take me for a canoe ride one of these days,
to see the wildlife." Her sharp little tongue moved neatly
in and out of tidy lips. For some reason, the thought
brought a smile to Cory's lips and she turned to her and
said of course.

The water was like a dark glass in which the rock slopes
and stubby trees were reflected with perfect faithfulness.
The canoe travelled on a thin line of light between two
equal, identical worlds. It passed over the water and it rippled like a curtain hiding a stealthy intruder. Cory pulled
her paddle out of the water and let them drift. Miss del
Zotto was the perfect companion; she went quiet and still
when Cory lifted her camera. "Mink," she said, softly.

"Who gets to see your photographs?" she said, after.

"Nobody. My artist friend, in London," said Cory shortly.

"Is he the father of your child?"

She half believed that no one knew, just because they said nothing. Of course she heard whispers but those she ignored. This she couldn't. No one but the genteel Miss del Zotto said it to her face. It must be obvious now. She had no mirror and she avoided her reflection in the water. "Yes," said Cory. They paddled on. Cory was glad of her sunglasses.

"Lawrence's wife doesn't like to travel," said Miss del Zotto, seemingly offhanded.

"Hah!" said Cory. "I wondered." Nothing more was said; it was enough. There was a strange dignity in this thin-necked creature with her large black eyes, her square black glasses, her neat feathered hair around her face.

"I really run the gallery, I keep in touch with all the artists," she continued. "Lawrence is a great enthusiast but he's too busy with his other businesses."

At the end of the ride Miss del Zotto alighted, apparently weightless, and very grateful.

"Sorry about the wildlife. You have to hang around a long time," said Cory.

"I got to know you a little. And the mink too." She leaned down to shake Cory's hand. "I hope we see you again next year, and some of your photographs too."

FIGURE 11

Corinne Ditchburn

War Is Declared

September 4, 1939
Manitou Hotel, Ontario
Gelatin silver, 35 x 46 cm

In this panoramic view, we see the huge white wooden hotel with its wide verandah facing the dock and the boat channel. The porch swing is tipped back as if someone has just vacated it. The news itself becomes visible, passing from boat to boat through hand signals and the unfurling of flags in the cluttered channel before the vacation hotel. Frightened families stand on the Manitou dock with the bags and cases, waiting to be transported back home. More than a summer holiday is over.

સ્જ

IT WAS LABOUR DAY WEEKEND. HOT, DRY AND STILL. CORY stood on the dock watching. The channel between Safe Harbour and the Manitou was chock full of boats. The water was so stirred up the waves met each other head on. The cottagers were closing up and heading home to Toronto, Cleveland, Pittsburgh. Jimmie Pamajong paddled up to Cory's dock. He was a guide now, as his father had been before him.

"They've gone and done it now and I guess that's it for us too," he said and she knew what he meant: Britain had declared war, and Canada had followed.

Cory ached for London. Just to be there, to hear the postman and the newsagent's voice, to catch the hushed frightened voices of the mothers gathered around the park swings, the children's taunts. In the centre of the fear, where the crowds surged. But war meant war and she felt the blood draining out of her. Would she be cut off from London forever? The baby kicked in the hard blown ball of her stomach.

"They've done it, have they?" she said calmly, squatting on the edge of the dock and putting one hand — one hand that wasn't needed, he drew up so sweetly — on his gunwale. "Well, I guess we'll have to wait and see how long it takes us to feel it."

She gave Jimmie a beer and sat silent on the dock.

St. Pierre's boat taxi drew up at last, a big, square boat with a huge hull to combat Georgian Bay water. St. Pierre was a transplanted Frenchman with a ponytail and an aquiline nose, who liked to use the time he held guests and cottagers captive in his boat to buy and sell any islands he could find. He jumped out and began to toss the baggage on board.

"He's thinking this war's not going to be any good for business," said Jimmie. "You gonna leave too?"

"Got nowhere to go. I'll stay over winter with you guys," said Cory.

Chapter Twelve

CORY BENT FURIOUSLY OVER THE OLD TIN BATHTUB SHE'D hauled from the dump, pulling prints, although Marge warned the fumes would hurt the baby.

"Pickled, you'll have him, in your old chemicals, before he gets his head out into the world," Marge said. "Bad smells, make you feel sick, give bad luck for mother to be."

But she did not feel ill. She felt large, which was different. As if she housed a globe, a water-filled globe that rolled within her, its weighted continent sliding this way and that as she worked. Impossible to write Albert, pretending this was not happening. How long could he keep up this charade? She hated to imagine. She even tried to stop thinking of him. She pulled out the print and hung it to dry. She peered at it, as it dangled from its clothespin. She was pleased with it.

FIGURE 12

Corinne Ditchburn

Self-portrait, Pregnant

1939
Pointe au Baril, Ontario
15 x 24 cm
Printed by the photographer

Ditchburn discovers her swollen body as a naturally occurring shape on which light plays. A stranger to herself behind the lens, she is also the stranger in front, to whom she exposes her pregnant body. Her face, impassive, dares a response in the viewer: The effect is somewhere between monstrous and angelic.

℘

HERE WAS ONE PHOTOGRAPH SHE DID NOT KEEP HIDDEN. TYKE came upon it in the portfolio, and lifted it without a word. There she was, starkers, just about, wearing only some kind of veiling thing, a transparent muslin shift it was. There they both were, in fact, because he was the water balloon in her stomach.

She was standing behind the cottage in the sun, face on to the camera, her gourd-like abdomen pressed out in front, the light falling on, and bouncing off the blind visage of that belly she carried. Her breasts were as small as ears in comparison; her pubic hair just visible below the curve. Her shift was so fine as to be transparent, and she'd caught it filled with light and air, so that it surrounded her like a caul.

"What is it?" he said. It was a small, old print, and he passed it over so she could see it under the light.

"What do you think? Self-portrait," said Cory.

"Mother!" he protested.

She gaped at him. "What's wrong? Are you embarrassed?" His face was scarlet. She giggled. "You're only fifty-five."

"Isn't this one of the ones you want to keep private?" He hoped so.

"I was private. Utterly. I never felt so private."

It was not easy to say who was the more astonished, he at her boldness, or she at his shame.

"This is not a self-portrait," he said. "It's a portrait of me. And my mother," he said.

She laughed. "I suppose it depends on your point of view!"

He laughed too. His reaction was ridiculous, all right. But why did she need to make everything so public? Why did she never realize that she implicated him in her bold moves?

"Have you no shame?" he challenged, half humorously. "You're so huge I can practically see myself in there, sucking my thumb."

"When you take photographs for a living you learn to be objective. Do you know," she said, "how I see every single shot of myself? As another person. The person she was is gone. Dead. I feel compassion for her, as I would for anyone who is gone. But she is not me. Put it aside," said Cory. "Maybe we'll use it."

Tyke put it aside. Maybe they would, indeed. He looked at the woman in the photograph, objectively. He was moved, after all, by her bravery, and her youth.

Dearest Coree —
The vice is tight around my chest: War is on us,
with all its glamour and ruin heading this way like

a train off its tracks. Sunday was the first bomb raid. In broad daylight the Germans flew up the Thames. Their aircraft glittered in the sun as they came, then they curved around and, even as our ack-ack began, dropped their load. Square on they hit the oil tanks at the docks: Smoke rose sulphuric yellow and puce, flames followed. I watched enthralled; only you could have shared this horror with me, its beauty.

Your man Beaverbrook has taken over all factory space for aircraft production. People are buying up all the bicycles, Liss continues the blackout curtains though you'd think by now one had enough. All my letters bring polite evasive responses: I can't get a war job. My tea is bitter as sugar is rationed. Women and babies are packed off in trains for the country. It could be worse: The Athenia was sunk by a German torpedo on its way to Canada, and you could have been on it.

It's back to the Middle Ages; one creeps down the streets of Soho by feeling the walls. In the early hours of the morning we listen to howling sirens at our gates. We wake to see the barrage balloons floating over Hampstead like a lofted fishnet with pearls. It's very romantic but I am useless without you. Let me try your Latin. Turpe senex miles turpe seniles amor. Ovid said it. "An old soldier is a wretched thing, so also is senile love."

There was a note from Liss, too, brave as ever.

> *I'm sitting at home by the wireless. The news is*
> *completely flat, we all feel as if we're being told*
> *nothing. Theatres, music halls all closed, you can*
> *imagine Albert at night, pacing like a caged ani-*
> *mal. I told him he should get on as a searchlight*
> *operator in the Territorial Service, but he's angling*
> *for more.*

The sun was in full retreat to the south. September's drowsy nostalgic daylight turned: Now on darker days the sullen cooling water drank its glow; the rocks were hidden under the surface. In October, the winds began to blow. The open was a snarling grey beast that broke through the channel, over the rocks, and nearly consumed Safe Harbour. When the waves became so strong they parted around Safe Harbour and attacked from the back as well, she stayed in and ate tinned beans, tea and apples. When calm came again, she shot over to the Manitou for provisions and company.

The Pamajongs were keeping an eye on her; as long as they didn't boss her around she didn't mind. No one else dared try.

"G'won with you!" Marge's voice would ring out from the kitchen at the back of the Hotel. "I know your kind! You only come to see us when you're hungry." Cory would sit down for tea biscuits and fish soup, no matter what time of day, and for once she'd be hungry.

"I don't know how you do it," Cory would say to Marge. "Provide this comfort. It's a talent, I guess. I'm going to have to try."

Marge scoffed. "Talent is what you use for taking those photographs." She backed away from the table. "But I know a thing or two about this other business you're in." She scanned Cory with a practised eye. "What's the trouble? You forgotten how to fish?" said Marge. "You haven't got any flesh on your haunches. You're never gonna be able to sit down and feed the boy."

"Who say's it's a boy?"

"I know it, the way you're carrying him."

Marge Pamajong had a big voice and was built to match it. Her long black hair was scraped back in a ponytail from a fierce widow's peak. Her forehead was wide, her face round. Her eyes were velvety brown but her chin protruded in an argumentative way. After her husband died she lived on her own, off the reserve. She raised her own kids, and some of her sisters'. It was always a game to get Marge mad. Spirit of the devil in that one, the men said.

Marge gave Cory strong tea in a tin mug. She offered the tin of Carnation.

"Don't like it."

"You seen a doctor?"

"I'm not sick," said Cory.

"Most of you white women prefer it that way."

Jimmie prowled around behind them, his hands in his pockets. "I guess we better start thinking about closing Safe Harbour, come Thanksgiving," said Jimmie.

"I'm not leaving."

"You'll never heat that cabin."

"I can't keep it very warm even now," Cory admitted. "It's the wind from the open, takes away any heat the wood stove builds up."

"Wasn't built to be lived in more than summer. None of those places were."

"But I don't have anyplace else to live."

"Tough here on your own with a baby. All winter? You got the baby to think of."

"Anywhere else, I'm going to need money."

"Lots of jobs on the mainland. Men going to war opens them up."

"Yeah, maybe." Cory listened to Jimmie the way she wouldn't to anyone else.

Filled with Thanksgiving turkey and carrying her cameras, Cory handed her suitcase into St. Pierre's boat. Her city coat, which she hadn't worn since she'd left London five months ago, wouldn't do up around her middle.

"You're going to do this thing in a hospital, I hope," he said, hauling the suitcase aboard. She looked over her shoulder at her cabin. Shuttered and bolted against the assault of snow and wind, it would stand through the winter as it had stood through twenty winters before.

"Do you think I should?" she grinned.

"I guess nobody here would call you a coward."

She gave him an arch look, if you can be arch with your cheeks puffed out and a double chin. Even her ankles now were thick and painful. Maybe she was filled up inside with tears that she couldn't cry. Her bravado was left behind at Safe Harbour. There were things that could go wrong; women died in childbirth, didn't they? She knew the baby was coming; it had gone still and heavy as bricks inside her. Trying to be brave, she'd left it too late. And she was angry. To have to live in town for the winter, to have to ask for help. She was angry at Albert for keeping his word: He never mentioned the baby. She'd imagined that by now he would back down. But if he didn't, neither would she.

St. Pierre carried her bag up the tin steps and guided her elbow in an unfamiliar, protective way as she climbed onto the train. His anxious face, for once its avariciousness gone, peered up through the window to make sure she was seated. She waved her hand. To be travelling again, to be leaving, going into another emptiness, made her want Albert.

Dear Albert —

Here's something I never told you. The day I left London, I became a species of angel. I had been bathed in the waters of our love and beneficence flowed off me. On the train I saw a black man holding his little daughter; he made for the seat beside me but lost out to a pokerfaced gent in a black coat. I touched his arm and offered him mine — would he like to sit with the baby? It was the way he held her, such tenderness in his hands around her little body, her legs against his chest, that moved me.

He asked was I certain and then sat. I gladly
stood halfway to my station, when he touched me,
offering the seat beside; the gent rose, twitching
with irritation, and left. We spoke a little, I tried to
make friends with "Sheila" but she showed a degree
of suspicion, and reluctance to have her idyll with
Dad interrupted. It seemed a prophecy to me and I
thought, yes, Albert will be won over. He will be a
father to my child. He cannot do otherwise, if I help
this man. Oh yes, I engaged in magical thinking, as
you would say. Oh well, maybe I can be forgiven, in
my state. Kindness, more kindness is needed — but
who will help me?

I am doomed to be on train journeys in a state
of shock: Remember that?

It wasn't much of a walk from Parry Sound Station to her
mother's house, but sweat burst from Cory's brow under
the brown felt hat as she trudged the two short blocks
uphill; her coat felt like an intolerable weight. By the time
she stood on her mother's doorstep, she was seeing spots.
She dropped her bag, leaned against the doorjamb and
knocked. Her eyes were closed when she heard the door
open. There was a long silence.

"Well," said Eliza, in the familiar, feared voice. "I'd heard
about this."

Cory smiled. Of course she had heard. Pointe au Baril
to Parry Sound: forty miles, that was all. "I should have
told you myself."

"Are you coming in?" The voice was marginally warmer.

Cory raised her eyes to see her mother. Her grey-blue eyes, her straight nose and cleft chin all conspired to make her an icon of directness. Eliza Ditchburn was small, efficient and perfectly made. She shot forth a look of great intelligence, and little flexibility. The Free Methodist Church ruled her days and she ruled everyone else's. Her lips were pursed with the lifelong effort of getting her family in line. The mystery was that, despite her scorn of fainter hearts, she had married the romantic, inarticulate Robert Ditchburn.

"Give me your coat. Take off whatever's binding around your chest and stomach: It's too tight. Walk a bit down the hall, that's it, keep walking."

Cory did as she was told. Walking that narrow hall, gazing into that small parlour, Cory remembered a night long ago. She must have been eight or ten. There was music on the radio.

"Eliza!" her father had laughed. "It's simple. One, two and quickstep, one, two and quickstep." Eliza had stumbled. "You've got Methodist feet," he said.

"What's that, may I ask?" She had looked at her dainty, narrow toes so tightly laced in their boots.

"They can't dance."

They had laughed and the house was merry, but Eliza did not dance then, or ever. And there was precious little laughter. My mother, she thought now, as Eliza seated her at the perfectly scrubbed table in a unsentimental kitchen, and forgave her: Someone had to. Eliza put Cory's hand around a cup of water, and draped a towel on her forehead. Then she put on her coat to go for an uncle: He'd call the doctor.

"I won't, I will not, I don't want to go to the hospital," said Cory, between gasps.

"You don't have to. The doctor can come here. He did when you were born."

If it was an arm or a leg she'd have cut it off, but this pain, right in the centre of her, skewering her, she could not escape. Something was wrong. Her uterus wasn't contracting, the cervix wasn't opening, it was all taking too long.

"Hold on, hold on, just a little while longer," the doctor said.

Cory was belligerent. "Make this baby come, can't you?" she demanded of him. The doctor fled the room, Eliza following. In the hallway, he murmured about taking Cory to hospital.

"I'm not going anywhere!" Cory shouted, between contractions. Now her mother sailed back to her side.

"Get yourself under control, Corinne," said Eliza. "You've got to get ahold of yourself and manage this thing. Don't let this child get the better of you already, you hear?"

The pain descended like a hawk and went straight to her core; she screamed and fought under it. When it receded, she whimpered sickly, anticipating its return. She tried to catch herself at the edge, and pull herself back to a place where she was human.

"That's better, that's better."

She leaned over and vomited in a basin. She fought for control.

"It's coming, Cory. I can see the head now."

Head? She did not imagine a head. This was not a baby; it was a force to be reckoned with. But she would not be bested. She was soaked in sweat. Her mother put her hand on Cory's own. "I'm praying for you."

"What good did that ever do?"

Her mother's head vanished; the door closed.

Now there was a burning rock against Cory's spine, spreading her legs, breaking her pubis. She gave in to sobs. Her body had begun to erupt.

"Push now," said the doctor, "push harder. For the little one." The little one! With each surge he descended. This was Albert's baby then, who she'd carried, at first in defiance, then with tenderness. Becoming real, no longer a condition of her body, but a being. Was it such a fight, then, life, from the very beginning? She gritted her teeth, held her breath and pushed, as if she could push out everything inside her, and be emptied.

Finally, she lay on dry sheets. The boy — Marge had been right, he was a boy — was gone somewhere with Eliza. Her body was limp, deflated, the struggle over. She had gone slack; the continent she had carried was separate. There was nothing but her own heartbeat.

When he was laid on her chest, tiny, bundled, prune-faced, a shudder of relief went through her. He could breathe, it appeared, open his eyes even. He was still, wary. They assessed one another. My child. Spy. Interloper. Stowaway. She felt pity. She moved the top of his head up against her mouth. It was fragrant, hot, downy. She was afraid she couldn't love him. Afraid that she was burned out, cut off, frozen out of her own heart. But his purple bud of a mouth sought her nipple, blindly. And she laughed for joy.

Chapter Thirteen

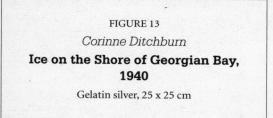

Sculpted by wind and water, the ice that built up in caves at the shore, with its great spears dripping down, and great teeth rising, stands as testament to the violence of the weather. Its shapes form a chorus, mirroring the photographer's rage, and her loneliness, and the stark silence of this winter world.

❦

THE WIND WAS BITTER AND STRONG, FUNNELLED UP THE Sound from the open water of Georgian Bay. With Tyke slung on her back, the Leica around her neck, Cory hiked along the North Road. Its surface was glass; her boots skittered under her. It was four thirty in the afternoon, and dark already. The winter days were dark at either end, napless, a lost space of time, baby time. Walking, she felt the pain still, at the base of her spine, in the space he had occupied. The warm heavy lump of him, outside, did not account for his absence within. He too seemed to be suffering from an irretrievable loss.

They had two rooms and a bedroom above a store; he slept beside her. There was a kind of knitting going on, her rhythm to his. She slept and ate when he slept and ate; in return, he was supposed to let her work. But at four in the afternoon, Tyke turned purple and cried until he choked. Nothing stopped him but walking. Cory wanted to read, write a letter, take a photograph; she wanted not to have her hands full of ten pounds of baby with milk running down his chin. But when she put him down he shrieked and the woman downstairs pounded on the wall. Tears of frustration drying on her cheeks, she slung him over her shoulder, pacing her room. "It's you or me, kid," she said. "One of us has to give in."

Eliza saw them from the window of her store, tramping one way, tramping back. She called them in for tea. "You look like strikers on a picket line," she said.

By six o'clock, nothing but the breast would console him. At seven he collapsed into sleep, sated with tears and milk. That was when Cory sat, alone in the dark, too tired to eat. She listened to the doom-calling voices of news announcers on CBC. It was "the phony war," in London, she learned from the metalized, whipped-up sound of the radio. No real fighting yet, not there. At newsreels in the high school she'd seen pictures to put with it: Canadian troops loading onto trains at Union Station; girls with their fur-trimmed coats running along the platform to wave goodbye.

She watched the empty road in front of her house. Now and then a set of car's light beams swung past. No one came by. She went to look at Christopher, who Eliza called Tyke, sleeping. He was so new and perfect, unscarred, a rosebud, a star about to explode into galaxies, constellations of light. What was she to do with him? This was all a dreadful mistake. She knew what she was. She was a photographer. She was not meant to be a mother.

Ice was her new fascination, her delight. Ice at the rink, forming and forming under the ripples of water hosed on to make a surface. Ice on branches, birds' wings, doorsteps. When the ice was hard Cory skied up and down the shore with Tyke on her back over hard ridges of snow and into the hidden caves where the trees grew out of rock crevices. She set her lens to capture an array of ice-coated twigs against the sun, or the cracking bark on a tree, with snow lines in it like hair.

At Pointe au Baril Station, St. Pierre met her in his scoot. The scoot was a local invention, a small wooden boat fitted out with an airplane motor and a big triangular rudder, which stuck out into the air behind. Amphibious, it rode over the ice, or floated on open water.

He handed her the ear protectors. "You gotta tuck up under those blankets," he said, "especially with your babe there. You know it's kinda loud." He set out driving across the Bay to the Manitou. The frozen surface was flat, with stiffened snow flipped up like beaten egg whites along the way.

"You sure you know where you're going?" Cory looked out over the windscreen. Familiar cottages and tree-lines had all been altered, set on a field of white.

"I just gotta watch the turns, eh? 'Cause it likes to tip. But the only times we gotta worry is if the motor goes. Then we're walking," he said.

But the motor blasted away without cease, St. Pierre's rapt visage behind the wheel. Tyke, in her arms, went stiff with fear but he did not cry. In Manitou Bay there were three dark mounds on the ice: fishing huts.

"See the nice hut Jimmie built?" said St. Pierre. "He made it out of old siding a cottager took to the dump; he even filled in the chinks so the wind didn't tear through. Good man, Jimmie."

"Sure he is," said Cory, wondering why her old friend should need this reference. Marge came out the door when the scoot roared up beside one of the huts.

"You back?" she said, squinting in the smoke of their fire. Without a word, Marge took Tyke and laid him across her knee. She took each leg, and each arm, pulled the joint straight and let it loose again, the way she did with a duck she was about to stuff. She held him before her eyes, propping his head erect with two fingers. She let the fingers drop. His head wobbled but held. "Strong back," she said. "Good baby. You've done well."

"Is that all you've got to say?"

The fire crackled, and the fishing lines bobbed. The dogs lay at their feet, making a homey feel. Heaving snow struck the side of the fishing hut.

"That's all I got to say. You've got your son."

"Now I've got him, yes, but what do I do?" Cory wanted to cry.

"What can we give you?" asked Jimmie gently. He stood gazing down at the baby, drinking rye from a bottle.

"Tea," she said.

Marge reached for a piece of wood and threw it on the fire. "I learned something getting these grey hairs," said Marge. "It's not what you do so much as what you don't do that'll get you in trouble." She gazed through the open door into the wind, the swirls and paisley shapes of snow that circled around.

Jimmie said nothing, staring down at the black hole in the ice, the line that bobbed gently there. Cory paced inside the hut. "I feel like I'm stuck out here in the backwater where nothing's happening. I keep thinking I should be over in Europe to see the war."

Marge's big midriff shuddered with laughter.

"Take the way for heroes, will you? You know something? Some people who like to think they go big places and face enemies look in the wrong place. Sometimes it's harder to stay still," said Marge.

Jimmie's eyes remained fastened on the ice.

Cory stopped pacing. She hugged herself. Jimmie picked up Tyke and began to fit him into the backboard cradle he'd made.

"You got your danger enough in being a mother." Marge rocked and smiled, watching Jimmie with the baby.

Dearest Coree —

There were no children here for Christmas; they've all been sent to Canada. There are hardly any young men either. It has a biblical feel, as if the angel of death has passed over. And I've been passed over, too — the first three war artists are named, all were with me in the Great War, I am left here at home listening to Lord Hawhaw, who has a great talent and a greater following than anyone admits. But no pounding overhead, no gunfire in the streets, though Parliament is sandbagged nicely and all the county squires have signed up for the Home Guard so they can parade with guns. Maybe I can get a job painting camouflage on the ships — Heraldo did. It sounds mad, but it might be just the thing to revivify the failing artist. I suppose the last twenty years have been only an extended vacation between one's real task, which is killing and destruction.

I've been reading Nietzsche, whom I dislike of course, but he seems to know me when he says that the real standard of the artist is to uphold resilience, courage and cheerfulness of spirit while at the same time absorbing full quotients of morbidity. It's like some scientific experiment worthy of Hitler himself — how much death and brutishness can one dose on, and still wake fresh in the morn? I can't paint

*now. For there's a balance that, once gone past, you
can't reclaim.*

*I think I hear your voice telling me this is the
most monstrous of all my excuses to drink, smoke
and dwell on misery, and yet — you're not here, are
you darling, so why should I not?*

Cory read with mixed joy and outrage: How could he go
on as if they still loved? After this, after Tyke's birth, which
he must know had happened, months ago now. Of course,
she hadn't written to tell him. She hadn't made a telephone call, which she could have done. Even though she
cried hoarsely, alone in her little apartment, with Tyke,
cried and ached and raged. In the morning when Tyke
reached out to touch her cheek she swatted his hand away.
His eyes flew open wide and his arms jerked with fear.

She was nearly out of money. Aunt Eunice sent a little,
with a card of congratulations: "This is for the boy, not for
you, since you're too proud to take it." And then she added,
somewhat more plaintively, "Leary's taken a job with the
Land Girls and I'm doing the shopping myself: Why
haven't I been doing this for years? Everyone's coming
back to London," she wrote. "Nothing to worry about. You
know what they say about the English. They never start
well, but they finish first."

Cory sent the money back, with a picture of Tyke.

On Sundays she dined with her mother. It was the only
meal now for which she sat down. Usually she had to hold

Tyke and walk around the room while she ate. Tonight Eliza held him, and he reached, dazzled, for her chin, her nose, laughing.

"Why do you go around with that camera all day when you should be making money?" said Eliza.

"I suppose I could go back to teaching," said Cory dully.

Eliza hooted. "You know this place better than that. You'd never get your job back, bad example to the girls, an unmarried mother."

"You're probably right."

"You know, they've reopened the explosives plant up at Nobel. They're making TNT to keep the Germans out of England, and nitroglycerin and guncotton. I hear they're lining up outside for jobs from five o'clock in the morning. They're coming in on the train and sleeping outside the office door. Not a good sort of people the most of them but you can't fault them for eagerness. The McIntyre boys walked the whole eight miles there before sunrise, got hired right off," she said. "Women too."

Cory got a lift up to Nobel. It was a cold March day with a clear blue sky. The sheds stretched half a mile along to the east of the highway. They were low and ramshackle, with a creek running between them. Hundreds of men and a few women were lined up outside the office. The sound of hammering on wood rattled the cold empty air: A dormitory was going up. Some of the men waiting couldn't do military service — they were too old, or tubercular, or nearsighted. Some were not shaving yet, and some were veterans of the Great War. The end of the line snaked out of sight behind the sheds.

"You shouldn't bring your baby around here," grumbled the woman ahead of her in the line. "What if the place blows up?"

"I need a job, just like anyone," said Cory. "If they hire me, I'll leave him at home." But she stepped away, and pretended she had a job already. She put up the camera and got a few shots of the queue, the bundled, ragtag hopefuls.

A man came out of the office and waved her camera down. "Defence Industries," he shouted. "No pictures! Off limits! You don't want to give Gerry ideas, do you?"

"It's just for the *North Star*," she said. "All I want is to show how many are waiting."

"You don't work for the *North Star*," he said.

"No, but I sure try."

Tyke began to cry; her breasts began to ache in response. She could feel the hot trickle leaking into her blouse, chilling in the layer of air between her flesh and her clothing.

"It's the cold air hurting his lungs," she said. "Can I just bring him in the office for a minute?"

He moved aside uneasily. Cory knew now that men mostly panicked in front of a crying baby. They'd do just about anything for someone to get him to stop. In the office the air was still and hot; Tyke went silent, wary; his legs stopped mid-kick. It was astonishing how attuned he was to what was needed. He sensed an emergency and co-operated. He rose to occasions like his father, she had to admit.

"You don't mind if I just sit here?" Cory said, and pulled one of the typist's chairs around behind a cabinet. They were all girls or young married women from Parry Sound in the office. Half of them had been in school behind her.

"He doesn't look like his father's an Indian," whispered the girl.

Cory undid her coat and lifted her sweater. She pushed Tyke under in the general direction of her left nipple. He was a voracious nurser.

"Jesus, Ma'am, we're making explosives here," said the manager, averting his eyes.

"He has a problem emptying his bowels," said Cory, with the candour of an absorbed mother. She rounded her eyes and engaged the man with her little problem, aping the innocence of more enthusiastic mothers: Of course, he'd want to know all about her baby. "Once he gets on the breast, though, he loosens right up."

The manager reddened.

Loud sucking sounds began to emerge from under Cory's blouse. She heard Tyke's familiar grunts. His lips popped on and off her nipple as he pushed and grimaced. She lifted the sweater. His face had gone the sudden livid purple that presaged a bowel movement. Then it came. With a blubbering, squirting honk, he shot it out into his diaper.

"Jesus Christ, who let her in here?" The manager stormed through the door, away from all the tittering stenographers. Outside, cold and anxious faces strained to see through the frost on the window. Cory switched Tyke to her other breast.

A high-pitched whistle signalled the end of a shift. Workers in blue overalls emerged from the doors at the end of the sheds, donning their shapeless thick coats, their hats with ear flaps. A bus panted on the pavement, loading to go back to Parry Sound.

The manager appeared in front of Cory, braced for anything. "Are you nearly finished?"

"If you put me on the list I'll go home now," said Cory.

He gave her the afternoon shift, four o'clock till midnight. That meant catching the bus at three o'clock in town. Before she left, she fed Tyke until milk ran from the corners of his mouth and then, holding him gingerly like an over-full balloon, transferred him to Parisian Fashions, where Eliza waited, trim in her navy frock, arms open. When the shop closed at five o'clock, Eliza was to take him home, there to break him to a bottle.

She was back in the world.

Chapter Fourteen

FIGURE 14

Corinne Ditchburn

**Women's Shower at
Defence Industries Limited**

1940
Nobel, Ontario
25 x 45 cm

The camera angle, almost straight upward from the feet of a massive nude woman into the mingled streams of sun and water falling from above, lets us know the photographer got on her knees to capture this image. And so she should have: The vision of three women under a shower, which, in the sunlight falling from roofline windows, appears as the mist of creation, has a religious power. The long, white upturned throat of the woman nearest and her sunlit breasts and belly speak of power and vulnerability in equal parts.

ॐ

BEFORE SHE STARTED, SHE GOT HERSELF A TOUR. NO ONE FORbade the camera: Maybe they just didn't notice. It was amazing what you could do if you looked as if you had a reason, Cory was discovering. In the cold air she caught the steam from the coffee, the rough expectant faces and, in the background, the hump of the TNT building.

A grizzled former logger, now in charge of maintenance, walked her around the whole enclosure, a frozen expanse of cleared bush, train tracks and mud above the rocky shore of Georgian Bay. Dave Clark was slow and almost apologetic. You could trust him with your life, they told her, and you had to.

The grounds were spread along the railway track, where the munitions factory had been during the Great War. They were flat, laced with pathways between flat-roofed sheds; men in overalls crisscrossed the beaten earth, full of purpose. It was all heated by water and steam, other methods being judged too flammable. Water ran to every building in above-ground pipes. The powerhouse burnt three carloads of coal, Dave told her, to heat the ten million gallons of water required. The workers had built shanty houses by the creek that took the run-off; they siphoned off the water, so its leftover heat kept them warm.

There was a staff house, an office building, switchboard and maintenance sheds, and the long, narrow sheds that looked like hangars. Inside these, under the bare bulbs that hung from the roof, were the guncotton lines. A chain of men stretched from the front door to the back; they were passing a rope of nitroglycerin-laden cotton batten hand to hand from wringer to wringer. She saw the TNT, a dark paste, wheeled out in metal boxes; crates of them stood by the train tracks awaiting pickup.

"This here's Angel Walk," said Dave.

A narrow path of beaten earth led from the railway tracks to the TNT sheds. "That's Billy. Bound for the cordite lines."

A muscle-bound youth of about eighteen scooted surely along Angel Walk, harnessed to a handcart behind him. He gave a cocky grin. He had a dimple in his cheek, visible through the soot that darkened his face.

"Don't let Billy fool you, it's no picnic toting that stuff. That's five hundred pounds of nitroglycerin balanced behind him. Hey, can you guess why we call it Angel Walk? One spark and you're on your way to heaven."

They followed Billy at a respectful distance. Dave slapped the base of TNT buildings. "This here embankment's eighteen feet thick. The roofs are just floating on top of the walls see, barely attached, so that if there's a big blow, the walls will hold but the roof will fly off. So the blast will go upward. Into the sky, instead of along the ground. You got me?"

Inside, two operators worked on an elevated track, mixing and controlling the temperature of the liquid nitroglycerin. A tin trough of water ran below them. "See here, if the temperature of the mix gets too high," said Dave, "the operators let the water flow in to drown it. 'Cause if they don't get that temperature down, the mix will blow. And if it blows, they dive into their escape hatches. They got individual metal chutes like a kid's playground slide. And that'll carry them over the banked walls and outside to the ground."

In the welding shop Cory ran into Wade Johnstone, the

blacksmith in Parry Sound, and a friend of her father's. Once, she taught his son. Now Wade ran the welding shop, where they made cast iron utensils and bins that could withstand acid.

"These guys are our heroes," said Dave, punching Wade softly in the shoulder. "It takes balls to go into a TNT shed with a lighted torch, eh?"

Wade pressed his hands along the hips of his overalls in a fruitless effort to clean them before he shook hers. "So you got yourself a job here, didja? Wanna have a look at that boy of yours too. You know your dad would've given his eye-teeth to take him fishing."

In the personnel office, they took Cory's fingerprints. She got her overalls, and a scarf to tie around her head. She drew it over her ears and knotted it in front, enjoying the loss of herself. She was joining an army. She punched the time-clock and was frisked for matches. She went through the guard house and lifted her shoe like a horse so the guards could examine the bottom for anything that might give a spark.

"You know what cordite is?"

The foreman stood with his feet wide apart; his nostrils were flat and wide and hairs sprouted out of them. Like every other person in sight, he wore a white coverall zipped up the front and a puffy white cap.

"Not really, no."

"Cordite is a propellant for artillery shells, the big ones, five to eight inches. First thing you gotta know, it's a highly inflammable explosive. Second thing you've gotta know, it's even more dangerous than that. If it's lit in the open, it'll burn. If it's confined, it'll explode. That's why we want it."

The cordite line was like an elongated night kitchen for the bakers of bombs. It was warm and dry with the buzz of sound associated with preparatory activity for some large event. Scrawled on the wall was a poem:

Here's to the girls who dress in black
They dress so neat they never get slack
And when they kiss they kiss so sweet
They makes things stand that have no feet.

A cheerful bustle on the floor belied the gravity of the mission. Cory thought of Albert: "One begins to understand even the surrealists."

Huge mounds of moist dough appeared by moving belt through a hutch. Swaggering in their coveralls, the men approached it and began by slapping and pulling the pale batter into thick ropes. By turns they pulled thick snakes of dough to where an operator with no chin and eyes permanently trained downward to his work took rope after rope of the elastic stuff and forced it through a metal funnel like a meat-grinder. "Follow!" said the foreman, and Cory stepped up to the grinder.

"Lookee here, girl," said the operator. "It's likely to be your only chance. Might as well know what you're handling, eh?" He had a wheezing cough and his eyes watered.

Cory put her face over top it: Inside, yellow cylinders pumped.

"Those pistons are beryllium bronze," he said proudly. His voice was high when he cleared it. "Steel might make a spark. Inside there's dies, so that the dough comes out the other end as threads. Like spaghetti, see, depending on which setting I use, sixteen or twenty of them. And each of these dies has a set of little plugs, you know what I mean, so that each strand of spaghetti is just like a flower stem: hollow with six or eight tiny holes right through the middle. Bet you didn't know that. There she comes."

The spaghetti straws of cordite emerged from the bottom of the grinder. Two workers slid sticks under to pull them out straight. The foreman shouted over the cheerful clatter.

"You make the straws like that and you don't have to wait for it to burn. Lets the air get in — spontaneous combustion. Don't you forget for a minute this is serious work. You got a soldier out there on the line and he's counting on you. He's got to get the right size for his shell. Got to be a mixture: Too fast and it'll blow up in your guy's hand; too slow and he'll be hit by the enemy before he gets it shot."

On a long table, cutters lopped the straws into thirty-inch lengths. "Just like how the Eye-ties make their macaroni, huh?" said the foreman. "Only they skip this part. We put 'em in the oven."

Boys loaded the stiffening strands onto a conveyor belt. The belt rattled to the wall that adjoined the stove-houses, and the cordite disappeared into the dark half-circle. The foreman walked her around the heated area to a final shed. Straws of cordite, hardened and yellowed, rode out of the ovens on a belt. Three operators stood on either side bundling the strands in thirties, forties and fifties.

"This part's for the intellectuals. Know you're a teacher so we figure you can count. You want ten of each kind, make two bundles of thirty, then two of fifty. The exact mix you get is going to set the timing of the ammunition," said the foreman. "Every bundle is life and death for someone else. So don't you forget it."

Cory took her place along the line, another woman diagonally across from her, and two men much farther down.

"Do it wrong and somebody's son, somebody's husband gets blasted into smithereens. Before their time. If they're gonna get it, we prefer it to be from the enemy." Those were his parting words.

Cory thought her arms were stronger than most, but in two hours her biceps felt as if they were being torn from her shoulders. Timing them with the rattle of the conveyor, she let out a few huge groans she thought no one could hear. A bell rang; the belt jerked three times and then stopped. The woman opposite wiped the sweat from her face with the back of her hand.

"We got a screamer in here this time!" Her smile showed teeth that were yellowed and crooked. "You oughta join the choir."

"You heard me?"

"I gotta admit I was listening for it. Betty's my name. I recognized ya', ya're the one came in here with the baby."

"You heard that too?"

"Oh, we heard!" Her laugh was like a ballyhoo behind the backs of the men as they went for their break. "We all loved that story. Don't you know they had to put up a sign 'No Babies,' so many girls tried to copy ya'?"

Betty had come from Manitoba with her man. He had a place in the dormitories, but women weren't allowed there. Right now she boarded in Nobel.

At seven o'clock, Cory knew, Tyke would fall asleep. When the hour came, Cory felt a burden of guilt lifted; her arms too seemed lighter. She dozed on the bus ride home, and at one o'clock in the morning she crawled into bed beside Tyke at her mother's house. His fat, unconscious frown reproached her; she woke him to empty her hard, painful breasts. When he cried at 6:30 she nursed him again. He was asleep on her chest, and she with him, when Eliza pulled the curtains sharply open to daylight. She scooped up Tyke and hustled him out of the room.

"He wouldn't take the bottle," said Eliza. "He's as stubborn as you are. He may starve himself to death."

This was her routine: Mornings with Tyke, during which he fed almost constantly. Bus ride to Nobel, four to midnight on the job, bending and sorting the delicate, deadly straws. Breaks with Betty and the boys, ping-pong till the bus left. End of the week, twenty-five dollars in an envelope.

One morning when Cory crawled into bed Tyke wouldn't wake up to nurse.

"You fed him?"

"He was hungry," Eliza said defiantly, when Cory confronted her with the evidence of Pablum, applesauce, mashed potatoes. "You can't expect me to watch him starve. Anyway, it's time you took him off the breast. You've got poisons in your system from that plant. I've heard them talk about how the men get headaches from the nitroglycerin."

"Well I guess he's mine to poison." Tyke rode on her hip now: Strong backed, he kicked his legs for emphasis. But Eliza won. Once the baby had tasted food, there was no turning back. Anyway, by that time they'd built married quarters; now that Tyke was off the breast, Cory could sleep over with Betty and her husband. Then she'd get up in the morning and roam the site with her camera. They were used to her now. Sometimes they even printed her shots in the plant newsletter.

She made a pest of herself with her camera. She loved the machinery, the cylinders and pistons, the water pipes running over the ground for steam heat, the funnels and wheels and drums. She wanted to shoot the workers too, but she didn't know how to approach them. Some of them were people she'd known all her life who'd acquired a new dignity as they played with fire. But most of them had come from east or west looking for the only work there was. She walked the Back Road where, a few hundred yards out of sight of the plant, workers lived in salvaged packing crates and tents. One family posed for her in their flap doorway, a muddy, sewage-clogged Guncotton Creek flowing past their feet.

"What's this?" asked Tyke. He held up the photograph without a label. "It must be in the wrong box."

"How should I know what it is: I can't *see*," Cory griped. The process was wearing on her: Today her eyes felt raw inside the lids, and the muscles that let them focus ached even at the thought of trying to read. She put her face right up to the print. "Oh, that." She remembered. "It's a roomful of naked women, I'd say. In the showers." And the memory brought a laugh with it, a laugh that bellied out like a sail into the stillness of the sunroom.

"You might share the joke," said Tyke, wonderingly. It wasn't often his mother laughed these days.

It was one time she had gone too far. She surprised the women in the compulsory shower where they changed their clothes before leaving the plant. The shapes and the steam were what interested her, but she forgot, that time, about reticence, forgot that not everyone shared her passion to document, especially when they were part of the evidence.

The women had their own shower at the far end of the grounds, and there was no shortage of hot water. It became a place where they let out their frustrations and shed their fatigue along with the dust of explosives. The wooden room was lit by big ceiling lights; three women clustered under each circular showerhead that curved over like a drooping sunflower. Cory got in there at the end of the day shift when the good sun streamed from the west through the windows which, for modesty's sake, were away up under the roofline.

She didn't know these girls the way she did the ones on her own shift, and when she stepped onto the wet cedar plank, shading her lens from the steam with one hand, heads began to turn. A dark, olive-skinned woman sounded the alarm.

"What the sam hill's she doing?" she yelled, instantly turning her back to Cory. "Hey girls!"

The husky redhead they called Norma, who was known as a fiendish ping-pong player, was standing in profile to Cory, her face upturned to the downpouring water, a wash of filtered sun whitening her breasts and belly. It was too tempting and Cory took a step forward, bent her knees and shot, thankful for the Leica's speed.

"She got you, Norma!"

It was hard to tell whether the shrieks were outrage or hilarity, but Cory didn't have much time to decide before Norma caught her and pulled her under the showerheads. They ripped off her clothes and held her under the cold for a minute. The dark-haired one got the camera and was going to pull out the film but Norma stopped her.

"Ain't too often folks want a picture of me starkers," she said, wonderingly, tossing Cory her trousers. "You shoulda asked, that's all." It was lucky she rescued the film because after, some of the women asked for pictures to show their guys.

Chapter Fifteen

FIGURE 15

Corinne Ditchburn

The Dream Catcher

(portrait of Christopher Ditchburn, age two,
under netting)
1941
Pointe au Baril, Ontario
Gelatin silver, 23 x 34 cm
Mounted on cardboard

An eerie and provocative photograph of an infant. The child, eyes shut, appears to be having a nightmare. The net that has been draped over him to protect him from insects becomes a sinister trap that he must try to escape, but similarly transforms him into geometric shapes that are themselves beautiful. Thus it is the beauty of the pattern we feel rather than the terror of the child.

❧

BY MAY, GERMANY HAD DENMARK, HOLLAND, BELGIUM, NORWAY and Luxembourg. The plant got new orders for TNT: They weren't supposed to know where it was going but everyone did. It was for landmines to cover the south of England against invasion. Cory went to see more newsreels at the high school. They showed the Canadian First churning up Cornish fields, unrolling bales of barbed wire on beaches. Still training for the big moment.

"We do not choose to be ruled by try-ants," said a volunteer soldier into the camera.

Albert's letter was a dash of pure self-pity.

> *I have lost my will to live, dear Cory, without you, and there is no hope to get it back. I am growing old at the rate of speeding aircraft and shall soon die.*

Cory heard the imperative double *brring* of his telephone set in Hampstead. The receiver was snatched up roughly. Albert's voice was wild, elated, cruel.

"What do you want, whoever you are?"

He was drunk. In the background she could hear a woman's raucous sobs. Liss.

"Where did you get the money?" Liss cried. "Where did you put it?"

Cory could not speak.

"Hello, who are you?" Albert sounded like a roused crow.

The long scoop of telephone wire leading from William Street to some transformer, across northern North America, to be beamed across the Atlantic, yawned before her. It crackled.

"Albert, I've had the baby. He's a boy!"

"Cory? Is that you?" boomed Albert.

She could hear a woman's voice in the background, crying. Liss. She panicked. Her news would make a bad scene worse.

"It is not," she shouted. "Albert, it's your sister."

"Cory!"

"It's not me, remember it's your sister calling to see if you're better —" There was more raw accusatory speech from Liss.

Albert was silent.

"Well," he muttered at last. "It's nice to talk to a human being, at least."

She hung up.

The longing was back and it was bad. Weekends she listened to opera on the radio and thought of Albert, leaning into the flower bed at Regent's Park, his eyes squeezed tight, the better to savour some esoteric scent. Albert rolling a cigarette with his blunt, beautiful fingers, whiskers of tobacco escaping the sienna-smudged white paper, much in the same way white hairs spurted out from the funnel of his ears. Albert padding down the stairs in his carpet slippers, with his frayed silk kimono tied over his stomach. Albert watching her dress after they'd made love on the studio bed. "Your legs are so strong, it's a marvel. I suppose that's what you get for growing up in a philistine country is legs like that —" Never again, she thought. Never again.

Bundling cordite straws with a depression-busted Saskatchewan farmer on one side and a local logger on the other, Cory raged. A woman's fate had been handed to her: She was tied to a seven-month-old baby. Albert went on, unaltered, unfettered, his passions in full play. And everyone around her signed up.

Betty's husband shipped out for Europe.

"Gives them an excuse to dress exactly like one another and to run into walls of fire, don't it?" she said.

The sun rose red at seven a.m. through grey mists. The islands came into sight one after another like a pealing of bells, some closer, some farther, too intricately related to give themselves up entirely to measurement. While she fed Tyke in his improvised highchair, Albert was already at the pub, if it still stood. As she sat in the sweet sunlight, the sound of the open always faintly heard, darkness fell on London. While Tyke smacked at tadpoles in the trapped pools of water, palm-sized, armless, legless, their swollen white bellies flashing, tracer bullets arced over Primrose Hill. And Albert stalked the streets of London, in his cape and his black hat, wanting his eyes.

Tyke got on his knees and crawled the entire width of the smooth rocks on the west of Safe Harbour and back, and Cory hardly noticed.

A letter never sent:

> *Dear Albert —*
>   *This summer the Manitou crowd is smaller. Only old men and boys fishing. The card tables at*

night reverberate with talk of war; the boys are lined up with fallen tree branches held over their shoulders, drilling, to be ready for the fighting. In the late blue light their voices ring over the rocks. "Attent-shun! Fall out! Man the lifeboats!" The boats are launched, and the fleeing soldiers dive to the floorboards to escape the hail of stones coming from up the rocks where the girls are.

The east wind of this morning has turned to west, cleared the sky, and now has gone. In front of the Manitou the ensign hangs limp on the flagpole. The surface of the Bay has turned white under the sun. Out toward the open, the water bulges here and there, in memory of waves.

Tyke is flat in his iron cot, at last, his damp nape sun-red and his fist denting his burnt cheek. The stars wink through thinning cloud. Before long there'll be a splash of them. The pine trees are arrested in their spread panic, branches splayed, trunks curved, reaching east out of the blast of the habitual west winds, which now, in the huge still-ness, seem impossible to conjure. Like all hysterics, pines bear false witness. It's so quiet that when I put my ear to the rock I can hear the bombs in Europe.

But who could she talk to, truly talk? He did not write. She didn't know if he remembered about Tyke's birth: He'd been drunk during that phone call. There was no word and it was too painful to think of him.

She caught the scrape of a canoe on the rock and an almost inaudible footfall. Only one man knew how to land at Safe Harbour from that side. "Jimmie?"

She couldn't see into the dark.

"You're not at the dance," she said evenly, when, finally, she could make him out in the dark. He stopped, courteous, five feet in front of her.

"The ladies dance together now," he said. And then, "I knew you wouldn't go."

She laughed. "I've got Tyke," she said, jerking her head inside.

"You wouldn't anyway," he said.

"That's right, I guess." She paused. They walked together over the rocks, their feet sure in the dark.

"The more I'm alone, the more I want to be alone."

"Are you asking me to go?"

"No."

They lay on their backs and watched the stars wheel over. They hardly spoke; there was nothing to say. His touch was gentle. It seemed, as his fingers travelled over her skin, that she was new to him, while to her his hard body felt like some talisman she had held and stroked many times before.

The innocent passion of Jimmie Pamajong surprised her. She had to be very careful. She was so practised. Each time she shifted her body he groaned, as if the imaginative possibilities were too powerful for him to contain. He was holding himself back, biting his lip, biting her lip. When her hand came near his groin he told her no. They waited,

waited, under the night sky, until Cory dozed under the curious, persistent stroking of his fingers. She woke to find her body rippling with his in a climax as unexpected as a soft rain.

Cory breathed her gratitude into the side of his neck. They did not open their eyes. He was young, Jimmie, perhaps that was it, and they'd been friends so long.

"This is good, Jimmie," Cory managed to say. "You're a good man, Jimmie."

Darling —

London has gone all surreal and I thought I would hate it but I don't — it has the feel of a masked ball before the gates of hell, and wouldn't you know it I'd be there. People in black masks and metal helmets climbing down holes to spend the night sleeping, shoulder to shoulder, under grey blankets. A doorway with a waterfall of bricks coming out. The barrage balloons like great slippery udders bobbing over Hampstead. One came down on Heraldo's house, neatly, as if to snuff it out, which mightn't be so bad considering.

The hell is not sleeping, not a single night through. I begin to wish, in the dead centre of the flashing over the docks and the sirens, I'd be hit and have it over with. But then it's morning and I walk the streets, stepping over the fire-hoses, slopping through the water, catching a voyeur's glimpse of naked dead limbs being pulled from somewhere.

Liss has the house packed with tinned sardines and spices, says if she's going to have to eat rat it will be tasty. Nothing works of course, either the gas is out or the electricity or the telephone.

Since your friend the Beaver has been put in charge of Aircraft Production we all feel safer; do you think he can make as many airplanes as he has newspapers? Apparently he will do it out of our saucepans, for he has called for us all to turn them in. Would that he could turn back the seas: Geography has turned traitor, the Channel keeps us but a hop and a skip from brutal destruction and planes take no notice of what's an island. Countries are falling like dominoes. After France we'll be next, no one doubts it. If you were here we'd be travelling around with a Leica catching the moments of madness but as it is I tramp the streets when I can, but the heart fails, the eye fails, you aren't here, I cannot work —

She'd put Tyke's bed out on the screen porch. He fought his demons there, in the mosquito netting, arms punching, back twisting. Tonight he sat up in his cot and screamed. Cory climbed out of bed and watched him in the moonlight. She stood back and saw the painful beauty of it. Tyke's nightmare, struggling with the net that he did not see.

She got the Speed Graphic and lay on the floor. The moon was so bright she thought maybe she could shoot without flash. But the shot would only work if she were outside the screen. She ran past him and out onto the rock and tried it from there. All the while Tyke was screaming and boxing with the white net that enveloped him in his bed.

He had his eyes open now. He saw her, his mother running by. Out the door, where he couldn't follow. He stopped in pure astonishment. He stood, with his arms outstretched, his face drawn and exhausted, understanding that she had passed him by in his distress to point the box at him, and stare into its black hole.

She got some shots. After, she went in and picked him up, held his shuddering body to her heart.

Chapter Sixteen

Propaganda poster.

ॐ

THE PLANT'S DANCE HALL HAD BEEN MADE OVER INTO A CIN-
ema, with chairs and a projector. The workers were dusted
with the flour of cordite still; their hair and forearms glittered. Everyone called them human firecrackers, but truth
was they were casual. They knew their explosive; they had
tamed and domesticated it. They were its bakers, shapers
and packers; it was banal as bread.

The screen filled with the giant machinery, a worm's
eye view of the nose of a plane, a bird's eye view of five
bombers in formation. Now London under bombardment; rows of east-end tenements mowed down; boarded-
up windows at Buckingham Palace. Troops throwing
themselves headfirst over bales of barbed wire.

"The Tigermoths are old, but the men are young." The canned voice was vivid with hate. "The fascist superman and his twisted following..." There were pictures of laughing German youth banging drums. "The most evil of all civilizations of mankind."

Cory could feel war stirring the loins of the men, as the fraught words did their work. Onscreen, the massing troops and jutting military shapes in black and white stirred her. She wanted it as much as they did. To join the effort. To work, to help, to pit oneself against the monstrous unseen.

The summons had come through the plant office.

"I got a letter about you from the National Film Board. It's a little job but you might not want it," said Dave Clark. He smirked. "I think they're playing a trick on you."

Cory showed the letter to Betty.

"You're the only one I know who's got the nerve," she said.

She borrowed a city dress and a wide-brimmed hat from Parisian Fashions and practised sitting with her legs crossed in front of the shop's full length mirror.

"Putting a little more effort into your appearance, are you?" said Eliza in a tone of grudging pleasure. "It's not too late. You're still young enough to find a husband."

Cory tried looking over her shoulder and stepping out, as if off a curb, to hail a taxi. Farewells had a poignancy these days. When she was ready, she got Betty into the dress. She put the Speed Graphic on a tripod and made

Betty stand there for hours to get the light right. She liked her in front of the shop mirror, because you could see her reflected back too. Betty worked for the price of her smokes: She consumed fifteen while Cory moved the window shades up and down, and held the flashgun here or there. Everything was right but the look on Betty's face and nothing Cory said — "Imagine your husband's coming home on leave tonight" or "Think about going to Eaton's and buying silk underwear" — could fix it.

Finally she stripped Betty of the dress, put it on herself, stood in front of the mirror, cast a glance over her shoulder and said shoot. Betty lined her up through the lens, laughing all the while, and pressed the shutter. She took five shots and prayed one was good enough. Film was expensive and hard to get.

She sent it off and heard nothing. One day a huge package arrived by postal express, a roll of three foot by five foot posters. There was the photograph of Cory, and in red script over her hip and into the grey backdrop ran the words "*She may look like your sister but...*" A line of print at the bottom announced: *Watch Out for Syphilis.*

Eliza cried from vexation. Betty wanted the credit for pressing the shutter. Cory put one up at the D.I.L. canteen. Most of the men didn't recognize her. But Dave did. All he said was, "Cory, I didn't know you had a dress."

When the check arrived it was worth ten weeks' work at the factory: $200. She gave half of it to Betty, who cried and kissed her hand.

New sheds were going up; the carpenter's tools rang dully in the cold air. Six huge steam boilers rose like dull moons into the air; extending from them, and snaking underground for miles, were the water pipes. Squatters' children, heads wrapped in lumpy scarves, played in puddles where the snow melted around the taps off the Back Road; the run-off was brown and smelled evil. In the lean-tos, off-shift workers sat at packing-crate tables playing cards and drinking. The steam whistle blew the shift change, and the sun rose orange and set red. The train rumbled in bringing supplies and rumbled out bearing explosives.

The welders' shop was set off from the rest of the plant. It was always dark inside, and warm with the glow of the torch, the iron's clang, and the calm flow of Wade Johnstone's talk. Cory sat and watched as the sparks sailed over his head like some demonic plumage. Wade wanted Cory to see his new car.

"Drove four fellows up here for a full year, charged 'em five cents a ride. And I saved enough to get an almost new Buick. You wanna come for a ride, girl?"

"Sometime," she said.

"Gotta get that boy of yours on skates."

"He's only been walking since September."

"I'll make him some blades. You can take some of the old bridle straps from the shop down in Parry Sound and 'tach them to his boots."

"It can wait for next winter, Wade. If I'm here."

"Where else d'ya think you're gonna be?"

"You know. Over there."

"You lost your heart in London, girl, that's bad enough. Don't need to go losing your life too. And you've got that boy to think about. You bring the sled in and we'll sharpen the runners, you hear me?"

"OK, Wade, I will." She gazed as he expertly merged two broken pieces of cast iron, patching a hole in a great melting pot. The phone rang. Wade and Billy looked at each other.

"Every time it rings I wonder if my number's up," said Billy, ambling over. He listened, said "uh-huh" a couple of times and hung up.

"Welding job in one of the nitroglycerin tanks."

It was their least favourite place to work. Nitroglycerin went up so fast you didn't have a chance. The buildings where they made it were lined with lead, everything — floors, walls — was all covered with lead. You needed three signatures to go in there with a torch.

"Yup, that's for me," said Wade. "My turn today."

Wade took the paper where Billy'd written down instructions: Nitro 3. "I'll take this over to Dave to get it signed."

Cory went for her dinner break in Gregory & Greek's across the road from the plant. She had in front of her a plate of runny shepherd's pie and a glass of milk. Two mechanics beside her were talking about hunting moose.

The blast turned the dark windows white, then orange. The room went dead; everyone's eyes and ears numbed. Next the chairs scraped back; there was an instant logjam of bodies at the door.

The night air rippled with orange flame. You had to know one of the TNT sheds had gone up. Nobody spoke; they were turned to stone at the size of it.

Finally someone shouted over the crackle and wind. "Which number was it?"

Cory knew but couldn't speak.

"Looks like three."

TNT Three was beside Nitro Three. She ran toward it, her arms over her brows. The roof of TNT Three had flown off as intended and lay burning savagely thirty feet away. The shed itself crackled and melted like fat. The flames flapped overhead like great gold wings, giving the streaky, leftover snowbanks a lurid glow. Voices flew back and forth through the roar, and the orders for hoses, buckets, trucks. The flat ground was crisscrossed with the dark figures of men running to shut down a line, move a wheelbarrow. The train cars sat a thousand yards away, loaded.

"Someone get those boxcars out of here!"

Cory stood, visualizing the inside of TNT Three. She saw the men at their stations, the gutter flowing with water beneath them. If the mixture got too hot they were to drown it. "Drown it!" one of them would have shouted. They'd tip the water in, sound the alarm bell by their feet, and dive for their escape hatches. The operators would be out.

But a welder working on the nitro tank next door? No warning. No escape.

Billy was dead. He had been climbing up the outside of the tank; a bolt flying off the TNT shed had gone neatly through his temple. Wade had been inside, where he'd gone so Billy wouldn't have to. He was burned all over his face and back, but he was alive. Cory went to stand beside him. "Boy, you caught it bad," she said. He couldn't hear. His lips were black and open. His clothes were licked off; there was no skin on his skull. She watched his chest. It barely rose and fell.

They had no hospital at the plant, only a little infirmary, with beds and some plasma and dressing. They had to take Wade in his new car the twenty miles to Parry Sound and most of them thought he'd die on the way, which, given his condition, wouldn't be so bad. The car set off, its headlights reaching forlorn into the bush.

A third man was lost. He'd been going for dinner break, walking past the shed. His pals had seen him lofted by the blast and carried westward. A dozen men dug frantically along the creek. The pyre sent a cascade of sparks down over them; steam and smoke belched out periodically as water pipes burst. The high, goose-necked overhead lights came on, turning the whole area between the highway, the railway tracks and the creek, down to the rocky slope that led to the shore, into daylight. She could shoot without flash.

They dug all night, but it wasn't until daylight erased the shadows that they discovered him where he'd been thrown into the swampy water of the run-off. He was recovered whole, unblemished and quite dead.

When Cory developed her film, it was nothing but black

shapes and blobs of light. She went to the hospital to see Wade. He had no face left to mention, no lips, no eyelids. The pain put him beyond speaking, but he knew her, and heard Tyke clamber around the legs of his hospital bed. One day when she came in the nurse said they were moving him to Toronto for skin grafts. They had all kinds of new ways to heal the skin, and the government would pay. She said goodbye to Wade. He made movements with his hands: What was he trying to show? Skates. Tyke. Next year.

My dearest Coree —

The war machine blunders on, carrying all of us on its fenders. September's mad nights of bombardment have given way to last week's total destruction of Coventry. You'd have loved it the night the bomb fell outside the Café Royal but did not explode: Everyone cleared off and it was just as if I owned the maze of streets behind, where I prowled telling all I was a war artist out of uniform.

The North African campaign rather attracts me, it's the colours I suppose, all that ochre and sienna, the gold dust, the horizons of sand. But I'm not there. I feel like an old rump of a man, useless. It's the worst of what this madness does to one, makes you feel like you don't deserve to live if you're not set to die.

PS Met some of your soldiers down in the pub. Asked if they knew you for the sheer pleasure of

*speaking your name, maybe even having a few
minutes conversation about you — but of course
that's mad. It's only that at home you've become the
unmentionable. I don't know how it happened, but
for over a year now there's been a positive edict
against uttering the C-word.*

Miss del Zotto, who had come alone this summer, walked
the length of Manitou verandah, swatting mosquitoes. Old
men, rosy with sunburn and beer, stretched out in the
wicker chairs. The ladies sat in circles knitting for Bundles
for Britain. "Lawrence is gone," Lydia said. "Back to his
wife. Back to his business. Art was just a fling with him.
The gallery was his parting gift to me."

"Too bad," mumbled Cory.

"No, it isn't," said Lydia. "Let me see your pictures."

Cory stood by while Lydia looked. There was Tyke
having his night terror in the white netting. There was
one of the back of Jimmie's hand on the striped rock; the
strata had come up beautifully, feldspar and mica and
granite with depths of light and dark and the shadow of
his arm somehow ominous, like a guillotine falling across
the space.

"Very *gneiss* picture," said Lydia.

"Ha ha," said Cory.

Then, because she didn't appear very excited, Cory produced the one of the shanty town by Guncotton Creek.
She imagined Lydia wouldn't buy, so she lowered the price
in her mind from thirty dollars each to twenty-five.

"A touch of Margaret Bourke-White," she said. "Maybe more Ansel Adams."

Cory had seen some of theirs in *Life* magazine.

"Just as good," said Miss del Zotto. "Just as good but nobody knows you. Nobody knows these places. I'd like to see what you could do out there in the world."

Cory bit her lip. This was the world.

Lydia said twenty-five dollars was far too low and she'd take all five and give her two hundred dollars. She said it was a deposit. She'd show the pictures in her gallery, and later she'd get more. She went upstairs to her room and came down to hand her the cash directly. The two hundred dollars felt potent in Cory's hands, full of mischief and hope. That made four hundred she'd earned from her pictures, and three hundred saved.

It was pitch black by then, the blackest time because the moon wasn't up yet, nearly ten o'clock and most everyone had gone to bed. She thanked Lydia maybe thirty times. Then she remembered Tyke had been somewhere around. She ran down to the dock and there was Jimmie. He smiled and pointed to her canoe, still resting in the water. Tyke was asleep in the bow, using the bunched up life-jackets as a pillow.

Jimmie and Cory took the fishing launch up to Head Island for a picnic. It was a big, beautiful expanse of flat smooth rock, with a few stands of elegant pine and cedar rooted in the low spots. Three hundred years before it had been the site of an Indian massacre. Like Cory, Jimmie paid most of his attention to the rocks and water while he fished. Cory walked with a stick, poking ahead for rattlesnakes. The rocks were coral, pink, silver. Black like something molten, flowing between the stiffer strata, mica gleaming like gunmetal and a stripe of quartz with the glint of money. There was electric lime green moss in the cracks, and scratchy, hospital green lichen sitting like dried scabs on the rocks. She lay down in a hollow. She looked through a branch of cedar to pink granite undulations stretching forward to blue line-end. Horizon. Her-eye-zone. She held her eye there until it burned, and she closed it, and slept.

Jimmie's foot fell beside her face on the rock. Look. And he handed her the skull. Small, delicate, hollow. It sat in the palm of her hand like something carved and polished. Cory knew it wasn't human but it had a spiritual look.

"Beaver," he laughed. He showed her the long, yellow teeth, which slid in and out of their sockets.

"In two days I leave," said Jimmie, "for the bone-fields of Europe."

She was angry. Her heart pounded. "You too? You never said." She squeezed the beaver skull. It wouldn't break. It was as strong as glass. She opened her hand and gazed at it.

"Will I be beautiful to you when I'm dead too?" said Jimmie.

"Is that what you want, too?" She didn't know herself what she meant, that he wanted to die, or to be beautiful to her.

She strode away to the edge of the water. She picked up

a stone and threw it as hard and as far as she could. Jimmie stayed behind. She could feel him, silent, waiting. The
gust of rage that took her chest slowly dissipated, leaving
a great hole.

"I'm sorry," she said. "I don't want you to leave me."

"Why?" He didn't move. Wary, he watched her. There
was such truth in the way he did not speak. But she could
not love him. How could she dare try to keep him here?

"I'm jealous, that's all. I want to go."

Still he said nothing.

"I'll be alone," she said.

A frog vanished from a rock before she saw him, only
a dark green shape and then the cluck of water absorbing
him, the cloud of muck on the bottom of the little
trapped pool.

Everyone was on the wrong side of the Atlantic. Little
yellow-bellied birds in pairs chased each other from one
side of the channel to the other. Come home! Albert
wrote. And he meant by that, come to the house where I
live with my wife. Where I am is your home too.

What conceit! Why didn't he come here? No, it was
impossible. She could not imagine him here, his topcoat,
his bowler, his cane, his need for layers and layers of
human expression, words on images, appliqué, floral walls.
He could never find the comfort he needed here.

What on earth are you doing there? It's all so new, he
wrote.

A letter never sent:

> *It isn't new at all, there's nothing new about it. In fact, these rocks are the oldest part of the earth; you could not find them anywhere else without going down ten miles underground. And I think every shape concocted by humans was anticipated here. If you came I could show you a perfectly spherical pothole, drilled by a rock being whirled between several mile-thicknesses of moving ice. I could take you out to make an offering to the Sacred Turtle. But no one comes here. Everyone leaves.*

She lay chest down on the rocks in front of the cabin, her ear flat against the rock. She strained to hear the roar of aircraft, the rattle of gunfire, the dynamite blasts in Europe. Army boots clattering over hastily constructed bridges, men's voices in anguish and the death rattle of tanks.

She was going to get herself over there. She would do it, she absolutely would. She almost knew the way.

Chapter Seventeen

CHRISTOPHER-KNOWN-AS-TYKE REMEMBERED.

He was low down, at the level of his mother's thighs. But he was agile; he could get up a tree and down off a rock now. It was the end of summer, the day they were moving back to town for the winter. St. Pierre was waiting to take them in to Pointe au Baril Station to the train. He and his mother stood on the dock. The light was rich, like in a painting, deep gold and blue. Tyke's body for that summer, for ever and ever, it seemed, had included the yellow, canvas-covered kapok slabs that went over his neck and were belted around his middle. At first he hated the lifejacket: He couldn't bend forward or twist; it was hard to throw a rock. But now he was used to it. And if he wore it, his mother would let him go anywhere. She would allow him to sit in the canoe while she waited with her camera poised for the blue heron. She would let him jump off the rocks into deep water, and she would even let him paddle the canoe alone, his upper arms propped too far from his chest by the spongy slabs. From morning to night he wore that kapok lifejacket. Until now.

"I'm sick of that old jacket, aren't you?" said his mother. "Let's get rid of it."

She undid the straps and lifted it over his head.

"Bye, lifejacket."

"Bye, lifejacket!" He jumped up and down.

Cory flung her arm in a big arc. At the height of it she let go. Like some fat yellow-winged butterfly it sailed through the air, hit the water, and bobbed once. But it did not bob again. As it got wet, it seemed to get heavy, and began to disappear beneath the surface. They watched the last bit of yellow go down. The wind was blowing toward the dock.

Tyke's face pickled up with doubt. "Can you see it?"

"No," said Cory. They stood, realizing what it meant as the jacket that was to keep him up sunk like a brick.

"Lucky you're not in it," said Cory. "The damn thing doesn't even float." She laughed and laughed, pointing her finger. Tyke stared into the silver green water.

The deep chug of St. Pierre's low wooden launch made them lift their heads. St. Pierre made a circle in front of them and expertly let the square back end of his boat swing up against the edge of the dock. Cory was paralyzed with hilarity, tears running down her face. She stamped one foot and pointed helplessly, unable to speak, till St. Pierre located the yellow shape on the bottom.

"Nice of you to provide the boy with an anchor," he said.

Tyke ran down the dock to the shore. He lay on his stomach and peered beneath the water: He could not reach his lifejacket, its siren yellow. His stuffed toy, part of himself. Tears welled. "I want it back."

Cory howled louder than he did. "It's no good, Tyke! It never was."

He ran away from her up the rocks. He hated it when she laughed at him.

She called: "Tyke, we're leaving!" The motor echoed in the stillness. He would never trust her again. He sat under the steps. She knew where. Let her come and find him. He squeezed his eyes shut.

When Cory took Tyke up in her arms and hugged him against her face the wetness of her cheeks against his was a puzzle. Was it her laughter or his tears? He thought his mother's face beautiful: Her soft short brown hair ended just at her jawbone, her eyes were big and clear and saw everything, her lips were wide and her shoulders too; she was strong as a man and quick as a fish.

"Did you see that Tyke? Don't you understand? The damn thing doesn't even float! You might as well never have worn it."

No record keeping is fair; memory is perhaps the least. Cory didn't know the lifejacket was defunct. Who thinks to test a lifejacket, after all? He had asked himself this over the years. She had done her best, he also told himself.

How early had she begun to tell the stories? Your Daddy's a soldier. Your Daddy had to stay in England because he had work to do. I'm saving you for your Daddy as a surprise. Sometimes, he thought, she simply adopted the rumours that went around the Manitou. Your Daddy was a ballet dancer who had to go back to Denmark. Your Daddy didn't know you were born. Your Daddy's an Indian. And even, when she was angry —

your Daddy's a bad man, he doesn't care about me or about you.

"Is that a letter from Daddy?" asked Tyke, to whom everything far away and mysterious had become Daddy.

"Yes."

"Did he go to the war too?"

"He's too old to go to the war. But the war came to him, you know."

And when she decided to get herself over to Europe to the war, who thought of "Daddy" first — did she, or did Tyke? He'd been as happy as if he could see Albert himself. You're going to find my Daddy. Only later did he learn to blame Albert for the fact that she left him behind. If Albert had been a normal father he'd have welcomed his child, or at least provided for him. But then if he'd been normal she would never have fallen in love with him.

That was the beginning of his memory, and the end of his mother. Images he had: the frozen surface of the Bay, pocked, ridged and grey-white under a faithless sky. Sliding down the hill at Pointe au Baril Station on toboggans made from the slats of grocery boxes. Sleeping on cots with three Pamajong kids: scared out of bed by Marge when the wood-stove burst and the cabin began to burn. One year, two years, three years.

But his mother was an absence, a burnt-out place, a fallen tree. In Marge's cabin he tried to save a space for her, a seat at the chipped green linoleum table where he ate. But she never came to sit there. Sometimes, rarely, there was a letter on his plate, a thin blue paper folded to make its own envelope, which Marge would read to him.

Later, much later, he would know everything about where she went. After he had dropped out of high school, gone to Northern Alberta to work on the tar sands, lived in the commune, grown mushrooms and become a student of the Second World War to discover her. After he had watched all the films, read the biographies, and had even gone to the archives to read the letters soldiers sent home. She sent so very few herself, and he hadn't saved them.

He knew she would have taken a train from Union Station. (In fact, Wade went down with her from Parry Sound, the new, unrecognizable Wade with his rubbery, unfeatured face and his white cane.) She would have crossed the Atlantic on a freighter, in a convoy, protected by the Corvettes. June and July of 1943 marked a lull in the battle in the Atlantic; she was lucky and her ship made it through.

He could see her in London. He knew her so well. After all, he'd studied her leave-takings and her arrivals all his life. She must have deposited her luggage and walked alone through the darkened, half-demolished city, a London full of whispers, a restless city eager to strike out, to invade Europe, beat those Germans back. She'd have taken a room in some lodging house full of soldiers on leave from the front.

He knew that for a day she would not call Aunt Eunice, or even Albert. She would sleep long and hard and rise up without hesitation, her eye on the goal: to get over to the fighting. He could picture her, his lean, determined mother with her muscled arms from her job on the cordite line. Her neck would grow a little longer, her chin push forward an inch, and her pupils contract. Her voice would soften as if in pity of anyone who got in her way.

She would be methodical, calm unless opposed. Swatting down her pride she'd go to the one man who could get her what she wanted. It was not Albert. Love might have been the first to draw her but it was not all for Cory. Tyke could not imagine it would ever be.

FIGURE 17
Corinne Ditchburn
London, June '43
23 x 45 cm

Where the row houses earlier set their unbroken face to the street, now there are jagged holes, gaps, pits, views into the back gardens, alleys, hallways even. Broken toilets, dangling curtains, whole mirrors reflect back the empty street. Had the permanence of London been merely a facade? A street is transformed by a hole in its middle, and a church is another statement when the roof is gone.

ℰⱭ

THE TRAIN PULLED OUT THROUGH THE DARK HUSTINGS OF Victoria Station late on Friday afternoon for Cherkley.

Ahead, glinting in the dim headlight, was a river of criss-crossing tracks. Four smokestacks protruded into an orange sky. On the horizon the chimney pots asserted themselves, disorderly, circling, crowded throngs of them, like armies encamped. The train picked up speed. The back ends of every row and garden were exposed to its plunge.

How different it was from home! Not pines with half a dozen sparse stretching limbs, but thick, knotted, vine-covered trees lined the track. She had forgotten the industry in the English landscape, the metal strips that defined it; fences, bridges, curving tracks, culverts.

Stornoway having been bombed, Lord Beaverbrook now had a flat in Arlington House. But he spent most of his time in the country, at Cherkley. By this time, he had resigned as Minister of Aircraft Production. He was covered with glory: Without him they could not have won the Battle of Britain, but they could not stand to work with him. His enemies had caught up with him and his tactics had exhausted even his friends. Later this same year, on September 28, he would be installed as Lord Privy Seal, with an office in Gwydyr House in Whitehall, a short stroll from Downing Street. Despite the grand title, it wasn't much of a job. However, he still had his newspapers.

At Leatherhead Station Max's driver awaited her. He tipped his hat and extracted her bag from her grip. They drove down the curving High Street. She had a brief panic: What will I do at Beaverbrook's home? she wondered. How can I carry this off?

"If you'll excuse me, I must make a stop," he said.

In front of the butcher he beeped the horn. A boy in a bloodied apron ran out, bearing paper-wrapped packages. Then they drove on through gently sloping fields and turned off the road to the private drive. The road betrayed nothing of what lay ahead. Fields, the usual outbuildings, a man with a scythe. Then the driver made a sudden hard turn to the right and drew up. The place had no prospect, it was simply there, dark, above them; it was as if they'd been thrown against its wall and had fallen into the courtyard.

A very tall, scraggy pine tree stood beside the front door on the left. The driver opened the door for Cory. As she stepped onto the paving stones she came face to face with a peculiar stone figure. He seemed to be an alms beggar, hooded, with his arm stretched out. How tactless and unfortunate it was that such a statue had been in place when he bought the house! Or had Max put it there, as his little joke aimed at friends who came asking for favours?

Towering bookshelves and a large painting of a horse by Stubbs covered the side walls of the room where Beaverbrook sat in an armchair with a tumbler of amber liquid in his small fist, head sunk despondently into his chest. He was smaller, his head larger. The leprechaun in his looks was accentuated, perhaps by petulance.

"Good evening, my dear," he said. "Do you know these people?"

She said she didn't, but he did not introduce her. One

reason was that Caruso was on the gramophone, singing at foghorn level. The other guests stood about in anxious small groups. Mimi Gluck floated from one klatch to another, easing nothing but her own need to move, leaving behind her a circling and aimless trail. Max solved the problem by bursting into apparently undirected monologue.

"Do you see, I've got my old shoes on? Shortage of shoe leather, you see. I do my best to help." He wore patent lace-up boots open to his ankle above which he revealed, lifting his cuff, an expanse of white tennis sock with a blue stripe. "Do you know they've cut the length of men's hose? The only size I can get is these. Don't you think they're downright mean?"

Cory said it had been some time since she'd thought about men's hose, since it was not worn with any particular sense of style in Parry Sound. He nodded sagely.

"Of course, I forgot, you've been away. Have you seen the place? Never mind, it's nearly dark," Max said to Cory. "But come with me while I do a little job. Nockles! Are they ready?"

Nockles inclined his impressive head on its stringy stalk and said he would inquire in the kitchen. In a moment, he returned with a large can. He winked at Cory as he presented it.

"Your Lordship," he said.

Cory caught the smell of earth. Inside the can was a grey clot of worms, twining and intertwining, weaving and burrowing in the loose soil.

"My fish are hungry!" he announced.

He opened the French doors at the end of the room, and together they stepped out onto a terrace. The bill of a stone pelican beside the door brushed her leg; the damp air of English summer pressed up against Cory's cheeks. Ahead was an ornamental pool, nearly blanketed with enormous lily pads. She'd heard about these lily pads. They were large enough to be a skirt, a loin cloth. It was one of Albert's persistent fancies that, amongst the lily pads, the rich and the famous disported themselves in the nude in nightly revels. She tried to elicit a confession.

"I like your lilies. In Georgian Bay these have white and yellow blooms that sit on top of the pad like eggs on a plate."

"Ours are purple. All gone now," said Max. "Hold this for me." Cory found the can in her hand while he thrust his hands into the soil and pulled out fistful of worms. Then he stepped over to the pond, and, crooning to the fishes, dangled the worms over the water.

"Here you are — do you see, little fishes? Come on now, oh yes, you'll like it." Fat carp shot out of the shadows like jungle tigers and hung open-mouthed at the shadow of his hand. One by one he dropped the worms. "My only pleasure these days. That and settling old scores." A flash of orange accompanied each tiny splash. "You want something," he said. His reptilian glamour was not lost on her. Power was a magnet with two ends: It attracted and repelled.

"Now is when you get to remind me I said there was nothing you could do for me," said Cory.

He laughed, in the way she knew he would — superior, pleased to be proven right in his cynicism. "I don't recall *anyone* ever saying that."

Of course he wouldn't, would he? But she didn't need him to admit it.

"I've got this war under my skin. I want to see it."

"You could always enlist. The Canadians would probably train you up and give you credentials. They might even send you over to Italy eventually."

"More likely they'd keep me here taking pictures of the servicemen's Christmas teas and regimental parades. You owe me a favour."

Beaverbrook only grunted and reached for more worms. "Remind me."

"I brought back Albert Bloom's portrait of you," she began.

"It's too late now to play that card. Timing is all. You're not a card player, I think. You must learn to take your advantages when you see them."

"All right, I'll just ask. No favours. I want to work for you." She took a swallow of her sherry. There, it was done. It was not so difficult.

His laugh was the laugh of a man whose view of life was always borne out. "That's all very well, but what can you do?"

"I told you. I can take pictures. For your newspapers."

The last of the worms escaped his clenched knuckles. She could tell he enjoyed the feel of it.

The fish waited, hanging. No more worms dropped. In

the failing light he turned his attention to her face. His smile was wide, full of innocent pleasure at her discomfort. They all came to him finally, didn't they?

"You are the devil," she blurted.

"No, I'm not. I'm known as the devil, but that's different. My friend Valentine said I was the devil. He's gone, you know, did you know? He was my friend, and I miss him very much."

She had not known. Valentine, the turnip-shaped gentleman, so courtly and so vile. Valentine, Beaverbrook's apologist, who pointed out how easy it was, with such a man, to hold him responsible for all the worst compromises in life.

"How did he die?"

"Heart, of course. He was warned. But to him there would have been no point in living if he had to practise moderation." But Max's mind had gone past Valentine now. He was thinking about Cory's request. "This war, my dear. You know you're very late. To want to get in."

"I know. But war eats people. They need more all the time. And the Americans have women correspondents now."

He became enlivened suddenly; his feet tapping on the terrace, he shifted his weight in front of her. Someone came out the door. It was Nockles to take the tin. Beaverbrook waved him back.

"Why do you want to do this?"

She began hesitantly. "I want to do my bit for the war. I want to be there. I want to see it. I can't sit by any more, when I know we have to win this, or there'll be no more world. And I'm good. I know I can *show* people the killing. Photographers can fight as well as the troops. So this will be the *last* war."

He nodded, as if it were the least she could say.

"If there were one place you could go to?" he said.

"It would be the place called Dachau."

"It's rumours, of course," said Max. "People will tell you anything in wartime." He seemed to be dismissing her but then thought again.

"You're late, and yet, you're in perfect time," he said, turning Mad Hatter. "That's how I know you're a journalist at heart. A good journalist is born. Not made. He phones up just because he's got a hunch, and sure enough, the King's about to abdicate. He takes a shortcut home and the convent is bombed in front of his eyes. *Things happen to him.* Or her. In your case, her. You are a natural-born practitioner of the Black Art. If things don't happen you can make them happen, but you get into trouble that way."

Beaverbrook spun his glass in her face. "You're at the right moment because, although nobody knows it yet, the Canadians are finally going to get out of England and into the war. I could let you cover them. They need something extra to get the public attention, languishing in the countryside, nursing their wounds from Dieppe!" He began to pace. "And this is the big one. Sending you might be a good gimmick."

A surge of desire very like lust blotted out thought.

Cory went weak. "I've got to go with them. Please. Hire me. I've got to go."

He was flattered, and she hated giving him that. But it was only this once. The future be damned.

"I could argue that you have no experience, you might not have any talent, and dozens of others are lined up waiting."

She said nothing.

"That's laying aside the fact that you're a woman and they won't let you see combat, and the forces will scream bloody murder about how tough it will be to keep you safe."

"I don't want anything special. Just get me there, so I can see. I can do it. I'm good."

His hands were empty. Nockles stood a few paces off, not interrupting, but seeming to listen intently, a lapse on his part. Cory rattled the worm can, and the dirt shifted. "There's a few more in here," she said.

"You do it."

The fish were gone. No flash of their orange-lit backs betrayed the life under the surface. Max bent down to rinse his hands in the water. Cory upended the can and suddenly the fish were there, sliding between and over his hands so it seemed he wrung his hands with their light.

It was now almost completely dark. The blackout curtains had been drawn; through the chink in the door Cory could see candles being carried across the room.

"Wait here with me for a minute," said Max. He stepped

off the terrace. He walked a few steps and disappeared. She heard the unmistakable sound of a zipper.

"I just have to make water," he called.

The dinner table conversation centred on deathbed conversions. Max announced that when the time came he would repent of everything.

"I can't imagine what you'd have to repent of, except of course the women," said Anthony, a businessman who had suffered reverses and who Beaverbrook had bailed out.

There was laughter. Mimi inclined her head as if she did not understand.

Mimi was serene and modest with her now-obvious role as lady of the house, but it was a calculated simplicity; she attended to every word and gesture, as if to lose the thread even momentarily would be to be woven out of the picture. Still, all Max's remarks seemed to end in hooks that went back her way. Everything he said asserted the universal need for the money and protection that were his to give.

"Cory," she said, "is back in England after living in the wilds of Canada, where she was taking photographs."

"Isn't that where Wyndham Lewis went too?" said Anthony.

"She found she couldn't practise her art in Canada. She needs a job. And so she's come to me," said Max.

"Needs money, does she?"

"Very useful for an artist, money. You take Wyndham Lewis. He'd never have done what he did without a trust fund," said Beaverbrook.

"That's not so!" The new male secretary was called George. He wouldn't last long. He was emotional, pink-cheeked with indignation. "That's not giving Mr. Lewis credit. He didn't have access to those funds until after his father's death, a long time after he'd written all those novels. He lived on nothing. In a shack."

"Did you know he was able to drink himself silly all his life and when he died his liver was absolutely clear? While his father, who never drank, died of sclerosis of the liver — there's no justice," said someone else.

"What sort of job?" inquired Mimi.

"She wants to be a war correspondent."

"Why should women go to war, for heavens sake? Here they've got their sex, the best protection of all from hell, and they're heaving it off." Anthony turned angrily to Cory. "What do you think you're going to find? The meaning of life? Not at all. You'll find death, death and more death." He wiped his mouth with his napkin, disgusted. "I thought you girls were more sensible."

"Why do you want to keep us out of it?" said Cory.

"Perhaps," said Mimi gaily in her careful English, "you men do not want women to see what goes on at the heart of wars. Perhaps you feel we will not admire men so much, after that!"

"I want to be there," said Cory. "It's where life is now. The rest is only waiting."

"That's what you think," said Anthony. "You won't know what waiting is until you're in the army." Then he abruptly dropped his line of argument, as if he'd forgotten why he even cared. "I'll probably never even see you again," he mumbled.

"Come with me to my office," Max said to Cory when the meal ended. "The boys can take their port down here. I'll take mine up."

There was the trumpet-shaped Dictaphone, and there was the telephone from which he was reputed to bawl out Churchill, when he called for moral support. Cory went faint. She could not believe she'd come this far. She forced herself to sit straighter. She thought of the open water on a calm day, of Jimmie's hand with the beaver skull.

Max picked up the phone, though it was now eleven o'clock Saturday night. Cory could hear the weary voice of the editor come down the wire.

Beaverbrook did not bother to identify himself. "Sir!" he shouted, the port in his throat giving it an extra rumble. "Do you believe women are different from the rest of us?" He held the phone away from his ear so Cory could hear the answer.

"Of course they are, Lord, but it's too late at night for me to answer riddles."

Max winked and brought the receiver up against his head again.

"Well, maybe they are and maybe they aren't. I've got an idea we should send one over to have a look at the fighting."

Rumble on the line. Cory took it the man imagined problems.

"If it's difficult, so much the better. Isn't being difficult what picture journalism is all about? You yourself said it was a photographer's war."

Max listened for a bit.

He stuck his chin over toward Cory. "He says you'll never get to see the fighting."

"*Life* magazine gets a woman to see it."

"So you think you're Margaret Bourke-White?"

"No, I don't. She shoots big. I think I'm Cory Ditchburn."

Beaverbrook laughed and repeated it into the phone. Then he lifted his head. "He says he appreciates your spirit but you're going to have to do something that makes people sit up and take notice." He held out the phone for Cory to shout into.

"Give me a chance and I will."

"This is not about giving people chances," came the voice out of the telephone. "It's about covering a WAR!"

"Oh that's bosh," said Beaverbrook, suddenly tired of the game. "It's news like anything else. Why do you have to be so timid? Why am I the one with all the good ideas here?" he said, petulantly.

"Because your good ideas are the only good ideas you'll listen to," came the weary voice back.

Max flared to a fine, fast rage. "What do I pay you for anyway? To tell me my instincts are wrong? Well, they're right, God damn you, and don't you forget it."

He slammed down the receiver. His face had purpled. Still, he gave Cory a cheerful wink and then preceded her out the door.

"Pay no attention to that. I don't know why he bothers to argue with me," he said. "You shouldn't think me rude," and, standing and hitching his pants up over his still-trim waist, "I am not a rude man."

"Nockles," he said to the butler, appearing in the hall. "Would you make the room ready now for the screening?" He turned to Cory.

Best, if you must be near this man, to be his servant, Cory thought. He got on well with his servants. It was important to him to be seen to be a gentleman. And a gentleman did not berate those who were inferior in social status. He had intimacy with servants. They knew him. He allowed them to know him, a little, because it was not dangerous, because they *were* servants. He had his place and they theirs. A junior was different, an aspirant to his position: He, or anyone like him, Beaverbrook was bound to demolish. At least then your job would end. But if you were his son or daughter, God help you, the destruction would last over a lifetime.

The company dutifully followed Max to watch "Destry Rides Again."

"I've become fatalistic," said one man. "On my deathbed I shall recite lines from the script."

"Don't you like it?" Max seemed truly astonished.

"In times like this, we find the familiar is very soothing." Nockles turned over a piece of white card beside the door, such as one might receive while waiting in line at the butcher shop. The new number said 239. "Number of viewings," he explained.

Max settled happily into the front row, his arm linked to Mimi's. Soon the room was full of snoring, Anthony's in particular, jerky, troubled, occasionally horrifying, so that the people dozing on the chairs next to him were jolted upright. Mimi slept silently, her head on Max's shoulder. When she cried out, from time to time, as if in a fearful dream, Max patted her arm. In the funnel of light that fell from the screen onto their faces, he grinned with delight at his memorized images. Cory sat awake, seeing nothing, her heart pounding at the hollow of her throat.

Chapter Eighteen

*Portrait of the photographer in uniform with Speed
Graphic held up before one eye, her left hand support-
ing the camera, her right clasping the flashgun with its
reflecting shield. Second of her self-portraits. She has
taken the photo with her time-delay Leica, most likely
using a tripod, in the same manner in which she took
her self-portraits of '39.*

CORY HAD PASSED THE MILITARY TAILOR IN PICCADILLY DOZENS
of times, before the war. It had appeared to her a kind of
museum, with the stiff models in the window, the gold
braid, the brass buttons, the serge and blue, the stuffed
models like wax figures dressed for some far-off theatrical
performance that she never wished to see. Now she was

inside and a terrifying man moved around her with a consoling air and a tape measure, which he wielded with all the skill of a cowboy's lariat.

"I don't want to wear a uniform," she had said to the war office. "I'm not fighting."

"Regulations," the man had snapped at her. "War correspondents are given the rank of officer. You must dress the part."

"There must be exceptions. Perhaps I could be an exception."

"Perhaps you'd like to get shot," he had snapped.

"No, that won't be necessary," she murmured.

She walked until the light faded, until, in the soft summer air, the unlit city was black, medieval, Albert had called it. Darkness soaked up Cory's footsteps as she paced the curves of Regent's Park. Voices, men's and women's, laughing softly, came from benches, all unseen. She crossed the road and entered Fitzroy Avenue. She saw the lights on in her garden flat: She wondered who the Stooks had let it to. She turned and set off toward the cone of Primrose Hill, shaven now of its crest of trees. An anti-aircraft light was mounted there.

The night had brought coolness, and there was a murky fog on the hill. Cars were little red-eyed monsters looming out of the black; the space in front of her foot was unfathomable. The row of plane trees against the road, fragrant even in the stink of motionless city air, stood like large cold spirits.

In front of Albert's house there were two forms beside a rumbling taxi. Surely that was his voice, and his hat, the shape of it just visible against the lesser black of the garden. He was in an uxorious posture, handing Liss, that adored, heavy figure, slowly into a car. She leaned on him before she stepped outward. How perfect they were together, even when their performance, as here, was carried out solely for the benefit of the driver and the night air. Even the knife-like edges of the love letters that had crossed the ocean for these past four years could not slip between these two.

How had she imagined that she and Albert had carried on their affair in secret? That even their letters were private? She realized now what she ought to have known always: Albert would have let his wife see them, concocting some accident, needing her to find this hidden part of himself, because it, like everything else, was for her.

"Liss darling, you haven't seen my receipt from the bank, have you? I thought I left it —" And Liss would go through the pockets of his waistcoat, his old and baggy trench, the piles of paper that regularly built up on the hall table, and find it. The handwriting, the Canadian stamp. She would read it without flinching. Then later — "Albert, what does Cory say?" her voice varnishing the hurt, her eyes a melted surface with the force of glaciers behind. And of course she would know about Tyke.

This was why they'd fought so bitterly when Cory had telephoned, that once. And this was why, also, it had become impossible, as Albert wrote, to say her name. It was Liss's only recourse.

So her hand came down and she turned her collar up, angled her head and crossed the road but not without a fleeting, powerful impression that Albert, as he dispatched her in the taxi, was tender to his wife. Perhaps they'd had a row. He was always tender after brutality. She fully intended to walk away.

But the taxi's door shut, and its little red eyes swept across Cory shortsightedly. Albert stood on the pavement as if uncertain which way to turn, to go back in to the dark house, or out, to the sleeping city.

"Albert."

His body registered the voice. He was alerted, he stood cocked forward, a gun on the trigger.

"It's me, Cory."

"Can't be."

"Yes it is."

She could hear his hissing intake of breath. "Can't be. You're teasing me. Who is it?"

She stepped closer. He was almost angry, as he saw her.

"How long have you been standing there? What are you doing here?"

"Where did you send Liss?"

They both began to laugh.

"But where did you come from?" He fell forward to her in astonishment, arms open.

"Across the sea."

"Ah. You've come back to life then. You stopped writing. I thought you were dead."

"Why should I be?"

"I killed you off, I think. It made it easier."

In the house he clasped both her hands in his and gazed into her face. The kitchen was filled with Liss's blue and yellow painted dishes. The smoky smell always associated with Albert and his hands enveloped her. On the bed in the corner was one of Liss's quilts, crumpled; in a jam jar, tulips arched and gaping in their death poses.

He put the kettle on, and came back with two mugs of tea, wordlessly handing her one. She searched him for clues: What, aside from the ongoing marital engagement, had been happening? His face was different, the cheeks were slim but not sunken, the effects of drink had drained off.

"You look so well. What is it? Money? Have you sold some work?"

"I'm purified by suffering," he said. "And war. We're under assault, you know. It's shocking to most. But life has always been this violent to me. So now everyone lives on the same plane as I do. It's oddly comforting."

He set his tea on the table and took her face in his hands. "I forget about young people. You change. You're still growing up."

They had not really touched, before that, beyond the first embrace. Now, he was tender. She felt an awful hunger to embrace him. She put her arms around him and he slid a stuffed chair on its claw feet toward the sofa bed.

"Sit."

"After the telephone call, I was so worried. Did you and Liss —"

"I don't remember."

"— fight because of me?"

"I don't remember."

She could hear a car door slam a long way away, and knew she wouldn't get an answer. He sat on the bed and she in the chair. Eventually, she laid her head on his lap. He stroked her hair. He hadn't said a word about Tyke. The bastard. She wanted to punch him. Such woeful consistency, on this matter, of all things, she'd never encountered. It was tantamount to madness. But she could smell his lap, his chest. Her thoughts were blotted out by rushes of blood to her head; her heart hit and hit her rib cage, bruising it. Between her legs, she throbbed, hot and painful.

"I think I hate you," she said. "But I won't go into it now. Just take me to bed."

"My dearest," he said, "that's all over for me. It's out of my life. And it's a relief, actually. Not to have to think about it."

She had imagined hundreds of times how she would lie with him, even when she also was certain she'd never go back to him. But she never dreamed that he would refuse her.

"It's too, too distracting. How long did I spend in that adolescent madness, lusting, when you were gone? I got thoroughly sick of myself. It's best we don't. Really, I'm over it."

She stood, and pulled him up after her. She pressed her waist and the hollow of her pelvis against his firm protruding belly. Both his arms went behind her back. He squeezed her hard, twice, as if in reprimand, thumping her breastbone against his. Then he pushed her off. She grabbed his arm. He tried to get away but tripped on the chair's claw foot, and they fell together across the sofa bed. She put her hand in his trousers, and pulled the shirt out of his pants. How easily he gave in. All their clothes were scratchy and difficult. His skin underneath was warm and even clammy, and he was thinner. There was the mat of chest hair. Remotely she recalled Jimmie's hairless, satin chest. But Albert had words.

"I've made you into some kind of object," he mumbled. "Your breasts. They ought to be in pornographic pictures."

He made noises like a little bird. Cory kept silent.

"My lust for you is like a fatal disease," he said. "It advances even in remission. What is it? Four years? We begin even farther along than where we left off."

When they were done, Albert lay asleep, or feigning it, on his back, his forearm across his brow. Cory's rage came back. She took his chin in her hands and shook it.

"Albert. You never even asked. How could you not?"

He whined. "It's unfair to take men to task after sex. We're so helpless. Especially when we've just gone back on a pledge of abstinence."

She pounded his breastbone. "Bastard."

They wrestled. She was as strong as him now.

"You never said one word about it," she cried. "The baby. He's your son, Albert. Don't you care? His name is Christopher but we call him Tyke."

She wrenched her hand free to hit him again. Albert sat up. That beautiful voice.

"Darling, no wonder you feel so bad. You've left him behind, haven't you? Left him behind in Canada."

In the morning, the door opened. Liss was older, her brow crumpled down, her white face shining like dough.

"Look who's come back." said Albert. "It's Cory."

I thought I would never look this woman in the face, Cory thought as she embraced Liss. And see how easy it is. At the same time she felt in her bones that Liss was aware. She knows about us, she's read every word. She tried to kill me off by disallowing my name to be spoken. All without ever uttering a word of her feelings. So that, when I present myself, she is compelled, by her own policies, to accept me back.

"We missed you," said Liss, her voice thick with feeling. "We really missed you."

"I thought I just dropped out of your life like last week's newspapers, or maybe an old pot."

Albert was rocking, smiling, so pleased. You'd never have known that last night he'd buried his head in Cory's pubic hair and wept. Under his eyes were thin horizontal lines that existed, it seemed, to divide those expressive orbs from the rogue smile.

"Are you staying here with us?" said Liss.

"I leave town in the morning. And I'm afraid I can't tell you where I'm going."

"Off to war, are we?" said Albert bleakly. "Do we have

your Lord Beaverbrook to thank for this? I shan't even say you've sold yourself, Cory. I know his Lordship doesn't have a chance with you. You were already bought and paid for when you came. Art owns you Cory, doesn't it, art with a capital A?"

Cory looked at Liss for sympathy. They could not hold each other's eyes, but stood, transfixed. Liss's lips drifted apart slightly: A flicker of pain crossed her face and was gone. "He's jealous, don't you see?" said Liss.

"My wife expresses my feelings precisely, as always," said Albert. "There's another surprise. Cory has a child, my dear."

Liss inclined her head. "Where is he?"

Cory stiffened. *He.* So she did know. Albert would have made sure she knew. And now it seemed to her that Liss too had abandoned the boy, that she abrogated a duty: Unfair, irrational though it might be, Cory expected Liss to play grandmother. "With friends," she mumbled.

Both Liss and Albert turned cheerful, obtuse faces into the ragged silence.

"You are a wonder," said Albert. "Here you've turned out a baby and you've turned yourself into a soldier all at once, and now, as if that weren't enough, you're going off to take photographs of men doing what they do best, which is kill each other. You girls can do everything. I'm nothing compared to you."

His voice ran on. He was a nomad and it was his carpet, Cory thought, all his richness: his protection from storms, his cloak, his packing trunk, his vehicle. He unfurled it to get himself out of trouble, to disguise himself, to ensnare his enemies. Was it possible to be in love with a voice, with words? The carpet was luxurious, it was magnificent, but hid, as her mother would say, "a multitude of sins."

"No doubt you'll do brilliantly with your photographs. I knew you could, you know, that first day we met."

"You didn't say so."

"No, forgive me, darling, I didn't want to spoil you. But I knew it and that's why I didn't want to interfere with you. You mustn't blame me for that. Talent is rare. I knew you had important work to do."

Yet you did interfere with me, she wanted to say. And now you wound me by brushing me off, using my work as the excuse. But she said nothing. She protected Albert. Protected his vision. Never mind the why. Your truth, he'd said before, isn't what everyone wants to hear. Save it for your art.

"Can you take a bit of advice from an old man?"

She nodded, wordless.

"Get yourself a shell. You'll need one."

"A shell?" She thought of mortars, but it was not what he meant.

"To protect yourself. You're too open, and easy. It's that Canadian innocence. Get yourself a shell. And one more thing. Don't forget me. Don't forget that I gave you your eyes."

Chapter Nineteen

CORY STOOD AT THE WINDOW, HER BACK TO TYKE.

It seemed to him, arranging the prints, that his mother had seen all the globe offered in her lifetime, that she had been everywhere. She had attacked her span of years with a vengeance, and it had not escaped her. But the very strength of the photographs, several hundred of them, selected from thousands, from a lifetime of stolen images, was too great. Would they claim all the saying there was? Whatever else had been present, whatever subtleties, were gone from history. The other witnesses were silent, and it was as if they had been blind as well.

He moved one up, the other down, replaced another. Perhaps, like a set of mahjong tiles, they would make sense when placed in a particular order. But order revealed nothing: Each photo remained a resolute, momentary shout, framed, isolated, final. Cory did not turn from the window. He put them back in their boxes and opened other boxes. Perhaps if he sorted by theme? He wanted to lift them, to look through from behind, to find what they screened out.

He had four self-portraits. The teacher who went to London. Herself in a cheesecloth cocoon, pregnant — Corinne Ditchburn as pagan fertility goddess. Then, newly energized, the soldier in uniform, wearing her steel helmet with an arc cut in the front to allow space for the camera to fit up against her eye — Corinne Ditchburn as war photographer. Finally, Corinne as she was today.

One, two, three. Innocent, fertility goddess, soldier, old woman. She remade herself for the camera, gathered all the accoutrements of each state of being; she put herself on the record, seemingly perfectly reconciled to each new incarnation. Between these bold statements of being, she left few clues. How had she made the metamorphosis? Like the Greek gods, her alterations in form appeared effortless, sudden. Then she disappeared, until the next manifestation.

Of course, these were still photographs, not film: Instants might be profound, but they did not move forward, they were not action. She materialized, and then she faded. When next she became evident, she was rearranged. She had shed her story; like the rattlesnake on the island she left each skin, each incarnation, each chapter behind on the rocks to shrivel and dry in the sun. Clearly, she had never wished to be followed, or caught out, or understood.

Her voice floated over him, irritated. "What are you looking at?" She hated for him to see, when she could not.

"I'm just trying to piece together your story, Mother."

"A woman alone has no story," Cory said.

Late a feminist, she kept herself apart. Her mentor was Albert, as dangerous an enemy as he was powerful a lover. A story needed witnesses. What she meant was that she had no witnesses, no cohorts, no support group. Except for Tyke.

He lifted a print out of the new box.

He was looking at a great ship sinking sideways into the sea, and small people on ropes clinging to the side.

"It's a ship going down." He was excited: an adventure his mother had been on, without his knowing.

"Darling," said Cory, affecting the upper class drawl she used for fun. "It's only *film*. Transparencies, you see. Something laid over. You are wrong. It is not a ship going down. It is merely a photograph of a ship going down."

In that moment he got a glimpse of her, and understood her. For Cory too the images were tyrants. It must be like having lived one's whole life alongside a seemingly subservient twin, only to discover, when all was coming to a close, that the twin forcefully put forth a version of events contrary to one's own. Her whole life she had believed in the moment, in what it revealed. But now these moments, frozen in their original verve, shrieking their unfaded message, were history, and stood like impostors between herself and memory.

Looking at the photographs now, forced to, by age, by her son, by her own unwelcome impulse to make some sense of what had kept her so busy all her life, Cory saw the screen slip aside. The still, gelled image melted and ran off the surface of the exhibition print paper. Underneath, there was water.

FIGURE 19

Corinne Ditchburn

Torpedoed Ship

July 2, 1943
Enroute to Sicily
Water-damaged negative
The National Archives of Canada, reproduced
from censored film by Orestes Hrudy, 1993

---

*Ditchburn's daringly captured angle shot of the raked
deck of a ship which is about to sink established her as a
new star of war photography before she even reached
her first destination. She has captured in this image both
the surprise of the attack, and the order of troops under
attack. One is aware, as one is so often with her photographs, of a degree of personal danger incurred by the
photographer in order to create the image.*

✧✧

THROUGH THE BARROOM SMOKE, REG MORRIS WINKED AT
Cory; he was tall, long-limbed, with a bony nose and pale
blond hair. He had the classic handsomeness and good
manners of the well-bred Scots-Canadian, a type for
whose gentlemanly behaviour she had, thanks to Albert,
only scorn.

The ship rose gamely on the walls of water; as each wall
fell away, the deck plunged. The sailors were able to hold
their weight above their waists and saunter like dancers
while the nurses and soldiers staggered and fell and lost
their dinners. They were four nights out already, and

tomorrow they were to land. The troops in the fast assault convoy were far ahead. Cory had been put in the follow-up, slow assault convoy, with the Tank Brigade. It was supposed to be safer.

The ship was a channel ferry, hurriedly converted. Etched into the glass partitions downstairs in the bar were women in pencil thin gowns holding small dogs on leashes. The benches were upholstered in red leather. At night the troops sat around singing "Bless Them All" and drinking ginger beer.

She managed to avoid Reg Morris until she had a run-in with the second-in-command. She was on the deck shooting the troops as they played marbles on a table when a pimpled, squashy-nosed little guy with a voice that sailed out of his throat like an air raid siren approached. "Put it down! Put it down! Put it down, put it down!" he sang. Clearly he never said a thing once if he could repeat it four times.

"Why should I?" Cory asked, not removing her eye from the lens. "This is my job!"

The officer was momentarily at a loss for words.

"Who the hell are you? You? You?" he shouted.

Cory lowered her camera as the 2IC took a step backward. Reg Morris stepped between them. He pulled out two cigarettes, pointing one of them at her. She shook her head. "Save it for when you need it," he said. She didn't know if he meant her film or her temper. She stopped shooting. The 2IC hitched his trousers and went.

"Easier if you don't fight our guys," he said. "There'll be enemy soon. I'm Reg Morris."

He took his own offered cigarette and put it in his mouth.

"You can just admit you're scared."

Cory stared at him. "I'm not."

"That's just inexperience," he said. "Never mind, you will be." Then he drew on his cigarette in silence.

She stopped to watch a soldier rub oil into his boots, polishing, polishing the leather until it took on a shine, like the shine of his bare upper arm, glazed with sweat.

"Gerry submarines been following us for the past day," he said.

"No kidding," said Cory. And because she didn't know what else to say, she added, "where are you from?" She always wrote their names and their towns for her captions.

"You won't have heard of it. Little town called Preston. On the railway, not far from York."

Cory laughed. "Oh, but I have. I've even been there. I had peas and chips at the platform tea shop. There was a man there who'd been bitten by a camel." And because it was too painful to remember that day where everything shimmered in the north English sun, she walked away from him.

Dear Albert —
   There's an officer who says I can't use my cam-
era and a correspondent who wants me to learn

*what fear is. But you won't believe, I met a soldier
who comes from our town. Remember the tea shop
on the platform and the man who'd been bitten by
a camel? You said I had courage. But what I feel is
nothing. Having gone beyond, is all. Having left the
land. Sailed out.*

The torpedo hit in the darkest part of the night. The
boat immediately rose up on a slant, as if it had run up
on a rock. Cory's face hit the wall of her bunk. Dizzy, she
climbed out of bed with the nurses and felt around in
the dark for her clothes and cameras. She got out the
Leica, but she couldn't find the Speed Graphic. It was
crashing around on the floor underneath her bunk, she
thought. Anyway, it was too awkward for shooting under
attack, which must have been what they were. She left it,
glad to feel the reassuring leather and metal of her Leica
in her palm. Apparently the lights were not going to
come on.

The ship plunged again. Now the deck ran downhill
and the guns were aimed at the sky. The soldiers had
lapsed directly into their drill and a voice overhead bawled
instructions that she could not understand. She sidestepped farther uphill and tried to shoot the exodus. There
was not enough light, and her flash was somewhere rolling
around under her bunk. Then she saw Morris.

"Get over to your lifeboat station," he said. "You'll get
your chance when the sun comes up. Can't you see the
deck is flooding?"

"If the ship is sinking I should have shots," said Cory stupidly.

"They'll stay in your camera if you go down to the bottom of the sea, won't they?"

Still Cory stood.

This was it. The war you wanted, said Cory to herself. Maybe you thought you could go along and take pictures from the sidelines? But there are no sidelines. Over the rails, tiny lifeboats were dropping, packed with sixty people each. Some of these boats were already in the water, bouncing on the swells and falling into the troughs between. The soldiers flung a net over the ship's side and men the size of spiders began to climb down it.

She could feel her hair follicles separate and her scalp shrink. She thought of Tyke. Would he forgive her for dying in the war? For wanting to risk it? Because it was part of what she wanted, why she had come: to feel this terror. Move, she told herself, go! She reached her lifeboat station just as the last few nurses were climbing in.

A hand reached out to steady Cory. It belonged to a red-haired nurse. They gripped each other tightly as the wooden lifeboat began to drop, banging against the side of the ship. The water felt like concrete when they hit. They bounced twice and then slid into a trough between waves where everything else disappeared. When they rode up on a crest, clinging to the gunwales, they could see no other lifeboats, only hills and valleys of angry water. But voices carried, like yodellers' across the peaks.

"Save me! I'm over here!"

"We're going over! We're in the water."

The ship was dark. The sea was dark, and the sky only a little lighter. The moon went into a rim of clouds. A soldier had a grip on the oars and would not let go, but could make no headway.

"Let me row," Cory kept saying. "I live on water." The others were alternately vomiting in, and bailing with, their helmets. The nurse who'd taken Cory's hand now reached over and touched the shocked soldier's arm.

"We'll take a turn," she said calmly and pried his hands off the oars. In that moment the group found its leader.

She faced Cory on the seat, and they both threw their weight on the oars. Occasionally their heads banged as the lifeboat rocked. "I'm Donalda," the nurse said after the third such bang.

"Cory."

Donalda was freckled and had a gaze of such calm and such dignity that Cory was grateful every time the woman's eyes lit on her. Donalda divided them into relays for bailing, for tending the hurt and for rowing.

The moon came out of the clouds, higher up now. Cory strained over her shoulder to see the great wedge of their ship's stern climbing out of the waves as the bow sank. The other ships in their convoy had scattered for cover. She gave up the oars and bailed for what seemed hours. As the water began to calm she could see life rafts loaded with men, and capsized lifeboats with people clinging to the ropes. They picked up four survivors.

Finally a thin line of brightness appeared along the eastern horizon. They rowed on, trying to stay in one place. When they were desperately tired, Donalda started to sing. "You are my sunshine." People from the nearby boats joined in.

Cory pulled her Leica from the inside of her jacket and began to shoot in the pale dawn glow. She shot the seascape, and the lifeboat passengers, their faces shattered, alive when others had died. She caught Donalda's disgusted gaze at her soaked shoes where they sat up to her ankles in water. She caught the way the dead soldier's body fishtailed as they hoisted him over the gunwales.

By mid-morning the old channel ferry had begun to burn. They rowed constantly to keep a distance from it, mesmerized as the metal deck begin to melt, the glass portholes too, dripping down the sides. Cory had run out of film, so all she could do was watch. The ship's guns got so hot they ignited and began to fire themselves, one after another, in a grotesque salute. Then, with a roll and great groan and a heave, it went over on its side and sunk beneath the water.

From somewhere behind came the high buzz that meant an airplane. It came down from the north, flew over them, tipped its wings, and disappeared. Then the quiet was deeper.

"They'll be coming for us. It won't be long now," said Donalda. But the other survivors, slapping their arms to shake out the water from their clothes, and looking to the sun for warmth, did not seem so convinced.

By noon the sun was painful to them. It was too bright to see over the water; the splinters of light were blinding. No planes.

"Why didn't they come back for us?" asked one of the CWACS, a plaintive note breaking her voice.

"They will!" cried Donalda. But a moment later she leaned toward Cory. "Are we hallucinating?" she whispered. "Did we really see that plane?"

"Maybe he got shot down before he radioed."

One man retched on a dry stomach. There were some with broken ankles and legs, and one man with a horribly bruised, swollen head. Mysteriously, a flask of whisky was produced and handed around to the worst affected. They took turns rowing, directing the boat eastward, as that was where land ought to be. Sometimes Cory thought she saw it, but then she wasn't sure if what she saw was land, or perhaps cloud. At last, from over the waves, came the call.

"A ship!"

The destroyer seemed at first to be bearing down on them. But then it veered sharply to the left. It veered back right, again, zigzagging, picking up survivors, their crafts so small they couldn't be seen on the surface of the ocean. By the time it reached Cory's lifeboat, the sun was over in the west and sinking, a blazing yellow orb alone in its pristine sky.

When they rejoined the rest of the convoy off the Sicilian beach, there was a telegram from Max.

TORPEDOED FIRST TIME OUT STOP IMPRESSIVE
WORK STOP JOURNALISTS BORN NOT MADE STOP
SEND PICTURES AND STORY END

Not, "are you all right? We've been praying for you."
Not, "what do you need?" Just, "send pictures and story."
She had only one roll of film and she doubted it was any
good. Send story? No one told her she had to write. She
didn't know how to write. She had lost everything, including her paper and pens, her uniforms, the Speed Graphic
and most of her equipment. She was useless. They should
never have sent her. And she didn't even have a bunk to
cry in. She still felt the swells of the sea rocking the
lifeboat, watching death pick this one and not that one,
here a wave catching a nurse off balance and sweeping her
into the sea, there an oar breaking a man's skull.

There in front of her was Reg Morris, handing her
something white. "Here, do you need this?"

"What kind of man has a dry handkerchief in his
pocket after spending all night in the water?" she sniffed.

"I got it from the infirmary, for you," he said, hurt.

She took the handkerchief and showed him the
telegram, by way of apology.

"I don't have a story," she said. "I missed all the good
pictures. And look what he says."

Reg read the message. "Let me guess. You expected this
man's first concern to be you? You expected to be loved
because of what you've gone through?"

"Not really," she said, although he was right.

"News," he said. "It's news. Hey, remember, you're not the main event. And the reason we're alive is that our number isn't up. When the torpedo comes with your name on it, there'll be nothing you can do."

Chapter Twenty

A rare glimpse into the workings of a field hospital under canvas. Ditchburn enters into the work of the nurses, this one comforting a severely injured man. Suspended overhead operating table lights have been used as flash. The jumble of wires belies the efficient organization, as it portrays the spontaneous response to the casualties of war.

৪৯

IN THE MORNING THE WIND WAS HIGH, AND THE WATER STILL churned; the waves, running fore and aft at once, collided with each other. At first light a solemn, crackling voice over the loudspeaker had ordered crews to their craft, and craft to sail toward the Sicilian beach. The rejected ones — the public relations officers, the chaplains, the reinforcements and war correspondents — sat at breakfast drinking coffee.

Cory stared off toward shore.

"Don't worry, Cory," said Will. Will was a war artist, thin, seedy, in his forties, older than Cory by a decade, old enough to be a father to most of the soldiers. "There'll be plenty left for us to see. I daresay they'll put someone in charge of you. That is if they don't forget in the rush. But in a pinch you can run along with me."

Over Syracuse there was heavy bombing, flares and ack-ack, which looked, in the dark sky, like exhaltations. Whoever called the place of war a theatre was not far wrong, Cory thought. By mid-morning no one had come for them. The water as far as the eye could see was littered with warships. The shore remained peaceful. Soldiers had begun to return in their boats by the time the call came over the loudspeaker. "Warcos and PR, permission to land. Proceed to station Q." Cory ran after Will. In a few minutes their landing craft pressed out over the surly water.

It was a breeze, to set down on the beach. There was no enemy to be seen, the bombers having gone with the morning light. Cory and Will waded through foaming surf up to the sand. The soldiers were in short pants but for Cory there was no choice but the khaki trousers that had been specially tailored for women. Better than a skirt, at least. As they stood squeezing the water out of their socks, they saw Reg Morris approaching shore by means of a presentable one-armed crawl. With the other arm, he towed his typewriter.

"Would you believe it? There was an idiot in charge of

my landing craft. He read the compass wrong and we hit a sandbar." He spouted sea-water under his mustache.

The Sicilian sun beat down on the beach. The soldiers, knees reddening in their tropical kit, were salt-crusted, dry and breathing hard. The three warcos walked up the road heading inland. There were walled groves of olive trees, lemon and orange trees bearing tiny unripe fruit. By the sides of the road they passed the occasional dead body, German. Testing herself, Cory got close and pressed the shutter.

"Don't even bother," said Reg. "It'll never pass the censor."

"Who is this censor?" said Cory.

"Oh he's quite a guy," said Reg. "Officer. He was wounded out at Dieppe. Name of Hrudy. Picturesque — only has one eye."

A wounded man got up on his elbow and asked when the ambulance was coming for him.

"Any minute now, I'd think," said Will cheerfully. "We saw them unloading a way back." He produced a flask of wine from his pocket and gave him a drink.

After a mile or two, they met some other Canadians who had commandeered a donkey and cart and were pulling a load of rations. Cory sat beside the driver, a young farmer from Edmunston, New Brunswick. The road widened and grew flatter as they entered a plain. Old olive trees, their crisp khaki leaves like desert survivors, lined the track. Suddenly the space around them went dead;

there was the instinct to hide, but there was no shelter.

Their cart rattled forward. No one spoke. They waited for the drone of aircraft, for the spit of shellfire, but nothing came. Cory kept her hand on the Leica. It protected her. They rolled on helpless, silently through the open space, and were still alive at the end.

"What did I tell you? Number's not up yet," said Reg.

Rocking with the uncushioned bounces of the cart, Cory felt as if it were all too casual.

"Do they always just leave you like this?" she said to Will.

"Unless you qualify for transport." He looked at her orders. "Doesn't say anything about transport here. You've got to hitchhike."

"But I'll miss everything!"

"Everyone feels like that, until they've got a piece of shrapnel in their chest."

A ruddy Sicilian farmer, his teeth black and his face accordion-pleated, invited them to his house to eat bread, goat's cheese, tomatoes. Cory declined the wine but could get no water. Because she could see them eye her, trying to decide what it was about her, she raised her helmet. Yes, it is a woman.

The war felt spotty and skin deep. She said so, to Will.

"You've hit upon the tragedy of it. It feels normal, but it is utterly abnormal. You aren't meant to be able to get used to this. But you do."

The next turn in the road brought into sight the village of Azzra, built of grey stone, impossibly beautiful. Already the scrawny children had spotted them, and ran forward.

"Caramelle! Caramelle!"

Now it came, what they had felt, eerily, to be approaching all afternoon. That sawing, buzzing noise. First the airplane was a black swallow, then it was a hawk, and then it was so close they could see the black cross underneath its wings. The bomb dropped between their cart and the village. A farmhouse exploded slowly, like a fan unfolding, and all other movement ended, while the frail silhouettes of children ascended, shimmering in the haze.

Cory walked shakily into the village, every nerve seemingly disconnected and buzzing. She heard a tap-tap-tap. Irregular in rhythm, it went faster, then disappeared leaving silence, and then began again, more slowly. She took a turn in the road and saw the open square, the baroque front of a church. The tapping came again. Cory trod carefully, wary, spooked. There was the well, and on the far side of it, a deep-eyed child with a stick and a stone, and a loose dress around her knees. She ran around the well in the central square, banging her rock from place to place with the stick, running a few steps to reach it again.

"Hello," said Cory. "Ciao." She pulled out her camera.

A door opened somewhere and a stream of Italian was loosed. The child was motionless, open-mouthed, watching Cory. She snapped three shots in quick succession, as the girl ran to her mother. Shrieking in outrage, the woman folded her inside her skirts, inside the door. Cory removed her helmet.

"Canadian," she said, showing the red patch on her arm.

The woman shut the door in her face.

Cory sat on the edge of the well. She looked down. There was a black glimmer at the bottom, but no bucket, and no chain. She rested against the well. There were children here too. She hadn't planned on that. *Dear Tyke*, she thought. Then, how can I write him? What can I say? She wanted to cry, but she couldn't.

As they left Azzra, the stench of dead bodies was heavy in the air. They passed a line of mule-drawn carts, where dead Germans were stacked like flour sacks.

That night Cory wrapped her canisters of film and wrote her captions. An army public relations officer would give them to a dispatch rider who would take them to the airport at Pachino. "Child of Azzra," "Women of Lentini crown British soldier with wreath of flowers."

"Put some in for One-eyed Hrudy," said Reg.

"Bodies of Germans stacked like cordwood."

Cory woke with her head under the jeep. She remembered, as in the jumble of dreams, an air raid in the night, and bits and pieces falling around her, until she had crawled here, neither awake nor asleep, for protection.

She leaned up on an elbow. Reg's rough cap of dark blond hair protruded from a bedroll between her and the tents of the camp. He had appointed himself her bodyguard. She slid out of her bedroll, stepped over his body and ran to the little track that led up through scrub and thorn to a spring-fed pond.

It was just after dawn; after the mayhem of the night she hoped the others slept. She pulled off her dirty uniform and slid down the rock until she was submerged to her neck. The water was as cold as if it had flowed here through ice. As the cold sucked the breath from her chest, she heard a footstep on the rock-strewn path. Just one footstep, and no other sound.

"Reg?" she said. "Reg, you needn't bother, go back to sleep."

There was no answer. Cory turned, treading water, to look at the bushes all around: Had the whole camp followed her, and were they about to jump out and jeer? She almost convinced herself the sound had been a lizard. Then she heard two more footsteps. A German soldier stood in the gap where she'd entered the grotto. He had the paratrooper's grease-blackened face: He must have bailed out of his plane in the night. She caught his eyes and stayed caught, barely moving; the connected gaze was enough to keep her afloat.

"Reg," she said, more loudly than she needed to. "You always follow me and I'm not sure you need to."

She jerked her head backward, away, to let the German know he should go. His hands had reached forward, as if to grasp something, an invisible weapon, but now he froze, listening to the sound of her words.

"The whole camp will be coming to wash soon, Reg," she continued, "and I'll have to get out. Too bad they don't supply towels."

The German soldier stepped to the edge of the water.

His eyes were red-rimmed, in the sooty face, the whites bulging. For one moment she thought he was going to jump in on her. But she felt that as long as she held his eyes, no harm could be done. She went on treading water, without moving her head. Perhaps he thought she was a Sicilian. But her uniform lay on the rocks. She stared into his black-streaked face, projecting, she hoped, not-fear. And not-running.

The soldier held his ground, but not as firmly as she. He seemed to be completely puzzled: What was she? Whereas Cory had him categorized. That was her advantage. Their eyes continued to hold until slowly his face began to melt, and his white teeth, in what might have been, what must have been a smile, became visible. Cory raised her knees in front of her chest and sculled. With his eyes still locked on hers, the German began to bend his knees. He sank lower until, squatting, he stared straight across the water at her. Suddenly he plunged his face into the water. The mirroring surface shattered. She stifled a scream and her body shrank as if from his touch. He began to rub his face with his hands. He was washing.

Cory heard steps. Or did she? "Reg," she called trying to hold her voice firm, "Reg, please don't bother. I'm bathing."

The German lifted his face. It was white now, like the daylight. He had a better chance of getting away. His eyes clapped to hers. Still watching her, he circled the grotto, leaping from rock to rock. With one last jump and a brilliant white smile, he disappeared into the thorns.

Cory was dry and dressed when she heard Reg's discreet cough.

"Coming in for a bathe?"

"Who were you talking to?" Reg's morning voice was sulky.

"You heard?" She kept her eyes on the rock where the German had stood. He might have killed her. But perhaps he had not been real.

"I was talking to you," she said. "Because I knew if you weren't there already you would be soon."

CORY

YOUR PHOTOGRAPHS ATTRACTED ATTENTION STOP
NO ONE SAYS I'M A FOOL FOR SENDING A WOMAN
STOP NEED MORE OVERVIEW STOP BE MORE PER-
SONAL STOP SHOTS YOU WITH MEN STOP KEEP IT
UP END

MAX

In the back of a fifteen-hundredweight jeep they jolted over an overgrown goat track. Demolition had blocked the highway: Great slabs of cliff face were blasted out and lay like fallen walls over the trail. Mount Etna rose in the distance, sharp in the sunlight, unperturbed while from the bushes came smoke and a foul sweetness. A tank was burning.

"Someone's in there. Smell that? It's human flesh cooking." Will's voice was soft. The odour was cloying, revolting.

Cory leaned over the back of the jeep to vomit as Will peered more closely. "It's one of ours."

"Doesn't it smell the same if it's a German?"

"You haven't learned to hate," he complained.

The doors and shutters of the house stood open. It had a raped, shot-through look.

"Gerry stayed here, but he went off in a rush," said Will. He put his hand on the door-frame and raised his foot to step across the lintel. In the split second before he crossed the threshold Reg leapt up, ran and tackled him and threw him out of the doorway. Will lay crumpled on the dry earth.

"I guess you play gridiron," he grumbled, as he got up on his skinny legs.

"Tight end. You gotta watch." Reg went in on tiptoe. "Let me check it out first."

"Fiendish, the way Gerry wires it up when he leaves." Reg's voice floated eerily out through the doors and windows in the high mountain air. "We've had some real surprises. Once it was a photograph of Hitler. Naturally the first guy in tore it off the wall. He bought it, and his two buddies behind him. Another time it was the water pump."

Will and Cory sat on a rock by the front step while Reg felt his way in to de-wire the farmhouse. The yellow sun pricked their dry eyes to tears. For a minute it seemed they were on a picnic. The whole valley spread open in a semi-circle in front of them. A low black cloud straggled over the high rocky outcrops across the gap. When there were shell bursts, they saw the orange light; a few seconds later came the first clap of the explosion, followed by its echo against the rock face. On the upward slope was a zigzag of roads and pathways. Some were blocked, and some were thick with tanks and trucks. The air was clear, swept by a sea wind that came through this valley: It sharpened the focus on this map of war so that it seemed as if Cory could reach out and move the figures by hand, like toys.

Reg filled the door-frame.

"Don't see anything here. Looks like he was an officer. Books on art, strange stuff in there. A few bottles of wine, you'll be glad to know."

That night, Will got drunk.

"It rots the soul, being exempt. It does. Rots the soul. You wait, you'll see. If you sit and watch them all get killed, it rots you right through. That's all I have to say."

But next morning, waiting for transport, Will sat in splendour overlooking his amphitheatre and sketching, while Cory prowled around the ledges, trying various long shots of the hillside opposite. No one came to take them to the front. That night they drank the rest of the German officer's wine. Will wove out the farmhouse door, addressing the valley.

"God-damned war won't stay pat long enough for me to paint it," he repeated. "You and your bloody click click, you get everything."

When they caught up to the brigade, Will threw a tantrum with the commander.

"I am charged to see this war. We are here, and it is not.

You've got to get me transport so I can get near the bloody front."

"We got you near the front two days ago," his aide mentioned.

"But sir, it's in the nature of the beast to keep moving..."

Even with the fifteen-hundredweight truck at their disposal Will was sunk in apathy, his skinny haunches propped on a sack of issue rice to cushion the bumps. Between Will and Reg was a web of unarticulated hostilities, which had something to do with a struggle for Cory's mind, or soul: certainly not, it appeared, her body. By July 25, they came, by circuitous mountain road, to Enna.

Dear Albert —

As you point out, I've never been anywhere. Now I'm seeing medieval villages and cathedrals, as a tourist. My luck to get a view of the classics while we're busy blowing them up!

Today I had a ride at least, in a 15cwt jeep driven by a sombre Nova Scotian who can imitate a bagpipe by putting his thumb across his lips and squeezing his ribs. When you smell rotten eggs you know it's sulphur mines. We're at Enna. On its height, with steep rock dropping off on every side, it's a natural fortress. Will says it's not Enna, but Henna. Persephone was raped and carried off by Ceres here, says Will.

When we entered the town, everyone was shouting and women in the street threw flowers at us. A

British soldier told us the fascists had put down
Mussolini and that he was in jail.

   We ran with the whole town into the Piazza Vit-
torio Emanuele. The shuttered windows above
opened and dark-haired girls leaned down, giggling
and pointing at the soldiers.

   And Will said, "If it's true that Mussolini is gone,
they will sleep tonight with Will Renzetti." Reg got
disgusted and can't wait to get rid of him.

   When the British soldier saw the Canadian
flashes on our sleeves he said, "But you're in the
wrong spot! The Canadians have been in a huge
dustup at Agira. Five hundred dead, at least." So
we're moving on —

She wanted to tell him about Reg but she couldn't. Somehow she knew Albert would seize on him and grow vitri-
olic with jealousy. Will she would sacrifice to Albert's
insults, but Reg seemed somehow too vulnerable. What
could she do about Albert? Only a battalion of nuns would
satisfy him, and likely not even that. To Albert there was
no innocence.

"Can't do it," said the driver. "Orders. This far only."

   Will grinned as he hopped out. "Leave me here tonight
then. You'll take me back? Tomorrow?"

   The driver waved over his shoulder as he disappeared
into his own dust cloud.

   "Goddamn," Reg said. "I've got to get to Agira."

"I'll come with you." Cory didn't fancy hanging around with Will in his pursuit of Sicilian maidens.

"I'll find us transport," said Reg quickly, avoiding Will's eyes.

They pushed through the crowds. The next, smaller piazza opened up to a staggering view across the open valley and to the perfect cone of Etna beyond. In front of the statue of Persephone the people danced and sang; the soldiers, bleary-eyed and joyous, joined in. Cory climbed the steps of the church to get her angle. Will climbed up beside her.

"Don't go with him," he said. "And don't fall in love."

"I won't," she said, meaning fall in love.

"Listen to me," said Will. "I'll tell you what he is. He's just one of those beautiful young men you meet in wars. You get to know them and the next time you see them, they're dead. Steer clear."

"I'm going," said Cory. "It's my job. I've got to find the Canadians." She backed away from him.

In the melee Will raised his revolver and shot two doves off the walls. He ran down to get them. "Dinner!" she heard him call triumphantly. From the edge of the square he raised a dead bird by its feet in salute.

Reg tried to negotiate the purchase of a car, and ended up with a bicycle and a bladder of cheese. Cory hopped on the seat behind him, and he pedalled standing up. They wobbled along the goat track cut into the side of the mountain. The long summer twilight was brooding and still. On the uphill stretches they walked, with the smell of death coming in on the winds.

At dark they reached Calascibetta, across the valley, its red bricks soft under a crescent moon. The last trattoria was closing its doors as they entered the town. Its owner, a bearded giant in a blood — or was it tomato? — spattered apron, let them sleep inside his gated courtyard.

Next morning they commandeered a car and its owner, a leather-faced man with teeth worn to stubs and a pin-striped jacket over his overalls. The bicycle they strapped to the roof, not knowing when they might need it.

The road looped and wound steadily to the east, toward Agira, although never fast enough. They passed through the valley of the River Dittaino, with its tiny dry tributaries, and the railway tracks of the San Stefano line, neatly plucked from a gravel bed like a fish skeleton lifted from its flesh and thrown aside. Everywhere were the signs of recent battle, exploded stone barns, burnt-out tanks, fly-covered bodies, emptied villages. Then, in the late afternoon, the land began to climb again.

"Do you think we'll ever catch them?" asked Cory.

There was no answer, but the driver, who might in some other life have made history at the wheel of a rally car, pelted onward, an expression of manic determination never leaving his face. They passed farmers, women and children leading mules and goats through ravaged fields, returning to their homes. At Leonforte, people ran alongside their car throwing flowers they'd reaped from their gardens. Mussolini had fallen! "But if Mussolini has fallen, why haven't the Germans stopped fighting?" asked Cory.

"They don't work that way," said Reg.

That night they slept in an abandoned hospital dispensary, together with the troops they'd passed on the road. Reg doggedly sought and found a partitioned corner for Cory, and then stationed himself outside.

"Thank you, Reg. Good night," she said, rather shortly. She could feel his fragility. There was a high, nervous strain in him. More than her needing his protection, it seemed that he needed to protect her, he needed the task to steady him. She propped herself up, and, taking a clipboard on her knees stared out the window into the darkness.

> *Albert —*
>
> *I shoot everything I can get, but I can't complete the process. My film goes out in canisters, I don't see the contacts, don't do the enlarging. So I don't know what I've shot, maybe just frames and frames of dust clouds over the town square —*

"Who are you writing to?" asked Reg through the wall.

"Do you want the truth, or what I tell everyone?"

"The truth, of course."

Silence. She stared at the place where his voice came from. She pictured his long, handsome face. Too perfect, it seemed to her. That noble visage, tufted eyebrows, splendid cheekbones, cleft chin. And when she shot disapproval in his direction, it began to crumble, as if made of soft stone, eroding little by little.

"Who's the lucky guy?" he said, presently.

"He's an old man and he's married to my friend," she said, just to completely shatter his illusions of her.

"That's not a pretty picture," he said, gamely. And then, "Good night, Cory."

One of those beautiful young men, Will had said, who you meet and the next time you see them, they're dead.

They knew they'd nearly caught up to the troops when they saw the hospital tent with the Canadian ensign flying. Saying goodbye to their driver, they walked into the encampment. Cory caught sight of a red-haired nurse: Donalda. They held each other at arms' length.

"What took you so long?" said Donalda.

"Trying to get transport!" said Cory. "And then they probably gave you directions. We had to find it ourselves."

They dined on bully beef cooked with local tomatoes. Cory was billeted in the nurses' tent. The shelling began as darkness fell. It was frighteningly near. The first thuds took out the hospital electricity; the nurses moved from litter to litter by flashlight checking on "their boys." All the medics wore helmets, and their boots were covered in mud. In the corners were piles of empty plasma cans.

Cory took as much of it as she could and then stepped out beyond the tent flaps to see the sky, torn up as it was with streaks of light and flame. An ambulance drew up with three cases; one had blown out half of his abdomen and chest, exposing a lung. The last was bleeding from the head and had a crushed foot. He was Archie MacDougal from the Edmontons.

"Go for it!" the soldier cried, trying to roll off the bed. "He's on the run, he's on the run. Now, throw. Duck!" The soldier managed to strip off his restraints, and sat up, where he began a series of stiff, urgent moves with his arms — opening the gun's breach, ramming the charge down, jerking the trigger.

"Somebody turn that guy off, will you?" came a voice out of the corner, a new doctor on shift.

They began to pump quarts of blood and plasma. Cory put down her camera to help.

"You want to try to make him breathe more deeply," said Donalda. She showed her how the balloon under the mask that covered his nose should expand and contract with each breath. But Cory felt helpless and as she watched, the balloon grew more and more slack until it hardly moved at all.

Donalda went from cot to cot, portioning out the morphine. "We wait all day for this hour to give it to them. Don't know if it's for their benefit or for ours. I think it's harder for us to bear their screams in the darkness."

They were running short of blood. An ambulance driver came back in with two more unconscious, bleeding men. After they were lifted onto litters, and the hookup over their bed began to drip blood, the driver lined up to donate his.

"Sometimes it gets so bad we get the soldiers walking in here from their hideouts in the rocks, to give blood," she said. "Then they go back and shoot some more."

"I'd like some Saskatoon berry pie," said Archie Mac-Dougal clearly, through lips the colour of sand.

Donalda came to his side to adjust his oxygen intake. She bent over to speak into his ear.

"We'll make you some, love, as soon as the kids come back from picking."

He was silent then, but his lips moved.

The cluster of medics hung over a flashlit operating table. Cory focussed on the operation, which was to remove shrapnel from a man's chest and stomach. When she dropped the camera she had to turn away; the sight of his abdominal cavity rimmed with red flesh was one she could face through a lens, but not unprotected.

When she looked at Archie his balloon was flat. "Archie's gone."

Donalda pulled off his mask and the corps men lifted his rifle away from where it had lain by his side.

"It wouldn't have been much of a life, anyway," said a doctor. "No leg, no arm."

"Well, he wanted it."

At Brigade Headquarters there was mail. Cory opened the letter first. It was from Pointe au Baril. The solid heft of Marge's handwriting called back to Cory the older woman's sure-footed, bear-like clamber over rock.

> *Dear Cory —*
> *This is just to tell you your boy is fine. He had a*

couple of teeth knocked out playing ball the other night, but I reckon they was baby teeth and due for it. He looked for hours but he couldn't find 'em on the rocks, so no nickels from the tooth fairy.

He's got the wandering spirit, we have to go out and find him half the nights walking in his sleep all around down by the dock. He doesn't say much but I know he misses you lots. Us too —

We don't hear much news but Mr. Thompson there by Outlook tells me they use your pictures in the newspapers in Toronto. Don't go getting too famous on us. Jimmie's unit goes into action by fall.
love,
Marge

Then the telegram. "Sicily's done," Max wrote, "get back to London by first available transport."

"All right! Well done, Cory," said Reg. "You've survived your first tour of duty. Your personal guardian angel does care! Go back to London." There was a trace of self-pity in his voice. "You shall be praised. And you'll be drinking champagne before you know it."

Cory left. Left Reg and Donalda to their jobs and Will to "rot" and all the fighting men to their deaths slow or sudden, or to an increasingly disbelieving survival. Though she had no choice, she felt guilty. As guilty as she did about leaving Tyke. She left people: That was what she did; it had become her name.

Chapter Twenty-One

*The censor with his black eye-patch and curious gravity
yearns to be a metaphor. Yet we know he is an ordinary
man charged with keeping extraordinary secrets. He
wears the mask and the rank of his office while com-
menting ironically on it. His one eye twinkles and his hair
curls exuberantly. He asks us to "turn a blind eye."*

⁂

IN LONDON CORY TOOK TEA WITH AUNT EUNICE, A EUNICE
enlivened by war and Cory's part in it.

"I wish your father had lived to see this," she said, waving away the birds that came to nibble on the dry toast
crumbs. "They miss Leary's cakes." Thinner, even more
erect, Eunice's white wave of hair stood above her like a
cap she could not doff. "If I can't get what I want to eat, I

shan't eat at all," she said. "If I can't have something good, better to have nothing. Wouldn't you agree? Or are you one of those whom base hunger takes by storm?"

Cory laughed, accustomed to her aunt. "You'd starve to death at the front," she said. "By the way, most people are glad their loved ones didn't live to see this war." She was not used to praise.

"Nonsense," said Eunice. "There are always wars. We need them. You've seen the inside of it now, haven't you? I envy you that. There can't be many women in the world who've gone where you have gone. I always knew you could make something of yourself."

"Thank Max," said Cory.

"No, not at all. He's an opportunist, an opportunist and a scoundrel and he took you on as a prank, Cory. You must never waste yourself in gratitude."

"Does that go for you too, Aunt Eunice?"

"But of course," she said coolly. "And I'll remind you I've found myself a job. Isn't it marvellous? At sixty!" She was working in Sarah Churchill's canteen for officers. "Opportunist? I wouldn't have it any other way, my dear."

Cory looked over the back fence: The house to the rear was gone, as was half of the vicarage outside of which they'd burned the Christmas trees at Epiphany that first year she was in London.

"I wish I were like you," said Cory slowly. She was not even certain what she meant, except that the older woman had such clarity of mind, and seemed immune to the muck and mire of feeling that dogged the rest of humankind.

"And so you shall be! You've managed to stay unencumbered of the normal weights and drags on women's lives — husbands, children and the like. You can't be encumbered by sentiment, can you now?"

"I'm not unencumbered. I have a child," said Cory.

There was a small, prim silence. "Yes, of course. I tend to forget the child, my dear. But you know I'm anxious to help. You don't want him to hold you back. I assume you've left him in proper hands."

Cory did something she'd never done. She drew the snapshots she carried out of her purse. "There he is, Aunt Eunice."

The garden was still, silent except for the buzzing of a bee as Eunice looked slowly and carefully over each shot. "A Ditchburn through and through," Cory half expected to hear; the boy was still tow-headed but his steady eyes were dead giveaways. But Eunice handed them back without a word. Still, something had happened. She had not refused to look. She had not.

In London she drank champagne, as Reg had predicted. The Beaverbrook crowd hailed her now as one of them. Cory was even, in her small way, famous. The Soho pubs were bursting with soldiers, and she was known to them: the girl photographer. But best were the joyous long days with Albert. He viewed her with amazement, as if she'd been reborn; he was tender, witty, even solicitous. They lived dangerously. Cory was on furlough, soon to be back at the front (she hoped); it was her duty to take chances.

They walked arm in arm through the parks in broad daylight, telling one another the stories of their early lives, stories that always ended when Albert groaned and said he wished he'd been there to see her then, or Cory clung to him and wondered how she'd be different, if she'd met him ten years before. Sometimes they slept overnight in the studio, risking a visit from a worried Liss. But Liss kept her own counsel, the glimmer of a smile always on her lips as she knit her afghans and soft grey socks. In the evenings at England's Lane, Albert walked in a circle around her chair as if she were some domestic idol whose peace he dared not trouble.

According to the papers, the war was nearly over. The Germans had stopped bombing London, and now Britain would be sending coal and chocolate to Sicily.

One day Cory got a telephone call at the *Express*. It was Lydia del Zotto in New York.

"Any wildlife there worth investigating?" she began. "So I see you got yourself into the action?"

"How did you find me?" cried Cory. She assumed she was untraceable on her private vector.

"I go to England now and then, business, you know. Even with this wretched war on. I picked up an *Express*. And right away I saw your shots. They're wonderful, Cory."

There was a wash of static. "But I've got news. It's about your photographs. We've sold three of the four. You're being collected, Cory. And guess what? The Curator of the Museum of Modern Art is very impressed with your work.

We told him you were off with the forces now. 'Even better,' he says. 'Let me see some.'"

The line went bad again.

"Curator?" she shouted. "Well I've got a curator here too, he's called the Military Censor, and he won't let me have any of the shots I've taken. I guess the *Express* owns them, and after that the Army. Just about everyone but me. I don't even get to see them."

"Never mind," she said. "Send what you can, darling, when you've got it. One day this will all be over, right? We'll go canoeing and see a few minks. Just remember, you've got an audience here. Oh, and I've got money for you."

"Money? Send it to Marge, at the Manitou."

It was inhuman to have so neat a desk. Everyone else in this war was swamped with entreaties, purchase orders, carbon copies of forms, and packaging of supplies. Orestes Hrudy was the great drying agent of the flood: The deluge of printed matter flowed in and evaporated. In his office there were metal trays, empty, wooden surfaces, polished and dust-free, a silent telephone. What did he do with all the material that crossed his desk — destroy it? File it? Incinerate it with a cold beam of sunlight refracted in the lens of his single eyeglass?

"Hello, Mr. Hrudy? I'm Corinne Ditchburn."

Cory had expected a bigger man: He was just over five foot two, with a black eye-patch and squash-coloured hair that rose from his temples and curled, on top, in an unmilitary way. When she appeared in his doorway, he unfolded his short rounded limbs in one quick movement and was out of his chair like a balletic prince whose first chord had been played. His one blue eye lit with mirth. His voice was precise, paced.

"I'm delighted you've come in," he said. "We've all seen so much of your work, of course. Come and meet the gang."

He led her to the doorway of another office room where two women sat at desks under long box-like lamps suspended from the ceiling on chains. Small easels stood on their desktops, and a set of sharp instruments like a surgeon's tools lay close at their hands. They were poring over contact prints in intense concentration, which ended abruptly when Orestes sang out.

"Ladies! We have a visitor. Who do you think this is? Guess!"

The woman nearest looked up. Cory saw the outline of dark hair and shirt collar, but the features that should have graced the face were wiped out by the light, which not only fell from above but rose from the box on her desk.

"May I present Miss Esther Upshall from Newfoundland. Come, Esther, who do you think this is?"

As Esther stood, Cory could see that she had a permanent wave and wore dangling earrings and a shirtwaist with puffed sleeves.

"And this is our retoucher, Alma. Alma was an artist, too, you know, in Toronto, before she signed up."

The women both downed their sharp tools and inspected Cory. Cory found she could barely restrain herself from telling them to get their hands off her work. As if they felt her wishing it, both women stood up, pushing the contact sheets out of the light. They all laughed a little self-consciously.

"How about we repair to the canteen for a cup of tea?"

Orestes beamed across the table at Cory. His eye-patch drew Cory's eyes: It was like a huge dilated pupil. It seemed to see, to perceive, independently and deeply.

"I was at Dieppe," he said, touching it. "There aren't too many of us left to tell the tale," he said. "I signed up and came over in August of '39. I did that long sit-out in the sheep pasture with the rest of the troops. And didn't it just turn out that the wait was as extreme in its length as my fighting career was extreme in its brevity? Faulty gun. Exploded in my face. I fell. I was lucky; most of 'em were mowed down by the time they got another few yards up the beach."

During this tale Esther looked appropriately sympathetic, and Alma, abstracted: They'd heard this before. It wasn't hard to see which one he was dating.

"I lay there for a couple of hours. It seemed unwise to move when I couldn't see. I only sat up when I heard the Chaplain's voice. He walked me back to ship with my eye dangling down my cheek." He delivered this melancholy tale so promptly and with such apparent cheer that Cory was unable to respond. She leaned into her tea.

He carried on. Orestes was part Greek, part Ukrainian, from Edmonton: He'd been in a folk dance troupe. It gave him his *ballon*, as he called it: a balletic term for bounce. In London he'd hoped to go to Covent Garden regularly but the war had stopped all that.

"I'm here," said Cory finally. "To have a look at my negatives."

"Oh, how too bad. That's not going to be possible," said Orestes. He popped a smile into the silence. "Perhaps you should get back to work, ladies?"

"All of us admire your work tremendously," said Alma, by way of a formal leave-taking. She extended her hand.

"I only wish I could admire it myself."

"Indeed," said Orestes, still beaming. "Of course you do."

"There were a couple of pictures of the injured at that field hospital in Italy." She was thinking of Archie Mac-Dougal. "There was a shot of a pile of amputated legs."

"Indeed there was," said Orestes. "And it was most interesting. Perhaps you would like to see it after the war?"

Cory flushed. A flood of new workers entered the tea shop, banging their trays on the metal rails leading along to the till.

"Many of you want to see all the photographs. Newspapers write us regularly asking for what they call 'realistic war photographs.' They claim such photographs will be helpful to them in persuading the public that there should be no more war."

He laughed merrily and, using his short arms as levers, bounced up and out of his seat. "Shall we walk back?"

"And wouldn't they be?" pressed Cory. Then, realizing

she'd caught his interrogative style, she reversed her words. "They would be."

He made rapid progress down the hall, his shoes clicking on the brown linoleum.

"These men are dead," he added, at his doorway. "They have families. Have you thought of that?"

Cory groaned audibly. "I know that. But we print pictures of dead Germans and dead Japanese."

"But isn't that very very different?"

"So people keep telling me."

"Miss Ditchburn," said Orestes, finally coming to rest and gazing directly with his one eye into her two. "Only my great admiration for you keeps me here chatting. It isn't exactly our style in the military to explain our rationale, have you noticed that? But since you came by to visit, I don't mind telling you. You know about 'Maggot Beach'? The *Life* magazine photograph? The three dead soldiers at Buna face down in the sand? Oh well, you remember, there were maggots in their backs. It was one of those powerful, evocative images you do so well. A wonderful photograph, I don't deny it. But the week it was published, American enlistment dropped off by five thousand. So what, Miss Ditchburn, would you define as the public good?"

She bristled. "I think my pictures are for the public good."

He acknowledged her with a dip of his chin. "Perhaps. One day. But we have to win this war and at the moment that means keeping up a supply of soldiers."

"I don't define anything," she said. "I just want to see my photographs."

"My dear. You can't. They're top secret."

She laughed. He had to be joking. "How can they be secret from me? I took them."

"Well, yes, but secrets are secrets from everyone in a war. Even from the people who make them up, sometimes. That's how we keep going." Orestes giggled. "You've hit upon one of the great conundrums. Yes. If circumstances dictate, then I am afraid so, they are secrets from you."

Cory gritted her teeth and paced a little away from him. He was so jolly, so impossible to fight. "What can I possibly learn that I don't already know?" she countered. "Because of course, I *have* seen them."

"And as a matter of fact you haven't seen them. They were not developed when they left you."

"Well I *took* them."

"Yes, you took them. But you might not have known *what* you took, isn't that correct? And if you did know, why would you be coming back right now, asking to see them?"

Hateful little man, she thought furiously, drawing herself up to full height and looking down on him. She knew that Orestes Hrudy was having fun, that he was not about to change his mind. "I am a professional," she said, knowing she sounded pompous but feeling, under the circumstances, that it was called for. "In whatever I did I was carrying out the Allied cause. I composed those photographs deliberately, and I would like to see the results."

He stepped back a pace and peered at her, as if fascinated to see what her next move would be. "Yes, of course, Miss Ditchburn," he soothed. "But who knows what you actually caught in your frame? We can't afford to publish what might prove, unbeknownst to you, to be crucial information to, as you put it, the Allied cause."

"But they're two months old. Those battles are fought and won. I just want to know if there were any better ones than the one the *Express* used. Do you understand? I need to see them to learn."

He appeared touched by this last appeal. "My dear Miss Ditchburn, could I advise you on this small matter? Perhaps your employer wishes to sell papers. Perhaps you wish to improve your craft. But perhaps you are in fact a spy. You laugh, but the possibility exists. Whatever your reasons are, they cannot be as good as ours. We wish to win a war. Contrary to public opinion, that mission is not yet accomplished. Until it is, you'll have to listen to what I say. Have I mentioned that I adore strong-minded women?" He smiled at her blandly in a way almost, but not quite, flirtatious. "Is there anything else I can do for you?"

"Anything else? You've done precisely nothing."

He extended his hand, as courteous as ever. "Truly, I'd love to help you. But I haven't that luxury now. Later, I will think about that. And about your art. For now, I'm afraid we look at a photograph as information. Classified information." He raised his single eyebrow. "I would be delighted to carry on this conversation at another time, in another place, Miss Ditchburn. But for now the answer is no."

Cory spun around and walked away, her heels resounding like a series of little gunshots going off down the long brown hallway. Fool: She'd gone and fought with the censor. Now even less of her work would get through. When she heard Orestes Hrudy call her back, his voice as sweet as ever, she kept walking. He caught up with her.

"Oh I wonder, Miss Ditchburn, if I might ask you a very great favour. I wonder if we could meet again, and if you could take my photograph."

She paused. "I'm astonished."

"I've changed a great deal with my eye, you know. And I need to know what I look like. Don't you think that it's essential, that we become aware of the image we present to the world? And my mother, at home. A portrait. Could I tempt you? We all have our vanities."

She did not crack a smile.

"The censor is human." The squash-coloured curls bobbed as he ducked his head.

Albert lay on his back, his white beard trembling with the out-rush of his breath. The dense whorls of his chest hair made a pillow for Cory's cheek. She curled her head under his chin, laying her ear on his heartbeat.

"And everyone has seen your photographs," he said.

"Some people have noticed them," she said.

He waved this modesty aside. "And everyone has told you they're good?"

"Yes," she said. Her unprotected body drew his sullen heat. She knew what was coming.

"Of course they are dreadful. Do you know how dreadful they are, and why?"

"Perhaps you would like to remind me."

He let out an explosive breath. "I? What am I? Not your teacher. I would be ashamed to be your teacher. They are — how shall I begin —" He became too agitated to remain flat on his back; he raised himself on one elbow. She drew away, curling her knees into her stomach.

"It's not only that you're green. You have no scope. No vision. You've looked on death and destruction and brought false witness. It is as I always feared. You are trivial, I think I can say. A clever liar."

He seized a copy of the *Express*; above the fold was her shot of a soldier walking forward out of a haze of smoke.

"What have you made him? A hero? A new god? You and everyone else!"

"There *are* moments of hope, even at the front." It was difficult to defend herself because she was naked. "You weren't there."

"No, no, stupid girl, I don't need to be. I have been there. If you must show us this individual, this 'person,' this little pathetic hero, then also show us what he has wrought. Make your scale twice as large. Shoot the destruction. It has all been done before, of course, but that seems your only hope —"

She pulled another paper from his pile. Evidently he saved them, bad as they might be. The newsprint was yellowed already. She remembered only running for cover when the whine came, then the blasting, bowel-burning fear, cowering under the camp bed with kit bag over her ears. Now this too had begun to fade. Each of her photographs she'd seen in the newspaper was organized into two dimensions, rectangled, captioned. It was as if some better regulated person had followed her, and harnessed from fugitive moments that which had been too present for her to see.

"What about this?" It was the widow in the square at Lentini, the one who'd come forward crying: Her husband had been blown up only minutes before. "Is she an individual? She stands for all the victims —"

"Victims! You speak in clichés, no wonder you photograph clichés! What you don't show is that the world has been turned upside down — and that is what happens in war and every single face you see is in a state of shock *including your own* — which you must keep in mind. Where is the rage and the hatred? Where are the injured, where is the breakdown, the chaos? Why all this neatness, these patterns, this sentiment, this womanly thing —"

She climbed out of bed, wrapped herself in a blanket and stood by the coal fire chaffing her hands. She let him go on for a while, but then she could stand it no longer.

"Albert," she said coolly. "Don't you have to go home to your wife?"

It rocked him for a moment, but not for long. His eyes grew long and narrow.

"You've changed."

She cocked her head.

"You aren't the same wild girl I knew."

"I've got my shell. Remember?"

"Shell. Shells are for war correspondents, not for lovers," he complained as he searched for his pants.

Cory was invited to Cherkley for the weekend. Somehow, Albert wangled his own invitation. They needed to have a life outside Liss's circle, to escape her ken; the thrill was the danger of it, of appearing together, secret lovers amongst their friends.

They took the same train, and rode in from the station with Max's driver, gone loquacious in his distress.

"Cherkley's not a happy ship, not a happy ship," he said. "You're friends of his Lordship, you've been here and you must know. Not a happy ship."

Albert had bought a bottle and consumed it on the train. He was dangerous, sloppy and elated.

"Not a happy ship," he mocked. "Well, we can't have that, can we?"

The lounge was half empty. A man with a perfect bald circle on the top of his head played "Roll Out the Barrel" on the piano. But no one gathered at his back to sing. Whether he was a friend, or a hireling, or vibrating on some continuum between the two seemed immaterial.

As they reached for the sherry glasses from Nockles's tray, Mimi Gluck rushed forward, the ends of her white shirt and tasseled shawl like little kite-tails in the wind. "You've come together," she said. "What a lovely coincidence." She now wore a look of entitlement, of being at home. Such women always made Albert misbehave.

"You look marvellous as well, Mimi," he said. "All the young ladies thrive here. It's not surprising," he said. "It does wonders for people, especially at the beginning, to be bought."

Mimi laughed in a robust way as they faced the room together.

"Oh, we're all for sale," she said lightly.

Cory rose to the bait. "Why do you say that? You're so ready to debase everyone, even yourself."

"You mean you're not for sale?" laughed Mimi. "I suppose you're better than all the rest of us."

"She is. She's bought and sold for Art's sake, I told her already. She just hasn't realized it yet," said Albert.

Cory stepped away from her lover. "Albert and I met by accident in the train," she said. Then she flushed: Had she explained too much? She could feel the electricity in her back. Though their cover was for his benefit, strictly speaking, not hers, she was the one who had to be careful: He might say or do anything.

"But how marvellous," Mimi cooed, apparently unconcerned. "You must miss your assistant, now that she's off to war."

"Indeed I do," said Albert. "But perhaps you could come and help me out." Mimi's giggle rose like a burst of birdsong over his puff of smoke.

Cory pushed into a tight circle to get near Max.

"So," he said when he saw her. "What do you hear? Will the Italian campaign go on all winter? Is weather going to defeat the Canadians?"

"The weather won't defeat them and they'll fight until they can't fight any more," she said. "But I hear from my friends that the Germans have orders straight from Hitler not to withdraw. That's not what your newspaper says, by the way."

"I never interfere with my editors," he said.

There was laughter all around.

"They just don't call it interference any more. They call it mind-reading. Max doesn't tell them what he wants. The editors just *know*," said someone.

It pleased Max to hear his despotism so discussed. The grin grew wide across his face, and became that laugh, that statement: I recognize humour. This is where the laugh comes in the script. But there was no mirth in it.

"It's hard on a man," he said, "sitting here with nothing to do but meddle." He had a way of making you feel sorry for him. Perhaps that was what women fell for.

"While you're at it, can't you meddle me back into action?" said Cory. "I've got this war under my skin now. I want to photograph it."

"I know about Italy," said Max, suddenly. "The men are fighting hard. The conditions are terrible. Trouble is, we've been spoiled. The public is bored with it. People want faster results."

"Send me back."

"You did a fine job. Couldn't have asked for better," he said. He mused some more. "But that was a one off. A novelty. Sending a woman."

"Who says?"

The blackout curtains had been drawn; through the chink in the door Cory could see Albert flirting with Mimi.

"Come and look out the window," Max said suddenly. "Can you see my big cross down there?"

Part way down the slope there was a cross perhaps thirty feet high, rimmed with electric lights.

"It's there to remind me of my sins. I put it up when Lady Beaverbrook died." He gazed at it, admiringly.

"It's very large," she said.

"It lights up. But I've had to have it disconnected, for the blackout, you know."

They laughed together, that time.

Dinner began with pig's head jelly. Then lamb and potatoes that had been cooked in hay.

"We're eating the same as the people," Max said. "Got this recipe off the wireless. Told the cook to make it up. Saves on fuel, don't you know, cooking in hay. How is it?"

"Delicious," murmured the man with the bald circle on his head. At that moment Cory decided that he must be a paid member of the group. Albert, across the table from Cory, was glittery-eyed, in love with the deception they worked on the crowd. He flirted with Cory, with Mimi, with anyone.

"Two lovely women. I couldn't be happier," he said, stretching his arm out as Nockles walked by, for more wine.

Nockles refilled it at once. Albert downed it again. As

Nockles began to look reluctant, Albert's arm went out once more.

"Would you mind?" Nockles had no choice but to oblige. Albert's energy made the others at the table pale: Only Cory understood that he was charged by the delight of malfeasance.

"How is Liss?" asked someone.

Albert didn't answer. Instead he started an argument about Monte Cassino. The Germans were on top of the mountain, blocking the way to Rome.

"So what do you think, do you think we should bomb the monastery? After all, there's only a lot of books and art in there," said Albert, leading them on in his raw, smoky voice.

"It would be the most dreadful sacrilege," said the bald man vehemently.

"They say the Germans aren't actually *using* the monastery. Perhaps they respect the art and the books?"

"Chances are they wrote a fair number of them."

"It's the entire history of our civilization."

"All right, let me ask you a question. What good have books and art been if they've led us to this?" said Max. "I say blow it up!"

The table went dead.

"I'd rather my own son die in battle, than we should destroy Monte Cassino," said Albert. He looked defiantly into Cory's eyes. She went cold.

Cory wrung her napkin in her lap to stop the tears. She hated Albert. She wanted to kill him, shoot him, leap across the table and put her hands around his throat and throttle him until he turned blue and his eyes bulged out and he went slack in her hands. That he should invoke his son, at this moment and no other, showed more perversity than even she imagined him capable of. She prayed for someone to change the subject. She understood him then: He was *afraid* of his son. Afraid that a child brought him closer to irrelevance and the death on which he constantly dilated.

It was Mimi who cried out. "You only say that because you have no son!" She looked around the table for confirmation. "You see? That's the trouble, don't you see? All our thinkers, our politicians and generals, they're men and they're intellectuals and they'd rather preserve a few dusty old books than all those beautiful young boys —" She was agreeing with Max. "It's lives we must save. It's children who matter, not..."

Down the table the bald man choked and had to be slapped on the back. "You're calling Monte Cassino a few dusty old books?"

Mimi was on to something and she knew it. Her voice fluted above the clatter of cutlery on china.

"In fact, they are all old men and maybe they're even jealous of the young ones and they're *enjoying* — I should not say enjoying, but there's something deliberate — something obscene in the way they send them out, boatloads and planeloads of them just to be ripped to pieces. There's something perverse, there's something sexual —" She began to wrap her arms around her waist, first the left over, then the right over, rocking herself, and just as she got to the point of saying, "There'll be nothing but old men *left!*" her eyes spilled out tears and her small mouth worked into a knot and she went silent. She reached for her wineglass.

When Cory reached for her glass in sympathy, she knocked it over with her forearm. A red spot blossomed on the table. The maid swiftly covered it with a napkin, then another napkin. Cory flushed and asked for water. He drinks, I spill, she thought. Albert, triumphant, sat back to watch what he'd wrought.

"Look at all this *seeping*, ladies!" he said. "Tears, wine, what have you..."

In the toilet Cory found Mimi weeping over the sink as she bathed her face with cold water. She stood behind, watching, in the oval mirror with its thick gilt frame, the other woman's inverted nape. "Are you all right?"

"They're horrid. Horrid. I don't know. No, I'm not all right. My whole family is lost, everything is lost," Mimi sobbed.

Cory stood for a minute saying nothing. Then, when she saw her friend's face rise in the mirror, washed of its tears and cooler now, she spoke.

"Mimi," she continued, forced onward by some irresistible need from within, "you said Albert had no son. That's not true. He does have a son. Who is also my son."

Mimi stared at her in the mirror.

"What are you saying?"

Cory told her again.

Mimi turned and opened her arms. Cory moved into

them, and cried, because there was no one else on this island, save Albert no one else on this side of the ocean who knew what Mimi knew now, and it was such a comfort. She told her about Tyke, she showed the little picture she always carried, she even explained where he was living. Mimi peered into the little snapshot, and praised him. "How beautiful he is," she said. "So blond."

Then she fumbled in her tiny bag. She pulled out her own photograph, which was curled and creased with many tiny lines, like the palm of a hand. Cory found herself staring into the face of a dark-haired, beautiful girl of about thirteen.

"I am so glad you told me. Because you see, that is why we are like one another. My daughter is also left behind. You know that too? It is my secret as well. I have a daughter. Yes! She I left in France, when Max helped me to escape. Now my daughter is in Austria. And Jewish! I could not get her out. I had to save myself."

The maid came in and Mimi was silent until she left, the door swinging shut behind her. "And now that I am here, I try to help her. You will understand me, because you too have left your son."

Cory bridled. I judge her, she heard, silently, in her head, the words of the cripple on the train. And she did: She was repelled by Mimi's tale. Surely their cases were different! To leave a half-grown girl behind in a war! To save herself! Cory struggled for compassion.

"In Canada, a safe place with plenty of food and no Germans."

"But for how long is it safe?" said Mimi. "And what is the difference between us? Only that you are lucky, am I right?"

Cory took her turn at the basin, bathing the teary blotches off her face. Too late, she wondered what she had done. "You tell one person, you've told everyone," Eliza always said.

The men were braying in the hallway. "Are you ladies coming out? What's going on in there?"

"They're waiting for dessert," said Mimi, mopping her eyes.

Cory turned on the cold water tap. "Let them wait."

When they rejoined the table the mood had turned black. Albert's drinking had moved him out of reach now: He muttered to himself under his breath and poked with his fork at the linen tablecloth. Cory watched him with something like relief. For tonight, he was no longer dangerous. She felt detached. How nice to be not Liss, not his wife, not responsible for his behaviour.

"Does anyone know the way to Hell?" Max asked, abruptly. He stopped a maid carrying a tray out of the room.

"Nobody knows the way to anything any more," said the bald man. "They took down all the road signs to confound the Germans and they've confounded us all!"

"No, no," said Max. "The way to Hell!" He snatched a large puffy loaf of bread off the maid's tray. "Watch!"

He pushed back his chair, walked to a spot behind the

table where he could be seen by everyone, and put the loaf on the carpet. Then he took two large steps and jumped on the middle of the loaf with both feet, collapsing it completely. When he stepped off it was flat, mushy. He picked a little bit off his shoe and laughed merrily. "The floor is supposed to open up and take me down. Right through the floor, to Hell! My father told me that and I never forgot it." He picked up the loaf, shedding flakes of crust, and pulled its two halves apart in his hand. He tossed one onto the table and took a hunk of the other half and put it in his mouth. Then he spat it out.

"Max, I don't understand," said Mimi.

"I'm telling you," he insisted. "I'm telling you as a boy I had a temper. Once my mother brought in some baking and I wasn't happy so I jumped on her loaf of bread. My father was a clergyman. He came in shaking his fist and roared at me, 'Now that's the way to Hell!'"

There was laughter. "You're a card, Max."

Nockles came in with a silver broom and dustpan. Max subsided to a brood and resumed his place at the head of the table. Cory's coffee spoon rattled into her saucer.

Albert looked across at Cory. "Shall we go up?" he said.

People looked away, pretending not to hear.

"I don't understand," said Cory shakily. Mimi rose and put her arm on Cory's shoulder.

"What's to understand?" Albert roared in sudden, alarming jubilation. "Let's just go up to bed!"

It was the moment Nockles had been waiting for. "I'm afraid, Mr. Bloom, you've had too much wine," he said, handing the silver dustpan to the maid and advancing on Albert's chair.

"Yes, I think so," said Mimi, nodding. "You, Albert, are ready to retire. But not our Cory," she said.

Roaring like a madman, Albert was led away.

Cory's eyes smarted. Immediately after he was gone she missed his huge presence in the room. She felt guilt: She had disowned him. Oh, why had they come, wasting their precious time together? Better to be in a room somewhere, lying down with his arms wrapped across her back, his black heart on hers.

After coffee the company went out on the terrace. They could hear the bombers heading east. Max had a son up there, flying.

"Each time the pilots go out on a mission they believe it will be their last. Of course, if they kept on going out, eventually they would be correct," said the man with the bald spot.

The roar came out of the dark sky and quieted them for a few seconds.

"By the law of averages."

"Or the law of diminishing returns."

"One of those laws."

"Give it to 'em, God speed!" cried the tipsy crowd.

In the morning when Cory came down to the breakfast table Albert was up and gone, they said, walking. The room was full of sunlight; the tablecloth was yellow. There was a silver rack of toast on the table. She asked for tea, and went to the window to look over the Downs.

"Have you had a tour of the area? Down there is the River Mole," said the bald man in his pedantic way. "You can't see it, but it is there, all the way down at the bottom. It comes from Molesly. The Surrey hunt goes all along there, on the South Downs, right to Guildford. And down there is Bocketts Farm. It's in the Domesday Book."

"So peaceful," said Cory. "This morning."

"After last night."

"Not a happy ship."

"He told you that too." They laughed, recalling the driver with his bleeding packages of meat.

Mimi drifted into the room, a wraith in a black satin pyjama, twisting her hands and skirting along the draperies. She smiled fleetingly in Cory's direction but did not speak.

The bald man persisted. "Do you know the Chalk Downs? When you dig in the earth it looks like a grave, it's so chalky white."

Cory was ready to ask how many graves he had looked into, but the bald man waved cheerily and walked out into the hallway. There was a draft by the window, and her hands were cold despite the cup of tea she carried.

Cory wanted to call him back. Mimi's peaked face flickered like a small bird's in and out of the solid yellow light. Cory regretted, this morning, her tears and confession of last night. Albert's refusal to recognize Tyke made her vulnerable, in need of a confidant. She had to get over it, let it go, or she would become a liability. This circle of people was like a secret service, an underground: You had to be without a weak spot to survive in it. Practitioners of the black arts, indeed. If you let them know your secrets, the soft and unprotected places where arrows hit flesh instead of shell, you put yourself in danger.

Mimi sighed heavily and looked as though she were about to cry. "I'm so terribly unhappy here."

Cory felt impatient. "Perhaps you ought to leave, then."

Mimi's eyes flew open and fear came onto her face. "Oh no, I could not, you see, he rescued me, I am a refugee, I must get my daughter."

"You're free, I should think."

Mimi simply shook her head. "No. I am not. But you are. You have a big important mission. You will go flying off to war again. I heard all about it from Max."

"You did?"

"And you will leave Albert behind. Like you left his son in Canada."

"I told you that in strictest confidence."

"Of course, there is no other way you would speak," Mimi cried. Cory looked down the long fall of the downs and saw Albert's black figure, his cloak flying out behind him, his walking stick ahead, so that he looked like some hieroglyph, some Japanese character of obscure meaning inked onto the landscape.

Chapter Twenty-Two

The Seaforth Highlanders sit down to a Christmas dinner served on tables made of planks in the Church of Santa Maria di Constantinopoli. For most it is a two-hour respite from fighting. Ditchburn climbed a scaffold inside the bomb-scarred church to get the whole group in her sights. The upturned faces of the men are a study in mixed emotion.

ℰᴖ

CORY SCANNED THE SOLDIERS' FACES. THEY WERE ODDS AND sods, replacement troops — English, New Zealanders, Sikhs in turbans. She felt she'd met them all before. Their faces wore youth underscored with fear, overwritten with bravado.

Weighted down with her kit bag and two cameras, her bag of lenses, flashbulbs, film-packs and a bedroll, Cory made for a bench. The temperature hovered at the freezing point. Three times they'd tried to take off for Italy, and three times the wings had iced up and they'd been sent back to wait over the coal fire in the otherwise unheated tin hut.

A skinny redhead approached, wearing the red shoulder flashes of the Canadians. Under his trousers could be seen the pointy toes and high heels of a well-worn pair of cowboy boots.

"Miss Ditchburn? I'm Lieutenant Baldwin Moench. That's M-o-e-n-c-h. Looks like 'munch.' Rhymes with clinic! Let me take those for you," he said, neatly lifting the leather straps off her shoulder.

"Not my cameras!" She grabbed the straps as they passed down her arm and up his.

"They'll be as close as the first word you utter," said Moench. "I'm assigned to you."

"I did all this before without having someone assigned to me," she grumbled. But Baldwin's good spirits seemed unlikely to be quenched by a Ditchburn scowl. Also, the new Speed Graphic, no lighter than Old Reliable, did make it hard for her to move. She kicked her kit bag over toward his feet. "That's the heavy one, if you want to carry something. I'll take my Leica back."

As the sleet turned to heavy rain, a static overhead voice advised them to board the plane. Inside the stripped-down metal shell they pulled down discs the size of dinner plates from the inside wall of the plane. Looking over the crates of baggage stashed in the centre aisle they could just about see fellow travellers on the opposite side of the aircraft. Each and every one braced himself for jolts, and pulled his chin into the collar of his greatcoat.

"Where're ya from?" said Baldwin. "Northern Ontario? Heard that's some kinda fine country there. I'm from Red Deer. Prairie, eh?"

At Montecorvino Airport the rain continued, heavy and cold. The Americans had taken over. Bales and crates of goods stamped in the names of Allied nations stood in small pyramids. Behind the track-crossed plain and landing strips the mountains rose, steep, and shrouded in dark cloud. With a Liaison Officer from the British Eighth, Baldwin Moench and Cory set off for Naples over a narrow track, which quickly ascended into the mountains and folded back and forth on itself through the Chiunzi Pass.

"Reminds me of the Banff Coach Road," said Baldwin.

From time to time they swung past an open spot offering a rain-swept vista of sea and sky, then swung again up against the hillsides. As usual all the original bridges had been blown away by departing Germans, and the metallic hum of their tires crossing the metal straps of each Bailey bridge sent tingles through Cory's feet. Finally the hills subsided, their last reaches running directly to the ocean where they ended in cliffs and pebbled beaches.

Naples was bleak. There were bomb craters in every street, and hastily cleared demolitions at corners. Enormous piles of half-burnt refuse graced the public spaces. Scruffy, mean-looking children ran beside their jeep, crying for candy and cigarettes. The Italians were pale and grimed;

their much-vaunted joy at receiving the Allies seemed to have been drained off with the cold, the hunger and the wet.

"Sugar is five dollars a pound," said the Liaison Officer. "Eggs cost maybe a dollar each, though these people have no way of getting a dollar, unless they sell their sister."

"What about the supplies we saw at the airport? Flour and powdered milk, from the Allies?"

"They come in all right, but the racketeers get it and sell it and nobody lifts a finger to stop them."

Cory wanted to get out of town, but it took two days before an information officer from the Edmontons showed up with a jeep and a map. In drenching rain, they set out. Baldwin hung out the side of the windshield to peer at the passing landscape, while Cory crouched behind it, changing lenses.

"It rains like this at home, in May," he said.

At the Eighth Army headquarters they were confronted by an officer. "Hey, where do you think you're going? You can't take a woman out to the front."

"You can if you've got a letter like we do," said Baldwin. Cory produced her credential, which she'd had coated in plastic; folded under it was a letter from General Crerar. The officer handed it back and shook his head.

"See this bit about regard for safety? I figure someone's gonna stop you somewhere before you get to the front, but it won't be me."

On the roads were armoured cars and tanks bogged in mud, and civilians carrying bags bulging with goods, their eyes black with fatigue.

"Sometimes you see traffic like this around Stampede Days down in Calgary," said Baldwin. "You get horses, cattle, Indians, tractors all pushing through at once."

"I guess you must be homesick," said Cory. "You haven't seen one thing that didn't remind you of there. Where did you say you were born?"

"Red Deer," he said. "Naw, I ain't homesick."

"Just 'cause you're not, we'll call you Red Deer," said Cory.

They passed the mobile bath station with a long queue of men snapping their soggy towels at each other to pass the time. Those who had finished their shower shaved in little bowls of water at mirrors, which ran with rainwater. Red Deer swung in and out of the truck on one leg, holding on to the roof, peering around the next turn to see how long was the defile of trucks and armour. He impatiently hopped out and jump-kicked the side of the jeep, to the amusement of other soldiers, stoically waiting for a sign to roll ahead.

"Used to be a nice olive grove here. This could have been a corn field. Everything stripped, not a leaf left. Reminds me of home, after a really bad hailstorm, you know?"

As darkness became complete the road emptied. Red Deer talked about being a cowboy. "I've harvested in Ontario. I've driven with cattle all the way down to Colorado. Great country." His narrow, lantern-jawed face opened up in a delighted grin. "When I get back I'm gonna go on the rodeo circuit."

"Won't your family want you back on that farm?"

Red Deer swallowed, and his Adam's apple moved painfully up and down. "You know, that's the darn thing about this business. When I went to war I kinda cut loose. It's easier maybe just to keep on moving."

Their second night out they pulled into a Canadian field hospital. Under soggy canvas, gas lights swayed in the wind. The tin cans of gasoline-soaked earth that the soldiers lit to boil water for tea popped and bounced as they heated. When Red Deer pulled off his jacket to dry his neck Cory noticed his collar bone, fragile and fine, inside the neck of his loosened shirt.

"Are you a kid?" she said. "Don't tell me I'm driving through this with a kid."

"Ain't no kids around here any more," he said.

Someone had hooked up a radio. Lili Marlene was on, in German. Just before the night's bombing began the ambulance brought in an officer who'd had his leg blown off when he stepped out of his jeep to inspect a site.

"You ought to get a herd of goats to go in and set off those mines," said Red Deer. By way of explanation he said to Cory, "Goats is what they've got here instead of cattle."

"There's more shells in those fields than there are goats in all Italy," said a wounded soldier. Another one piped up.

"Hey, goats are worth something. Eye-ties need their goats. Infantry's better. Blow us up, you get replacements." The cynical one, head bandaged and arm in a sling, stood by the canvas tent flap sucking on a cigarette. Cory was arrested by the bitterness that saturated his voice, and by something else, a Northern Ontario twang. She took off her helmet and looked at him.

"I guess I know you," the kid said to Cory.

She stepped closer.

"You used to teach me school, Miss Ditchburn," he said. "Either that or I'm crazier than I thought. Or maybe I'm dead. It doesn't make no sense, you being here."

It was dark, and his face was half hidden by the white wrappings on his temple. When Cory got close enough she recognized Willie Johnstone, Wade's son. He'd done grades seven and eight, maybe, before disappearing up north into a logging camp. She held out her hand.

"I guess I don't hafta call you *Miss* Ditchburn here," he said.

She remembered the chilly schoolroom down by the salt docks as he said her name, recalled its clapboard walls shaking when the storms came in off the Bay. As if from another lifetime, she saw the picture of Queen Elizabeth hanging over the blackboard, the Mercator map of the world, with its parallels of longitude pulling out the width of the land masses at the north and south poles, so that Canada and the Arctic loomed enormous above all the rest. To get here they had crossed the unbridgeable vacancy of the Atlantic Ocean.

"Willie Johnstone," she said, wonderingly. "Who'd have thought, back then, we'd meet here?" She held out her hand. His smile nudged his head dressing up an inch on his brow.

"Caught a sniper's bullet at the River Sangro," he said.

"My buddy bought it. I only got shipped in here two nights ago. Now I guess they're going to send me back." He sounded mournful. "I wish I could stay and finish the job."

"Maybe you'll be back."

After he finished his cigarette he went back in. The nurse offered Cory a cup of tea. "You know him well?" she said.

"I know his dad," she said, simply. "Willie was a boy with a dirty jersey and a fishing rod. It can't have been more than eight years ago." She let the tea burn her throat.

"He's got a bullet in his brain," said the nurse. "We can't understand how he's still standing. Sometimes they do this with brain injuries. They're talking and laughing right till the end. Pain centre is blocked, I guess. We'll try to get him out in the morning."

The ambulance pulled away at dawn, but it was too late for Willie Johnstone: He had fallen into a coma and died in the night.

A letter never sent:

> *Dear Wade, I saw Willie just before*
> *Dear Wade, what can I*
> *Dear Albert —*
> *How can it be the world is organized this way? I want to see you and I cannot bridge this intractable distance. I tried so hard today to stretch over the Atlantic and embrace my friend whose son died here, but that too is impossible. Tell me it's a cliché*

*if you want, but what I know, now, is that our lives
have their limits. Every day is one off the total. The
trouble is you don't know how many you had to
begin with. But it's my war, and I have to see it
through. The worst thing is how calm we get.*

Brigade Headquarters was a grisly mud-hole, surrounded
by two-foot trenches like moats, in which water stood. Last
year's crop of corn was trampled, pulled out by its roots,
and water ran unimpeded from the higher end to the
lower of the camp. At one end was the mess hall and the
men's quarters. In the centre, under the flag, where the
urgent, static sounds of the radio could be heard, was the
office. It was the week before Christmas. Somebody had
built a crèche of corn husks and bits of wood; the Babe lay
in a manger made of the sliced-off half of a tin can.

Red Deer ducked his head and grinned engagingly. "Do
you think we might step in out of the wet?"

The Public Relations chief was Mahoney, a large red-
whiskered Lieutenant Colonel with a rubbery, blustering
face. He took one look at Cory and threw his hands over
his head.

"So now they're sending us women. We don't have
enough trouble." He turned over his shoulder and yelled
back into the tent, from which came the clacking of a
portable typewriter, sporadic and intense. "Least they
could have done was tell us in advance. Why didn't they
give us some warning? Now I gotta get you a female conducting officer."

"How do you do," said Cory. "We're on our way to —"

But the big man was busy roaring. "What is this war coming to, I ask you?"

"You've heard of Corinne Ditchburn?" said Red Deer.

"I've heard of alla' them. We've got Mrs. Hemingway somewhere and Miss Bourke-White somewhere else. We've got no female conducting officers! I tell you, I can't send you out there. You'll get raped!"

A voice came from inside the tent. "The Americans and the British have the same problem, sir."

"I was all through Sicily and I never got raped, Sir," said Cory.

"Is that a complaint?"

A snigger from the tent. Cory stared at Mahoney until he dropped his eyes.

"You're all the same," said Mahoney to Cory. "You haven't seen enough danger. Can't wait to play the hero. Wait until you've been around here awhile. Sicily was a picnic compared to the Gustav Line."

"I guess your men don't need their actions to be recognized," she said, handing him her papers.

"What's your newspaper? The *Daily Express*? Never read it!" He scanned her ID, swallowing and pulling on the mahogany-coloured handlebar mustaches that overhung his lips. "That's the trouble with you women!" he roared. "You get yourself a position like this, with some newspaper organization, you make yourself indispensable, and then you expect the rest of us to deal with it!"

Then he glared at Red Deer. "It's a waste of any good

Category A man to give him the task of shepherding a woman. If I let you go through I'll get screams from all the other warcos I've got stashed behind lines that *they* should be allowed into battle zone."

"Maybe they should be."

"I've half a mind to send them all home! It's like a kindergarten here. Griffin of the *Star* has a virus and can't talk, I've got another one who's had dysentery so bad he's got to be airlifted out. Morris from CP is pushing the limits every minute, running ahead of me —"

"Reg is there?" said Cory.

Mahoney's eyes gleamed. "Is he a friend of yours? It figures. Well for tonight I'm going to find you a nice convent well in the rear," he snapped. "Tomorrow you'll go."

There being no convent close at hand, Cory was billeted overnight in the home of the mayor of the battered little town of San Leonardo. Attended by a sharp-featured wife, he played the piano and sang "O Sole Mio," like a bellows, ceasing only to bow and to gesture expansively from the heart. He was so effusive Cory decided he must have been a fascist. In the morning Red Deer was at the door with an I-officer and the promised car.

"We're going forward," he said.

They drove on silently. "If you want to make it home," said a road sign. A few hairpins later it continued.

"To the virgins you left behind you."

They drove on for several hundred yards, up a hill and down it again.

"Don't drive on the verge, soldier."

Across the valleys the grey rocky stutters of campanile and basilica were darker than the mist. Sounds of gunfire that had been a low rumble in the background were now ear-splitting. Puffs of smoke and ash rose up from hits down the other side of the hill.

They came to the River Moro. It was a little creek, over a small valley. The I-officer began to warm up. "See this bridge?" It was a corduroy bridge. "Our engineers built it at night, under constant shellfire. When one was killed, we put in another. We started on December sixth. We got through on the eighth. But they never stopped trying to hit us. When you crossed it you held your breath."

They held their breath, and rumbled over to the other side.

"We took it inch by inch and German by German. Our prisoners tell us Hitler's given them precise instructions: Fight until you die on the road to Rome."

On this side of the Moro, no houses were left standing. The trees were skeletal, splintered in two, thrusting upward like javelins aimed at the sky. Aircraft went over, diving through the clouds, swooping down in an arc and delivering their moaning bombs. Then the ack-ack began. Red Deer and Cory jumped down into a pit. Every nerve in Cory's body stood on end and screamed for it to stop. Finally the guns were silent.

"That's giving you an idea," said the I-officer. They clambered out of their trenches and drove on.

The Canadians were within a mile of Ortona. From their bleak outlook they could see the old town set on the top of a rocky promontory; between here and there the roads were three feet deep in mud. The fields were spotted with ruined tank turrets and abandoned gun-sites.

"I say Merry Christmas to you," said the commanding officer, giving Cory the once over. "But you're on a fool's errand. There's nothing to see. We're fighting a hidden war. It's cat and mouse. The guns are hidden, the men are in slit trenches, the rain covers everything."

At nightfall the magnesium flares and green streaks began to lace the sky. When the clouds cleared enough for stars to come through, Red Deer and Cory stood out under them, by the door of the mess tent.

"Hey, which one is the star of Bethlehem? Isn't it supposed to be the brightest?"

"I don't know this sky," said Cory. The whole firmament had revolved; she was disoriented, a wanderer in an overturned landscape. Death grew here like a famine, an infestation.

"It's over there," came a voice from behind. "Look over the top of the boulder at the turn in the road, lift your eyes directly overhead, keep lifting them."

She knew the voice. "Reg! If I hadn't seen your byline I'd have sworn for sure you were dead by now."

He loped up and strapped his long arms around her back, and laughing. "It's not as bad as all that. Well, yes it is. But contrary to popular belief, the Gerries are human. I saw them stop today for a whole three minutes to let an

Italian woman and child get out when they'd been caught in crossfire."

Outside there was the far-off firing sound — a hollow whumpf! — and the silence that followed it, then the declining scream as the missile fell. Then it landed, and there was a crack, followed by a thundering echo.

"They got a new toy a few days early for Christmas — this tank that throws out flames. Still, when you capture them they'll tell you they know they're losing the war."

On Christmas Eve they sang carols in the men's mess tent. "Maybe the enemy will walk out of its foxholes and we'll all shake hands?" said someone.

"No chance. That was the last war."

Red Deer pulled a Bible out of his kit and they read the Christmas story from the book of Luke. "And she brought forth her firstborn son and wrapped him in swaddling clothes…" His voice was slow and easy. After the reading, Cory wanted to keep him talking.

"Tell me about Red Deer," she said.

"You really want me to? Okay. Let's see. There'll be lots of snow at our place, provided we didn't get one of those chinooks to dry it off. That's what they could use here. Come to think of it, the arch in that cloud formation tonight around sunset *looked* like a chinook arch."

Cory watched him. He was an incredible creature, long and rope-like in the arms and legs. He needed someone to tell him, as Albert had told her, to get a shell. He couldn't be nineteen, even, she thought, eyeing the hard, muscled leg in his too-short breeches, his thin rump as he bent over the coal burning stove. She decided to go to bed. He stood up after her and hiked his pants.

"I don't need an escort. I'll get myself out there on my own."

"My job, Ma'am," he said. The men in the mess grinned.

"It's dirty work but, hey, someone's got to do it."

"Why go to bed when you know you won't sleep?"

"Because morning comes anyway."

Together they walked out into the cold dark mist. You could see nothing, feel nothing. Cory's ears, dulled by shelling, seemed not to register Red Deer's voice as he spoke, and they walked together across the slick ground. His arm caught hers; they sidestepped a trench. A boy, just a boy, she thought, but he seemed more alone than the others. She turned and put her arms around his neck, leaned into him and caught his lips with hers. She kissed his dry, soft mouth deeply and for a long time.

"Merry Christmas," she whispered.

He had lifted her already and she was astride one of his legs, split by it. She was reduced to pure sensation. Without having taken a step on her own, she found she was down in her tent on the sleeping roll he'd carried for her into the plane.

Under his rough clothes his skin was hot, dry and perfect. His body had the density of clay; stripped so clean were his bones that it was like making love to an essence, not a man. Cory's own flesh felt like extraneous matter, but in the heat of making love it all melted away.

"Red Deer," she said, "Red Deer." He was long and thin and so strong it was as if she were tied up with electric wire. They tried to be silent but when the shelling started they thought it was cover. There were no hours to the night, and the darkness had no peace in it, and there seemed no reason on earth why they should not be using each other's bodies to produce these beauties, when all around them was mud and death. He cried and she wiped his tears and began again.

The men would be up at six. He stood, and in the darkness found his uniform and dressed. Cory crawled to the door of the tent to watch him go. The darkness had turned to before-dawn grey, but she could only see his silhouette. He took two steps from her door and disappeared. He seemed to have dropped off the edge of the earth.

"Red Deer!" she screamed.

She cowered in the tent. She hadn't heard a bomb, a shell or a gun, but there was nothing left of him. What had happened? Had he been brought down by a sniper? Had a prisoner escaped?

Then she heard groaning. Heaving up at ground level, a dripping figure slowly growing to full height.

"Jesus Christ!"

"Oh, God," said Cory, "I thought you were dead!" Her greatcoat around her, she ran out and embraced him as he stepped, streaming rancid water, from the drainage trench.

"Where ya' been?" The ribald voice of a soldier.

"Fell down a hole."

Laughter from all around.

"Guess you thought you'd sneak away quiet like."

"Well Merry Christmas to you, Red Deer!"

Laughter rocked the camp that morning until the Take Post whistle blew.

For Christmas dinner the supply trucks brought in turkey with dressing. A dozen Italian women braved the donkey track above the sea to carry in white table linen. They set out long tables from the convent in the hollow centre of the church, in a large square. Soldiers sat to eat in shifts, said grace, and talked of home.

"My wife will have taken the kids up to see my folks; they always open their gifts Christmas Eve — that'll be right now. I hope she spent the money they're paying me on that table-hockey game they wanted."

"I always go back to the farm and kill the turkey myself. Maybe two weeks ahead, let it hang. It's not good if it's too fresh."

"We pick the cranberries in summer, by the cottage at Lake Joseph. Gloria makes the sauce and cans it."

There was an organ, the pipes miraculously still in good order. After the carols the men wiped their chins on Italian napkins and went back out to fight. The next shift washed and came in quietly. When they picked up the King's speech on the radio it was as if civilities from some long-forgotten and alien civilization had been leaked in.

Chapter Twenty-Three

FIGURE 23

Corinne Ditchburn

At the Well

January, 1944
Ortona, Italy
Gelatin silver, 34 x 45 cm
Reprinted from original negative by Orestes Hrudy
National Archives of Canada, Ottawa

This photograph caught press correspondent Reg Morris at the moment when he was hit by a last grenade after the Canadians cleared the town of Germans. Amid the dust and bricks flying around his head Morris remains visible, lifted into the air, his face opened into a gape of astonishment. The wide angle allowed Ditchburn to also catch, at the far left corner of the picture, the rounded shape of the helmet and forearm of the lone soldier who threw the grenade.

❧

THE RAIN STILL FELL. CORY LAY IN HER SLEEPING BAG WITH HER greatcoat on top of it. Reg Morris came to the flap of her tent, emanating a stiff hurt; his lips barely moved but his voice cut through her. It was obvious he knew Red Deer had been with her. Reg still bore his dog-like devotion which had so irritated her. He'd been kicked but he wasn't going away.

"I'm going in with a recce patrol," said Reg. "They'd let you come if you wanted."

She scrambled to her feet. "I'm coming," she said.

"You don't have to."

He stood with one hand on her tent flap, looking away. "Apart from anything else," she heard him say, "it's downright unsafe. All these men out here. Are you mad?" He was not talking about the recce patrol.

Cory rode behind the muleteer because her mule, Rico, wouldn't move without instructions from the boss. After came Reg Morris, and after him Red Deer, his heels so low they were cocked just over the path on either side of the stocky animal. The path ran above the Adriatic along a road plugged with demolitions, wasted tanks and dead men. They tripped along the white tape which had been laid by sappers to keep people out of the mines that had been sewn liberally all around. When a shell sang through the air, its banshee moan made the mules shrink back against the wall.

"Get down!" someone shouted, but Cory was already off Rico's back and flat on the path. The explosion echoed off the walls of rock below.

The officer at forward headquarters was a pleasant surprise: He actually was glad to see her.

"That's Casa Berardi," he said, pointing ahead. "There

have been a dozen or more Germans holed up in there for a couple of days, shooting at us. We're trying to get them out."

Cory trained her camera on the collapsed buildings and the pitted fields. Only the cold kept the whole place from smelling like a charnel house. They watched as a couple of Canadian infantrymen made a run for the shelter of a half-demolished wall.

"They can't stay there long, Gerry's going to hit it," said the CO, and, just as the soldiers threw themselves forward on their stomachs, worming their way to the next position of "safety," the wall exploded, bricks and stones flying in every direction. When the dust settled the soldiers were still moving.

"It won't be healthy for ya," he said. "But I guarantee if you get to Ortona you'll see some heroics."

The mules had been walked back to where a pasture used to be; a child was feeding them dried grass.

"I'm going on," said Reg. He had his coiled reporter's pad in his hand. "You coming?"

Cory looked at Red Deer.

"I'm happy in the rear," he grinned.

"You don't have to come," said Reg to Cory.

"You don't have to come, either," she said to Red Deer. He just grinned.

"Yeah, we're coming," said Cory.

She was scared, so scared that fear burned her gut. If you give in to fear even once, you're dead, Albert said. Stupid, the voice inside countered. It's not fear that kills, but lack of fear. Sure, Reg can write the story of the fighting, he can send back his dispatches and say it was all taken down under fire, he can get the names and even record the deeds of the heroic as they fell, and even with censorship, eventually it would be published. But if there were no pictures of what was happening in Ortona, how real would it be?

Walking on, she forgot her burning stomach. Red Deer followed as she knew he would. There was a lull in the shooting; it was a novelty to hear a voice that wasn't punctuated and broken by bursting shells.

"I'll take you around through the old gardens," said their leader. "You know how to hit the ground when you hear a shell coming over. There's no shortage of holes for cover."

They made it easily to a knoll behind Casa Berardi where three soldiers with Bren guns were reclining behind a wall of brick and sandbags.

"If we don't get some more shooting in the next half hour I say they're either dead or gone," said one soldier. Reg took his name and his hometown, and they talked for a while about the German and how he fought. You could not fault them, said the soldiers, except that they wouldn't give up. By this time they ought to have given up.

"This one guy, he held out behind his wall for four hours, we thought there were two of them but it was only him. Then he ran for it. We hit his shoulder strap and his gun came off. He rolled into a trench and we hit him three, four times. When the stretcher bearers carried him in, he was laughing."

"What was he laughing about?"

"How it took four of us to get him, I guess," said one.

The firing started again. Cory hit the ground; she held her hands over her ears and shook as the ground shook. Reg jostled her with his foot. She could see his mouth moving. Then he was up and running. She followed, her camera banging against her chest; ahead through the smoke she could barely see the khaki figure of Reg and the feet of the officer ahead of him. Then they were against a wall, panting.

They were in a narrow street. There was a corner a hundred yards up, a house with open windows, and a doorway. The air was still filled with the inhuman screech of the mortar. But now there was a new sound, the sound of a plane. Its roar increased, swooped down on them. Reg's mouth was against her face.

"Those are ours!"

She started to move out across the street but the house they ran to wasn't on the ground any more. It was liquid, undulating. The lower part of the wall burst forward, spitting bricks. Cory had her camera on it. The door burst open and men ran out, Germans, she supposed, but there wasn't time to think of more than — alive! — as the top of the house began to rain down over them. She shot as fast as she could, it went on forever, this ballet of the collapsing house, the way the men's limbs stretched forward out of the dust cloud, the way the first one began to fly, of his own volition it seemed, across the road, like some huge, steel-toed turkey.

Then it was over and Reg had gone, where she didn't know. She stood up and began to walk forward, disoriented. She must have been in the open because Red Deer tackled her, so that his shoulder and back caught her in the stomach. His mouth was twisted out of shape. She could see rather than hear his words; get back!

She found herself against the wall. She held her cameras to her chest and began to crawl on her elbows back toward where she'd come from. Coming to a slit trench, she dropped into it. She was lying on something padded, but hard in places. It was wet but she didn't care. Keeping her cameras under her she put her hands over her head and lay still. Maybe she even slept.

When she woke it was nearly dark. The gunfire was farther away. It was the closest to quiet this place had been, she realized, and it had been for some time. She moved her arms, and lifted her head. She was lying on a dead body. The scream came up her throat like gorge.

At first she saw no one. Had they left her? Mourned her little life and gone back? Then, in the dusk she picked out small figures moving. They weren't running or ducking. They were engaged in some ritual or dance; bending and lifting, one at either side. They faced each other, bowed, then straightened. She watched them, puzzling it out: They were stretcher bearers, working their way toward her. She sat up, pulling out the Leica. The stretcher bearers were close to her now. She rolled off the corpse and out of the trench.

"Get down!" someone shouted.

She got down.

When he was above her she asked the stretcher bearer if he knew where Reg and Red Deer were.

"Where were they fighting?"

"They weren't. They're warcos," she said stupidly. "Not armed."

The man looked at her with pity. "This him?"

She looked at the stretcher. She couldn't recognize his face but she knew the boots.

"This fellow here's bought it."

Dear Albert —

My conducting officer wanted to do the rodeo circuit. He was maybe eighteen years old and today he died, throwing me out of the way of a bomb blast. I feel ashamed. Ashamed not to be fighting and killing people? I think not. Ashamed of the pictures I got, thinking they're not good enough to be worth his life? I don't know if I'll ever even see those pictures. I don't know if anyone will. But I know Red Deer will never see the Rockies again.—

They buried him in the cemetery beyond the town. The Loyal Edmontons had a piper, and he played his tune — Red River Valley, in honour of the west, as he marched back and forth beside the grave — but it wasn't Red Deer's regiment and the guys hadn't known him. The shellfire never let up.

She found Reg trying to write copy. His arms were shaking and he couldn't get words on paper. "It's the noise," he said. "Do you think they'd stop for just a moment, so I can hear myself think?" He began to laugh.

At first Cory laughed with him. "I'll go ask, okay? Who shall I start with, our guys or theirs?"

Tears began to run down his cheeks. Then the laughter turned deep into his chest and became hiccups and he was sobbing. He held his head between two cupped hands. "Go away. I don't want you watching me."

She gave him the line about how many stories he'd filed, stories that would pass the censor, maybe without dates and maybe without names of regiments, but finally they would reach Canada. "You've given a guy like Red Deer dignity."

"What's a little dignity when you're dead?" said Reg bitterly.

"Pretty well everything."

Reg said nothing.

"You want to watch out," said Cory. "Your nerves are shot. Maybe you should get out."

He'd written about that, the men who finally broke, whose desire to live went up, evaporated, like the coil of smoke after a plane in a tailspin. "You want me to go?" he said.

"I can't afford to lose you," she said with difficulty. "You know I never count on anybody. But I count on you."

His face twisted. "You mean now that you've lost Red Deer?"

She slapped his face. "That's vicious."

He looked at her with academic interest. "I know," he said. "I'm sorry. I just can't feel anything. I thought I'd be dead by now," he said. "At least when you're dead it's not so noisy."

The people of Ortona were gone, but not their furniture. It was a curiously domestic battle, this one, fought behind curtains, with bits of broken mirror, altar statues of the Virgin Mary, and upholstered chairs as props. Broken ends of kitchen chairs stubbornly reasserted themselves when soldiers dove over windowsills. Cellar doors burst, and wine bottles rolled out into the street. When layers of rock dust flew into the air the framed portraits of Jesus Christ went cockeyed but remained.

The rain persisted. The men knew they were winning; they were dug in now and couldn't be dislodged. Every German captured or killed was one less. They crawled over a haystack and caught four off-guard on the other side — killing them one by one. They captured the man who'd held them off one corner for three days. The day after Christmas they got the tanks in. Like huge blank snails they ploughed through the streets, guns swirling.

Finally it was the end. Cory stood in the command post across from the main square.

"If we don't hear back from them soon it means they're all gone, or all dead," the voice crackled out. No one moved in that sandbagged stone room. Two minutes passed and then four.

"I think we've got 'em all," said the voice on the radio.

"That's the last of 'em." The place erupted in cheers and whistles.

Reg went out to the well where four or five soldiers had dropped their weapons and were pulling up water and throwing it on their faces. Cory watched as he meticulously wrote their names in his notebook. Then he looked up, as if he'd heard a sound. He seemed to be watching a movement, down at the end of the clogged street. He walked away from the well, forward, as if to investigate. She lifted the heavy Speed Graphic, peering into its depths. Time seemed to wait for her.

The new silence cracked then. The soldiers threw themselves into the rubble beside the well. Reg looked up over his head, unsurprised, his right arm thrown across his brow as a protection against the weak sun. He remained standing and the grenade came down just in front of him, as if it were aimed. A direct hit.

They packed him into the ambulance, the last of their wounded. Cory stood by his side, clutching his hand.

"You can't go, I need you." She hadn't sobbed aloud since after Tyke was born but she did now.

He was conscious, but his voice came from far away.

"I'll just be out a little while. I'll see you at the next place."

She wondered what he meant by "the next place."

Tyke remembered Christmas, 1944. He was four-and-a-half years old. He'd been at his grandmother's in town. It was almost New Year's Eve, and he was going home to

Marge's house on the island in St. Pierre's scoot from Pointe au Baril Station. Tyke was frightened of the scoot. It had square sides and a tendency to tip on turns. But the ice wasn't good enough yet for the truck; there were still patches of open water. He had to wear special earmuffs to block the sound of the motor. The woman in the next seat shouted at him, so he had to shift the ear muffs to hear.

"I see your mother's been in Ortona," said the woman. "Saw the pictures in the paper."

Tyke nodded. He did not know what Ortona was, but he knew about her photographs in the paper. The scoot went past all the summer landmarks, covered with snow. Tyke could recognize the main channel, Blueberry Island, and the jumping rocks. In the whiteness and the sun the woman's face exploded in shards of light, which pained his eyes. He squinted. She had a pointy nose and bright red lips and her eyes seemed to take him all in.

"And don't worry, she won't get hurt. She'll come back," said the woman kindly.

Tyke turned away. He had never imagined before that she wouldn't, though he knew soldiers got killed. His mother wasn't a soldier, was she? He had a thought, and turned to this stranger, who didn't look like anyone he knew who came out to the islands in winter, not with that kind of shiny mouth, and asked, "Do you know her?"

"I do," she said. "And I know you, too. I'm Lydia del Zotto and I sell her photographs, and I've come out to see how you are because she asked me to."

Memory was a door that opened, a door that let in the

cold wind. The scoot turned around Round Island and headed across the open stretch leading toward the inside channel. He was afraid, suddenly. In winter the wind from the open gouges out waves that freeze solid as they arch. It tears the hair from your scalp, and turns your legs to blocks of ice.

A week before, Tyke had done this journey backward: He had gone with St. Pierre to the train and down to Parry Sound. She had been waiting for him, Grandmother Eliza in her fashionable black coat, her face screwed into something between anger and pity, the low sun casting her dark shadow across the snow at the station. "Your mother did not send you a letter for Christmas?" she accused, as if both he and his mother had done something wrong.

Tyke jumped off the platform crying and ran from her. After that he found himself on Eliza's thin slippery lap in the parlour of her home.

"She's not a bad girl, your mother," his grandmother told him, her own face wet with tears. "But she would do just as she pleased, she always would. Still she loves you, son, in her way."

The cold wind from the open blew that day, and the next. Then Eliza said, "A package came for you. She couldn't get you a present, but she sent you these." Inside were lots of newspapers with photographs by Corinne Ditchburn.

Tyke saw the photographs. Men charging down narrow lane-ways, houses without roofs. Tanks and guns and piles of stones in the street.

"Where is my mother?"

"You can't see her, because she's behind the camera. You're seeing what she saw."

More than anything, to Tyke his mother had been his physical world, the alive part. Legs on which he had pulled himself up to standing. A warm back against which he slept in his backpack while she hiked; a hip on which he could ride, arms into which he leapt from a dead run. He knew her movements even in the darkroom, in the barest available light, the quick, deliberate way she dipped the photographic paper in its bath, then lifted her lean arms, pegging the prints to the line.

When she left him, a door opened and the world rushed at him before he was ready to block it. He hid a lot, that year, when he was four, in the trees, behind the fallen logs, where the old sheds gently rotted back to earth behind the hotel. In hiding, he memorized the way his mother looked, her narrowed eyes sizing up a negative, her long-fingered hands spread on the hips of her trousers; the way she bent to scoop him up when he ran at her. Every picture he had of her in his mind he called up, and gazed at, and tried to put himself inside. He was cold, and he cried in the night.

Marge held him, then, and told him he would get stronger, that he would be a man as strong as a bear because he had learned to live with missing his mother.

Now, when he saw the pictures of Ortona, he was back with her, beside her, inside her. He could see with her eyes. He could feel his mother's fear, and see her hand shake as she held the camera.

Eliza gave Tyke the newspaper. Tyke kept it under his pillow for Christmas week. So when the woman riding in the scoot said to Tyke, "I saw the pictures of Ortona. Don't worry, she won't get hurt," Tyke wondered how she knew that he was hiding the pictures in his knapsack. He would not let her take them away and sell them, either.

Finally the scoot roared with its cockscomb of snow into Manitou Bay and he saw Marge's cabin under its hat of snow. Lydia del Zotto stayed for two days and taught him how to play gin rummy. If this was where his mother sent her friends to see him, Tyke reasoned, then he'd better be there. He made up his mind that he would not leave Marge's again until his mother came home.

"I remember these," said Tyke, when they came to the pictures of Ortona. "You sent me clippings that Christmas I was four. Your mother thought it was a strange present."

"It was maybe all I could do at the time. I had no other way of communicating."

Cory wasn't fighting him any more, that was the good part. She waited, expectant, to see what each box brought back. Their mutual task had become a kind of truce. At any moment it could break down, but it kept them at the table.

"More soldier boys," said Tyke cheerily as he lifted the veiling page off this new batch.

"Oh yes, an inexhaustible supply."

She was drinking scotch from a crystal glass. Her eyesight was bad now, worsening. And she had a virus, which made her cough. She hated to be sick. Her way of dealing with it was to blame the doctors: "Flaming idiots, the whole lot of them." This in itself was invigorating, and finally, the illness had the effect of keeping her oddly merry.

"One thing about you, Mother, you never say they were the best years of your life."

"I *detest* people who say that! Profiteering from the war."

"Why do they say it?"

"Because it was. It *was* for them." She took a pensive swallow. Tyke raised his own glass. "You see, there are some people who go through life like sleepwalkers. They're thick, and loutish, and it takes an enormous overdose of sensation to wake them up to life. And for those people war is a great adventure, because it is so extreme that even they can finally feel. But for people who are already sensate, you know, who feel a little more, it is a catastrophe."

"A *catastrophe*. In every way?"

She turned her head sharply. She was looking at him but he could not tell if she were seeing him. "Are you asking me where I'd have been without it? I have no idea. I can't play that game. I suppose it made me. But then if it hadn't been war I'd run off to, it would have been something else."

He looked at the young men in the photographs, halfway between the age he'd been then, and the age she'd been.

"Do you suppose I was a bad mother? I know Eliza thought so."

"She didn't," said Tyke.

Cory's eyes welled with tears. She was like that now. You never knew what would cut through her defences. "What do you think? That's more important."

"What do I think?" He became arch. "I think you're marvellous, dear. But of course, you screwed up. On this one. The mother thing."

A tear had spilled over and now sat, glittering, on her withered cheek. "You know what Albert used to say," she began shakily. Tyke hated it when she cried. He always had. He produced a handkerchief and wiped the tear away. "What did he say, Mother?"

"He said I needed to 'screw up,' as you put it. He said it was the great artistic principle. That I was afraid of it, of cracking open, of being terribly wrong, of looking on the worst I could do. He said if I didn't let myself fuck up then I'd never be great."

"Well, there you are. You're great, and I'm the proof."

She stood, wanting to move. She wanted to go to the little parkette where the metal deer cutouts stood amongst squat pines. The deer always incited her scorn but he noticed she was energized by the confrontation with this urban parody of the wild. She would not take his arm but walked, spindly, without a hint of shuffle, though he knew she could not see where she put her feet.

"Do you know what Tom Thomson used to do? He had an old copper tub full of water at his knee in the studio over there on Severn." She gestured with her hand; it was just around the corner. "He sat with his paddle and dipped it in and he paddled sometimes, for an hour."

"I don't believe it," said Tyke.

"Well, he did. My father took me to see him when I was a girl. My father sketched, you know."

Outside the house they were hit by a roar of traffic heading down valley through the Rosedale Ravine.

They were halfway through their task. Portfolio boxes remained stacked beside the pine table, dozens of them still locked. Tyke wondered if memory itself was made that way, of a series of closed portfolio cases, each with its key; if locked inside were images delicately laid one on top of the other, a sheet of onion skin between, each scene vivid and frozen and separated from the others: a pressed flower, a waxed leaf.

His memory was not so discrete; it was fluid. His images escaped their boundaries, at times, and became polluted with other memories, their disposition thus changing. He knew this process to be going on, without being able to stop it. For instance, he remembered his mother's lover Jimmie as being stern, cold and even frightening, while at the same time he remembered Jimmie carrying him on his back through the undergrowth behind the Manitou, hooting and laughing and crashing through the pine trees in pursuit of some other boy who'd been designated the wild bear. This first memory had no location, it floated on the surface, the sharp-beaked, black-eyed profile, the long ponytail, Jimmie looking down the sight of his gun. The second memory had location, but in it Jimmie had no face, he simply knew it was Jimmie.

In the same way, when he began to bring his lovers to Cory, he remembered, or thought he remembered, that she did her silent routine, pressing her lips together and brooding in corners. However, other scenes fought their way to the surface: Cory and the lovely Lily from his mushroom co-op, laughing until they peed their pants while gutting the fish Tyke caught.

He dared to take her arm as they crossed Park Street. The tiny parkette was empty but for the pigeons and a scattering of newspapers flying around the hooves of the metal deer. She felt behind her for the seat of the bench and then backed up to sit on it.

"That's all it was, a life in pictures," Cory said, cranky at retrospective, at seeing her life in hindsight, mostly at being reminded that so much was *behind* her. But she had conveniently forgotten that she had spoken, for hours, about the war. Now Tyke understood something, which was that Cory needed these words, this audience, this prodding.

A life in pictures, a life of split seconds needed synthesis, didn't it? How had Cory got this far, this old, on the theory that all that counted were the flashpoints, those captioned, black and white gestures that she trapped in her lens and printed with light?

If Tyke had to slice his memories and lie them on sheets of cardboard, he would not know where the truth lay either.

In the parkette they met up with the metal deer. They

were as thin as a piece of paper. "Talk about slice of life," he muttered.

She snorted. "How do these photographs feel to you? True? Or like traps? I feel they attack me," she said.

"And you fight back?"

"I have to fight back."

"People always said your pictures were strong."

"Now they seem too strong, even for me. They're shouting, they're drowning out the other voices I want to hear. They steal all the saying there is about my life. I can't," she said, her cloudy eyes lowered to the ground, "stand by them. I can't be sure," she said.

"You can't be sure what?"

"I can't be sure they're true. They are a thirty-year-old's photographs. I have an eighty-five-year-old's mind. I remember shots I didn't get."

Tyke loved his mother then. He loved her for fighting back. He could say to the curator, that Maida Kirk who called so regularly now, asking how it was going, he could say with great pride, that Cory Ditchburn was never easy. She never went along with orthodoxies, not even her own.

He laughed out loud there in the ridiculous parkette where the metal slivers of deer trembled in the blasts of city air tunneled through the high-rises.

"What's so funny?" she said, though she had already caught the chuckles, because it was contagious.

"You are," he said. She lifted her fist and punched him in the shoulder.

"*You* are!"

Tyke felt the laughter loosen the muscles in his back and a shiver of delight travel up the nape of his neck. How perverse she was, but how right, to choose allegiance to this other truth, this uncaptured and uncollected moment, which dwelt in the mind all these years, which faded, grew, was coloured, sullied, filtered through a lifetime, but which was never erased, and finally, now, might come to the surface. She had not frozen on the shutter's impulse; only her subject had done that. And perhaps her son.

There was something cold in Cory, and yet — because of those flashes of excoriating self-revelation, because of that rough, determined truth-telling — she was a woman for whom many people, too many people, felt the most passionate love and ownership. Of course, thought Tyke, you can add me to the list.

He watched her face, itself a retrospective. Grown crafty with age, but childlike too, she was unable to entirely disguise the feelings that ran under the surface. Anger, at being invaded, and through the auspices of her son; pride in having her work praised; a struggle to discover remnants of truth tucked up in all these retained memories, and their obverse, the images in boxes. All this but most of all letting go, letting the shell slip away, the shell she'd had for war, for Albert, and forever.

They were back in the studio.

"I'll give you an example. This one," she said, pointing at the picture of Reg at the well in Ortona. "You see, it was not like that. Not like that at all."

"How was it, then?"

She went alert, silent. Before she ever went to war, she'd dreamed explosions. At the munitions plant, she knew those cordite straws she cut and sifted would pack into a gun barrel — but she thought they would propel the world out of darkness and into the light.

She had loved the acrid smell of the cordite. It was invasive. It got up your nose, everywhere. Crumbled cordite was shed all over the plant. They wore it in their eyelashes like stardust. They blessed their foreheads with nitroglycerin every day they didn't work, to keep up their exposure. If they didn't, the headaches came.

They never thought they were making death. Not until the night the TNT shed exploded, and in the darkness she searched the run-off ditch for bodies. When she found one — her first war casualty in Nobel, Ontario — she raised the camera and took him prisoner.

In Europe she wore her camera like a shield. She could not be hurt because she was charged with a task. She was there, Kilroy, her name scrawled on the wall. Corinne Ditchburn pressed this shutter.

Tracer bullets made a white arc on the black sky, as if a razor had sliced the dome and let in a hairline of heaven. You thought of what was beyond — yes, even she did, raised a Methodist and in permanent rebellion from the otherworldly. But when bombs hit it was so bright your eyes went black. When you opened them, seconds or maybe years later, you could only see white — smoke, dust, refractions. Sound travelled more slowly, ricocheting from stone walls and mountainsides, arriving at last disconnected from its origin. Could she explain to her son that she felt at peace there? She'd already learned this violence; it felt like home.

Blind, deaf, they crouched in the low-ceiling world below explosions. Some new world was being born overhead, licked with fire, swaddled in smoke and thunder. The soldiers became mud. They lay waiting to die, even hoping for it, something quick, manageable, a respite. Cory knew that she wouldn't die, that when the darkness seeped off, the smoke had blown past, and the world she knew was gone, she'd pick up the dead, and begin again.

"The photograph tells a different story, sometimes."

"How?"

"Well, to start with," — her eyes took a sudden sharp focus, but she wasn't looking outward, she was concentrating — "there he was. The German whose grenade got Reg."

To the far right of the photograph, near the edge of the square where the street was blocked by an abandoned tank, the just visible bent forearm, and the top of a helmet. "Can you see it? The last German in town. Nobody knew where that grenade came from. He must have crawled away in the confusion, after Reg was hit. We never found him. But the camera saw it."

"And so?"

"And so," she said, "the photograph shows you this was a planned attack. What it felt like was the stupidest, most random bolt out of the blue, striking Reg down the minute we'd finally relaxed. What I saw was him flying through the air, coming down to land like a broken sack of bones. I never thought he'd live."

"So the photograph is false?"

"No," she said. "But it makes my memory speak, finally. What I knew then, but I couldn't let myself know, was that Reg *saw* the last German. He knew something was coming, and he walked right out to meet it."

Chapter Twenty-Four

FIGURE 24

Corinne Ditchburn

The Guinea Pig Club,
Queen Victoria Hospital

1944
East Grinstead, Surrey
Gelatin silver, 23 x 35 cm
Express Newspapers

After Ortona, Ditchburn began to drop her insistence on being at the front. As much courage was needed to depict the "new world" left by war as it did to face what is known in today's parlance as "the bang-bang." This photograph of soldiers who have suffered facial burns and disfiguring injuries brings us face to face with what no one wanted to see, after the heroics.

"HERE'S THE GIRL PHOTOGRAPHER," SAID THE OWNER OF THE Soho trattoria when she went in for lunch. Soldiers would wave to her, talk to her as if they knew her, as if she were one of them. "Is it true, Miss Ditchburn, that you never felt fear?" asked a woman who stood behind her in the post-office line. How did she recognize Cory? Perhaps she read the return address on the letter she sent home.

The Stooks brothers had her pages from the *Express* tacked up on the ends of their shelves and when she went in to the warehouse under the railway overpass, they blushed and went all formal.

"Miss Ditchburn has dropped in," called George to Harry.

"Oh, Miss Ditchburn, what a *pleasure*."

They surveyed her, rocking on their heels. Several dismantled radio sets lay on the counter. There was a bird's nest of copper wire there too, and a stack of order forms, curling in the humidity.

"You've made a name for yourself. You can't go back now, can you?" said George. "Got to see it through."

She wanted them to call her "colonial lady" again, and advise her to use lots of film. But now they stood in awe of her and would give no advice. They had no small talk and there was nothing to say.

London was being bombed again. Now it was the doodle-bugs, the unmanned missiles that came down with their heinous cry, flew along the street, and hit at random. It was almost a relief to feel she was at risk again. Sometimes the smell of cordite woke her in the night, and she saw the November sky over Nobel, that dove-grey, stone-cold layer of cloud, and the flame bursting out from under the eaves of the TNT shed. She saw the shock of it run down the trees and force the roots up through the shallow soil, the way a lightning strike can do. And again she was shouting over the barking of dogs and digging in the snow-laden bushes for her first war casualty.

Sometimes, after a night drinking in Soho, she saw ahead of her in the crowd on Oxford Street Red Deer's impossible lanky legs, his loping slow walk, which carried him faster than anyone could hurry. She'd be certain, from the tilt of his back, that it was him, and she'd quicken her pace, push through the standing throngs at the traffic lights, and race across Regent Street, dodging the homeward-turning barrows and the news vendors. Finally she would come up beside the boy. He'd be a Texan, maybe, sympathetic but uninterested in her stammered tale about her friend who'd been hit —

Well, died actually. At this point the Texan would swing his long arm and give her shoulders a squeeze and offer to buy her a drink.

Because the dead don't go away, just like that, she discovered. Their faces, their silhouettes, and the particular sound their throat and larynx makes are peculiar in nature, and they have made a place for themselves on earth. Accustomed to seeing or hearing this essence we continue to for a time, until at last we are ready to forget.

Cory was not ready. Her eyes had memorized Red Deer's long neck, the arrowhead of his Adam's apple, the shallow cheekbones and wide pale lips, the light blue eyes, which had no shading, only candour. And her eyes conjured him, amongst the living. Her ears tricked her and played his voice amongst the cacophony of the ruthless living. Each time she fell for it, sprung out of her everyday by thoughts of him, alive, before her, within reach.

Cory's editor sent her down to East Grinstead in Surrey, where a surgeon was putting the faces back on men who'd been burned.

"Watch out. It's where they sent Virginia Woolf when she went mad," Albert said. "Of course it only made her worse."

"They've come along to the point where they can go down into town," said the surgeon. "Try themselves out on the population."

In the massive foyer of the Queen Victoria Hospital, Cory lifted the camera to hide her eyes. For once it did not protect her. There were men without lips and eyelashes, men with half a face. There were men whose eyes were gone, behind a gauze of whited skin. Men whose entire body surface was clotted, tortured with the bulges and knots of scar tissue. The method was to take men whose skin was gone, and soak them in acid baths. The acid, though painful, stimulated growth. The new skin, when it came, was pink and rubbery and without lines. The men called themselves the Guinea Pig Club. A few of the guinea pigs laughed and talked. But most were silent, and you could not find any expression on what remained of their faces.

"They're so much better than when they came in, you see," said the doctor. "But they have to get used to the fact that they don't look normal. They never will."

"But surely the local people are used to it by now?" said Cory.

"The people of East Grinstead? They know what we're doing. But get used to it? I don't think so. You see, each man is so very different."

Cory let the camera fall.

"How can you let me take these pictures?" she said.

"You photographed the combat, am I correct?"

"That was different."

"There, of course, you have the excitement of action."

"It's not exciting. It's terrifying."

"Yes of course, but there is the adrenaline of the fight, the illusion of winning, at least." The doctor's face was smooth and clear. Ugliness or grief, all the reconstructed faces in the world were not going to jar him, and he didn't need a camera to be composed.

"How would they feel, to see their picture in the *Daily Express*?"

"It's no worse than a mirror. No pun intended." He laughed.

"Do any of them wish they'd died?"

"A few. Especially the ones who were beautiful. But they get over it. They prefer, finally, to be alive. And then they discover someone else is worse. They're not alone."

The doctor waited, and watched. Cory kept her camera at the level of her chest.

"Please, take pictures. They feel, and with some justification, that the world does not want to see them. That people are not prepared for the consequences. But we must prepare. This is what will remain, when the drama is passed. This is what we have made. They are the new world."

Cory walked ahead of the men down the winding, green-edged road. It was spring, and the bushes were full of twittering birds, the ponds edged with bluebells. There was one man in a wheelchair. The man pushing him had no chin; his face ended with the bottom of his nose, then slanted inward to his collar bone. His mouth was a receding hole. He bent over his chair-bound friend, whose arms drew parabolas in the air, the two of them deep in debate. Though she couldn't hear what they were saying, the angles of their heads showed that a joke had been made, that someone was laughing.

The little parade turned onto the High Street, its destination the tea shop. Pubs were out of bounds. A beer might loosen up the guinea pigs or the townsfolk to the point where someone regretted it.

Reg was the one she never saw in dreams. She remembered Reg lifting a cup beside the well, not knowing that what he was about to drink was all-but-death, and then the way he looked up, saw something coming, and stepped forward into it, away from the others. He'd sustained a head and back injury that would have kept any sane man out of the war for good but only stopped Reg for five months. Like the men he wrote about, he wanted to see it through. He was convalescing at Watford.

First he begged her not to come to see him, and then he begged her to come.

"I've given you no warning," she said, as she put her head into his room.

"You don't need to," Reg said. He didn't sound surprised. "I knew you'd be along some day."

He dressed and they sat over a low tea table overlooking a garden, which fell away in stages to the road below. She told him he looked better than the burn victims.

"If you're interested in beauty," he said, "then you must be fascinated by its opposite."

"Who said I was interested in beauty?"

"You didn't have to say. Your war was so handsome. You found the shape, the light, the position for heroics. It's what I had against you. If I had anything," he said. Then, after a pause, "other than the fact that you wouldn't have me."

Her heart thudded. Move on, she thought, move on quickly.

"How long will you stay here?"

"Not much longer. I hardly merit medical attention now. You see, I am physically whole. I can walk. It's only —" he tried to move his arm and wrist in circles. "I can't do this. Write."

He stood to shake her hand as she left.

"You'll be back," she said. "We'll be together."

He ducked his chin in the way he had, half an acknowledgment and half an evasion.

Because it was near East Grinstead, on the way home Cory revisited the Stable Cottage, where Albert and Liss had repaired to escape the doodlebugs.

Liss removed the tangle of camera bag straps from Cory's shoulder while, as usual, Albert stood back, smiling.

"I'm so pleased," he said. "I'm so pleased you're here."

The Stable Cottage was as she remembered it, except more crowded. Tea sprang from the spout of the tea pot into the yellow French cups with the blue rim. Cory tucked her feet under her on the sofa. She noticed that Liss had re-covered it in canvas, and said so, but that gave Albert the opportunity to accuse his wife of stealing his materials so that he couldn't paint. As they bickered, Cory tasted her tea and felt the comfort enter her belly.

"We saved your photographs from the *Express*," said Liss. "Albert would run down to the newsagent as soon as the papers came in. And if they didn't have one he'd be so cross —"

"Were there any you liked?"

Albert glared at his wife before answering.

"I liked the soldier reading the Bible with his cowboy boots propped up against the collapsed stone wall."

"That was my accompanying officer in Ortona."

Immediately Albert's eyes went black and dull as arrowheads. "Did you fuck him?"

Liss picked up her needlepoint and put on the look that said that she was an artist's spouse, listening to the music that fed her soul. "You don't need to answer, Cory."

Cory's face heated up. Every time he turned on her she was taken by surprise. Why could she not learn to expect it, and to know it for what it was? To have Liss taking her side made her feel ill.

"War, war," Albert roared. "I saw it all in 1914, 1915, 1917, and tell me what good it ever did for me? Death and destruction are the easiest things in the world to make your subject. That's what you don't understand. It's all laid out for you. Automatic. The work's done. The odds are so much in your favour you can't lose. You think you've travelled to some new frontier. You haven't."

Liss lifted the teapot, felt that it was light, and signalled silently that she would go to refill it. The two combatants were left staring at one another. Albert took three silent steps toward Cory, slid his arm under her buttocks, squeezed her, and then kissed her roughly on the mouth. She couldn't speak.

> *Dear Albert —*
> *I sleep in dreams of you —*
> *I cringe in my damp bag under dripping canvas and hug to myself the image of the white flag of hair on your chest. I love you. I hate you.*

Had their love affair become a series of silent prayers, a form of religion?

> *I hate your cunning, and your confidence that you can slay my resistance, even my decency. Stop! your wife is listening. See — only your desire to protect yourself stops you from going further. Watch out! There will be a point when even Liss has to react.*

Liss came back into the room with the teapot, her plait newly drawn over her shoulder in such determined repose that Cory had to believe she had waited, listening, for a few seconds outside the doorway, and then adjusted the plait, moistened her lips, and entered. Albert stepped away.

They made a bed for Cory on the sofa, and readied themselves for their night stroll.

"I shall miss all these lighting effects when it's over," he said. "A night sky won't be the same without tracers and flares and duelling ghostly bombers."

Cory lay as she had so often lain, wide awake in the sitting room under Liss's coverlet. She was warm and dry. Mangled bodies troubled her closed eyes, but no more than usual, and in a few minutes she banished them, and slept.

Albert opened the door to the sitting room. Without warning he was on her, his harsh prickly face unwelcome against her breast. He began to speak. It was as if he were drunk, but there was nothing on his breath.

"I'm so dreadfully sorry, I treat you abominably, there's no excuse for it, absolutely none. But you don't know how I suffered, you in tents with all those boys. They're mad for sex, you know, when they're dying all around, it's a known fact." He pulled up her nightgown.

She tried to shift him off.

"You're absolutely wrong, it's not like that."

His practised fingers rolled her nipples.

"Albert, I can't do this. Not with Liss right here."

"What difference does it make?" he mumbled, his mouth full of breast. "You do it everywhere else."

She was shamed. Her stomach began to contract, her hips to lift obediently with the small of his hand.

Silent now, Albert fitted himself into her and began to thrust. She gave up resisting. They were licked by some kind of fire, and forgot everything but this avidity. Silence was their only restraint, until they'd tried every remembered way, and they were wet, slippery, smelling of mingled sweat and musk as they tried to finish it. Finally it was over and the sofa was wet, the coverlet twisted and tangled, their limbs limp and sticky. Without another word Albert extricated himself and padded to the loo. Cory lay still until she heard him go through the doorway into Liss's room. Then she got up to wash. In the bathroom she vomited. Never again, she swore. Not in Liss's house.

In the morning Cory was exhausted. Liss was sympathetic.

"Sometimes in the thick of it we endure more than we actually can. Then later the terror returns," she said.

She smiled at Cory and in her eyes there was nothing, absolutely nothing to be seen.

Albert's cigarette like an angry red fly dotted the air between them in the dusky studio. "Look what you've printed there. It's just a tank. A dumb, actual tank with nothing more to claim than the fact of its existence. A tank-tank. You have taken its photograph; therefore it is assumed to have significance. This is precisely what I have against photography, and what your little art shares with the even blacker art of newspapering."

"This is not a tank. It is a photograph of a tank. It begins with me."

"You speak as if people were in fact interested in what you think! What you feel! As if you were a great artist! When all you are is the vulgar man on the spot with a camera."

"Maybe you don't have to be a great artist for people to be interested in how you feel," she said mildly.

He looked astonished and his chest swelled up like a bellows.

"Of course you must. Otherwise what will we have? All sorts of minor characters running around filling every corner of the world with their beastly little impressions. No, no, no. It's too easy." He scoffed. "Anyway why should we be interested in your thoughts about a tank?"

"'The most objective image comes from the most personal approach.'"

Albert roared with laughter. "Now the schoolteacher from Parry Sound is going to go quoting Goethe to me."

Cory paced around the studio. She would stand up to him, she would.

"The only thing that gets you noticed, Cory," Albert said, as if kindly, "is that you get the photograph first and print it first. That, I admit, in a national emergency, is a useful tendency. But you must understand that your picture is not important; the war is. Everything is overwhelmed by war."

"I can agree with you," said Cory as if she too were conciliatory, "that photographs are all about time. The instant it has been exposed, the instant it will be developed —"

Albert sneered. "You can add to that the instant — and it will only *be* an instant — the very brief instant when you will have the public's attention. What is so quickly produced will be just as quickly rejected. A painting must be *regarded* with attention, to allow its depth to be perceived. The trouble with photography is it has no depth. It's two dimensional. And furthermore, too many people will look at it for too little time."

"I suppose now you're going to come out against the printing press, as well? All those 'minor little people' cluttering up the world with their ideas?"

Albert blew out an untidy circle of smoke.

"Oh, Cory, let's face it. All your photographs do is sell papers. That's what they're for. To make money for Max Aitken Lord Beaverbrook."

Cory wanted to cry, which would end this, but she couldn't give him the satisfaction. "Oh, Albert," she said, finally, "why are you so angry with me?"

"Because you're a stupid girl and you won't learn!"

Until now she'd never dared to speak the truth. But now she did.

"If I didn't know you better I'd think you were jealous." She expected an explosion. She sneaked a glance at him. With a great show of serenity he pulled his cigarette out of his mouth and looked at it as if it were something entirely foreign.

"Is it true? Are you? Because you feel old, and passed over? Do you hate my photographs because they're all you can 'see' of that war?"

The silence grew more ominous. By now she was pleading.

"I learned to see from you, it's true. But something else has happened in this war. The art that I practise has become very powerful. You're right: It's not really me anyone wants. Photography is for the new world."

He fell silent. It was the worst thing he could do to her, withdraw. Even in their most vicious jousts Cory was exhilarated by the irresistible pull of his mind, the way they spoke to each other, from the bottom of some well where no voice had penetrated, nothing but pale echoes had issued, before Albert came into her life. She waited.

He walked to the top of the stairs, poised to leave. "Darling of the press!" he called out dismissively. "They love you because you are one of them. It's all about the press making itself into demigods. You've fallen for it. Fallen for your employer's own publicity stunts."

"Oh, Max! I'm so sick of the way you use him as an excuse for everything that ever goes wrong."

Albert's exit was arrested.

Cory danced in the studio with rage. "That's right. If your work doesn't sell, if the war goes on too long, if the public's taste changes, blame Beaverbrook, press baron. If your protégée has a success, blame Beaverbrook."

She retreated in tears to the toilet off the studio. It was

more painful for Cory to see Albert ridiculous than to have him ridicule her. She still needed him to be great, to be above her, to be right and true and admirable. Shut inside, she heard Albert cross back to his desk: He had not gone back to Liss. She washed her face with cold water and came out the door.

"Max is wrong about most things," she said, conciliatory.

"The man is simple-minded. But we're entering a simple-minded age. He's a harbinger."

"He never actually made my career, either. He just gave me a chance." This was mostly what Albert hated Max for, of course, his championing of Cory.

"You weren't ready. All this came too soon," he said, restored to his jovial self as he toyed with brushes and paint. "No matter. No matter. You're your own woman now. And now you have the gleam in your eye, to please the public, to make yourself rich. And you'll leave your old Albert, your old bear."

She clambered through the stacked canvases then to stand before him, draw him upward, entice him to make love. And love was the same, a practised thing. They knew how to do it so well.

She should have known. Whenever Albert attacked her it was out of guilt, and she would soon discover why. This time it was the portrait.

Cory met Aunt Eunice after her shift serving tea at the Churchill Club in the Houses of Parliament. They set off together for home along the Embankment, there to make a meal of their rations.

It was September, 1944. Those who were still living in London regarded themselves as survivors against ever-increasing odds. Although the big bombing raids were over, the harassment of the population continued through other means, which, depending on one's wants, were either physically terrifying, or simply a drain on one's spirit. No beer in the pub, a bad egg once a month for rations, or the simple death of friendship, because one was afraid to go across town of an evening: You could take your pick.

Aunt Eunice reacted to privations with a spirited anger, as if the enemy were attempting to spite her personally, and had made a study of her needs in order to frustrate them in particular.

"There's no need, simply no need to add an uncivil tongue to the lashings of wartime life," Eunice was saying. One of the other women working in the club had made the mistake of telling her she got up too slowly from her chair.

"It's the wretched hips," said Eunice. "They don't bend any more. Not that I'd tell her that."

"What did you tell her, then?"

"I told her to mind her manners, but I can't see she'll ever change her style. She's a disagreeable little tramp, Lady Whatever, like it or not that's all she is."

The dirty Thames sloshed against the walls of the Embankment under Cory's feet. The blackouts were over, and now a dim-out had taken their place. So, although night would soon fall, there were feeble lights coming from overhead standards. The wind assailed them as it moved up the Thames. She turned her shoulder to it and walked backward, breaking the blast, and also allowing herself a lingering view of her beloved Westminster. Into the darkening sky the tower of Big Ben rose like an exclamation mark, and the fine gothic points of the Houses of Parliament and the Cathedral danced an irregular but stately tune.

"You could give it up and move out to the country, Aunt Eunice. Certainly no one would call you a coward."

"What? And not make it to the end?" she said. "I don't know how you can suggest such a thing. I've been in London since this war began and I'll be here when it ends." She strode facing the wind, its teeth drawing her hair away from her high forehead and temples like a fine comb. She led with her chin and the long arms and legs, which swung forward, step after step, as if she were on parade.

"In fact, one might even argue I've seen more action than you," she said, "simply by staying home."

It was an echo of what Marge had told her, the day they sat drinking in the ice fishing hut. "You'll find more danger by staying home."

"One might," she said mildly. She never felt inclined to argue when Eunice told her what, from other lips, would have caused great offence. Was it because, she wondered, stealing a look at the great grey profile — high, firm cheekbones, cavernous cheeks, the chin that pushed forward like a small shovel — she knew Eunice, despite her gruffness, was loyal?

"You might at least have the courtesy to disagree," said Eunice tartly. "You make me feel as if I am of no account at all."

"You're tired," said Cory.

"Of course, I'm not."

"What do you eat?"

Taking care of her aunt was difficult because the woman refused to be taken care of. Cory suspected she existed on the scraps of sandwiches she took off plates at the Churchill Club, and had nothing in her house at all. Tonight she would find a way to examine the inside of the icebox and to make sure that the cats were not drinking whatever milk Eunice managed to get.

"I eat," said Eunice.

"There's talk of standing down the Home Guard," Cory said cautiously. "Perhaps Leary will come back."

"Leary!" Eunice said, as if speaking of one who had passed on to Elysian fields. Cory understood. The very idea of Leary seemed to come from another era altogether, an era of scones with cream, and ruffled aprons, and a warm parlour with logs on the grate.

Tired of tripping backward, with reluctance Cory turned her face into the grimy wind. When they reached Chelsea they could turn, at least, northward and away from its blast. It was nearly dark when they strode into Eunice's row. The old orange London aura was troubled with surges of fog and murk, and against a sky of this disagreeable blend of colours the ravaged housetops looked angry and bleak. But Eunice brightened as they turned up her walk: The house she'd occupied all this time, sitting out her own private siege, had become her partner in defiance. There was no light on, but a brightness came from within; the blackout curtains had been taken off, or were not drawn, and the unaccustomed vision of lace curtains behind the several-times-replaced glass offered hope.

Eunice reached into her bag for the keys. Cory mounted the walk behind her, breathing the night air for a few seconds longer before she climbed the step. "One reason I'm not dying is that I know, when this war is over, they'll come up with some cure for my arthritis and then I'll be able to bend my knees and bend over at my hips again. We can light some candles," Eunice said, "and I'll tuck you in with a few of these little sandwiches I've managed to save —"

"I knew it," muttered Cory.

"— and then you must tell me everything, everything you've been up to since —"

There was a sudden gap in the air, as if some large spirit had joined them, or departed, leaving in its wake a gulf, which sound and wind and a massive flare of light then rushed to fill. Cory, nerves trained in Italy, hit the ground on the other side of the stair just in time to see the front door of Eunice's house burst out of its frame foursquare to the corners, scoop Eunice up on its white expanse, and disappear.

Cory lay there, her face pressed into the cool fragrant

grass, for perhaps ten seconds. There were no more projectiles overhead, only a serious crackling sound somewhere on the other side of the house, and silence. She knew what had happened. A V2 bomb had landed, presumably in the back garden, and the force of the explosion had forced the door out the front of the house. The V1s, or doodlebugs, had terrorized people because they were preceded by a great whining tooth-grinding sound. But the V2s came down without warning, in silence, which was worse, Cory thought. She lay with her nose pressed into the grass, almost forgetting that she needed to rise and find out what had become of her aunt, carried off on that door.

Yet she could summon no sense of urgency for this task. She dreamed a little, of the garden, which must now be in ruins, of the tea table there, the door off the entrance, which led to the pantry where Leary had presided. They were talking about Leary, weren't they? And she realized that she was suffering some kind of shock. She found her feet, took a minute to get herself balanced on them, and then set off toward the street, looking for the white door, which would surely show up well even in this gloom, and for her aunt's sensible navy coat upon it.

"Aunt Eunice!" Cory called. "Aunt Eunice, where are you?"

There seemed to be no one about, as she went along the street. But then there hadn't been for months, had there? London was emptied, those people who still lived here entrenched in whatever niche they had found, whatever represented safety to them.

"Aunt Eunice!" she called. There was nothing on the street, and very little damage, either. She looked back and saw the dark entrance to Eunice's house yawning. How she would hate it, having lost her front door to the public like that! And then she began to blubber, realizing that Eunice herself might be lost.

She saw no white rectangle, no navy trench coat, and the gloom settled lower over the bricks and stones of the Chelsea street. She redoubled her steps, back toward the house. Definitely, the white door that had been there only minutes before was gone. And Eunice too, who had been reaching into her handbag to unlock this door, was most decidedly wiped off the landscape.

The white curtains fluttered in the parlour window: A breeze was moving through. At the back of the house was a glow, something burning in the garden, no doubt. Where was the vicar, across the way? The firemen?

"Eunice," she called again, turning to the road. "Where are you?" Horrible images came to her mind. She might be impaled on any of these tall, spiked wrought-iron fences, which she had been so proud to save from the campaign to raise metal for aircraft. She might have flown over the housetops, her coat inflated with wind, her front door a magic carpet. She might be crushed somewhere, against a wall, the door slammed on her with a finality — goodbye and good night!

No, no, no, Cory howled, and began to run in circles like someone's little dog, around the bricked-in tree roots, the curved line of the wrought-iron fence, up and down the neighbours' steps, and across the darkened road. There was no place for a door to go, except upward, and why would it do that? No, she was wrong, the door could have flown free of the road itself and its phalanx of houses, into one of the gaps created by the real bombs of earlier war days, into this watery hole, for instance, which used to be Number Twelve. She peered past a feeble wire fence that had been imposed between the bomb cavity and the street, no doubt to dissuade children from wandering in, and thought she saw, there in the muddy six-foot hole, something white which could be a door, if it were not a downed mattress or a mantelpiece. When would houses ever look safe to her again, she who'd seen so much of their intimate dressing strewn about in public collapse? But no, that was a wedding dress, or a long spill of white paint. It was no door and there was no irate Aunt Eunice rising from it.

By now you would have thought the strike would have attracted some attention, and perhaps it had, over the back of the house. Perhaps the vicar had arrived, or some of Eunice's frequent dinner guests, from before the war, arrived like ghosts to dampen down the flames and flow backward into the house from the garden to the front door, like a reel of film played in reverse.

Cory looked back at the house and did see a figure in the darkened doorway, looking out inquisitively, for all the world like Leary, except for the ruffled white shell of an apron. Cory ran to the pathway.

"Is that you, Cory?" Leary cried. "Why don't you come here and help me lift her out of these bushes?"

It couldn't be true but Cory came, out of breath and grass-stained and wet and cold, and it *was* Leary, pointing over the curl of the metal banister into the bushes that grew three feet down, to the side of the door. "She's stuck down there, don't you see?"

Without bothering to ask Leary what she was doing there, Cory raced around the step and down the little side steps. There, neatly tilted up against the house on a forty-five degree angle, was the white door and lying back on it with her hands folded gazing back into the street with an expression of endurance, was Aunt Eunice. Dead or alive Cory couldn't be sure, until she reached the bottom step and held out a hand.

"Aunt Eunice?" She was trembling, past tears.

"I wondered when you'd notice," the old woman said dryly. "I've been here rather a long time, but then I thought it was luck, and should I move out I might put myself into greater danger. I can't hear a thing, mind you. My hearing aids are gone."

She grasped Cory's hand and pulled herself back to the vertical without bending at all.

"Hips," she said, and, "Knees too, as I was mentioning. It's a Ditchburn thing, arthritis, I hope it doesn't affect you when you're my age."

"Picked my time to visit, didn't I?" said Leary.

In the kitchen they inspected each of Eunice's joints, which did bend, with no greater difficulty than before. "Well, you haven't *fixed* your hips," said Cory. Leary found what she could for tea, all the while complaining that

Eunice didn't know how to take care of herself until finally the old woman roared, "Well, if we can't do it like you can I guess you'll just have to come back, then!"

And Leary stuck her hands on her hips in the middle of the kitchen and said, "My fiancé wouldn't like it."

"Fiancé?" crowed Aunt Eunice, not missing a beat, "When did this situation develop, Leary?"

It felt almost like before, only that everything in the house had been lifted up and shaken a bit and set down again, almost in its place but not quite. Cory supervised the setting of the door back on its hinges, just for tonight, until someone could be found to come and replace the pins.

"I believe we need a drink," said Eunice finally, and Cory took one before she left to get herself home. The taxi felt like only marginal cover and the sky above her hummed with danger at every turn.

Chapter Twenty-Five

FIGURE 25

Corinne Ditchburn

**Mimi Gluck, with Her Portrait,
Painted by Albert Bloom**

1944
London
Exhibition print
Gelatin silver, printed 1968, 30.6 x 20.6 cm
Estate of Max Aitken Lord Beaverbrook

This curious photograph can be taken in the context of Ditchburn's life to mean many things. It compares the powers of photography to the powers of portraiture in painting. It refers to an important formative character in Ditchburn's own artistic development, as well as being of interest for its own sake, considering the masks that are simultaneously donned when one sits for a portrait, and peeled off by the artist. Here a sitter, the refugee Mimi Gluck, who worked as a translator in London during the war, is unmasked twice in one photograph — first by the painter, and then by the photographer — to reveal two different faces, between which we may choose.

⅋

THE PUB DOOR OPENED, LETTING IN A BLAST OF COLD DAMPNESS and Mimi, wrapped in a muffler, under which could be seen her red nose. Dark-haired, elfin, she pushed into the space between Reg and Cory. She'd been crying, and she was tremulous. Her news bubbled from her lips untidily, without control.

"I have a letter; they tell me she is living now. She is not dead!"

"Who?" asked Reg.

Cory knew.

"My daughter."

Reg patted her on the back and ordered a round of beer.

"But who sends you letters?" said Cory, suspicious.

But Mimi did not answer anything directly. She had the little wrinkled photograph in her hand, and she kissed it.

"They've seen her, these people who write you letters?"

She gulped some beer. "Yes, yes. She has grown up. Now she is seventeen."

Across the counter, the bartender pulled down draft after draft, carrying on conversations with four people at once.

"*Where* have they seen her?"

Mimi dabbed her face with a tiny bar napkin.

"It is possible now that we find her. I think it is possible. What do you think?"

"I have no idea," said Cory. She cocked an eye at Reg. He was studying the ring of water around the place where his glass sat on the counter.

"Didn't you leave her your cabaret job in Vienna when you hopped to southern France and chanced upon that well-known music lover, Max Aitken? Look to the Nazis. She'll be working for them."

"Of course, they force her. It is the only reason she will do that."

Mimi's pointed face flushed all over again. The dark hair with its coppery lights swung around her cheeks as she plunged her face into her hands.

"But it makes it difficult," began Cory.

Mimi whirled on her. "Why are you so hard? I don't care what you say. I never stopped trying to get my Karin out." The hollows around her eyes were bluish and streaked. Her lips were stained as if she'd been gorging on grapes. "Your son lives in a safe country. There is no war there. In my case, I have left my child in a war, and she has done what she must to survive."

"I'm not criticizing you, I'm talking about —" began Cory, in the hubbub of the bar having to raise her voice. Reg had paled, and looked at Cory with astonished eyes. At least he did not say, "You have a son?" Mimi seized his arm.

"You must help me find Karin, now. We must bring her out now."

"It's next to impossible," said Cory, "from what I hear. You can't get her out. Unless you're prepared to go in —"

"They're walking out now, I know! Walking out on foot," cried Mimi indignantly. "People. Jews. The Dutch boys who were taken as forced labour. Into Holland, into

Belgium. The French who were prisoners in Germany, they too return on foot. Germany is in chaos. They are starving, there is no more money to feed them, there are no more guards for the factories, the Germans are giving up."

"You don't understand," said Cory. "Germans don't give up."

Such is the power of the black art; when you are a practitioner, you believe in its power even though you know it to be an illusion. You believe in your own version of events, that fortunes change overnight, that people are made one day and broken the next, that we are overwhelmed by events. You believe and they believe, which makes it possible. Mimi was gone then, dancing, in a crowd of soldiers, laughing, blending with the Soho crowd. And Cory watched her, thinking, anywhere she went, she would become one of the crowd. And Cory never would.

"When I was in my war phase," Tyke liked to say. Meaning when he was young and angry, he'd studied all this. When he was in his war phase he'd made scrapbooks, filled them with clippings and photocopied bits of books, paragraphs circled in red pen, about the Canadian Army in Sicily, in Italy, in the Netherlands. He'd become an expert, in the same way that later he'd become an expert in mushrooms. He'd learned to identify them, and to search them out; he'd studied all their characteristics, put the spores under a microscope. He'd even learned to lecture on mushrooms.

But first it had been war, and that was in the sixties when he'd worn hair down to his waist and lived in the commune at Britt with the draft dodgers. He'd found somewhere farther north, more isolated, and less populated than her home. He would drive down in the truck to Pointe au Baril and take St. Pierre's boat out to Safe Harbour to visit his mother.

"The co-op can spare you?" she would say, sardonically, narrowing her eyes in a way that made you expect to see smoke coming from her nostrils, although she had no cigarette.

"It's only the mushrooms that need me," he said modestly.

"Not the ladies?" She was never comfortable with this co-op. Whatever they did about sex did not particularly concern her, but she was afraid of Tyke being stuck with a woman with children, of whom there seemed to be a large number. He was too easily made to feel responsible, she thought. He could be trapped and used. Once Tyke had brought her that girl, Lily, in her long Indian skirt and braids, with lethargic movements, dragging a three-year-old by the hand.

"You'll end up having to keep her, and some other man's child as well if you're not careful. How do you know she's not just using you?" She had shouted at Tyke, who sat with bowed head.

"Mum, you don't understand," he said, looking at his two forefingers, which touched together in the gesture children use when saying here's the church, here's the steeple. Next to come would be "open the doors, and here's all the people," but he didn't go that far. "Mum, you really don't know what we're doing there. It isn't just me looking after them or working so they can eat. We all look after each other. She cooks, Tanya does, and she's great in the garden, and we dye fabrics and some of them we sell. I'm not the only one who brings in money —" Some of the dodgers got money from their families in the States, but he didn't say that. He didn't dare risk her scorn.

"Well I'm confident you bring in most of it," she said, unmollified.

"Mum," he said, still looking at his hands, "not everyone has to look after themselves alone, the way you did."

She put her lips together and stared at the water.

He might have added, "and Mum, no woman will ever take me away from you. I will look after you, because my father never did."

When Tyke was in his war phase he'd gone with his mother to Fredericton. It was in 1968. They flew in a twenty-seater plane filled with businessmen on their way to fish the Restigouche. Fishermen: the bane of Cory's existence. They followed her even here. In the taxi riding to town she gazed at the clapboard houses on their huge, flat lots. The town was couched in the valley of the Saint John River and unfolded up a series of hills on one side. The capacious Edwardian houses had steep roofs made of metal, so the snow could slide off. They were painted brilliantly in red and pastel blues, and sometimes yellow.

"Max talked so much about New Brunswick I somehow thought it had to be bigger than this."

The new Beaverbrook Art Gallery was festooned with streamers. Local dignitaries abounded; there were the usual art lovers, and advisers, and even a new Lady Beaverbrook, who'd married Max two years before he died. She'd been his secretary once, long ago, had married well and then been widowed. Her remarriage allowed her to live the life of the very rich; she had chartered a plane to bring over her two dogs. The Director shook Cory's hand: "We're so pleased that you could come," he said.

Tyke wandered off. When he found his mother again, she was gazing at a sombre oil painting of a woman and a man in a dim room. The man sat back in an armchair, his black eyes fixed on the elfin, shawl-draped woman. She was leaving. Half turned from him, she cast a despairing last look backward into a mirror. It was clear some petition she'd made, some plea, had met deaf ears. In the mirror could be seen a door, slightly ajar: her escape, or his. The painting was called Refugee.

"This is Albert," she said simply.

Tyke stared. He'd never gone to England, although he might have, once he finished school. She couldn't have stopped him then. But it seemed as if it had been too long and he was too far away, this putative father, this man who had denied him and never once sought him out. Why should he, Tyke, have made the first move? He told Cory she was mother enough for anyone and left it at that.

Well, not quite at that. In the university library he'd once looked up some catalogues. The potted biography of Albert Bloom made no mention of Cory — or himself, obviously. There were also reproductions of paintings, and a catalogue from some final exhibition.

❧

Albert Bloom was an artist in flight from his subject matter; his passions seem about to fly out of the frame at him, and us. His late works are characteristically ragged and opportunistic. In trying to escape the subject rather than examine it, he has not taken the care to compose the elements of the painting. What is achieved is a certain spontaneous, momentary quality of insight and feeling, but we lose the fine technique and poise for which Bloom was known.

❧

Frankly he had been a little surprised. His mother had led him to believe that Albert was a larger figure than the critical assessment indicated.

Now he saw his father's handiwork for the first time. Albert Bloom had stretched this canvas, drawn his square graph on its surface to get the composition right. In these colours he'd dipped his brush, roughed the surface. To his surprise Tyke was moved. All the emotive power of the idea "father" was stored for him in the voice of his mother's longing. As a child he had accepted that the struggle between his parents, one incarnate, the other merely an idea, was a battle of Titans, of gods. He did not understand his own need.

"Funny how his paintings age," said Cory calmly. "It's got a mouldy sort of feel to it, doesn't it? Strong emotion can go that way. And colour. It wears out, you see. Something about the base he used: Indian Red. The cheapest. It looked great at the time but over the years it does not do well."

She passed on to other canvases. Whereas Tyke fell into the mood of the painting, into decades ago, before his birth, into the smoky, gas-lit studio, the murderous unhappiness of this domestic scene, the tie between this man and this woman — not his mother, clearly. Perhaps it was Albert's wife. Or another of his mistresses. The painting was strong, but no stronger than his mother's photographs. He could see how their visions had been pitted against one another, opposed and yet rooted in passion. Cory judging, clear-eyed, outraged, and Albert tender, rueful, corrupt, revealing.

At that moment, the buoyant figure of Orestes Hrudy bore down on Cory with a delighted smile.

"Someone you know?" Tyke whispered out of the side of his mouth.

The man was short, and round, and carried his befuzzed pate high. His large blue eyes were oddly mismatched; one must be glass, but Tyke couldn't tell which.

"Miss Ditchburn, I believe? Do you remember me? I am Orestes Hrudy."

Cory took his hand. He defied being ignored.

"Of course I remember you," she said. "I hated you."

"I'm her son," Tyke said quickly. "Christopher Ditchburn."

Hrudy appeared not the least offended as he transferred his hand from mother to son.

"I recall our conversations in Pall Mall," he said. "They were most energizing." The false eye was fixed in its regard, while the other roamed in the normal way, which, by comparison, appeared wanton.

"You've left off your black patch," Cory said, warming a little.

"Ah yes, when it all ended and Esther and I came back to New Brunswick — you remember Esther, don't you? — the army got me this glass eye." He reached behind him and produced as if by magic the small and eager Esther.

"We've followed your career," she said.

It was the pleasantry Cory most disliked. The whole idea of a career was to Cory an affectation. Then, too, when people said this she felt instantly inadequate, as if she had not provided them with enough of a trail. As far as she was concerned, she worked. Occasionally she was lucky and got paid for it.

"Tyke, remember I told you I never saw most of my war shots?" she said to him. "This is the man — and the woman — who had the best look."

"Right," said Tyke. "I know they were — well, suppressed."

"They were not suppressed, ahh, exactly," said Esther defensively in her Newfoundland drawl. "Corinne

Ditchburn wasn't ahh singled out, you know. It was the same with everyone." Then she brightened. "We always loved that portrait you took of Orestes. I still keep it hanging, you know. We've had offers for it, too, haven't we? But we wouldn't part with it. You captured him."

As Cory was moving away, Esther took Tyke's hand. "Ahh, young man. Take Orestes's card," she said. "And do keep in touch. We just might have a try at getting those photographs released."

Which was why, while Tyke was still in his war phase, some months later, he visited Orestes Hrudy in Ottawa. "News!" he had said airily on the telephone the week before. "You'd asked about the war work. I've looked into it all and you'll be happy with what I have to say."

They were in an old grey stone building near the canal which looked as if it were originally an armoury for the fort. It was all much more casual than Tyke had expected. "Hrudy? Oh, his office is that way." First this man and then that had taken up Tyke's quest, leading him down the resonant hallways a little ahead of him. Now he had found, in a small, windowless room, Hrudy's tidy desk; only a black telephone with a circular dial sat on the blotter.

"It seems that all our film and photographs have not been seen since being sent back here from the London headquarters. People were sick of war, you see, in the forties and fifties. Nobody wanted to look at it. Not even your mother, I think! And there was no place to put it all.

At first they kept it at the Rockcliffe air station, but that was flooded."

Hrudy gripped the arms of his chair and crossed and re-crossed his short legs. His words gushed out of him; he was simply delighted. Tyke imagined he was fulfilling a long-cherished dream to please that angry young woman who'd stormed his wartime censorship office.

"It was winter and it froze. I gather they had to chop it out of the ice. Can you imagine? Such a valuable collection! Then they moved the cans to an abandoned hangar about thirty miles east of here. And finally, late in the fifties people got around to wanting to sort out the footage. There was something like fifty million feet of it, a lot confiscated from the Germans. And it had all been shrunk and rusted. They had to look at it with hand viewers. Then there was the problem of identification. Some of the reels had been separated from the information sheets: Who were these soldiers, where was it taken, when?

"By the end, though, we came up with quite a collection, plenty of it from Corinne Ditchburn," Hrudy said. "Of course, your mother will remember shots that aren't here. No doubt some favourite that has been in her mind all these years is lost. But what we've got is remarkable, I feel. Remarkable. Some of it too gruesome to show. Government property, of course. But yours to see."

"When can I start?" asked Tyke, beginning the long negotiation that would lead to the day when he and his mother left the Military Archives with a dolly cart loaded down with several dozen heavy black boxes. Cory's war photographs were free at last. By then, of course, nobody much was interested. There were other wars going on, Vietnam chiefly.

Tyke and his dodger friends called his mother "the war monger," affectionately.

The old fishing camp at Britt was drafty, cold and damp for all but six weeks of the year, and overrun with rattlesnakes. Tyke cultivated mushrooms in the former boat sheds. Others harvested blueberries on the nearby islands, and some made macramé hangings, which they sold around the province at craft shows. The main lodge had a farm-sized kitchen with an old wood stove, and around this they gathered every night with their guitars.

It wasn't much of a place, but he could offer a room, Tyke said to Lydia del Zotto over the telephone. Even a few rounds of gin rummy. If she really wanted to see war photographs. She certainly did, the New York voice crackled over the phone. She wouldn't miss it, would she, she'd been waiting to see those pictures for twenty-five years.

Lydia had grown in status if not in stature. She sported huge, thick, mauve-tinted aviator glasses and fuzzy hair. She'd abandoned the little suits and high heels of her youth and now wore designer denims. She could sing all the Peter, Paul and Mary songs they came up with, and cook brown rice. She even fished, a little.

Over the knife-scarred fish-cleaning table, Tyke spread the contact prints: Cory's war. Sicily, Italy, Normandy. The flooded Scheldt estuary, and the banks of the Rhine, burn victims in Surrey, German prisoners of war and returning vets.

"I'll take this and I'll take this," Lydia would say. "I think I have a buyer. Your mother could use the money I'm sure. War is out of fashion now, but it will come back. You understand, Tyke, the market for her rocks and trees is limited. It would help if you could get her off that island."

The last night of Lydia's stay, Cory came up to join them. Jimmie drove her in his fishing launch.

She just looked at the contact sheets, hundreds of little squares of dark and light, and heaved a weary sigh.

"It's like another lifetime," she said wonderingly. "It was something I had to do. And now it's gone from me. As if the person who did that is dead."

The dodgers gathered. Every night they sat by the wood-stove and reviled their government for killing people in Vietnam. It was 1970. To Tyke and his pals, there was no greater evil than the military establishment. It was a given that the fighting men were victims of the generals, the politicians. There was no enemy, none that could be believed in. Military conspiracies, the cynical sacrifice of human life, breakdown of discipline — this was the war that his friends fled. But Cory's war looked different.

"Are you saying it was a necessary war?"

"No," said Cory. "Spain was a necessary war." She remembered Heraldo's evenings, the boys and girls who left there for Madrid, not unlike these boys and girls.

"What about your war?"

"My war?" She grimaced. "I don't think it was necessary. I suppose the leaders could have saved us at the beginning. But they didn't. It wasn't until people saw the camps that we knew how justified we were."

Tyke watched his friends scan his mother's face: Did they long for his mother's life, for the legitimated hatreds, the lust for righteous violence that he read in her prints? Did they try, through her, to reconnect with their parents, most of whom were American military? She was approachable, while the generals were not. She had not only fought the Germans, she had fought the very idea of war.

Cory's war, only thirty years before, had been so simple, the soldiers decent, the victory essential. She told them that night about the two German brothers at Heraldo's, painters and Communists who had to learn to paint without fingers. About experiments carried out at Dachau in 1934, before the world knew. Hitler took in everyone he found inconvenient and worked them to death, or killed them slowly, scientifically. "That got me started. I wanted to win the war, and see Dachau fall. But I never made it there," she said. And no one asked her why.

They were large, well-proportioned rooms, with lofty ceilings and ornate plaster trim; there were wine carpets anchored with round mahogany tables and wing chairs upholstered in flowers and butterflies. The walls were burdened from high to low with oil portraits of actor-managers in waistcoats, their hands on the knob of a cane, and beef-fed men of the pen, even a few women with names like Mrs. Terry, Mrs. Ternan.

Cory asked for Lord Beaverbrook's party.

Mimi separated herself from the rose and taffeta background. She was a darker red, like a single drop of blood in velvet.

"My dear, you look marvellous. I'm so glad you're still in London, so you could come," Mimi said, cupping a gentle hand behind Cory's head and pressing her lips against Cory's damp forehead. It was as if the scene of three days ago in the pub had never occurred. Mimi was ravishing tonight; her shoulders were bare and around her neck was a chain of rhinestones, perhaps a gift from Max. Her voice fluted over the careful tones of the others in the high-ceilinged room. She was high, precariously so; one felt cautious near her, as if this glittering mold could crack and spill the raucous cries still fresh in Cory's mind.

A man hovered with a circular tray. Two women who were not in uniform, but managed still to look as if they were, nodded seriously together. Their only frivolity was dark crimson lipstick and shaded brows and rouged cheeks. Some underling scuttled free and out the door as Max emerged from an antechamber. His eyes lit on Mimi with paternal affection. The affair was over, and this made it easier for both of them. Then he saw Cory.

"Where have you been? Don't tell me again that you want to go back to the fighting," he said, insisting on a kiss.

"I won't send you any more if it ruins you for parties. We need to keep you safe now you're a celebrity."

"I might be safer there than here. Eunice and I had a close call in Chelsea," she said.

Max waved a hand in a gesture of dismissal; it was all small stuff to him. He was only mildly interested in other people's survival. The truly unfortunate death was the one that removed some old enemy from his black books, before he'd done harassing him in the pages of his newspaper.

Mimi grasped Cory's forearm in that way she had of insisting on attention.

"Albert's been here. You just missed him. Max had him deliver the new painting. My darling, you must come upstairs and see it. You'll be ever so surprised."

Surprised was the word. Albert had said nothing about a painting for Max. How he droned on about being bought! No doubt this was the reason. He'd done another painting for Max. He'd been bought himself.

Cory managed to say "I hadn't heard" while following Mimi's neat red suede heels up the turning staircase. When had this painting been completed? All the while as he complained of being unable to work.

And then she saw it. The painting was of a tiny, frightened but furious young woman rising from a couch. She had flyaway black hair, a piquant face, and clutched a fitted jacket far too big for her, gathering about her some dignity in distress. It was not the natural pride of the animal in which Albert was interested; no, it was in that other

thing, the sullen defiance after an unnatural use of a person — a woman, specifically — and the abused spirit.

"It's me," whispered Mimi, gazing at the canvas.

Cory could not speak.

"Do you know what it's called? Refugee." She finally
noticed Cory's silence. "What do you think?" she said
anxiously.

Cory knew that Albert only painted a woman like that
after he had bedded her. She could say nothing.

"Cory?" Mimi's voice rose high and her strange rictus
flashed from ear to ear.

"You're finished with him, is that not right? I thought
he said so," whispered Mimi. "Otherwise I wouldn't have."

Cory barely heard. She couldn't feel, either. She could
have watched blades slice into her anaesthetized flesh.
Albert and Mimi. He was so obvious, she thought. He did
this for money, she thought. The painting, that is. Sold out
to Max, the way he's always accusing me of doing. But why
did he sleep with Mimi too? To hurt me, she thought.
Because I went away? Or to hurt Max because he thought
Max had taken me away. To compete with me, to be in
Max's eye, as he imagined I was? Or to compete with Max?
It was dizzying. She could no longer imagine Albert's
attraction. With what did he seduce Mimi? The answer to
that was easy. He seduced her with her own desperation.
Did Mimi think Albert could find her daughter?

"Tell me you don't mind," Mimi insisted.

"I can't," said Cory. Then she retreated to the sofa, from
which she could examine Albert's painting. She tried to

banish the recent image of his lips grazing over her breasts and belly. The painting bore all the marks of a Bloom masterpiece — the sombre, nostalgic palette, the depth of perspective, the captured fine gesture, which seemed so evanescent yet here — stopped, preserved.

"What does the title mean, 'Refugee'? A refugee from war, or from him?"

Again Mimi caught Cory's forearm. Cory jerked her arm away.

"Stop whispering! Can't you speak out loud?"

Mimi shrank and looked as if she would break into tears.

Cory wondered how it had been carried out. Against a tree (his specialty), on a park bench? Perhaps they'd been conventional and had gone to a hotel. But more likely it was in the studio itself, on her horsehair sofa, under her scratchy blankets.

Mimi fluttered in front of her like a frantic butterfly. "Oh, what have I done? I've hurt you. My friend, how could I have done this thing?" Her narrow hands circled her hollow cheeks. "If I have destroyed this friendship, then I have destroyed myself! I thought it was over between you. I thought — oh, you must forgive me — I thought he might help me get my daughter back..."

"I'm a little weary of that excuse," Cory confessed.

Others were gathering in front of the portrait. Cory heard their insincere admiration. "There's a story behind it. That's what I like about Bloom," said someone. Mimi flitted toward them.

When Max came back, Cory put a hand on his arm. "You've done well. It's a lovely one." Max remained, holding her arm, gazing at the portrait. For no reason, Cory remembered the electrified cross he'd erected in the garden below Cherkley. "To remind me of my sins," he'd said. His puzzled round face like the Wizard of Oz beamed up at the portrait of his former mistress, disentangling from another man's embrace.

Cory began to laugh.

Mimi went quiet.

Cory wiped her eyes. She laughed until she was weak. Her stomach muscles ached and a feeling of lightness came over her. It was all too insane, too too insane. It was a circle. Some circle closing around her and Mimi, Albert, Max.

"If you want to know," Mimi was saying stiffly, "it hardly lasted a week — well, perhaps two weeks. I could not do it, you know, because of his wife. At least Max was a widower." She leaned closer, to whisper. "Albert does still have connections in Germany, Cory. You must know. He might be able to find her."

Cory waved her hand at Mimi, as if to say don't worry, this is not about you, but Mimi was not able to interpret the signal.

"I suppose you could say it's worth it. Max was so pleased to buy the painting. He thought it was brilliant."

Of course Max thought it was brilliant. The painting reproduced the exact form of suppressed sexuality, and the woman evinced just the degree of submission to forces greater than herself, for his taste. A taste he and Albert shared. Cory laughed until she was shaking and very cold, until the palms of her hands ran with sweat and the spasms made her stomach clench. Then she lay back on the couch.

"You're not well," announced Mimi, and ran from the room.

Max's head reappeared. "I've heard of this — battle fatigue is what they call it. Suddenly, the nerves give out."

The doctor, a red-faced gouty looking man with wisps of white hair standing all over his head, looked as if he rather regretted the glass of port he'd been called from, but he set about taking her pulse.

Dear Albert —

Cory began the letter in her head, but she started to giggle and to choke on the glass of water they brought her.

> *I thought it was only me who cheated, and he only a young soldier, dead the next day. How could I have been so stupid? I know what you'd say: Art makes it all necessary. But I've seen into you now and into myself as well and it is not, as my friend Reg would say, a pretty sight.*

Her brow had been wiped and her temperature seen to; she'd drunk two glasses of water and now begged to be let go home in a taxi. Mimi crept up, contrite, and put her bare arm around Cory's back.

"I admit. I stole what was yours. I was very wrong. But you see how it is for me? I've lost everything. I must take what I can get to save my daughter."

Cory patted Mimi's hand absently.

Chapter Twenty-Six

Working behind the lines after being banned from D-Day's dramatics, Ditchburn witnessed French retaliation against their own citizens in the wake of the German retreat. Here she has caught the exact moment of impact of multiple bullets from an impromptu firing squad. The force of the bullets lifts the man from his feet so that he seems almost to be flying, before his final collapse.

❧

FORESTS OF TENTS, THEIR WALLS OF CANVAS TILTED AT THE moon, massed along the south coast of England from Fowey to Dover. Press from New York and Chicago, from Liverpool and Toronto, restless reporters leaning on the deck railings in clean, pressed uniforms. There were women too, reporters who'd been given nicknames by the troops, like Blond Bombshell and the World's Oldest

Living Virgin, the latter being a forty-year-old named Glenda who represented the National Home Monthly.

From her prison-deck Cory looked over at the shore, the rows of tanks, the parade files of soldiers, the trucks in convoy loading supplies into the bellies of ships: It was as if the whole war massed here. She saw the waving lines of camouflage paint on the sides of the destroyers, the long oval chains around the base of the tanks, piles of circles, which were, on closer examination, bicycle tires. The war machine had multiplied, it had cell-divided and propagated in facets, like some cubist abstraction. And there was an avidity to the men, as if this elemental re-organizing introduced a magnetic charge. Transformed into part of the machine, they were relieved of the burden of their private selves. The Normandy landing was to be an excursion, an outing of huge proportion. And she was locked up.

When the whistles blew on the night of June 5, and the commands were fired into the air, all faces turned toward the south, to France. Men interrupted the Chaplains' prayers to vomit, and throw their seasick bags off the lee-ward side. At dusk the boats moved out, away from the English coast, minesweepers first.

It seemed impossible that the Germans could be surprised by the thousands of vessels, more thousands of planes. But in fact they were. In a scarlet dawn off the coast of Normandy, soldiers began loading off. The first deaths occurred when soldiers were dumped off the front end of their craft into eight feet of water and sank like stones. And there were other, more inventive deaths: the soldier who was cut in two when his lifeboat got under the propeller of a seaplane.

The next deaths occurred when soldiers hit the German mines. Not long after, a few German aircraft looped down over the beach, spraying the soldiers as they scrambled wet and heavy from the surf and began to run, dodging the upright black X's that blocked their progress across the sand. Underneath the sweep of the plane certain of the running men fell, and flipped, or dragged, or just lay where they landed. They became bodies on the beach, neutral, casualties.

Cory saw none of that. "That was the other story, the Hollywood story, the one everyone knows," she said. "It wasn't my story. I will have to disappoint you."

She had waited out the first day in a hospital ship, locked up for lipping off Colonel Mahoney. Punished, held back, when all the inexperienced press sailed out in the first ships.

To Cory, Normandy was a country entered in anger and left in peace. She had walked onto her ship with her whole body rigid with the rage she felt over Albert's betrayal, every nerve in mute rebellion. Normandy was the point when she knew she couldn't fight like a man. That that kind of fighting had no meaning for her. She was not a man, or a soldier either. Losing Albert, she finally learned what he had been trying to tell her.

Her hospital ship anchored several miles off Juno Beach,

in the lee of a French cruiser which was firing at a German pocket inland. It rocked furiously with each salvo, and so did Cory's ship. On the shore, through the drifting smoke, she could see Bernières sur Mer, captured now. It appeared a beacon of safety. The Germans had fled inland, though not far enough yet. Still she was made to wait.

Late in the afternoon of D-Day plus one, a small landing craft ploughed back through the water. The triumphant crew was from the Film and Photo Unit. Red-eyed from smoke, their hair standing in stiff salty spikes, they had a couple of wounded to deliver. She recognized Reg among them.

He boarded. Roughened by his night ashore, he looked almost the way she remembered him in Italy. But now there was a strange stiffness to him. He had a way of cocking his head as if he were listening to an offstage voice. And he no longer wrote; he couldn't. To get back to the fighting he'd joined the army. They put him in the Film and Photo Unit as a sound recorder.

Reg was jubilant: He had his soundtrack and the cameras had their pictures and, best of all, they'd already stuffed the film and the story in a can into one of the red and white press bags and seen it off across the Channel on an LCT.

"We'll beat the rest of 'em by at least a day! This is the greatest day of the war. How do you feel?" he said in his hearty way.

"Like I should have been there," she said. "What do you think?"

He ripped his hat off his head and slapped his forearm with it. "You can't miss this one," he said. "I'll see you ashore."

D-Day plus two, when the soldiers were sleeping in the wheat fields, and Cory finally came ashore, she saw Reg again. They drove with the 7th Brigade in a convoy of trucks along the road to Bayeux. There were tanks, jeeps and staff-cars. Although downed stone walls and dead cows blocked the way, it felt like a jamboree.

The sun was hot and bright. From behind them, sea light bled over the flat fields and inland. Their jeep rumbled on past honey-coloured stone walls, and down deep, winding streets. Ahead of them, inland, black smoke clouds and a rattle in the air signalled the conflict. Silently they passed under the remnants of a soldier and a parachute caught in a tree.

"Poor bastard. Had all the luck. Now he's going to explode in the sun," muttered Reg. "Doesn't anyone have the decency to take him down?"

"The mop-up teams aren't here yet. We're still fighting," said the World's Oldest Living Virgin. Her face was lined and animated, gnome-like, on a thin stalk of neck. Her short, colourless hair stood in tiny curls like those of a shorn lamb. She sat erect on the seat, bouncing on tight haunches and staring into the distance with narrowed, far-seeing eyes. "And by the way I'm not a virgin. They can call me that if they want. I find it's useful for getting myself around."

Cory looked at Reg sidelong. His rueful voice and

once-merry eyes gave him the look of the matinee war hero. His empathetic brows, perfect nose and chiselled chin sent tremors through the women's corps. But something was wrong with Reg; something was broken that had not been fixed. That too-protective soldier she'd met off Sicily only one year before, that pup she'd tripped over getting out of her tent, was gone. His temper was ragged. He couldn't rest. Now, Cory wanted to touch him, to comfort him, to be comforted, as if what had died in him had died in her as well, and together they might stir it back to life.

Brigade headquarters was set up in the courtyard of a seventeenth-century inn, which the German command had vacated only hours before. With its mustard stone walls and trampled greenery, the hotel had a romance its occupation had not entirely destroyed. Barn-sized wooden doors at curb-side opened on a courtyard where a couple of dusty palm trees clung to life.

At the water fountain, Reg, Cory and the Virgin filled their canteens.

"The hearthstones are still warm. The Gerries burned their files before they left," said Reg, poking with a stick to make the grey flakes light into the air. "Would that we could read these ashes."

Through the glass-paned doors strode Lieutenant Colonel Mahoney, as bilious as ever. His mustache still sprang out to the sides as if he waxed it. He was sounding off to his aide.

Their eyes met. He was no more happy to see Cory than she him.

"Good day," said Cory, smiling slowly. He barely paused in his tirade.

"Everybody wants photographs. They want stories. They want supplies and trucks. Well, they can't have them now. They'll have to wait. I'm getting all these women conducting officers. You, Ditchburn. You're lucky I let you in here at all. You've got to be billeted behind. And don't give me any of that guff. If you women don't learn army discipline, you're going to be bounced. Come back in an hour and I'll give you your orders."

The sun was hot, and the earth was dry, as if it had not drunk for all the years of war. Cory took a walk in the streets of Bayeux. Business went on in the post office, and the little cheese store, and the provisioner of cider and produce. The people looked small and pinched, their faces unable yet to give up the habit of holding secret defiance under blank submission. A Frenchwoman came out her doorway with a cup of foaming milk and presented it to a young soldier who sat on the curb in front of her door. He took it in both hands; his eyes moved up in his sweat-streaked face to thank her.

Near the centre of town there was a tiny stream with a mill and a fish market. A tremulous butcher was putting out his shingle again, shaking hands with his neighbours: They'd survived.

When she returned to the courtyard, soldiers had begun to gather, gesticulating. At the edge of town, they said, a crazy German holed up in a hayloft had shot their sergeant as he got out of bed to take a piss. They'd heard the Gerries were shooting prisoners, too.

On the beach, said a soldier, I saw one of ours take a wounded German behind a blown-up concrete bunker and stab him to death with his bayonet.

The others shouted him down. A fist fight broke out.

Reg came walking toward her. "It's true," he said. "At the Abbaye des Ardennes they shot our soldiers point blank with their arms in the air. All the rules, all the conventions, screwed. This General, Meyer, should be strung up for war crimes."

"War is hell. I'm not sure the rules hold, in Hell."

Reg cast her an angry sideways glance. "You've changed. You don't understand."

Maybe it was true. The World's Oldest Living Virgin could out-talk her and out-run her any day of the week. Killing had no particular meaning to her now. She was after something else. If men had given Hell a set of parameters, then perhaps she could find its co-ordinates, where it intersected with the world that once had been, where the corner was turned.

She found Mahoney. With his beefy back to her he stood, barking out orders in the courtyard.

"Colonel Mahoney!"

He swung on her.

"I'll work behind the lines. Find me a billet and I won't complain."

He was slow to register it. Then he laughed.

"Well I'll be damned," said Mahoney. "Something knocked sense into her."

"She heard one bang too many," came a voice from inside the hotel door.

"I don't mind, I can poke around and get some good atmosphere," said Cory. "As long as you give me transport."

"Are you trying to bargain with me?" Mahoney snapped belligerently.

Reg watched her silently while Mahoney fiddled with his paper and got her settled into a convent, only too eager to get rid of her while the getting was good. Then, waving to the collection of men, and to the World's Oldest, Cory headed for the street. Reg followed.

"Times like this I realize what a star you are," he said in a conciliatory way. "Look at what you've done to those poor guys. Now they're all scared as rabbits! When you decided to back off they figured you're on to some secret. You're so good they know it's a move to get ahead of the pack."

She watched as his tall khaki figure went around the gate post and blended into the soft brown stone of the walls. They never said goodbye; it was bad luck.

Cory woke, in the shimmering heat, to the smell of earth and damp straw. Above the partly destroyed convent walls the canvas parted to reveal a triangle of blue sky. Cory peered out and saw them, the nuns.

They were black and white, cone-shaped, and they floated six inches above the rich, ridged earth of the garden. They travelled as if on invisible wheels, whirring forward, twirling and dipping, and then setting off at angles, their heads bending over rows of erect, obedient vegetables.

Through half-opened eyes Cory watched these automatic creatures, their hems flying above the muck. They too were a machine, but there was mercy in it. She called out and waved. "You are awake," claimed a voice in triumphant English. They gestured that she should come to the kitchen.

Speaking no French, Cory made signs. She did not want to bother them, to interfere with whatever they were doing. (What could they be doing? The invasion interrupted everything, she had thought.) But still she felt, rather than saw, that they were waiting, sizing her up. They were handsome, lively women, not at all the downtrodden wives of God she imagined.

"Sit here, please," said the Abbess, showing Cory a corner with an open window. They gave her coffee with milk and bread fresh from their ovens. She could hear the nearby sound of pigeons cooing.

She met the young man, in his late teens, who tended the cows and the chickens. His name was Lucien.

"Where do you go?" he asked.

She halted with one foot on the running board. A small jeep and driver of her own awaited Cory, the reward from Mahoney for her compliant behaviour.

"To see what I can see. Do you have any ideas?" she said.

His sallow face instantly became opaque.

"*Il est curieux*," said one of the sisters, watching. "He likes to be photograph too."

"You want me to take your photograph?"

They both recoiled.

"*Non, non*," she laughed. "I mean, he likes to be like you, take photograph."

"Come along, then. You can help."

Lucien looked at the sister, who nodded. He dropped his canvas sack of chicken feed and stepped into the car.

She told the driver to go back toward the beaches, into territory the Allies had already taken over. The Germans were gone. Lucien sat in silence.

"I don't even know what I'm looking for," said Cory, "but together we might find something of interest."

In the little village of Longues sur Mer, Lucien pulled her arm.

"Follow by here," he said.

In the centre of the town, a sombre crowd surrounded a man tied to a stake. He stood with head hanging, his arms held up to shield a broad, pale face. His hair was brown, incongruously curling up in ringlets, giving him a childish look. He wore battered boots, soiled, stiffened pants with a stripe in the fabric, and a short, cuffed jacket that buckled at the side of his waist.

"*Collaborateur*."

"Why didn't he leave with the Germans?"

"Afraid to go. Afraid to stay. They are cowards, most of them. That's why they did it in the first place," said the driver.

The stake looked like a square of railway timber, perhaps from the train lines they'd blown up to confound the Germans on the night of the invasion. A young woman came forward with a blindfold, a large folded piece of grimy cloth. Once tied, the triangle covered his entire face, from his hairline to below his chin, over his ears.

Cory trained her lens on him.

The executioners shouted back and forth, setting up their guns. No one spoke to, or for, the condemned man. The silent crowd pressed nearer, as if to contain this necessary event, and close out the rest of the world. Lucien spoke to this one and that among the townsfolk, and the driver went back to sit in the jeep. As the gunners prepared their volley of fire, Cory trained her lens on the commander. He seemed to grow, his sense of importance swelling as she became his witness.

The first bullets hit the wooden post, and splinters shot out from the stake behind the collaborateur in a little false halo. With the next shots the cloth straps that had held him against the post burst, so that for a split second, he was airborne, untied, bursting his bonds. Then his body contracted and his feet hit the ground, limp.

Lucien rejoined her in the jeep.

"Is good?"

"Thank you, Lucien. It's good." She felt the tremors in her body.

The nuns served her tomatoes grown in the convent garden and preserved from last year, fresh lettuce and white radish. In her honour they had killed a duck, one of their dwindling flock. The Abbess presided, her chin firmly bound in starched white cotton. The watchful sisters ate in silence with maximum efficiency. Each one smiled quickly when Cory looked in her face.

She left the meal with a feeling; there was some key that she perhaps ought to have picked up. It had been left out in the air, for her to see, and then snatched away again because she had not reacted. She lay on her pallet in the annex envisioning the Abbess's kitchen: one onion, one duck, the viscera that had been removed from the bird. Her swift, clear-minded motions as she prepared the food. The three leaves of lettuce on each plate, and the long white radish with its thin hairy root, clipped just where it had to be, no extra flesh cut off, the tail in the pile of vegetable discard that would go back into the garden. The women were so unhurried, it seemed that no matter what conflagration went on outside, there would be enough here. However little there was would be enough, because they knew how to use what they had.

But there had been something else in the kitchen. A sense of preparedness, of anticipation. Cory remembered in the corner, on a little table, three colours: red, white and blue. They were not table napkins but flags, perhaps ten flags, a pile of flags that had not been there in the morning. It was very strange, those flags appearing. Perhaps they were the key.

In the night, Cory heard someone come to the convent, or leave it. The sounds were so small and muffled she couldn't tell. She thought there was the rumble of a car motor too. She strained her ears in the darkness but heard no more.

In the morning the Abbess again stood in her kitchen, motionless, smiling. Cory felt, obscurely again, that some secret eluded her. She breakfasted in silence.

"Lucien will not go driving with you today," said the Abbess.

Cory went out but didn't go far, and after an hour told the driver to stop in the lane close to the Abbey. The sun baked the earth; sweat and dust made her skin itchy. Perhaps it would be a wasted day, she thought. But suddenly out of a swirl of dust in front of the barn came Lucien waving his arms and shouting.

Two farmhands pushed open the wide wooden doors. From nowhere materialized a host of black cones: the nuns. Out of the barn came first one, then another and another — three long black cars. The tricolour waved from each hood. One by one the cars turned in the narrow lane and drew up to the door of the Abbey.

Cory leapt a ditch and ran, holding her camera high, trusting her nuns to know her. She was only a dozen feet away when, gaunt, with his immense nose, and wearing his round, flat-topped hat, General de Gaulle emerged from the Abbey door. He had spidery long legs and wore his uniform with boxy awkwardness, black-belted around a waist as big as his shoulders. As the roar went up, he turned to the people already collecting in the road and raised his long arms over his head, fists closed, in a victory sign.

While the crowd stood at attention, General de Gaulle walked slowly toward the Abbess, took her hand and bent over to kiss it. Then he was neatly marched into the second of the black cars. As he drove off, the Abbess at the door gazing after him with tears running down her face.

Cory took the film in to Mahoney at Brigade. "My scoop! Aren't you happy for me?"

He shook his fist. "Cunning little wench. You must have had some word, asking for that billet." The aide gave it to a dispatch rider. It would go to the beaches and be sent over by carrier pigeon, the fastest transport until they got an airport.

A telegram from Max:

> AMAZING SHOT STOP HOW DID YOU MANAGE TO
> DODGE THE REST OF THE PRESS STOP KEEP IT UP
> END

Chapter Twenty-Seven

FIGURE 27

Corinne Ditchburn

Boy with His Dog, Outside the Abbaye

June, 1944
Caen, France
23 x 45 cm
National Archives of Canada

At first glance this is not a war photograph at all, but a sentimental shot of a child and his pet. However, the rubble in which they stand, and the looming tower of a medieval cathedral behind, offer a sombre, spiritual context, and in turn, help explain the passionate bond we glimpse between child and animal: an effort to hang on to the normal in a collapsing world.

❧

"YOU HAVE LADY LUCK WITH YOU." REG DOFFED HIS HELMET wearily. Grime lined his forehead. "Here we've been going at it with your basic newspaper Nazi erupting in the fields. Hair as gold as the tassels on the corn, and just as young and fresh. Seventeen years old if they're a year. And you stay behind the lines to catch De Gaulle's whirlwind visit, and steal the front page."

"I was rewarded for good behaviour. Mahoney's frantic because his crop of war correspondents is becoming unruly. The World's Oldest made a break for it over to Cherbourg to see the Americans," said Cory. "He wants to bounce her."

They sat in the broiling sun. The cream from their pastries turned into a puddle on the plate. Suddenly he put his face into his open hands. Tears ran down the sides of his dirty cheeks, but his voice was flat. "I saw a shot for you. Over in Villeneuve they took a dead Canadian soldier and propped him up in the square with a German helmet on his head. They put a cigarette in his mouth and a beer bottle in his hand. Someone had pissed all over his feet.

"I'm there with my tape recorder. I talk with the gunfire in the background. All I can do is talk. I can talk but I can't remember. To write I'd have to keep it all in my head. I can't keep it in my head." He lifted his cup of coffee and toasted her with ironic pleading in his eyes. "Has it happened to you? Have you got fear in your gut where it never used to be?"

She tried to explain. "You're thinking like a soldier. I'm thinking some other way."

He opened his satchel to show the gun. "See what I'm carrying now? You should get one."

"Never," said Cory.

"Listen to me," he said. "We've got the beachhead but we haven't got France. The German equipment's still out there, hidden behind bluffs." Reg rolled the newspaper in his hand and used it to swat a fly that was crawling over the puddle of cream.

Dear Albert —

How strangely exhilarating it is to see something massive, permanent, even beautiful erased in one ear-blasting moment. Vistas open. Vistas of ruin and privation, but vistas nonetheless. You could almost laugh. Some do. Suddenly, you can see for miles.

When all the beautiful things we've made are going down, one after another, gardens, fields of grain, church spires, those that remain seem out of place. It's almost satisfying to see one more blown off the landscape. I feel like some kind of avenging angel. Clearing the way.

Caen had collapsed. It was entirely underfoot, a rolling surface of rubble three feet deep. Steel-helmeted and steel-booted, the soldiers stepped as delicate as ballet dancers through the waves of human refuse — roof-beams and awnings, chair-backs and bedsprings, factory chimneys like the noses of great cannons toppled. Dead these past two days were twelve hundred soldiers, and thousands of civilians. Each death had removed another pillar from the town, ripped out an artery or a tendon.

The silence was so deep you could almost hear the dead expire in the vapour. So Cory thought as she walked in that void. When she turned a corner she saw a dog regarding her from the jagged edge of a downed stone block. Most dogs she'd met in war zones were ferocious and she couldn't blame them; they'd been kicked, abandoned, and hounded away from houses where there was not enough to feed the children. But this dog — part terrier, it looked — panted gently, its head cocked. It gave cautious, inquisitive sniffs, by which it seemed to be determining whether Cory was friend or foe.

"Here pooch," she said, bending over it.

"Watch out," said the Sherbrooke Fusilier who walked with her. He lowered and primed his rifle.

Cory held her hand out, palm up. "Here pooch, here pooch."

The dog cocked his head and finally lay his face in her hand.

"You're mad," said the Fusilier, leaping one-footed onto a higher mound of jagged rubble. "He could be rabid."

"Bye pooch," Cory said. But when she tried to follow the soldier, the dog bounced on his front legs and yapped excitedly. He engaged her with bottomless black eyes; she had to follow. The dog pattered on lightly over the stones, and kept looking back to see if she were coming. They turned into a narrow passage that was so choked with debris she had to climb partly up the wall of the adjoining building. Like the dog, she looked over her shoulder. The Fusilier was following.

"Good man!" she said.

"You're mad," he grumbled, "but then so's all this."

The dog led them around the corner to where a

wrought-iron gate blocked the passageway. Inside were the large wooden doors of an intact building. Cory looked up. Towering overhead were the spires of a huge cathedral. On either side of it, in all directions, every building had been razed. But by some bizarre twist of fate the bombs had missed this one.

The dog barked twice. A woman appeared, her eyes underscored by deep pockets of black. Thanking God for the French-Canadian regiment, Cory let the Fusilier speak. They were at the Abbaye des Hommes, otherwise known as the Church of St. Etienne, and the doorkeeper was one of thousands of townspeople who had taken shelter there.

"Welcome to our shelter," she said in French and, stepping aside, let the dog run in.

They stepped into a low alcove, its stone ceiling just above their heads. Before they had gone many steps forward the towering vaults of the cathedral opened above them. The space stretched, in gloom, so far to left and right that the stained glass windows at either end were like distant lanterns. Cory and the Fusilier pushed back their helmets.

"We are rather crowded," said the woman. As their eyes adjusted to the darkness Cory could see hundreds and hundreds, indeed thousands, of men, women and children camped out. In pews, in alcoves, around the nave, they lay on pallets of straw or sat neatly with blankets folded beneath them. The place was rank, foul with the smell of unwashed bodies living too close, but at least it stunk of life rather than of death.

The dog waited, ready to lead onward. Cory gazed at the greyish stone, rising in several tiers to its gothic height. On the ends of each pew were faces carved in wood — urchins, mermaids, bearded gnomes.

Here the people of Caen, those who had survived the last day's onslaught of bombs, went quietly about their business, preparing now to walk out into the emptiness that was their town. Some clutched prizes with which they hoped to begin again: a wedding photograph, two silver goblets, a small leather case containing documents.

"It was our Curé who gave us the faith to come here. We knew the Cathedral would be saved," said the woman to the Fusilier.

The woman took Cory's arm. "William the Conqueror is buried here," she said. Picking her way over seated children and sleeping elderly people, Cory saw the place where the babies had been born during the month-long siege. The alcove over the Conqueror's tomb was a makeshift hospital.

The dog, meanwhile, circled possessively around one pad of blankets in the third pew. There, a boy of eleven or twelve lay on the floor. The dog took the boy's arm between his teeth and shook it, pretending to bite, but never letting his teeth dent the delicate skin. Cory began to shake. She raised her camera but she had no flash; it was too dim to shoot without it.

"Who is the boy?" Cory asked. "And how did he save his dog?"

"It was not his dog, before this," their guide explained.

"The boy lost his father and his house in the attack. The mother is somewhere, I believe in a hospital. The dog came to the church door several weeks ago. It was a stray. It is a happy story. Now he has adopted the boy, and the boy has adopted the dog."

The boy had the sort of energy that could not be stopped by sorrow for too long: His eyes were limpid and intelligent, his face radiant. He smiled in delight as Cory reached for her camera. "Come outside so I can take your picture."

A light rain had begun to fall, and in the ruins of Caen little columns of sullen smoke rose from the unseen fires.

Dear Albert —

We never speak about our son. As a father, you refused him existence. I tried to hate you for that and I tried to leave you for that. I was angry to be tied down by him.

Then I left him. I have no one to blame, and no excuses. I said I left Tyke for war, but really I left him for you, because I had not finished with you. This was your world, Europe, and your death, your war. I couldn't bear to miss it.

But it's my war now; I've earned that. Today for the first time I felt Tyke's aloneness, and I can see I've hurt him. I pray he will forgive me. My child was a weight, yes, he was, but none of us is made of air.

What can I say to Tyke, except perhaps that I

needed to get here to see him? I needed to see this beautiful boy of Caen with his dog. I love my son! I am filled with gratitude that he exists! I want to hold him in my arms, I want to watch the light dawn on his face, I want to begin all over again with him. And this time it will be you I leave behind.

Chapter Twenty-Eight

A portrait of the distinguished and weary journalist on leave, amid the shining fixings of the drinking cellar. His face shows five years of war, and a strange vulnerability to which his uniform gives the lie.

❧

AT THE END OF THE TERRIBLE HOT MONTHS OF FIGHTING IN Normandy came great surges that made victory palpable: Patton's Americans made their dramatic sweep from Paris into Luxembourg. There were liberation parties in Paris, in Brussels, in Antwerp. Without warning, wide reaches of ruined land in Belgium and the Netherlands were ceded by the Germans.

In London, the papers proclaimed that the Boche was beaten. How could he not be? He had no more fuel, he had no more planes, he had no more men. In London Cory was treated to a first look at Reg's newsreels, with canned liturgical voice track.

"The Hun is on the run," he intoned. "The fascist superman and his twisted following will soon be wrestled to the ground." He brought all his Scots-Canadian decency as well as a mad conviction to the camera. "Bringing an end to the most evil civilization mankind has ever seen."

Yet the war went on.

The pictures were by now familiar: planes soaring away into the horizon, leaving behind a spreading veil of parachutists: tiny black figures of firemen dwarfed by a great white plume of water — only this time it was a German city, not London. Deanna Durbin in a turban and well-filled coveralls, singing for the troops. "*When you begin to give in to what's under your skin.*" Housewives making do with rabbit stew.

Cory noticed something strange. The dirtier the war, the cleaner and neater the women. Perceptions had been inverted in this long war. A willful distortion of what was seemed to her everywhere, on every side, and it was as frightening as what they faced, out there, on the battlefield.

Cory had slid on rotting corpses in Italian mud; she had seen bodies burst in the heat of Normandy's summer. Now, in the winter of 1944-45, catching a ride with a British transport truck, she watched the dead float over the flooded land. They lay bloated, frozen and hideous for days after battle. Even if they were buried they came unburied again. No one seemed to care that dead animals lay in farmyards and burnt-out barns, along roadways and in sad clusters under splintered trees in the fields. Death was everywhere proliferating, but still it could take you by surprise. A family hid all night in their cellar from the bombing. In daylight when all was clear, they stepped out for air and a mine killed their child of five. To the boys who'd given her a ride, the soldiers in the Scheldt estuary, it seemed that war was not ending, but falling apart on its feet, becoming ever more sordid and unstoppable.

Cory was alone.

She preferred, by that time, to travel in the ranks of soldiers, without connecting to Army Public Relations. She filed her pictures when she could get someone to help her. She slept in bombed-out digs, and begged her transport. By the time Mahoney had figured out where she was, she'd moved on.

A week ago she'd left Reg with the troops in the muddy water of the Scheldt. He was seething. "I never saw such wonderful soldiers. Fierce on the assault, dedicated sloggers, great improvisers. And what does it get us? Because we're not glory hounds, we'll get stuck in the pockets, the cul de sacs where Germans fight to the death for ten feet of ground."

She didn't remember, now, why she had decided to go to Brussels. She had no orders to do so. She was adrift in a war zone, and it felt right. If she stumbled into an action, she could be arrested. But she made herself small, and the soldiers were good to her. They fed her and found her warm, dry places to sleep, and in return she heard their stories and took their pictures.

The soldiers driving this particular transport truck had a reckless habit of stopping in the middle of the road to brew up their rations. The road was a high, flat, diked track with ditches on either side. The truck, and the men cooking underneath its rear, were completely exposed. The soldiers were casual, loud. They stretched and boxed each other beside the vehicle. Cory sat hunched, her nerves vibrating, expecting any second the whine of a mortar.

Her friends of the moment were in Supplies. Their task was to drive back and forth from the fronts to liberated Brussels, with crates of first aid equipment and rations. From the soldiers she heard what happened at Nijmegen: The American 82nd Airborne made a drop and liberated the town, but the British, despite good Dutch intelligence that the Germans were across the river, met disaster. They dropped the paratroopers on the wrong side. The men died before they touched the ground, shot in their harnesses. Those who landed alive were massacred or taken prisoner. Some tried to escape back across the Waal. Now the Allies faced the Germans across the river, both watching the bridge; the Allies determined to save it for when they could force their way into Germany, the Germans still hoping to go the other way. It was a standoff.

But first was Brussels. One night in a town she'd never see again, would never want to see again, although it lived in her memory, was a crossroads in her life. For decades after the war, she could close her eyes and conjure the Grand'-Place as if it were some court of judgment, some higher place to which she had once been called.

Brussels was only one hundred miles from the front but it felt like another planet. Brilliantly lit, humming, it was full of soldiers on leave. And you could eat: Anyone could get food — eggs and bacon, the waffles called goffre, mussels cooked in cream with spaghetti.

There was a hotel and even a hot bath. A crowd of American soldiers and nurses, bursting with *bonhomie*, invited Cory out on the town. Cory had only her musette bag and no clean clothes, but Madame provided a shirt, and washed her trousers. Cory joined the gang, the kids, she thought of them, all dressed in their fresh clothes, and went out to the *caves*.

She found she had washed off the mud of battle but not the sweet-smelling slime of death. In the streets, she walked slowly, not accustomed to being clean, not sure she was clean. The population of Brussels made room for them, swelling around them, absorbing them.

"Gotcha," cried Herb, grabbing another boy's hat and ducking into the crowd. He was from Pittsburgh and he worked in a mill.

His buddy, a lean-faced college boy from New England, ran after him, laughing. He tagged his friend, and then dodged sideways. Herb feinted back and ran after him. He was maybe nineteen. "Hey, these are the people we're saving! Don't knock the population down!"

Streetcars were disgorging crowds of office workers;

women in hats and gloves skittered over cobblestones. It was five o'clock in November, the sky an unspecified mottled grey, half night, half cloud. Even as they walked, it darkened. Lights from store windows reflected blearily in the uneven stones of the street. One by one the shops began to put up their signs: *Fermé. Fermé.*

The narrow streets of slippery, rounded stones led downhill. They trudged beside the submerged gleam of streetcar rails. In the cold, a baker's window glowed. Cory was drawn to it, as to a hearth. There were gold and green ribbons, holly and candles, the enormous gingerbread dolls for the feast of St. Nicholas, and loaves of bread made in the shape of swaddled babies.

The narrow street wove toward something; it seemed to have a purpose, unassuming though it was. Then, after a sharp corner, all was revealed, this huge brilliant space with its guardian edifices: the Grand'Place.

On three sides they were faced by ancient, elaborately carved stone guildhalls, on the fourth by an enormous gothic facade that culminated in a slender central spire.

The soldiers stopped, feeling as if they'd stepped into a previous world. In their intense elaboration, the great hotels existed in another dimension. Their height shut out the ruins of war and they mused inward. Follies, to be sure. Yet they stood while the rest of Europe lay in heaps.

Bathed in gold and red lights, the ebullient stone leapt up to a charcoal sky. Everywhere on it were perched figures, men, women, angels. They stood on balustrades and cornices, loomed in niches at the corner of a street, hid under fountains, and over doorways, suspended themselves along balconies. Cory had the urge to laugh at all this stopped energy; it was as if a race of pygmies had overrun the place but had been frozen in their flight over housetops and parks.

Her friends surged on in search of a bar. There was a cellar cafe, "'t Kelderke": It was Flemish; no one knew what it meant. They found it under the sign of a wine barrel and a gnome with a pointed hat. In twos and threes they clattered down the stairs. The cellar was square timbered, hung with silver platters and beer steins, the mirrors steamy with smoke and body heat. In the strange heart of a strange city, it felt as familiar as a dream, one of those havens in which everyone one knows eventually will appear.

Beer in hand, Cory stood at the bar. Since Normandy, she'd barely seen another war correspondent. She hailed a bunch of newspapermen and asked after her friends.

"Haven't seen anyone. Except Morris. He got here today."

At six o'clock, the bar began to fill. Outside the narrow cellar windows, the rush of feet on the sidewalk was sudden, intense, like a flight of ducks. Then, as abruptly as it had begun, it abated: a stoplight. The flow of feet began again almost immediately. After the front, such order and restraint was quaint, laughable.

Yellow globes swam in the mirrors behind the bar. There was music, a three-piece band. The musicians swayed on their feet, seeming to be asleep except for the tapping of their feet, the automatic arm and finger movements that made the music.

Herb asked Cory to dance. For comfort, she leant her chin on his shoulder. She wrapped her arms around his neck; his arms went around her back. She tucked her face under his chin. The music let her move with him, and feel, for a time, that her membership among the living was guaranteed. The song was "A Nightingale Sang in Berkley Square." She felt a terrible pang for Albert.

"You've been around," Herb said. "Longer over here than me."

"I have." She quelled her maternal instincts.

"You're with the press."

"In a manner of speaking."

"I want to ask you something."

"Sure."

"You heard about these camps the Gerries have?"

"Yeah, I heard," she said. "Quite a long time ago."

He pulled his neck back to look her in the face, his eyes rolling as he told it. "I heard the Gerries kept a prison near the Dutch border," he said. "One day they loaded all the prisoners onto a train. I talked to the SS officer who went with them. He said they took 'em to a factory and gassed 'em all. Made them undress and crowd in together. Thousands dying standing up. He said he watched through a little window in the door. They were gagging and screaming as they fell."

Their bodies moved together within the music.

"Do you think it's true?"

"I think it's true, yeah."

Herb didn't look at her then. It was easier to keep dancing, looking over each other's shoulders. Finally he said, "So if you guys know, how come everybody doesn't know?"

"Ask my bosses that."

"How come they don't know in Pittsburgh?"

"Nobody's going to believe it."

He was silent.

"So we're keeping the Germans' secret," Herb said.

"The problem isn't knowing, it's telling. The problem is making anyone else believe. That's something you learn when you practise the black arts."

He laughed. "So that's what you call it," he said, leaning back again to look at her assessingly. "I never met too many journalists. You been all over this war?"

"A few places," said Cory.

"You sleep with the guys, then? If they ask you?" he said, leaning back and looking her in the face.

"I did once," she said. "But he died the next day."

She sat down at a table, waiting, uneasy: The night had a feeling of being set in place, planned. The high, delicately cut walls of the great square, which could have been made out of stage paste; Reg coming to town; Herb asking about what people knew and didn't know. She felt as if heavy game pieces were moving into place. All that was needed was the immense hand of the player overhead.

Now the windows at street level were shiny black. The

flocks of hurrying feet were gone; only pairs of pant legs, in twos and threes, went past, and soon they were the colour of the night. Before too long dinner appeared, mostly potatoes, and fat sausages, which were slashed along the sides to keep them from curling. The gang spoke of going out to find another bar, but no one moved.

It was ten o'clock, then later. Sleek little girls in hats, their lips like bubbles of black-red blood, came to sit on the soldiers' laps. Two of Reg's pals from the Film and Photo Unit showed up; she asked for him but they said they hadn't seen him since dark. Herb had a girl on his arm, but first he wanted to see Cory back to her room.

"I'm all right," said Cory. "It's only a short walk. I'm a quick study on memorized maps. I could find it in my sleep."

"I don't want to leave you here alone," said Herb. "You might take pity on someone and it wouldn't be me."

The girl gazed quizzically at Cory. She was about twenty. Her war still had glamour. She wasn't letting go of Herb's arm.

"All right, walk me to my door," Cory said.

On the cobblestones the girl tripped, unsteady in her high heels. Cory and Herb's boots rang out the same steady rhythm.

"Good night, Herb," she said, kissing him. Never good-bye. Herb grinned. Then he turned, ran a few steps and sprang up with one arm overhead, as if to dunk a basket-ball. The girl glimmered, watching him. Then he took her arm and they were off into the dim street. Perhaps Herb would find some respite there. Cory figured he had earned it.

But Cory remained on the street, her ears reaching into the dark. Sometimes she thought that all the explosions had made her deaf. Then at times like this she knew her ears were sharper than a bat's: They kept her alive. The footsteps were gone. The street was utterly silent. She had shaken Herb. But still, she was left with her sense that the day was not over; something had to happen. She listened to her instincts; they had saved her life more than once. Moreover, they found her the pictures she wanted. She began to walk back to the 't Kelderke.

From the entrance she saw the back of a man's head at the bar. With a little leap of gladness, she recognized the nape of Reg's neck. He turned and, in the mirror, she glimpsed his tense, blanched face. To see him from two directions at once set him off from the rest of the room: He was a prism, two faces reflecting outward from the centre.

She walked up behind him and he swung to face her, his arm lifting and falling again as if he would have embraced her, but for some inner reserve, or great fatigue. "They told me you'd been asking after me."

"You never said you were coming this way."

"I didn't know."

"When did you get here?" she said. "What's the story?" She lifted one hip up on the barstool.

Reg waved his hand vaguely toward the quiet street. "No story. I was thinking. This war will never end. It will always be going on, somewhere beyond the suburbs, while the cities brim with light. It's as if we have decided that killing young men, hell, killing ordinary civilians, is to be a sacrament. You know, a bleeding off, some kind of payment to the demon gods."

The beer glasses were piled high beside the sink. The bartender polished the marble bar with his cloth. Reg slid off his stool, putting one foot up on the rail. He drank two pints while she nursed her half. She stood in the triangle made by his thigh, his long torso, and his arm where it leaned over the counter. Heat radiated from his body.

When the bartender gave them his sign, last call, Reg ordered another. She covered her glass. She'd learned by experience that if she drank when she was with Reg, her hands would begin to lift off the table of their own accord and reach for him. But he never reached for her. She thought one day he would; desire seldom travels in one direction only. But Reg was tense, preoccupied. Tonight his moodiness felt personal; he was holding himself against her.

She remembered Sicily, when Reg had guarded her fiercely, devotedly. Obsessed with Albert, she didn't want him then. But after Reg was wounded, everything changed. Back in London from Ortona, she had fallen mindlessly into the postures she and Albert had invented. She healed herself with sex. Her body became concave, her legs and arms wrapped him, and her thoughts were obliterated while Albert was inside her. But as soon as he withdrew she thought of Reg, stepping forward to receive the

hit, going down beside the well; Reg, veiled in his own
blood; Reg, still as earth on the stretcher. Reg was left to
heal himself alone.

She was like a starving person. It had taken months for
the hunger to burn itself out. But once satisfied, her body
felt glutted. When Albert rolled off her, he became nothing. He snorted as he slept, reaching blindly for the blanket. She looked at him with a cold eye. He was old. Coarse
grey hairs sprouted at the base of his spine, and stretch
marks, like mounds revealing a worm burrow under his
skin, ran over his hip to his belly.

Cory was restless then, shut up in the studio when the
life of London revived at five o'clock. What before had
been delicious secrecy was now simple tedium. She even
stopped quarrelling with Albert; it wasn't necessary. To go
for dinner with Liss at home, to be the child at their table,
didn't offer the consolation it once had. More and more
she spent her evenings with Mimi, the other war correspondents, the soldiers. Then Reg came back. He was
released from the hospital at Watford. As soon as Cory saw
him, she knew what made her get up from Albert's bed.
The beginning and the end was this: desire.

She couldn't find a way to tell him. Reg was different:
angry, bitter, passionately engaged in a fight that seemed
to mean more than simple war. He picked fights with
friends about Monty's strategy, or PR field regulations.
Then he'd go off in search of newspapers or cigarettes.

"That man desperately needs to get laid," Mimi always
said. But Cory maintained he did get laid. There were

always women around him. He could have whoever he liked. And if he didn't like ordinary women, he could go off to the brothels. Who he slept with was a matter for speculation. Nobody knew for sure.

She had wondered then if she loved him, and in what way. Compared to his previous self, Reg was weary and bitter. Still, he was green compared to Albert. His story was being written, while Albert's had been written, Albert himself had scripted the end over and over. He would refuse regeneration itself if it were offered. But Reg could come alive again, she hoped: There was still time.

Cory watched him now, in the cellar bar, as she had watched him then, his elbow reflected in the surface of the bar, his thigh steady as a table, his huge knee-bone propped against a stool. He had no awareness of his powerful body. Something curious but quelled was in his face. He was full of this arching, quizzical, frustration: Why doesn't life reveal itself to me? Where is the valve, why can't I feel, why doesn't it all work for me? Still, Cory reasoned, he had fallen in love with her once: He must feel something. He might again.

He drained his last beer. "I got a message from Mimi."

"You did?" She knew what that meant. Some word about her daughter. Maybe the girl had escaped. These days you met people who had escaped. She felt uneasy. "Come on, let's walk," said Cory. "Where are you staying?"

When they opened the door, a sliver of the cellar's golden light preceded them into the dank night and then it was extinguished. Two steps took them to the middle of the narrow street. The mad baroque guildhalls on either side seemed about to collide overhead in their froth of cornices, cupolas and statuary. But the cobblestones demanded attention. It had rained while they were in the cellar and now the stones were shining, slightly iced. It was very cold.

They set out directionless, in faith that the street would lead them somewhere. It went uphill.

"You're up to something," Cory said. "You have no reason for being here."

"No reason for being anywhere," said Reg.

"It's got to do with Mimi, doesn't it?"

They continued walking. They always walked quickly, when they were together, feeding on each other's speed. Now the hairs were standing up on Cory's neck. She felt the way she had felt sitting in that convoy on a raised road, while the soldiers cooked in full view of the enemy. Reg put his arm around her.

"Don't worry, Cory," he said, patting his pistol. "I've got my gun." He knew she hated it. They'd had this argument before.

"You've crossed over."

"And so?"

"I have nothing against soldiers," she said easily. "It's just that as journalists they're lousy."

They crossed an open space, bomb damaged, and then the seventeenth-century houses reappeared. They saw no cars, but heard, from another street, the sound of tires on wet stone. When the car was gone, their footsteps were loud. Then it seemed to Cory that there were three sets of footsteps — her own, Reg's and another's. But perhaps it was echoes. Cory held Reg's arm. She synchronized her footsteps exactly with his. She listened and heard tramp, tramp, tramp. Yes, there was a third set.

She leaned her head alongside Reg's, which felt lovely; he was taller even than she was, they were temple to temple.

"I believe we are being followed," she said.

"The possibility exists," said Reg. "But remember, there are no Germans here."

Cory laughed. "How simple life has become. There is no danger but Germans. If no Germans, nothing to fear. Shall I look back?"

"If you like."

Reg was too calm, too easy. Cory stopped. He stopped, too, and put his hand in the pocket where the gun was. In the darkness the footsteps hesitated, and then came forward.

Chapter Twenty-Nine

> FIGURE 29
>
> *Corinne Ditchburn*
>
> **Wooden Angel**
>
> December, 1944
> Brussels, Belgium
> 23 x 45 cm
> *Collection of Reginald Morris*

This simple, almost primitive carved statue of the Virgin Mary, which stands in the Cathedral of Notre Dame in Brussels, acquires a powerful symbolic significance as she rocks in a simple open boat, nearly disappearing backward into the shadows. It is one in a series of interior shots Ditchburn took of the Cathedral before setting out again to the front lines.

❧

THE MAN WAS THIN-FACED AND BLOND WITH A MUSTACHE LIKE a shoe-brush above his upper lip. His cheeks were lean, his bones delicate, his chin sharp. It was a face one did not forget.

"Good evening, my friends. Would you care to walk with me to the Place du Grand Sablon?" His English was perfect, his accent Dutch and his voice neutral. He had a small gun; Cory could just see the glint of it above his coat pocket. Reg squeezed her arm, and they fell in step with him. The man led them around a curve to the left, and they came to a large square that sloped uphill. At its top stood a gothic cathedral; lit from the inside, the tall, stained glass windows glowed an eerie, underwater turquoise.

"Place du Grand Sablon," he announced, like a tour guide.

"What is this, Reg?" said Cory. But he only smiled at her.

"Hundreds of years ago this was a sandy marsh," remarked their captor — that was how Cory thought of him, as a captor — "where they buried the dead of the poor. Later, the great noble families built their homes overlooking the square. Before Notre Dame was built," he gestured to the cathedral, "there was a little chapel there, the Chapel of the Arbaletriers. I believe in English it is the crossbowmen."

They walked alongside the iron railings that enclosed the square, and then took the upward-climbing alley alongside.

"A fine example of the final stage of evolution of the gothic cathedral. Notre Dame des Victoires is its proper name," remarked the man. "But we call it Notre Dame du Sablon. It stands on sand. Not a promising basis, do you agree?"

Halfway up he stopped and, putting his elbows between the wrought-iron bars, leaned into the fence and gripped the standards as if they were the bars of his cell. Cory and Reg stopped behind him.

"Picture this. We are in the twelfth century. Here is the crossbowmen's small chapel. And beside it a poor hospital, and around the back the burial ground of the dead who could not be fit in the cemetery."

Nothing in this war frightened Cory any more, except landmines. But this man did. He had the cool cunning of one who traded between deadly foes and had no regard for the living or the dead, and he was under some presumption that they would hear him out.

"In the marsh? A bad spot to plant a corpse," Reg contributed, as if this conversation made sense and were expected.

The man shrugged. "They could not choose," he said.

Cory walked away from him, past the cathedral. The clouds had melted into the dark sky, and directly in front of her, rolling back onto its curved side, hung a huge crescent moon of the type used in children's book illustrations. Within its convex curve she could see a gnomish profile: indented eyes, pointed nose, thrusting chin. It threw its hollow glow down onto the small cleared space, which lay a little uphill, seeming to lead her there.

The grass was now frosted with white, and the borders holly-green. The wrought-iron fence was gated but not locked. She walked inside the little square. It was beautiful; two paths crossed in the centre beneath a shell-shaped pool and the hedges were cut in paisley curls. Standing there at the crossing of the paths, Cory looked around. The blond man had followed her.

"Do you see," said the unwelcome tour guide. "On every side? The little bronze statues of men, making guard around the square. These are the men who represent the guilds of Brussels. There are twelve per side, a small force of forty-eight. You see how they look, outward; they have their backs to you."

It was true, she was now surrounded by dainty men on pedestals with swords or scrolls, plumes or helmets. Two larger men stood arm in stone arm, over the high end of the square. The stranger touched her elbow, and they took the path that led to the edge of the square.

"This man makes the arms, you see, he holds a sword, and at his feet is a helmet. And this man is a plumber. Here is the one who represents the makers of chairs." In front of the man was a small chair. "And next to him but one is the shoemaker, and then the merchant of fish." They walked around the edge of the square. "The vegetable sellers, the tailor with his scissors. The wine merchant with a bottle and a glass."

Despite herself, and despite her fears, Cory smiled at the small figures. Their poise and their particularity was moving. They were not the great men of Brussels, but the tradesmen, burdened with tools, dwarfed by their pedestals. They stood like costumed actors with no lines to deliver, the painter with his palette, the barber, the glove-maker and the draper.

Reg caught up; together all three stood under the arms of a tree with rich green, rubbery leaves. The puck-faced moon appeared again, over the buildings behind them, its light cold and white.

"Now?" said the man.

"No, not now," said Reg. "Inside the church."

"What is this, Reg?" The mist of the night had seduced her here, but she didn't want to be drawn further into Reg's scheme. "Do you know this man?"

Reg took her arm, but didn't answer. They followed the Belgian across to the cathedral, where he stopped before the giant door. The high walls of Notre Dame rose starkly out of the misty earth. Rows of windows in the pointed arch lit the side; and the huge doorway was like the mouth of a cave.

"We have a charming story in this church," he went on, as if he had never stopped speaking. "A legend, in fact. We do not know its veracity," he said, bowing courteously to urge Cory to climb the steps of the church.

Reg took Cory's hand as if to reassure her.

"I shall recount the *histoire*," the mustached man said almost happily. They stepped inside the church.

"There once lived a very pious woman of Antwerp. This was in the middle of the fourteenth century. And her name was Beatrice Soetkens. And every day Beatrice went to the cathedral in her town to pray."

Cory stood looking down, reading the worn engraving on a tombstone embedded in the floor. The narration of their strange companion was magnetic, his voice aimed to soothe her, although in fact it alarmed her greatly.

"There was in this cathedral a little statue of the Virgin, all neglected, and covered in dust, and — how do you say it — *decoloré*. To Beatrice, in a dream, appeared the Virgin Mary, asking her to seize the little statue of herself. Many times over the Virgin appeared, making the same request."

At the far end of the cathedral, near the nave, a woman bustled in and out with mop and pail. She appeared to Cory like all the people of Brussels, a tiny figurine in an enormous amphitheatre, rendered deaf and insensate to any call for aid.

"Until finally Beatrice did as the Virgin asked. One day when she was alone, she took up the statue and carried it home. She painted it and gilded it and replaced it in the cathedral. And now that this was done, the people began to admire the little statue. No one was more happy about this than Beatrice."

"But again the Virgin came to her in a dream and asked that Beatrice should take the statue out of the church. Like an obedient servant, Beatrice carried out this dangerous task. How did she manage to carry away the statue of Our Lady from Antwerp?"

At his own rhetorical question, the man looked up, surveying the space around him, wanting to be certain he still held Cory and Reg in his grasp. Cory had moved a little too far away for his liking, so the man edged backward, including both of his followers in the reach of his voice.

"I shall tell you how. When Beatrice reached out her hands to grasp it, the Sacristain, who would have stopped her, was struck by a force, *a mysterious force*, which paralyzed him, and even prevented him from speaking until the next day!

"The Virgin told Beatrice she must transport Our Lady to Brussels by boat, and so she did. When she arrived in this city, at Brockere, she was greeted by a great crowd, and they walked here, to the Place du Grand Sablon, where the statue was placed in the Chapel of the Crossbowmen, which stood on this spot. And forever more, the statue was discovered to bring about miracles and healing."

The man with the blond mustache finished with a satisfied air. His voice disappeared upward into the cold air of the cathedral.

"Today, many people came here to pray to the Virgin. You may see a copy of the statue. The original was destroyed during the French Revolution."

"A delightful legend," said Reg.

"Thank you," said the man, as if he were a storyteller and not a thug. "Of course, there are other ideas about the miraculous statue. Some people do not believe in Beatrice, the pious woman of Antwerp. In one charming version that I believe you would particularly like, the miraculous statuette was found by a couple, in a tree in the forest. And it was said to have been adorned by the angels."

He smiled. "You will see on the other side of the cathedral there is a wooden copy of this couple, in their *barque*, with the virgin between them."

The man crossed the floor of the cathedral to where a wooden carving depicting the boat sat beneath a circular window. The boat was small and open; on slats at either end sat a man and woman, facing each other. And between them, standing, her child in her arms, was the statue of the Virgin Mary. The couple rocked back in awe. Uncertain light from somewhere overhead fell on the centre of the boat; the Virgin herself appeared to be floating on air.

Reg spoke into the silence. "No, you are mistaken. I don't like this version of the myth. I don't believe that the couple would find the virgin in a tree, 'adorned' as you say, 'by angels.' It is better that Beatrice steal the statue. I like the idea that an illegal act, perhaps even an immoral one, can be the first stage of a miracle."

Cory dropped Reg's hand and turned toward the altar. She was not about to be ambushed by angels. "You speak in parables," she said.

"It's cold in here," she called abruptly, and after one long look at the sacristy with its exultant wood sculptings she turned her back on it all and walked toward the door. On the steps of the church the blond Belgian overtook her. He cut in front of her, herding her against a tree trunk. Reg came up behind her. The evening jerked forward, into another cast. His tone of voice was utterly changed.

"We have got your people out to the border."

Reg's hands moved forward involuntarily. "They're out now?"

"They're still in Germany. Very near to Nijmegen. It is not clear that they will survive. They are very thin and tired, especially the girl."

"The girl?" said Cory.

"Soon," said Reg. "We must get them very soon."

"There are some others coming through now. Yesterday, an old Jewish man and his grandson who had been in hiding. Dutchmen who have been forced to work in German factories. People are running. But it is very dangerous. If they are found, they are shot. And of course, there is no one to help them on the way. No food, no fuel, in German towns, we're told. There will, of course, be a flood to follow before too long. And then your armies will march in. For now, it is all we can do to get a few across. Sometimes it is more than we can do. We have done well to get them this far. But at the river, all is lost or gained."

"Of course."

Cory understood everything. She'd been set up. She was caught. She felt the bristling presence, behind, in the darkness, of the little tradesmen who had closed her into the square.

"We are on our way to Nijmegen," said Reg.

She couldn't endanger him by saying, "We are?"

"I should like to be paid," said the Belgian, pleasantly.

"When they have safely arrived," Reg replied evenly.

The man stood with expressionless face, his eyes moving from one to the other. His hand flickered in the direction of the gun.

"It is not good." He did not move his lips; his eyes were cold.

"It is always possible they will not arrive," said Reg.

"You must be very careful. You would not want anything to happen to alert the border patrols," said the man.

"Other lives are at stake."

Reg crushed Cory's finger joints together, so hard she nearly cried out. Then he dropped her hand.

And so it was arranged. Reg and Cory stood in the street. The moon had climbed out of the tree and hung overhead, mirrored in the gleam of the wet pavement. They listened to the man's boots echo against the walls. Then it was very quiet.

"I suppose you're upset."

"Who are they, Reg?" As if she didn't know.

"Mimi's daughter. I don't know the other one."

"We're not allowed to participate in escapes! You can get me bounced from here. Slapped in detention again!" Cory railed. In the dead streets their words ricocheted like stones. They acted as if they were the only English-speakers in Brussels; they were behaving dangerously. They walked, feet racing, faster and faster.

"An illegal act. To facilitate a miracle."

"Fairy stories, Reg. Do you think I'm stupid enough to fall for parables about statues?"

"Now that the Virgin is here, she heals."

"They don't believe in miracles in the army."

"They should." He smiled at her once, then walked away from her, swinging his folded hat in his hand. He pulled a flask out of his hip pocket, a molded, silver mickey-sized flask she'd never seen before, and took a long drink. "What's the point of being a soldier if you can't stop people from dying?"

"We're the opposite of soldiers, Reg. We don't fight. We're not here to smuggle our friends over borders!"

He took a long, hard look at her over his mickey of spirits. "I always thought you were a cold fish," he said. "Moralizing, too." As if it were himself he had insulted, not her, Reg's face grew knotted and purple. His fingers dug into the flesh of Cory's forearm as he held her up against him. "I — think — you — are — dangerous!" he hissed. "What you think. How you see. What you have become."

Tears spurted to Cory's eyes.

He let go. Cory drew her forearm to her chest and rubbed the sore places where his fingers had dug in. He wiped the spit from his mouth. "Mimi was your friend before she was mine," he tried at last.

"This girl's been dancing and singing for the Nazis!"

"She had no choice. She was what — thirteen? I know what this is about. You're still angry with Mimi about Albert," Reg taunted. "That's why you won't help her get her daughter."

So he knew about Albert and Mimi! Cory knew he was trying to derail her argument by getting her angry.

"That's not true! How many of them are we going to meet in the next few months who had no choice? When we get into Germany, do you think they're going to admit to being Nazis? They'll all have been forced into it!"

"Oh, Cory," he said wearily, "there you go with your Ontario Methodist morality."

Cory faltered. Perhaps Reg was right.

Sometimes she was frightened by the image of herself

her friends reflected. She was like Eliza — rigid, self-righteous, judging. She was frightened, too, by just how alone she could become, how, to her, everyone could so quickly turn, become a burden, become dispensable. Mimi *was* her friend. But now she was ready to deny her because she'd made a mistake. Proven herself human, as Albert would say. She was frightened by her own inflexibility, by her little song: Nobody helps me, and I don't help anybody.

Perhaps this rescue of the girl — why didn't they ever call her by name? It was Karin — was exactly what they ought to be doing. Perhaps, despite being soldiers who should kill and journalists who should report, this was indeed their higher task. Perhaps it was why, out of all the trails in Europe, their two separate trails had brought them here. What was she really resisting?

"Why didn't you just ask me outright? You want me to get this girl out of Germany."

"I wanted you to hear the legend. To see the statue. The Virgin, carried by boat. It's so specific, it has to be meant for us. Can't you see? There are particles of spirit, glimmers of the divine, that cling there."

It was the way he said "us" that silenced her. She walked on, riven with emotion.

Reg stopped for a minute to take a drink and then caught up to her. "You always did want to fight with me," he said, lamely, and began to laugh.

She wiped her eyes, hoping he didn't notice the tears. Perhaps she *was* becoming dangerous. And who was she to talk of army discipline, she who, since D-Day, had meandered behind the lines, refusing to report to head-quarters, failing to pick up the telegrams from the *Express* that she knew must be piling up, somewhere?

Perhaps this war would be kicked into life, perhaps it would finally flare up and burn itself out, if people like herself crossed the lines. If the soldiers refused to shoot, and all the correspondents refused to send back their dispatches. If they decided to help their friends, and the children of their friends, and of their friends' friends. Even as she thought it, she knew it was a mad, childish notion. What then of the camps? Of Dachau? What of the prisoners locked in it, over the border in Germany? What of the people without friends? It was a mad notion to try to save Karin, and yet, tonight, in Brussels, under the gibbous moon, it seemed the only thing to do.

Reg drew her toward a street light. "Why do we fight?" he asked. And he did not mean the war. He meant the two of them.

"We fight because once, I was too stupid to go to bed with you."

Now, with the white glow coming over his shoulder onto her face, he examined her without smiling. "Is that it?" He leaned toward her, and she leaned herself, inside his waiting arms. The puck-faced moon was fully exposed now, bobbing up in front of them as they walked, embracing, down the narrow street. The night had become transparent, like a black day. He pulled the flask from his pocket and drew on it again.

"I'll take you home," he said.

But he was not as sober as before. He swung Cory up against him, squeezing her ribcage with his big hand. He leaned on her.

"*I'll* take *you* home," she said.

"Let's get back to where we were before," Reg countered. "Tell me again about being too stupid to go to bed with me?"

Clattering, shushing him, she got him up the stairs at Madame's place and put him in her bed. Then, while he lay unmoving, she pulled off his boots, his socks, and his shirt. She hesitated before undressing to get in beside him. There was only one bed, and she was tired. Besides, it was cold and she could not resist the comfort of his big, warm body. She stripped down to her underwear, lifted the sheets, rolled Reg under them and climbed wearily in herself.

In the early morning, Cory was wakened by a pair of large, cool hands exploring the hollow of her back. The hands ran up and down over the mounds of her buttocks and the small of her back, pressing on her spine, venturing further to investigate the closure of her brassiere, and the elastic tops and legs of her panties. As the hands pressed her closer to his body, the buckle of his belt dug into the soft mound of flesh around her navel. He held her there urgently for a few moments and then relaxed. It seemed he was drifting back to sleep.

"I refuse to do this while we're unconscious," said Cory. "Let's decide."

His laugh was a low, sleepy rumble. "Let's not decide. Then we're not responsible." He slid his hand under the strap of her brassiere. She got both her hands on his belt buckle. She was only a little nervous. After all Reg was her familiar and perhaps the only man she might have loved, after Albert.

The odour of his chest had come to her before, in cramped airplanes, steamy wet bomb shelters. She had clasped that back with her tensed fingers before, when the shellfire erupted around them. She felt she knew all about that belly, those large-boned elbows, but the long, heavy penis with its silky tip was a surprise.

They moved, curiously, all over each other's bodies. It was like exploring something they'd owned for a long time, but had never fully appreciated. How long his limbs were, and how beautifully formed. His chest was furred in a shield shape, his nipples were shy but sensitive, his belly hard. The long deep thighs trembled when her hands came near and his penis came to life like a stem that had been watered, and nudged her, patient, but insistent. Once she thought he had gone to sleep again, his hands were moving so slowly between her thighs. Once she thought *she* had gone to sleep again, but it was only a kind of meditation.

She pressed her mouth against his side, his scars, his chest. Somehow they became joined; she could not have named the moment and they rocked that way, it seemed forever, Reg slowly rolled, onto his back and she rode over the top of him. Then they changed again, and he was the rider.

A whole day was lost in there, between sleeping and waking. It was a day without signs, when escapees from Germany hid out at the river's edge at Nijmegen, a day when all that could be held off was held off. It was hunger, finally, that drove them out of Madame's house as the dark settled over Brussels again. That night, they went to the cellar and had dinner. Reg went off to pay the ferret-faced Belgian and then he came back and they went to bed. Tomorrow they would go to Nijmegen.

Chapter Thirty

FIGURE 30

Reginald Morris

Corinne Ditchburn, War Correspondent

December, 1944
Brussels, Belgium
Reproduced from the original negative
National Archives of Canada, Ottawa

The photographer is standing, dressed in her ordinary clothes, which are a pair of khaki pants, a shirt and a loose-fitting jacket. She is out of uniform, yet she seems to be at attention, ready for war. As if to remind us of a status she does not otherwise make apparent, she carries her helmet. The cameras are slung over her right shoulder. Her hands toying with the dangling cameras are long-fingered, tendony, capable.

Her hair springs thickly from her crown, as if escaping the repression of the tin hat. Tipped off by the hair, you feel her femaleness, also her soldierliness, in several ways: in the way she cradles her helmet, in the narrowness of her waist, in the wide pants that are gathered in to the belt. In the shoulders and upper arms, she looks small. But then there are boys in the army who are no bigger than she.

There is something else particular in the way she meets the camera's eye. She is conscious of what she appears to be: a phenomenon — the helmet, the cameras, her gender. She smiles. She would never be called beautiful, even on battlefields where women are so rarely encountered. She is aware of herself, but not set in her sexual power, a little beside it, quizzical, perhaps.

Getting past all these social indicators, we find the main interest of the photo: the face. The photographer's face reads like a map of the senses: pain, fear, passionate love and sorrow all played havoc here recently.

The hands are tools, but they are sensual. They have done their work, as have the eyes. She is a witness.

❦

THE SUN CAME OUT AS REG AND CORY RODE INTO NIJMEGEN. There were shaved plots of field with unshaven ovals in their centre, and trees with trunks of phosphorescent lime. The grass was turning from grey to green, as the snow melted in the furrows of the fields. On the outskirts of town, little red brick houses stood undamaged.

"I don't know what you're going to see here. This place has been hammered by both sides," said the driver of the truck. "You don't even want to know. There's nothing much to do, except watch the bombs fall at night. There's a hospital — they've got some Jews recuperating in there who were in hiding for four years."

In town few houses were standing. On every corner was a neat pyramid of swept-up stone and glass from the bombings of the day before. People climbed up out of their cellars carrying baskets for shopping, but there were no stores. The housewives stood in disconsolate groups, staring at the army vehicle as it passed.

"Still, they're lucky, they're liberated. Most of them know people to the north, in Amsterdam, who are starving to death, waiting for us to get the Germans out. You figure, they hold all the territory to the west, to the east and Amsterdam to the north. I tell you, we'll get to Berlin before we liberate Amsterdam."

They passed a bleak field where low sheds, like cattle sheds, were grouped inside a barbed wire fence.

Gazing out of the jeep Cory could see nothing to make a decent photograph. There was only brown water, fog, the dark skies and the flatness. There were no landmarks. Nothing but stripped trees rose above eye level.

"Now you're looking at the only reason we're here," he said. It was a long metal bridge with two arches, over the Waal. "We've been shoved up this ass end," he went on pleasantly. "Sitting at the top of this little alley from Brussels all charged up for the moment when we get this show on the road and get into Germany."

She was billeted at a farm where, despite the tanks trundling across its lands, the chickens were fed each morning and the cow milked. A woman whose eyes never lifted from her work swept the floor, mopped the counters and put the slops out for pigs. A day went by, then two days. Cory was not certain what she was waiting for, or watching for. She assumed Reg was in communication with the go-between. She wanted to know as little as possible. She did not know what she would be called upon to do but she'd promised to do it, and the promise lay upon her like some new landscape to be explored, disobedience of the sort she would not have undertaken previously but that now, in the absence of illusions, she almost looked forward to. In the meantime, she could pretend to do what she always did.

Then it snowed.

"I think God loves photographers," Cory told the young officer called Mickey Brennan who'd showed them around. The army brought out its white camouflage suits. Propped on their stomachs on the side of a dike with their rifles poised, invisible but for their faces, the troops were suddenly new, clean, bagged. In her viewfinder a soldier was reduced to a rifle and an indefinable weight that anchored it. In the background were the evenly spaced, straight rows of fruit trees, branches black on the bottom and loaded with snow above. To add to the photographic interest, she had landed in the one place in the war where the forces were actually using canoes. Swift and silent, the Lincoln and Welland Regiment had unsheathed their war machine, canoes.

The next day the weather alternated between sleet and snow, with a leaden, low sky and racing horizontal winds. The soldiers made shelter under ice-crested tree roots, and scooped out caves in the drifted snow. They patrolled the ridge above the river bank and returned to sleep in their ice-lined burrows, only lifting their heads to answer a field telephone that had been wired into the mud wall.

"It's a stalemate," said Mickey Brennan. "The Germans can barely defend their own border now. They believe, against all evidence, that they can still get out with what they had when they got into this. It should be over, but still — and this is the goddamn shame of it — we're losing men all the time. If we can see them across the river, we gotta presume they can see us," said the young infantry officer. "Stick your head up at the wrong time, or run along the edge of the hill attracting attention, and Gerry will pop you off."

After dark on the third day, Cory, Reg and Mickey Brennan went outside. Across the river lights were moving around on the flat ground behind the farmhouse.

"Either there's going to be an air attack, or they want us to think there's going to be an air attack. See that farmhouse, you see lights as if somebody's in there. Whereas I know it's abandoned," Mickey said.

Was that where the refugees were hiding — the man and Mimi's daughter? Cory felt cold and sick. A soldier came up to talk. "Sir, the phone lines have gone nuts. Everybody, platoons, companies, has called Brigade. Brigade has called everyone back so no one could get through."

Reg pulled Cory aside. He lit a cigarette and stared off across the river.

"How much of this is your doing?" she said.

"None of it," he said, staring at her with incomprehension. "How could it be? It's pure luck. I got a message this is the night," he said. "And the Gerries are creating a fantastic diversion."

He put a pistol into her hand.

She was a good shot. She used to go hunting with her father. She'd shot a few squirrels out of trees with a pellet gun, and even downed a deer once. But the gun offended her. It was wrong.

"Just in case," he said.

"No," she said.

Cory, Reg and Mickey Brennan walked out into the frosted fog and down toward the canal. Mickey thought something was going to happen. Cory had her cameras and Reg his tape recorder. It was late at night, after eleven. From the town of Nijmegen came not a sound or a flicker of light. Brigade headquarters, behind them, had also become one of many ghostly ruins against the sky.

"Let's go to the river," said Reg.

"It's none too healthy there," said Mickey.

"If there's fireworks, that'll be the best place. Cory should get shots of the bridge, don't you think?" Reg persisted.

"You seem to know more about what she needs than I do," said Mickey, acquiescing.

They walked along the side of the power plant toward the canal towpath, which would take them to the river's edge. It was slippery, a mixture of sleet and ice caked in irregular footprints, ridges, and pools. They watched their feet.

When they heard the bark and the whine of a Moaning Minnie they hit the ground. It was easy to see where the Minnies came from because they belched flame from their barrels as they were shot. Mickey Brennan got the bearings and ran for the nearest field telephone.

Reg and Cory lay there while six of the missiles sailed in. When they raised their heads they saw flames, a barn or a silo, a stack of hay burning.

"Before long, our side will hit back," said Reg. "It won't be any use, because they'll have moved on. But that will be our moment." He looked anxiously at his watch.

Mickey had returned. "You still game to walk to the river? I don't know what you're going to see there, but I'll take you."

On the half-frozen mud bank of the Waal, they waited. It had begun to snow again. Small, dry flakes spun in front of Cory's eyes, dancing like dust motes, seeming to rise as often as they fell. In the whiteness she picked out the dark figure of a man on the other side. He ran, hunched over, from the house where the German soldiers were holed up, along a fence where he must have thought he couldn't be seen, to a barn. She could see the barn door open a crack, just a crack, above the fence, and then shut again.

"He's gone to check the livestock. They've got chickens in there, or ducks, and maybe even a cow, but if it's a cow it's a mute one," said Mickey. "Either that or they're up to something."

Cory thought of Tyke: how some day she'd tell him the story of the pious woman who stole the statue of Our

Lady from the cathedral in Antwerp, and took it by boat to Brussels. How she'd tell him if she came back that it all had to do with him. How she was sorry. She thought of the Germans across the river, watching them as they watched in return. And she thought of the seventeen-year-old girl on the other bank. How, in a few minutes, she'd walk along the riverside path, a pleasant walk for the town's lovers, when there were lovers, when there was a town, just as if she didn't know that two armies were poised across the black cold winter water, either one lethal to her.

She wondered if Mimi got what she wanted from sleeping with Albert, if he gave her a pipeline to the girl.

Dear Albert —

The girl will wear white, we've been told, to be plainly visible in the darkness. But we weren't counting on snow. Reg is wringing his hands because of this reversal: What would have been her striking beacon is now camouflage. I didn't mention to him the rightness of this photographic reversal, negative image, black goes white and white goes black.

She'll walk down the road, appearing to be a local girl, perhaps demented from the war, harmless. And when she reaches the natural indentation before the bridge where the creek enters the flow of the Waal, she will step down the bank, carefully, because of the mines.

Then Reg will work his subterfuge on the hapless Mickey Brennan: "Who's that? Look, some crazy

girl. What's she doing? She could get herself killed."
He'll get into a canoe to save her. In its belly she'll
be invisible, and when she reaches our shore, we'll
smuggle her back along the treacherous tow path,
across that shell-pocked land on the edge of
Nijmegen: just another simple-minded civilian
wandering lost in no man's land.

On the surface of it, there is nothing wrong with
this plan. It's simple and manageable. But it has its
weak points. One is that we have to deceive our sol-
diers and risk their lives. But every plan has its
flaws, says Reg. This one will do, and the night is
like any other night.

But already it isn't. The snow has made it dif-
ferent. The little flakes fall up as well as down, and
we are confused...

When did it start to go wrong? First, Reg went out in the
canoe too soon. He was not supposed to be the one to spot
the two refugees.

"Hey! What's that?"

They were shouting, but the girl was not down yet, not
out of sight of the Germans. She was on the bank and the
soldiers saw her. Why should they care — she was on their
side. Even the Nazis are now running away from themselves.
But they began to shoot as she slid down the icy bank.

Reg shouted at the soldiers to get her. "Look, she'll be
killed. It's just some crazy girl trying to escape, can't we
pick her up?"

Cory saw the canoes cluster in the stream and knew the men were arguing. She floundered off the edge of the hillock, and down the bank, her feet feeling the chill of the black water. The river had its own expiring, ominous motion. What a stupid plan it was: Who would stroll along the river banks at this hour of the morning except a prisoner escaping?

There she was again. One minute the landscape was flat, submissive under the constant fall of heavy snowflakes, and the next minute she stood, a triangular black shawl marking her shoulders, her legs like a pedestal barely visible, under the bridge.

Two canoes spurted from under an overhanging tree. They moved silently on the water toward her. Then, for who knows what reason, little Bobby Forbes in his foxhole taking his option, perhaps, or soldiers believing she meant to blow up this highway into Germany, gunfire came from the Allied side. The bullets stuttered uselessly into the water and the canoes moved onward.

Cory stepped into the river. It was icy cold. She lifted her camera. Mickey Brennan must think she was getting her shot. She thought she saw the shawled figure jerk down, quickly, as if she'd been grabbed by the feet. Or perhaps she'd been hit in the now-steady rattle of shells?

The canoes that had sidled up, briefly, to the rampart, now sallied forth again, two paddlers in each, one lying more heavily on the water than the other. They came straight across the river toward Cory.

Now the Germans' attention had been drawn to the

canoes themselves, cutting across the current of the river. Cory could hear shouts and see lights flashing, then disappearing, then flashed again, fifty yards further along. They were trying to move the Moaning Minnie, but she was heavy and clumsy.

Mickey Brennan appeared beside Cory at the river's edge. "What are you doing? Are you nuts?" He yanked her back behind the tree roots.

At that moment the canoes went out of sight around the central base of the bridge. Cory and Mickey waited, frozen on their slippery bank, under shellfire. When it was quiet — how many minutes it had been she couldn't guess — the first canoe slipped out again from the shelter of the island and cut across to the Allied side. The moon and the falling snow gave a diffused light, as if the air itself was glittering. Suddenly Cory was overcome with a strange excitement, the feeling that she was attending a rite, a ritual, some holy sacrament. She stood and ran. Behind her, Mickey shouted at her to get down, but she saw Reg in the bow, bearing down on the paddle.

Into this holy feeling came a blast. The second canoe, darting from behind the pillar of the bridge, was hit. The explosion broke the slender craft in half and threw the sternsman out at an angle. A piece of the stern flew into the back of the bowsman's head, and he was boosted forward, as if he suddenly decided to stand, before he tipped out of the canoe. Reg continued to paddle. The girl in the belly of the canoe remained invisible.

One of the men from the hit canoe had floated into the

trees by the bridge piling. Reg, insanely, was trying to turn back to save the other man. She knew what Reg was thinking, that he had to get him. Otherwise he'd die and it would be Reg's fault. *Their* fault. But he was singling and the current was powerful, steady and flat. She could see he'd never make it. The sky only a hundred yards downstream was lit with the arcs of tracer bullets.

Another canoe appeared from around the bridge supports and streamed for the injured man. A shell fell in the water fifty feet downstream. Reg gave one last look at the injured man and spurted toward shore.

"You've got her?"

He didn't answer but her eyes took in the bundle on the bottom of Reg's canoe.

The girl was stiff, unmoving in her thin woollen shawl and her face was grey. But she knew their names. Reg — she said, and Cory — a high, stilted, German-accented voice. She cried a little, and then lapsed into a silence that could not be distinguished from unconsciousness.

In Brigade Headquarters, Mickey Brennan strode angrily back and forth, waiting for his superior. "We've been set up!" he said, over and over. "Two men injured. Who is this girl, anyway?" Reg and Cory waited together, shamefaced, for their reprimand. It seemed a time for joy but how could they celebrate? The girl was barely alive.

The skeleton in the boat was Karin, Mimi's daughter, and she would live. That was the miracle. But it happened slowly. That Reg would fall in love with her was perhaps obvious from the start, even as he took Karin's veined and pallid hand. But perhaps that is not true. Perhaps it was only that Cory knew she had lost him already, lost him the moment she learned she could love him. They were amiss and awry, off rhythm with each other. Cory, the practitioner of the black art with the magic timing, she who never missed a story or a shot, lost Reg because she had missed her own time. Now it was Karin's time.

That night, her old nemesis Mahoney got on the telephone from Antwerp.

"So that's where you've been hiding out, Miss Ditchburn!" Then she heard a lot of, "If you girls can't play by the rules," "endangering our men" and so forth.

Reg and Cory got forty-eight hours in detention, then they were both out of the war, for now, maybe for good.

And this time she had no recourse, no chance of going on by herself. No offer of staying away from the front lines would appease him; she'd tried that one. Which was why, although Karin was becalmed between life and death, the next day when they got to the hospital Cory insisted on getting the photograph of the two of them, side by side.

It was the nearest Cory would ever get to Dachau.

Chapter Thirty-One

That this toothless rag-decked bone rack beside Corinne Ditchburn is a person, we understand, because we have learned, by now, to recognize its condition as human. Other photographers, such as Margaret Bourke-White, entered the concentration camps on liberation, and presented similar images to a disbelieving public. But four months earlier, when this photograph was taken, the young woman beside the correspondent might be taken for some wraith, some propped-up mummy half unwound from her shroud, animal verging to vegetable or mineral.

But the creature is a young woman, and as we look at her more we see that she has intelligence, that she is aware of her condition, that she evinces a curious devastated dignity.

ℛ

TOGETHER, TYKE AND MAIDA, THE CURATOR, EXAMINED THE photograph, now redeveloped for the exhibition. They were silent, dumbstruck, unprepared for its power. The selection built toward this, it must be the climax, if one could use the word climax about a retrospective.

But Tyke wasn't sure. He wasn't sure that such a shape pertained to moments from a life, or from this life, in any case. What interested him in the picture, so difficult to look at, so painful to contemplate, was something quite opposite to the rise and fall of interest and suspense. "I'm not certain it does what you want it to do. Maybe we shouldn't use it," he said.

Here was his mother, and a half-dead, skeletal apparition that was, one somehow knew, a girl. Beside her, the fully dressed, well-nourished photojournalist stood unsmiling. To see the two figures side by side, apparently complacent, shocked Tyke. The alive woman did not even offer her jacket or a canteen of water to the victim but stood, apparently willing to go on the record as merely *having stood* beside her, in the way one stands by a monument. Looked at in this light, the photograph took on the quality of an obscene parody of the snapshot of tourist and native.

Consider the calculation involved; Cory had set her camera on remote, taken her place beside the young woman, and faced the flash. It was all in a day's work, and she would go back where she came from, unharmed, perhaps even unchanged by what she has visited.

Or would she?

It seemed to Tyke that he knew the face in the photograph, the face of the victim, that he had seen her in some dream, or some incarnation utterly unconnected.

It further occurred to Tyke, as he peered at it, that the photograph was about absence of desire. Ahead of its time, it would feel familiar to the modern viewer. Television news broadcasts, and oft-reprinted photographs of horrors that ought to move us to compassion but instead stun us to passivity, give the same message.

What, indeed, would he have his mother, this witness, this tourist, do? Take the chocolate out of her pocket and give it to the starving victim? She was so depleted that chocolate would kill her. Throw away her uniform and become one with the victim? What interests would be served?

He asked himself: Does this snapshot represent for Corinne Ditchburn an unprecedented bit of vanity?

He asked Maida the same question.

Together they examined the photograph.

"No," said Maida finally. "It illustrates her helplessness. You see, she's only a photographer."

Yes. She was only a photographer. Tyke felt peace descend on him with that pronouncement. He smiled at Maida gratefully. The photograph was a record of all that its creator could do about suffering: Be its mirror. She could not tend the sick, minister to the disaster-struck. If she had, she might have eased the victims momentarily, but the situation would have been unchanged. Her role was to be unaffected. It was the photograph that must act.

Karin was like a voodoo doll, or a graven image. There were tufts of dry hair on her scalp; her eyes were sunk in black pits, and her cheeks sunk too, because there were no teeth left in her mouth. Her limbs seemed impossibly long; racked out from the hangers of her pelvis and her shoulders, they dangled, skeletal things without motivation. Her ribs were bold as an abacus. Above them were the spots of what would have been breasts, and below the thin shavings of pubic hair covering a mound that appeared enormous. Her head was large and perfectly shaped. She weighed fifty-five pounds and she could not stand on her own.

The doctors would not allow her to eat. When she saw food, even the wretched hospital mush that went past in tin bowls for other patients, she sobbed. Sometimes she raved that they had kidnapped her, and were starving her to death, that her lover would come and shoot them all. At other times she fell into a dazed state, not sleeping, not appearing to see or hear, which the doctor felt was most dangerous of all.

Mimi sat for hours, revolted, mourning. "They have killed her," she insisted, "and sent me this dying thing by mistake." Grief for the child she had left behind drove Mimi from the room to cry outside. "It is an impostor," she cried.

"Mother," called Karin.

"No!" Mimi screamed. "Tell me it is not her."

But the girl had a string of dark brown moles, spaced as evenly as jewels on a chain, over her collar bones, and the fingernail on the forefinger of her left hand was rippled where it had been slammed in a door when she was a toddler. All of this Mimi had told Reg in advance. All of this he showed her now, lifting the long, skeletal arms from under the sheet and carefully holding the finger up to the light. The hand itself was translucent, like a leaf, veined, magical.

Then Mimi rocked by the door, half in and half out of the room. It was as if a sheet of glass lay over Karin. Magnified, she looked inward, to her dying. If she coughed out fragments of her story, she wasn't telling them so much as she was regurgitating. She had been someone's favourite. When he had to move on, he did not wish anyone else to enjoy her. In the camp, unaccustomed to work, she failed quickly. Despite her youth, she was classified with the dying, received less of the already pathetic rations, only rose from her bed to be counted.

In the end, it was Karin's voice that called her mother back. The voice came from the past, from now unreclaimable years of joy. It was a lovely voice. When Karin raised it, they who watched her looked around the room, to the walls, the cellar windows to find its origin. Perhaps a bird had flown in from another part of the world, and alighted. Certainly the voice bore no relation to the husk on the bed, with its sores, its self-absorption.

Cory got her punishment: bounced out of the theatre for the duration. In truth, her old friend Colonel Mahoney had not had his heart in it. They'd become strangely allied in their attitude. Lately she'd made no trouble for the forces, and she'd managed to get some good shots out. Still, you could not have war correspondents taking matters into their own hands and trying to help every German who tried to escape the Wehrmacht. Cory quite agreed.

Reg met the same fate. They were together again in Brussels before they flew out to London. Mimi and Karin were in the Nijmegen hospital until Karin was strong enough to be moved.

"The woman is impossible," said Reg, openly scornful of Mimi now that he had done what she wanted. He hated her shining hair, the fur collars of her coat, her "ill-begotten wealth" as he called it, waxing biblical. "Selfish, spoiled, deluded." But Cory felt pity for her. Mimi's heart could not take in what her eyes saw.

In a nursing home on the Cromwell Road, Karin lay supported by soft blankets. If she lay on a mattress, bearing her own weight, the skin of her haunches would tear open. She was allowed a mouthful of Pablum every few hours. Even that most often came back; her throat constricted on it, she began to spit. But drops and particles of nourishment must have slid down her throat, because she stayed alive.

Day by day she remained in her place, still as an effigy on the lid of her own coffin. Her head was like a stone, the high round end of it, the way it narrowed, past the cheek bones, past the chin, to a sharp point, and her far-apart eyes, which no longer quite moved together, had the look of beacons.

When Cory visited, she saw Mimi flit along the corridors. Under her eyes the skin was black, swollen. Cory caught her in the powder room with a piece of broken mirror, menacing her own reflection. She seized both her wrists, and held them by her ears as Mimi banged her head backward against the wall. "I should die. I don't deserve to live."

"Not you, too," said Cory, wearily.

"Perhaps she doesn't deserve to live," said Reg when she told him. "But it's not what she deserves that matters. It's what she's needed for," said Reg.

Resting in London, Cory was angry. No one was safe from her rancour. She was angry at Albert for betraying her. At Reg for getting her in trouble. At herself for going along with it. Max accepted with equanimity that she wouldn't work again.

"Cory, it's time you settled down. Go find yourself a good man to look after you. Marriage is a financial arrangement. It's based on the fact that men can earn plenty of money, and so they set up with women and the women live off them. The way Mimi lives off me..."

Cory knew she'd never give a man the right to say she lived off him. To belong to a man would mean captivity; it would force her into passivity. It was too familiar, like Liss with Albert. Find a man to survive? No, proximity to one of them would extinguish her. The only men she loved were both dangerous and unavailable.

She and Reg never spoke of their day and night in Brussels, which might have been the beginning of a life together. Karin had stopped it. She floated between them, obscene, a comment on lust, on love, on the miraculous and the vile. She was a grotesque of the Madonna in the boat: She was the old wooden statue that had not been cared for and must be adorned, perhaps by angels. Cory was like the sacristan, paralyzed temporarily by the mysterious force. Sex, love, passion, flesh: It was all over for her, thought Cory, as far away and unreachable as the moon.

Again, as when she had first come to London, eight years ago, she walked the streets in a welter of emotions. She pondered her own selfishness and her rage. Had her rapt attention, her love of the man who taught her, all along been a disguised envy?

Albert was drinking again. One day she walked past the Duke of Wellington at afternoon closing and watched him cross the street, and eventually crash against the wall. She could not go to him. He was lifted by some passerby, and she walked on.

Distanced, she began to weigh his influence. How much had he given her, and how much had he stolen? She wondered how she dared to go forth to war with his derision ringing in her ears. Only because she had been enabled, too, by the force of his passion. She had been enlarged by his adoration. She had been diminished by his judgment.

And Tyke. How to understand that? How to make anything of his utter refusal to know the child, although he was the one who'd raved on the train from Yorkshire: "We must have a child. Every time I fall in love I want to have a child."

She had tried to live by his rules, in leaving Tyke. What had she learned by doing that, except what we all must finally learn: to die. That was what Albert had meant about death being too easy. Absence of desire. She would not let death win.

Tyke would lead her back home.

Yet Cory did not leave London, not yet. Still she waited on in Europe as the news came in: Dachau was liberated. There was victory in Europe. The soldiers began to muster in London, ready for their journey back across the Atlantic, and home.

When the atom bomb was dropped on Hiroshima, Max wanted her to go.

"You are the only one to take these pictures," Max said. "Your last hurrah."

"I've seen enough."

"You told me you were a photographer."

They were at his flat in Arlington, up on the seventh floor. It was just possible, from the sitting room windows, to see Green Park, where in the old days before the war he had disported himself on horseback with young ladies. The Lord had just exited his water closet, his unfortunate secretary in tow. It was bad enough to be called into service while Max was in his bath or sitting on the toilet. That had happened to them all. But then to be observed, tripping in his wake as he exited, doing up the buckle of his belt — it was intolerable. The current flunky avoided Cory's eyes and busied himself with a coiled notebook, his face fuchsia.

"I don't think I need to prove that," Cory stood with her feet apart. There'd been a change in her dealings with Max. He needed her, and she made up her own mind: She was in a category of her own.

"Aren't you all for sale, well aren't you?" Max was famous for shouting at his employees at the *Express*. What Max did not understand was that he could only have as much power as his victim had need.

Absence of desire meant maximum control.

"If you're a photographer, you won't be able to stay away from this one," Max said. "It will be the event of the century."

Only a practitioner of the black art could say such a thing. Cory stood apart from him and his unfailing zeal for catastrophe. It wasn't even about selling papers, as was so often said. The catastrophes themselves had such resonance with him: They fit his inner world, filled some need.

"How can you say that? We're only at 1945," said Cory. But she sneaked a glimpse at the destruction wreaked by the new bomb.

"Look!" and he held up a copy of the newspaper. "It melted the metal on roofs. People were vaporized, simply turned to ash, it was so hot. There are bound to be sights —"

"I want to go home," was all Cory could think of. "I've been here too long. I want to see my son."

"Of course you do. You know I don't approve of a mother gallivanting like this, leaving her child at home. You should be off. Go to see your son. But do this first. Let's book you on a short trip. You can call me in a week. Then I'll fly you right back to Canada if you insist."

"Promise?" She could see it coming into sight now, her little cabin, the boy fishing on the dock.

"I never break 'em."

He turned into his bedchamber, where he proceeded to unbutton his shirt, pulling it out of his trousers. The unfortunate secretary began to back away.

"Hold it! Don't go off, George! I've got lots more to say to you!" He was down to his undershirt now, his wide chest with silver hairs reminding them he was a man and Cory was a woman.

The Stooks brothers came forward from their jungle of cartons and disused equipment to stand side by side, hands clasped in front of their waists, and look upon her, dismayed.

"Now we shall have no reason to look at the paper," said George, woebegone.

It was impossible to thank them. Her throat rose up painfully and tears stung the rims of her eyes.

"Colonial lady," Harry said.

"I have to go home."

"Not again! I absolutely forbid it!" Aunt Eunice shrieked. The war and her job had loosened her larynx. The new hips and knees still not available, she walked with a cane. She banged the tip of it on the bricks of her garden patio emphatically, once, twice, three times. "You must not!"

All Cory could do was repeat that she was sorry and help her aunt to a seat under her rubber-leafed tree, and leave her there, under Leary's new command, majestic behind the house whose top floor was still very much open to the heavens.

She went to say goodbye to Albert, but he was "unavailable," said Liss. The two women embraced with promises to write. And Albert did, the next day. But he had to chastise her, didn't he? He couldn't let her go in peace. He had to lecture, to impose, to intone.

> *Dear Cory —*
>
> *You really have changed, you know. You haven't got that cool, disguised feel, as if you were giving the day its due, knowing full well that once the moon was up, it would be off with the mask, caution thrown to the winds, daring the fates to catch up to you.*
>
> *It's more as if you and yourself have ceased relations with each other. As if you don't want to permit that wild bloody girl who's so much trouble and*

*so unpredictable to take over. You're so much less
dangerous now.*

*I console myself by thinking — one can't truly
lose oneself, can one? Even if I can no more see the
wild girl hiding in you, you can't have left her or
lost her. All you can do is choke her out for a season
or two. She'll come back, won't she? She'll love me
again. I have to believe that nothing truly significant can ever die.*

She went to Japan. When the second atomic bomb was
dropped on Nagasaki, she wondered if Max had known it
was going to happen. With his cunning, he might have
suspected that if Japan did not surrender there would be
another bomb. On the other hand, more likely, with his
supremely erratic judgment, he expected an American
invasion, a counterattack of thousands of suicide pilots, a
self-immolation of the Emperor, who knew? He sent Cory
to get photographs regardless. After all, he sold ten times
as many papers when he had photographs.

In Japan she did not take many photographs. She did
not want to. What she saw there made her decide she'd
taken her last war photograph.

It was a woman, a woman's body. The woman had been
800 yards from the epicentre in Nagasaki.

Cory saw this woman lying in a hospital ward atop the
hill from which one can see the harbour. Cory stopped in
front of her, bowing as she had learned to do already. Her
form was inert, her eyes shut, a tube coming through

black, sizzled lips. The doctor who was accompanying Cory explained that this woman had been wearing a dark-coloured kimono printed with large white flowers at the time of the blast. The kimono was no more. The flash of light as the bomb exploded was so intense that the fabric had been incinerated on her flesh. The dark-coloured background absorbed more of the light than did the white-flowered part, and so her skin, under it, was burnt more severely. The light-coloured fabric, in the shape of large flowers with five pointed petals, repelled more light. When the skin underneath the flowers burned, it did so with less severity. And so the pattern of the woman's kimono was repeated on her skin, in reverse. She became, herself, a photographic negative — her skin the paper, the cotton the emulsion, the great flash of the atomic bomb her light source.

Afterward she called Max from her hotel, and he was as good as his word. She flew out of Tokyo three days later on an American military plane. The airport was wild with American soldiers; the war was over. The Japanese were expressionless, terrified, waiting for the victors to exact revenge. She couldn't wait to get away.

That photograph, which she never took, was there, in her mind, as vivid and clear as if she had actually seen it, until the last day of her life.

She surprised Tyke on the rocks in front of the Manitou Hotel. He was six years old, and he had not seen her since he was three, but he knew her, perhaps more from pictures than from memory. He raced for her and leapt up on her waist, wrapping his legs around her body. She caught the substance of him, pulled it from the air, her hands automatically under his buttocks. Pure joy and astonishment filled her. How could she have left him for those macabre pursuits? This boy was made of light.

"I'm home. It's me, it's me."

They spun together, laughing, crying.

"Here, lock your feet!"

She put her hands underneath the small of his back. "Now, fall."

It was a trick they used to do. He arched backward, reaching overhead for the ground, screaming in delight, his torso falling through the air, his hair standing on end, reaching for the earth with his hands.

And she gagged, for suddenly he looked all too much like one of the dying soldiers she'd seen, stretched out, blown, vulnerable. She bent and gasped for air, letting his arms and then his body down to the ground.

He stood beside her as she bent, dry heaves wracking her body. His little hand was on her back. "Are you okay, Mum? Mum?" She pulled herself upward, her eyes watering, and lifted him up again for the game.

"I'm okay. Yeah. I'm okay." She wiped her eyes. "Just — dizzy."

He watched her, critically. Was something wrong with his brand new mother? She fought for control and won it.

"This time, we'll do it. Go!" She patted his rump and he trotted a little distance away.

"Now!"

He ran at her and jumped again, tucking his legs around her waist. He threw his arms over his head and swung backward so his hands could reach the floor. She leaned over and put her hands down to walk on all fours. He put his hands on top of her feet. They walked forward, marsupial like, then backward, chortling. Her hands gave out.

"You're so big, you're so heavy."

They rolled on the dock, embracing, and Cory cried as she had learned to cry only in the last two months, roaring and bellowing, tears spurting from her eyes, holding him to her breast. Tyke went still against her. He knew the war didn't send people back whole. A Pamajong uncle of his had returned without an arm. His mother cried.

There were footsteps on the hollow wooden stairs, and shouts from the rocks behind.

"She's here!"

"It's Cory Ditchburn, she's back!"

"Wouldn't you know, that sneaky old thing" — it was Marge's voice, booming over the rock — "she never even let us know!"

Then they were all on the dock, crowding onto the dried cedar planks above the water while a few bemused hotel guests gazed down from the verandah. It was all the homecoming she wanted. Tyke standing in front of her, holding both her hands, a grown boy, all that leg, fighting back his tears. "I knew you'd come back for me."

There was a visit she had to make. She hadn't been home three days before she took Tyke out to the plant at Nobel.

The guardhouse was manned by someone she'd never met, and when Cory asked to go in for a visit he called the plant manager. Dave Clark came out of the office squinting in the lemon sunshine, shaking his head with a crooked smile. He extended his hand solemnly to Tyke.

"How are you, young man?" he said. "I think we've met before. You were your mother's secret weapon for getting her job here, did you know?"

Inside the gates the plant grounds were quiet. "Oh yeah, we're out of business," said Dave. "Operations scaled down to practically nothing, except that in came a contract to disassemble a couple of million landmines. Stockpiled over there in England I guess. At some point, before V-E Day even, they realized they wasn't going to need 'em all. So they sent them to us for salvage. The shipments began to come in so fast, big steel boxes of them, and nobody knew how to get the TNT out. We didn't know anybody but Wade Johnstone could figure out a way. I expect it's Wade you've come to see," he said.

Again they had to pass through the checkpoint for matches or any steel, which could rub against steel to make a spark. Inside one of the old TNT lines they came upon the blind man seated on a stool, his face a mask of rubbery seams, his eyes half-sealed. Ten feet behind him lay his seeing-eye dog in harness; he broke off his snooze and growled. But Wade was busy, his foot operating a treadle like Eliza's old sewing machine, his hand rhythmically pumping on a handle, and he didn't raise his head.

"Couple of visitors here to see you, Wade," said Dave Clark.

There was a great tank of water next to Wade, and Tyke wanted to put his hand into it. Cory gripped his wrist. "It's dangerous," Cory said. "You can't."

Wade's face broke into a smile then. "Is that my boy I hear over there, and did you bring someone here with ya?" When he heard Cory's voice, he stood up and opened his arms to her.

"You better tell me what you're doing there," said Cory, wiping her eyes after the hug was over.

Wade explained that he'd been pretty depressed, not working, especially after they heard Willie was killed.

"Hadn't done much of anything. Then the landmines started coming in and Dave asked if I could work out how to defuse them. I went home and doodled a bit, on the weekend," he said, with what was intended to be a smile. "Yeah, I can doodle, just nobody can make sense of it, not even me, that's all. And I figured out this system here. Came in that week and we tested it for a few days till we could get a line up and running."

He showed her the mines, circular, like shoe polish tins, with their rimless lids pressed into the top. He'd fashioned a conveyor run by a foot treadle, which brought the tins up one by one in front of him, standing on their edge. Then all he had to do was fold down a handle, which inserted a blade between the tin and the lid, and roll back the lid. The conveyor carried the opened tin to a big tank of warm water and dumped it. In the water it overturned and the TNT, like a lump of hardened brown sugar, fell out. The empty tins bobbed up on the other side of the tank, harmless, and the TNT was left in a sludge on the bottom.

"Watch," he said, feeling his way back to his stool. He pumped the treadle again, and Cory watched as her greatest wartime fear was dismantled in front of her eyes, on her home turf.

"Pretty smart, eh?" said Dave Clark. "Company's got a patent pending on it."

"Gives me a job, eh? We haven't had too many problems with it," said Wade modestly. "Of course they were supposed to have had their detonators removed but they don't always."

Chapter Thirty-Two

FIGURE 32

Corinne Ditchburn

Christopher Tyke Ditchburn, at 10

1949

Pointe au Baril, Ontario

The photographer's son stands on the rocks near his island home. After the war, Ditchburn rarely photographed other places or strangers.

૪ટ

"WHY," ASKED MAIDA, "ARE THERE NO PICTURES OF YOU AFTER this one?"

"Because I refused to let her take any."

He and Maida sat together on the army cot in Cory's studio. Going through the boxes was dusty work. Tyke had brought a flask, and Maida made tea which they drank with his brandy. Then — dusk falling, the sound of people's footsteps rushing outside on the pavement — they rested.

"Why did you do that?"

"I've often asked myself the same question."

He swung off the bed. Whenever he talked about his

mother he became restless. He walked to the great uncurtained window, which hung wide and oblong over the Rosedale Valley Road.

"She took me over. Then she gave me back something which *she* had created."

The silence was deep, layered. Maida listened to all of it, and watched this man, his muscular legs, his expansive chest, the hanging belly, a localized expression of age. They hadn't known each other for long, but the work had been intimate, and he told her a great deal. Perhaps because he needed to.

"I couldn't bear to look at them." Tyke's eyes reddened with emotion. "Do you see? She saw a needy little orphan. She saw with her guilt. But I had made myself strong, so I could survive without her. I was proud of myself. I wanted her to be proud. I wanted her to see the man I was becoming. She saw the boy she had abandoned."

She heard the voice over the teacups clear across the wide verandah. "That's Cory Ditchburn. Her father was up here before any-one —

— drowned you know

— I know

— been away in the war, hasn't she"

And the bright smile focussed on her, the head revolving as she crossed the lobby to the clerk at the main desk.

"Any letters for me?"

He produced the one slim blue envelope. It seemed to float like a feather into her hand.

This particular, perfect day — maybe it was 1948 or 1949; her war had been over for almost as long as it had lasted. There weren't very many of those blue air mail forms any more: Most of her mail came from New York. But today this. And the old peacock blue ink, the spidery, man-running-in-a-rainstorm look of the handwriting was his.

She walked to the verandah and sat on a chair. The sun went behind a cloud and without it the shores of the islands opposite could not be separated one from the other: The separate mounds of rock with trees were massed, appearing like a solid shore. In an instant the water turned that choppy grey, solid, with no light in it.

These were the days she loved most, now. Anyone could see beauty here on a good day, but on a day like today only the subtle eye was rewarded. It had taken this long for her "vulgar" (Albert's word) love of sunshine to be sated. It was a love she had shared with Max Aitken: That had been enough to incur Albert's contemptuous comments. Sunshine was a luxury: England had little of it and that was as it should be. That was how, she reflected, Max had brought Mimi into all of their lives, lounging in the sun like a lizard on the Côte d'Azur.

"Dearest Coree —"

he wrote. Using the bird call he'd made of her name at the very beginning.

*They tell me you have taken no lover over there
in your wilderness. It seems a shame that you have
given up what is obviously your greatest talent in
life...*

She put her head back and laughed. She was seized by the
laughing, it drew in her stomach, it tightened her throat,
nothing could move. Then there were tears rolling down
her cheeks, and she thought she might wet her pants, but
she held on. She was clamped by this fit of merriment, this
explosion of mirth.

Who was this "they," so knowing about Cory's lovers?
And "her greatest talent"? For passion, was it? A seeming
tribute, but definitely not an expression of faith in her
photography. And Albert was always so sure of his judgment, of the way he summed her up, encircled her,
sketched her into the picture he had drawn.

*I knew from our first meeting that your heart
like your country was virgin forever. You fought
every takeover always, whether from a man or a
muse.*

*If you can hear a warning take this to heart. The
muse won't wait on you: A dragon in her lair, she's
demanding a tribute of love and sex, preferably
both. You're in great peril if you don't accede. Don't
imagine I'm giving you a great sales pitch on my
own behalf: What you need is me, that sort of thing.
On the contrary, I have only your interests at heart.*

But perhaps I have it all wrong, perhaps you have found love, sex and the font of your genius all there in the arms of whoever, your Red Indian voyeur or was it voyageur?

Dearest Coree, you haven't said, and, now that I think about it, I'd rather not know. Leave me believing your reasons for abandoning London and me were maternal, delusional and could have been melted under the burning imperatives of flesh, had I had one last chance. This is not a plea, though you must know I'd happily die for you on a moment's notice. Meanwhile, I'm bereft, but who's to care? Let me say this — I'm honoured if I bear the expense of our mistakes, rather than you.

She was briefly, passionately carried there by the voice that came through his words. But it was over with Albert. Over, except for moments of weakness when she grew so hot with longing she had to go in to Pointe au Baril Station to use the radio phone and call Liss, or Mimi, anyone with news of them: Max, Reg, Albert.

Jimmie saved her, because he had been there. Jimmie had come back from the war himself, miraculously, a whole man. He never talked about his fighting, or asked her about hers. But he saved her.

It had been impossible at first to sit through dinner with people who thought the hardships of war could be summed up in the fact that fishing guides had vacated or they couldn't get rubber bands for their children's hair. Jimmie made a set of eyes to connect with, while memory ran panicked through the range of images that were most often suppressed, except in the nightmares that periodically ravaged her sleep. Jimmie was there then, too. He folded easily into Cory's days and nights, sometimes there, sometimes gone for weeks on end.

"I don't suppose you could ever find yourself a white man," Eliza said, tremulous but still defiant, at her doorway in Parry Sound. She loved her daughter, she loved her grandson even more fiercely than before, but still, there was a way to live and a way not to live.

"I don't know where you get your information."

"My customers tell me things. Otherwise I'd never know, would I?" She cast a long, critical look at Tyke, who stood staunch, defending his mother against what he did not know. Finally she sighed and walked away, leaving the door open.

"I don't know," she called over her shoulder to a cautious Cory stepping over the threshold. "You're just like your father. What he saw in those islands, those Indians..."

"They're only people, mother."

Still Eliza helped Cory. She kept Tyke for weeks at a time when Cory went down to New York. Cory never knew nor thought to ask what they did together, but when Eliza died, in her small estate were many books, which she left to Tyke. It turned out they had sat together in the evening and read poetry: Sir Walter Scott, Poe and Whittier, Eliza's favourite. It was because of Eliza that Tyke was able, even as an adult, to recite most of the poem, "The Specter Ship."

> And lo! the vision passed away—
> The specter ship — the crew —
> The stranger and his pallid bride,
> Departed from their view;
> And nought was left upon the waves
> Beneath the arching blue.

In Tyke's adult voice Cory heard the formidable Methodist romantic who'd been her mother. Like Eliza, he reached for aphorisms to contain his strongest emotions.

> In vain the Sage,
> with Retrospective Eye,
> would from the apparent
> What conclude the Why.

> *You will be forgotten by the world,*

wrote Albert. She countered,

> *Fine, if it must be. I don't care for all that anyway. It's behind me, all behind me. What I know is this: I must make one place on earth my own, or I'll never work again.*
> *Little yellow-bellied birds in pairs chase each other from one side of the channel to the other. I*

have all this — miles of ancient rock twisted in lava layers, laid out in swirls, rolled into boulders, opened in crevices where the trees forced their roots down to water, using their own dead needles for soil. Every shape known to humans was first imagined here, in some creative tantrum of the earth's molten state.

They call it no-man's land. And it is that, just like the space between opposing armies. The forces this time are yours and mine. You could never find the comfort you need here. But I do, in the knowing of it. I know the shoals, where each one lies secret under the surface. I've memorized the water for dozens of miles around; I could run it by my eyes before sleep, like a farmer reviewing his fields, like the path to the sea we memorized at Heraldo's.

How can you stay there, my darling? It's all so new.

My dear Albert, it isn't new at all, there's nothing new about it. In fact, these rocks are the very oldest part of earth; to find them anywhere else you'd have to go down ten miles into the planet. Just come over, why don't you, and I'll show you a perfectly spherical pothole, drilled by a rock being whirled between several mile-thicknesses of moving glacier in the last ice age. Only come over and I'll take you out to make an offering to the Sacred Turtle.

But he never came. She'd said goodbye to him, hadn't she? Their love affair was over, it had been over since France. Still, his letters came, and his voice went on, speaking to her, and she spoke back to him. In this whole wide world, he was someone to talk to, a voice to still the silence inside.

There were, in the ten years following the war, a series of arrivals at the Manitou, each more improbable than the previous, as Cory's friends tried to dislodge her from her seat there, or at least tried to understand why she refused to go anywhere else.

Donalda came the preferred way. A red-headed woman in a yellow slicker, deftly steering a canoe, in the bow of which sat a couple of kids and a man. She simply came around the point and pulled up at the dock. "Hello, Cory," she said.

"Donalda? Is it you? How on earth did you find me?" Cory screamed. She was up to her knees in water, rinsing her laundry. The kids stood up, making the canoe teeter. Tyke helped the man pull it up on the rock. No one knew what to say, the way the women were dancing around, slapping each other's arms and shoulders.

"Cory Ditchburn, you haven't changed a whit, how dare you!"

The husband and kids announced they were thirsty.

"I still can't believe you found me."

"You've got a postal address, right? We started at Killbear and just kept asking."

The canoe was full of packs; there was a tent, too. There would be no way of avoiding a few days stay-over on the island. Tyke took a closer look at the kids: They both had red hair and freckles — a couple of girls.

Inside the two women watched the aluminum of Cory's coffee percolator bounce and jiggle on the propane burner. They repeated names to each other, in a slow roll call, at each one shaking their heads. Donalda had news of most: dead, dead, prisoner of war, not the same, made it back to Saskatchewan, perfectly okay that one, oh he lost a leg.

They poured their coffee into the chipped blue mugs, Donalda every now and then breaking into laughter at how she'd surprised Cory.

"It's the only way. I knew you'd never invite me. They said you'd gone to ground. You haven't got one comfortable chair in this place. Geez, Cory, you're so Canadian. You'd think having an upholstered chair was unpatriotic or something."

They sat in the sun on the deck and held their coffee to their chests. It was hot, and the stillness had changed from the perfection of earlier to an oppression.

"So this is your famous island."

"It's changed," said Cory.

All around, people were adding boathouses or building on additions. New cottages mushroomed from the rocks behind the originals, built to hold children and grandchildren. Many of them had electricity. Lights at night ruined the sky and beside that, they gave boaters false co-ordinates to steer by: Once the light was out, they didn't know where they were.

"It's the thin edge of the wedge. Don't you see?" The people down at the far end of her bay had added a yellow roof. "All you need is one of those to ruin the view, ruin it."

But she had given in on a flat cedar platform out in front of the cottage, facing the southwest, and on four bright yellow canvas folding chairs, around a table Tyke had made the summer he was thirteen. It was made of a cross-sectional slice of a giant pine that had fallen in a storm, sanded and varnished, and cedar logs (bark on) for legs.

As motorboats gnarled their way through IgoUgo Channel, splashing water up on the rock walls, Cory complained on behalf of the loons, which nested at the water's edge. The wakes could wipe out a generation in one splash.

"But you love it all," said Donalda.

"I do."

Clouds began to crowd onto the western sky. The heavy thug of the inboard motor travelled from the channel ahead of the sight of the boat. Then it appeared, a white wooden square-hulled boat with a flat cabin roof: Jimmie Pamajong's. He'd had people out for the day of fishing but had seen the weather and was running for home.

They ran to cover their gear and turn over the canoe. Donalda folded chairs as Cory pulled in the kitchen window, which opened on a hinge from the bottom and was suspended out at an angle by a chain. Tyke pulled his own canoe up on the rocks and flipped it. By this time they could hear the rumbling, and the sky was full of clouds of a rich purple-grey, tumbling quickly over one another.

The always-dark cabin was darker now, the usual squares of sunlight gone from the floor. They could see the rain approach, over the water, as a rising up, a dance on the surface. Then it reached them, falling in ragged sheets that swept and retreated, battering the walls of the cabin, then subsiding a minute before battering again. This dark descended upon them, heavy and close, an embrace unlike the dark of night, when the absence of light made the world more distant. The thunder rolled around them, sometimes to the east, sometimes to the north. The rain steadied to a thorough downpour, the wind dropped to nothing.

"Now," said Cory, "wait for it." Her beloved explosions of thunder and lightning. They sat through it together, smiling.

When Donalda left she promised to invite herself again. "I won't wait for you to call. You'll never change."

Lydia del Zotto came, and when she came it was with "clients" who bought photographs. The first time she arrived it was a muggy August day, at the tail end of a heat-wave. Every day for the five days previous, thunderstorms had been forecast to break the Bay area out of the vice of ninety-five degree temperatures, humidity of nearly one hundred percent, and complete stillness. And every day the thunderstorm did not happen; dawn came at six, pink and pale blue. The water was thick, a silvered turquoise, and the air too. The sky was cloudless and promising to encase them all once again in the kind of summer day which made one feel like a fly in aspic. At seven o'clock in the morning a leftover moon stood white as a bone in the western sky, and the trees were lying on the water, waving at their edges. The crows woke half the Bay, going after the compost behind the hotel.

Tyke was fifteen, working that summer as a dock boy at the Hotel. He'd have rather been a fishing guide but that job belonged to the Indians, he said, and even when the Pamajongs asked him to work with them, he refused. So every day from seven in the morning until six at night, he manned the docks, getting gas, loading the supplies into boats, helping children and old men step over the gun-wales into their canoes, bailing out leaky boats and what-ever else was needed.

He knew everything about boats, how to land them, how to fix them. He was the best canoeist the regatta had seen in a decade, regularly cadging the trophy for the canoe race. He was small, but strong in the upper body. There was nowhere he couldn't leap to, on the rocks, no dive he couldn't imitate, no combination of wind and water that could defeat him. Cottagers who'd been around for the last fifteen years took a possessive pride in Tyke, in his beauty, his joyousness. He was *their* boy.

That day the first three early boats had come for their eggs and their bread and had left again, in the post-dawn mist. Now the sun had worked free of the slight haze it had risen into, and was sending down its hot message. Into the sound of the greedy and quarrelsome crows came another, a hard beating, which could have been one of those new speedboats if it had not come from the air. Tyke looked up and there, circling into sight in the bay in front of the Hotel, was the plane.

In Tyke's memory another plane had come, bringing the Queen or maybe the Governor General, when they opened the National Park. And there was one very rich American, the president of a big oil company it was, who had flown in for his fishing holiday. But arrival by plane was frowned upon around Pointe au Baril. A plane stirred up a wind, disturbed the calm surface of the water, made a terrible noise, and attracted attention to itself, all undesirable activities according to local custom.

A plane was, furthermore, an ostentatious show of wealth, also frowned upon, especially by the wealthy, who more and more had come to populate Pointe au Baril. A plane was modern, and involved change, and change was looked at, by the cottagers at least, as a threat. The isolation of Manitou had turned on its head; once it had been a liability but now it was cachet. If one person could get in by plane, how many others might follow?

So this one must belong to a bigwig, thought Tyke, taking off his hat because the wind that was stirred up as the thing coasted up to the dock could have blown it away. It couldn't be a hotel guest, because they'd have told him, wouldn't you think? But desirable or expected or no, it was part of his job to deal with it. Whether it was a lost fisherman or a flock of ducks: "Whatever and whoever comes up to the dock" was his responsibility.

So Tyke found himself shaking hands with a man and a woman with dark hair and loud nasal voices, wearing shiny white tennis shoes, matching white blazers and ironed blue jeans. And after the "beautiful day"s, and the "quite a view from up there you know" and the "amazing part of the world," they let on they were looking for a Miss Corinne Ditchburn.

At this point Tyke had a choice: It was a familiar choice *vis à vis* his mother. He could claim her, instantly, "She's my mother!" and become the recipient of curious, mildly pitying looks, and thus identify himself by what she was, as being a part of her. Or he could play it cool, hang back, wait and see what they were after, and maintain his independence.

When he was smaller, anyone mentioning his mother's name drew him like a magnet. He loved to hear talk about Cory's photographs, about how brave she was to go off into that war with all the fighting men, and he felt proud. Then she had come back. "Miss Corinne Ditchburn, War Photographer, who had been in Europe, has now deigned to come back to us," they said, smiling widely, at the cocktail hour in the Hotel.

Having a war hero mother wasn't like having a war hero father, it seemed. It meant he was deprived. (Even his name came from "poor little Tyke," it seemed: All along they'd disapproved of her.) He hated to be felt sorry for.

"Cory Ditchburn?" he said. "You mean Cory Ditchburn, the photographer? She's on one of those islands out there," he waved his hand vaguely toward the west.

"How do we let her know we're here?"

"There's no phone, you know that."

"They're probably on the CB radio bands, right, son?"

People were starting to come down the stairs now from the hotel, curious about the plane.

"Actually," said Tyke, "I figure she won't be home, not on a morning like this. She'll be out in her canoe somewhere, with the camera. She likes this kind of calm."

Miss del Zotto cocked her head as if she were listening to something far away. And she ran her tongue into the side of her cheek and poked it, then she caught Tyke's hand and said, "I knew I recognized you. You're Tyke! How's your gin rummy? I never knew you'd turned into such a marvellous young man!"

Eunice arrived by train at Pointe au Baril Station, a straw hat tied on her head with a net scarf, for all the world as if she were about to go punting on the River Cam. When she saw Tyke and Cory she stepped down from the car with her long neck extended, her chin in, peering over the metal steps to the tracks below as if she disapproved of the very gravel they were set in.

"You drive a hard bargain, Cory Ditchburn. Never coming back to London! You ought to be ashamed. Well, I've come to you," she said, as Tyke picked up her ancient leather suitcase. "How many of your fancy friends can say that?" She hugged Cory briskly and avoided Tyke's eyes, or so it seemed to him.

The wind was blowing hard from the west as they set out. Down the long inlet they ploughed into a heavy chop touched at the crests with white. But the water didn't really get big until they turned to cross the open stretch beyond the lighthouse, before heading into the inner channel going north.

"Hang on!" shouted a gleeful St. Pierre into the wind as they swung around to head across the open. He loved to give newcomers a baptism of fire. The waves pitched the boat from side to side, occasionally slapping over the bow, and soaking them all. Eunice sat as erect as ever and did not flinch, not even when, for a moment or two, they couldn't see over the waves.

When they rounded Semaphore Point and entered a stretch of relative calm Cory and Tyke wiped their dripping faces with their sleeves. Eunice pretended she was bone dry and betrayed no relief, either, when the taxiboat pulled up at the Manitou. "Please find me appropriate accommodation," she had written. Cory had debated whether to have her aunt stay in the cabin, but the idea of Eunice using the outhouse was more than she could imagine.

The Manitou had grown prosperous too, this decade: The dock had been expanded to eight slips to accommodate all the boats, and newly painted white wicker chairs lined the verandah. "I hope you find this appropriate," said Cory.

She took a hand to step out of the boat, and allowed one of the kids to run ahead with her bag, but Eunice gave a long look across the Bay before she went in.

"You won't make me wait too long before you let me see my brother's fishing cabin," was all she said.

In the mornings when Tyke came to pick her up Eunice would be stalking along the dock, inveigling the fishermen to tell her their secret spots as they came back from their dawn runs. She showed off her new artificial hips and knees by climbing in and out of canoes. A stork of a woman she was, in her mid-calf khaki skirt, with a man's shirt tucked in at the waist and forever the straw hat tied down with chiffon. Her white Ditchburn wave only showed when she took off the hat for dinner, and then the oldtimers came around to talk about Robert. And once, as one of these gents approached deafly, hand extended to shake, Eunice included Tyke. "The next generation of Ditchburns to live at Safe Harbour," she said.

And that was enough for Cory: If she were ever to hear a note of forgiveness from Eunice that would be it. The old woman watched Tyke as he lightly stroked through the waves on his daily swim around the island. "You've got a golden boy there. What else is he good at?" she said, ironically. "Anything useful?"

"I never understood what you saw in this place," said Eunice, when her bag was packed and once again she was standing on the dock waiting for St. Pierre.

Cory grimaced: She heard Albert's voice, one of his favourite phrases — "*that fucking primeval photogenic island...*"

"But now I know. I wish I hadn't left it this long. I don't

suppose I'll live long enough to come back."

Reg Morris, too, came by helicopter. Tyke heard the crack-pounding, which could have been one of those new speed-boats if it had not come from the air. He looked up and there it was, circling into sight in the bay in front of the hotel, the helicopter. Landing on the big X painted on a bare rock, it made an ear-splitting noise, not to mention the wind, on account of which he had to grab his hat. A face grinned out the window, and the door opened. A tall man climbed out, followed by a young, dark woman; she hesitated and he offered her his hand.

"Beautiful day for it," Tyke said in the way of the locals.

"We don't mean to disturb you. We're looking for a Miss Corinne Ditchburn."

"Oh," said Tyke, still assessing. Reg Morris stood by looking down at the minnows under the dock. He was a big man, handsome, even distinguished, but there was something broken-looking about him. "Oh yeah, she's on one of those islands."

"How do you know she wants to see us?" the woman said to Reg. "Not everyone likes surprises."

"She likes surprises," said Reg. "She went to war, didn't she?"

Tyke decided they were friends. The woman had an accent, something European.

"I'll take you out in a few minutes," said Tyke. "Just let me get through with this grocery load, okay?"

He eased the runabout through the line of big cruisers

tied at the docks, rounded the corner and crossed the open bit. "That's it," he said, pointing out the dock on the back of Safe Harbour. He could see the canoe. "You're lucky. She's there."

Reg handed the woman his watch, his shirt and his shoes. He stripped off his khakis. Underneath he had bathing trunks. A scar that looked like a loop of messy purple worms wound from one side of his neck under his arm and down between his ribs.

"It's farther than it looks."

"I swam farther than this to land at Sicily, pulling my typewriter and about twenty pounds of kit," he said. "I figure I can do this little stretch."

Inside, Cory turned on the kitchen tap. The water gurgled, spat and ran down to nothing. She went out the back door and headed across the slant that led to the pumphouse. A fish jumped in the quiet channel behind her. Then a series of splashes — what was it, an osprey? She looked in the water and was astonished to see a man with a powerful front crawl ploughing her way.

"Hey!" she shouted, thinking it was a boater in trouble, or somebody's drunken house-guest who'd lost his way.

"Hey!" the man shouted back. The voice plucked an old chord in her. Smoothing back her hair with one hand, she walked down to the dock, and out to the end of it. His great leonine head grinned up at her out of the water.

"Take you by surprise?"

"You did, actually." She still didn't know who it was. To cover her embarrassment, she peered across the water, seeking something she could recognize. Who was it? The voice was like music, a modulated, professional voice. She knew it, she knew it so well.

"Reg!"

He was close to the dock now. She ran back in to shore and splashed in at the shallow, marshy spot, howling with joy. He got to his feet and they both tried to run, but they fell, so that finally they hugged each other on the surface, under the surface, and on the warm rocks as, together, they dried out.

"You bastard, you crazy bastard, you old rotter you, you scared me half to death," she kept saying.

Then she looked up and saw Karin in Tyke's runabout.

Tyke was maybe seventeen that year. He didn't ask too many questions of his mother, but he knew there was a story there, about how the war had ended for her. He had not become a scholar of the conflict, that was still to come: At the moment he was simply dead curious to know what it was in her that he didn't grasp.

Once he got Karin a drink, he led her down to the smooth, warm rocks looking out to the open where today there was not a breath of wind. Making an excuse, he left her. Then he crept alongside the cottage and stood under the kitchen window where he could hear everything that was said inside.

He could tell the man was holding his mother in to his chest, then out at arm's length and in to his chest again, as if she were some returned object of desire.

"You look so good. Why did I think you'd look older?"

"I look older? How could I? Hell, we were old then. Now we're younger."

They must have crossed the room then, because the voices disappeared. But Tyke knew exactly what to do: He followed the line of the cabin to the verandah, and crouched beside the little pine that was bent around the support beam.

"You brought her back to life, you waited for her, you married her," marvelled Cory.

"You knew that."

"I knew it but I had to see it to believe it."

Reg made a noise that sounded half whimper, half complaint. "Hey, be gentle with me. Cut me, I bleed, all of that."

She was quiet for a minute. Tyke could hear the ice rattle in their glasses.

"So much heroism in one man. It's almost as if you had something to atone for." Then swiftly moving on, so that he might not comment, "What on earth will the kids be like?"

"There won't be kids, Cory," said Reg. "Karin can't. Not after what she went through."

Cory was silent, perhaps shamed. "Explain to me," she said. Her voice trembled. Tyke did not understand. What did it all mean?

"What shall I explain? This?" He dipped his head in Karin's direction. "I suppose you'd call it perverse. Some people do. She was a child then. Only seventeen."

That was Tyke's age exactly. Jealously, he wondered

what part this seventeen-year-old had played in his mother's life.

"But I waited. You can't say I robbed the cradle. There's only a dozen years between us. I tried other women. I tried being without her. It didn't work. You were gone, Cory. And I guess — somehow as long as we're connected, I mean Karin and me, I have my past, it wasn't all for nothing.

"You know," Reg said, and now he had taken a different, more public tone, a tone of reminiscence, not confession. "In general, I like young people better than people my age. You and me, we're survivors. It's as if we know too much. Too much that's ugly. About us and the whole world. I'd rather spend time with the students, the nineteen- and twenty-year-olds who were going to school *without* a war sweeping them off to mayhem and death. I look at them and think, what would it be like to be nineteen, and not believe your country might ask for your life."

"Karin's like that?" said Cory, disbelieving.

"No. She's not innocent, but she shed her past with her flesh. She came back from the dead, you might say. Maybe I have it both ways," he said.

By one o'clock the haze had burned off and the water was perfectly still. They took the canoes and went out to the shoals in the open. Tyke cooked some smallmouth bass on a little fire in a crack in the rocks. Karin walked head down along the shoreline, poking with her toes at crayfish and broken shells. Cory told Reg about Donalda's visit and the thunderstorm.

"You know, don't you, that she had her camera out in

case the cottage got hit and you were about to burn up?" said Reg to Tyke. He had never quite forgiven her for taking the photograph of the moment when he was hit with the shell, standing by the well with the two soldiers.

Cory put down her beer and walked to meet Karin at the water's edge. They stood for a moment together, saying nothing, and then Cory took two steps and made a neat shallow dive into the swells. She surfaced and began to scull on her back, looking back at them all on shore. Then, almost in slow motion, Karin stripped off her top and shorts, and awkwardly walked after Cory, straight into the afternoon sun. They both — Reg from farther back on shore, and Cory from her swimming posture — watched Karin, saw the wholeness of her body, with pride.

This, too, Tyke witnessed, and he felt some message pass over him, felt that some balm was spread, and that a huge weight of years was shifted away.

Reg was slower. He did everything slowly, Cory thought, treading water and watching him. The scars on his chest and back were there like giant seams, like the scars in the rocks themselves, but they were only scars, not wounds. His bitterness was gone, but so was his passion. It was the way he walked, with care, without joy, thought Cory. He had been so big, so believing. He had run everywhere full of the confidence that life was for his understanding, for his consumption, that he could defeat evil. She thought how true it was that the losers of the war had perhaps won while the winners, the heroes, like Reg, had paid with a life that would never, quite, be real again.

He did his stately breaststroke to where she stood, one foot on an underwater boulder that rose up from the bottom, far away and green.

> *Dear Albert —*
>
> *Don't believe for a moment you were the only one I could have loved. You were just the only man on earth I could talk to. That's different.*
>
> *I can see there were possibilities. I could have lived with Reg in admiration, pity and friendship — what more does one need?_But instead I wrapped myself in the shroud you'd given me, that of the artist alone —*
>
> *Perhaps we are life cannibals. We feed off something that the rest of them prefer to ignore. We go too deep for anyone but us to bear and even we can't bear it. Yet we haven't done too badly, have we?*

They walked out on the porch and sat on the front step of the cabin with their drinks.

"We're supposed to be back in Ottawa by nightfall," said Reg. "Got meetings tomorrow." He was the head of a journalism school.

"The black arts," said Cory. "You still believe."

At the end of the day Cory said, "Now you know where I am."

"Sometimes you must leave here?"

"I do. But I'm never really myself anywhere else."

They said goodbye, with Karin and Tyke standing between them.

Chapter Thirty-Three

FIGURE 33

Corinne Ditchburn

Jimmie Pamajong

1978
Pointe au Baril, Ontario
Gelatin silver, 63 x 45 cm

A portrait of the photographer's longtime friend and neighbour.

҈

ALBERT NEVER CAME TO VISIT. NOT THAT SHE EXPECTED HIM. Liss, perhaps, but Liss died first.

When the news came, Cory realized that there was no longer any impediment to her being with Albert. But of course Liss had never been the impediment. Albert himself was. The great love of her life was an impossible man. When Tyke asked, "What is my father like?" Cory said, "He's just about bearable, for an evening."

Then Eunice died, and Cory went back to England for the funeral. In her will, Eunice left Cory the house in Chelsea. The upper stories still had bomb damage. Eunice had dealt with it by refusing to climb the stairs. Cory told

Leary and her husband to remain there: What was she going to do with a house?

Albert received her grandly in the house on England's Lane: He had a housekeeper who went silently through the house wearing a patterned dress. He was drunk, and wore carpet slippers. In fact, he seemed exactly the same. She was no longer so young in comparison; she was catching up.

"You must stay," he said. "Live here with me where you belong."

His paintings had escaped the studio and were invading the sitting room. They stood stacked along the hall and behind the sofa. Liss's flowered fabrics faded into the background in their presence. It seemed that in his old age, Albert had grown wilder, as if he were fighting himself, fighting the very furniture in the rooms he inhabited.

"I have to go back. I've got to work," said Cory. She couldn't help testing him, though she thought she cared no longer. "There's Tyke."

"Oh yes," he said, "the boy."

Albert would not die.

Albert who had threatened to die so many times. Who had promised to die, in fact. Albert for whom death was the next expected event throughout the entire time Cory had known him: "Well, that may be the last time I ever make love in my life. I may die before I see you again..." Albert who lived in the expectation and in the contemplation of death, who feared death extraordinarily, and who flirted with death extendedly. Death was always on his mind, and his friends, those who loved him, came to expect his death. He had educated them on the subject of his imminent death for so long that they came, without realizing it, to agree with him, to feel that death stalked Albert Bloom avidly, and in particular.

But in fact death was lax with Albert. They say people are too smart to die, or too mean to die. With Albert it seemed that living so intimately with the idea had inoculated him against it. He went on and on, past most of those he had terrorized with threats of his own demise. Certainly in his morbid way he was most tenacious about living.

The news came when they were on the island, having a quiet week at the end of summer, watching the sun colour the distant rocks pink, then white, then pink again at sundown, watching the wind swing from west to east bringing fog and stinging rain, then swing back again in five hours to the saving westerlies. It was their pleasure to sit on the porch and ponder the decline of the sun.

When they heard the soft rumble of a twenty horsepower, they sat up for a friend. Jimmie walked up the dock with a telegram in his hand. Cory went to him, while Tyke, on some instinct, held back.

"Don't go away," commanded Cory as she opened it. Her face showed no expression. When she'd read it top to bottom, turned it over and examined the time of sending, and reread it, she straightened her spine and lifted her chin. She touched Jimmie's shoulder and turned slowly away, to walk up the incline to the cabin. With her back to him she said again, "Stay here, Jimmie. Albert's dead."

The three of them sat in the screen porch as the sun became a pale liquid yellow, and then a fiery orange ball falling amongst the blackened spikes and west-leaning pine limbs of the next island west.

"I always used to think the sun went down into Rebecca," said Tyke. "But when I went to Rebecca I could not see any traces of it. So then I sat on Rebecca and realized that their sun goes down into Lost Island. So then I went to Lost and sat there, and I realized that it gets the real sunset. Its sun goes down into the open water."

"White folks like that open water, I guess," said Jimmie. "Never did understand why a view with nothing in it beat a view with a bit of land and some trees."

Cory was drinking steadily, and Jimmie too.

"I used to think he'd walk up those rocks one day; there was nothing I wanted more. I thought."

Later she said, "He made me what I am. For what it's worth."

"I don't think you ought to give anyone else the credit," said Tyke. He knew he should grieve but how could he, for a man who had denied him?

Dear Albert —
    Tonight I sat here and was ushered into the dark by the largest part of my life here, the sun, and our son, and my oldest friend Jimmie Pamajong, with whom I not once, not thrice, but many times betrayed

you. And all I could think of was the darkness you had gone into and wonder who ushered you there.

Of course it was your housekeeper who sent the telegram, but I wonder who else was there, and it's such a long darkness with nothing — I think it will be nothing — to come of it. And I have to say that with all of it, and our stupid passions and the pain we put them all to, that I am glad of you, and glad of me-with-you. It was just that in you I found, for once in my life, someone to talk to. Talking to you ever since, throughout it all, eased the loneliness. And I have been so lonely that even your savagery, because it touched me, was relief. I wonder if I made some disastrous mistake in my early life, that set me apart from everyone. You always said I needed you, that passion was my muse. But I felt if I couldn't be lonely I couldn't make art. I learned to live with absence of desire. Absence and desire.

The way we were together, something had to die. It wasn't going to be me, and it wasn't going to be you, and so I left. If you were here you'd tell me I killed you, and it would pass for normal conversation because that was the kind of thing you said. May I just say that, having killed you, I'll still be waiting for a note, from where you are. Because I refuse to believe it's over. Didn't you once tell me that nothing really significant (love and war included) is ever over —

And Albert did write. That was the strangest part. Like a miracle, the letter arrived the next week, having sat its requisite ten days in Her Majesty's postal service. Its inside date was only two days before Albert had suffered the massive heart attack that took him abruptly, dramatically, while lighting a pipe after his dinner.

My dearest Coree —

I feel you out there. But where is there? These days I wonder why I refused to come to that fucking photogenic island of yours, your "nowhere" which I always reviled because it claimed you and I could not. At least then I'd have set my foot upon it actually and wouldn't have to feed my starving imagination from your kindly presented prints.

I feel you out there, and I send messages, but these days I can sense my emanations growing weaker. It won't be long, perhaps. I shouldn't actually mind, if it weren't that in my old age, in my frailty, I have begun in fact to like this place, to feel very blessed, in my late wife, my work, my friends — and knowing you, once, in a way that stilled forever the loneliness of my soul. If I have wronged you (and I scarcely dare take up such authority, you have made yourself such an icon of independent womanhood) but if I have wronged you I am sorry from the very pit of my heart, and if I have wronged (which I much more surely have) another person who owes his existence to us, then I grieve in the

bottom of my black black heart and I shall attempt
in what life remains to me to repair that damage...

She handed the letter over to Tyke.

"Only the second time he ever mentioned you," she said, as if it were a small thing, and stepped away from him, suddenly very intent upon rubbing a speck off her sunglasses.

"Another person who owes his existence to us" — well that would be me, wouldn't it, Tyke thought. I can no more claim to have been disowned, can I? "I shall attempt in what life remains me to repair..." What would he have done, if he'd not been snuffed while sucking the flame down into his pipe-bowl? Tyke would never know, would he?

Cory was older than he had been when they met. But not too old to get in a canoe.

She headed out at sunset to the open, to where the islands on both sides dropped back and the water spread before her, a flat horizon.

The glare cut into her eyes, making it nearly impossible to look where she was going. She pulled on her J each stroke, keeping her bow in a straight line for the west. She passed two loons, floating together silently, their dignified profile black because it lay between Cory and the sun.

The brightness spilled out of the low sun onto the water. Not the yellow brick road of certain crisper days, but a large and widening wedge of lemon carried Cory, at last, past the edges of the last islands and beyond to where only a few isolated black shoals disturbed the surface.

She saw the colour working its way down to dark, and thought of Albert's palette, the rich, ripe colours — oranges, browns, maroons and greens — she had never wished to speak in. It had been, to her, a surfeit.

The water was at once blue and yellow. How could that be? She examined each tiny rough peak on the surface, evidence of a little motion in the air, memory of the storm that had been. Each tip was gold, but under it the solid blue of the water remained.

When she looked west, out toward the sun, the gold filled her eyes, her head, with a brightness, that felt like ambrosia. When she looked back where she had come from the difference was total. The wash of gold was gone; there remained only enough light to reflect the chalk and velvet of the deep blue water, the deep green trees, the rocks, now lustreless and grey.

There are insects who literally feed on colour, she understood: It was their nourishment; they were all eye. But the life of colour, although glorious, was short. The eye is overcome, and ceases to see. Witness how colour died, now, at sunset, before the light. Everything becomes black and white in the end.

She sat in her canoe, motionless, and turned her head. Ahead, the brilliance. Behind, the depth, the dark. When she looked into the sun she felt blessed, as if the richness of life were being poured down on her. When she looked back, to where the sun had gone, she felt that she'd been stolen from, that life was bereft of comfort.

The sun had gone into clouds. Cory was tired. She wanted to go home. She turned away from the light, and began to paddle. But that total absence of sun, the powdery dark, like the dry tempera paint that Albert used to use, frightened her. She swung the canoe around again, westward, toward the sun.

Here I sit, thought Cory, on the dividing line of darkness and light. If I go outward to the open, it is all brilliance. If I go back, it is without glitter. Oh, there was still enough light to see the cottages, the edges of islands, the rocks that jutted here and there out of the water making the channel hazardous to all but the initiated. But none of the brilliance remained.

How is it, she thought, that I have paddled to this exact point on the day of Albert's death? How have I chanced upon the very edge of the apron of sunset, the cusp of night? If she paddled farther out into the open, would the sunset retreat with her? Always the skirt of sun ending where she was; always the darkness beginning just at the eastern edge of her canoe?

She experimented for a moment or two, canoeing forward, canoeing back. It was absolutely true. Wherever she sat was the end of the sunset, the beginning of the plain dark blue, the homely, sunken last remnants of day.

It is not where I am but in which direction I look, Cory thought. If I look outward, I see gold. If I look backward, I see darkness. I can see humiliation and defeat or I can see glory. I can see what I have left in either way. The way the world looks to me is absolutely arbitrary. And where I am is the dividing point. "In vain the sage with Retrospective Eye," she quoted, "would from the apparent What conclude the Why."

Cory sat under the amber-shaded lamp staring into the drenched garden. The crisp, airborne leaves of brilliant orange and red declined like aviary birds from branch to earth. The long needles of the red pine were beaded with clear drops of water. The last purple blooms were scattered under the Rose of Sharon, and the Virginia creeper that rose up the side of the house across the way was red. Closer at hand, in the vase on the table in front of her, giant chrysanthemums sailed with their brave yellow into the grey, like a call to arms. A strangely self-possessed Tyke stood before her.

"Mother, I want to talk to you about the letters."

"Albert's?"

"No. Yours. To him."

"Mine? I don't know if he even kept them."

"Of course he did. I have them."

There was a time when Albert's keeping the letters might have exploded his little house of cards, so that all the eggs would be broken, as he used to inelegantly say, and the omelette would be made. Perhaps that was why he had kept them, so that the possibility of Liss finding them, and throwing him out, was always there. But of course Liss had him beaten. She already knew them by heart. She probably packaged them and filed them under "Albert — love letters," in her suffering way.

"How did you get them?"

"He sent them to me. Remember in the last letter what he said? That he would try 'In what life remains to me to repair that damage.'" Tyke looked momentarily smug. "I never told you because I thought you'd be angry."

"Angry?" She looked at him. "I suppose you've read them."

"Read them? I can quote... '*I don't see a future for us, but can't one be constructed by error...*'"

She wondered, as she sat for a long time absorbing the news, how he had managed to intuit once again something she wanted and didn't want: Albert to include Tyke, turning a love affair into a family. Yet she had permitted the exclusion, resenting, perhaps, that Albert should get fatherhood for free when motherhood had been so much work for her. "I suppose they'd hardly seem like mine now. This young woman in her thirties, so desperate, so adoring, so furiously angry — I'd hardly know it's me. What did you think when you read them?"

"You never mentioned me!"

She smiled. He would forever be looking for himself in places where he did not appear. "I did, too!"

"Well, hardly ever."

"And what will you do with them?"

"Nothing, without your permission. I'd like to put them together with his letters, which I know you have." He let his eyes drop, modestly.

"I don't have them," she said quickly.

"I don't believe you. You could never have brought yourself to give them up."

Albert's letters. How they clung to her, those frail scraps of paper. They had crossed the ocean and for decades they had ridden in her hip pocket, or lain forgotten in books, to be taken out once a year, and reread, sometimes aloud, like a joke or a prayer.

Even though she knew the words by heart, each time she went back to his letters they took on another colour. As she grew older without him, the physical existence of Albert's letters indicted her, called her back, invoked some other person who had lived in her body, who indeed, had ruled that body. They were worn at the edges and all out of order. She had memorized most of them. They were little works of art, robust and full of trickery. They were like his paintings: Over time, the cheap background paint of Indian Red showed through, the foreground faded, and they turned out to be quite different to what they at first seemed. Even now if she looked at them they'd have metamorphosed and let through yet another layer of meaning.

She thought on reading the letters that it was his love of her that she loved.

And perhaps it was his love of her that *he* loved too. Was that just because most often they lived with each other's absence? That they lived in a state of shock, travelling on trains, longing for one another? Because, for him, love became some kind of sustaining religion in a blasted world where he was not able to paint, or live with Liss, or with London's moods, without despair?

Old Albert. It was bad, wasn't it, when things went wrong? When he was famous and she wasn't. And then the reverse, when she could work, and he couldn't. When she had a child to raise, and he refused to know. It was bad, very bad. But still the extraordinary good outlasted everything. She wished she'd known him in his better days. And then she wished for nothing at all to have been different and she felt exceedingly blessed. Sometimes in a life these windows open between souls and light and life flows between. It was rare to enter another soul and to enter another body and to find oneself perfectly at home there.

"I don't have them," she repeated.

He stood stubbornly before her.

"All right," she said. "I'll tell you the truth. You're right. I couldn't bear to give them up. But I knew it would be dangerous, for me and for others, to keep them. And therefore, I ate them."

Tyke smiled in a tentative way.

"Oh yes?" he said.

"Yes, like Russian poets in the gulag. I ate them. First committing them to memory," she said a little primly.

"But why?" He almost was caught.

"It was better than burning them. They were part of me. I always felt that."

"You're certain?"

"Yes."

Tyke went off, infuriated, probably to call Maida and

complain. Cory laughed to herself until the tears came. She wished she *had* eaten them. But how could she? Surely she'd have gagged on Albert's words. Eating them would have meant she could not consult them again. I'm still alive, aren't I? I've not consigned my goods to the Flounders and the Tykes and the other custodians of this world? I still retain rights to my person.

Chapter Thirty-Four

FLAT, BLACK FIELDS STREAMED PAST THE CAR WINDOWS ON both sides: the Holland Marsh in October, harvested, dug up and ready for planting next spring. They would drive for half an hour more past settled southern Ontario farmland, and then the rocks would rear out of the earth, orange and angry where they'd been blasted to lay the road. More rocks, and finally, on their left would appear the choppy blue water of the Bay, and as if floating in it, the first few dollops of island bearing their burden of clapboard cottage and dock, with a martin house on a pole planted in front like a flag of occupation.

Tyke sped as he always did, tailgating, passing, naming his opponents on the road "dingbat," "leadfoot." Cory tolerated his hurry; in a car, she let him take charge. It would be their last time up this fall: In two months the ice and wind would wrap the cottage in its natural cloak, sealing off all but the stout-hearted year-rounders, of whom there were fewer and fewer. In the back seat were Maida and a thin, wire-haired young man named Joel, who was a new incarnation of Lydia del Zotto, from the gallery.

Executor: curator: agent. They trail me now, thought Cory, like vultures waiting for me to die. And one day I'll oblige them. But not yet.

Here I am, eighty-five years old and I own barely more than I inherited sixty years ago: a fishing cabin on a god-forsaken little island. Add to that about ten thousand photographs. And what I am, where I have been, what I brought back from there.

They say it is about the photographs, but they're avid for something more, they want my life's blood. I agreed to give them the photographs, but when did I say they could have my life too? That is my true valuable. It's all I have. I traded in dreams, like Max, I was a blue-sky drummer. Even Tyke joins the curious. But he'll get the rest, why should I give him the intangibles too?

All right, I admit, I've been tempted, I've been, in fact, unable to resist. Needing what people need from each other, acknowledgment, a moment's shared contemplation of the landscape of emotion behind the eyes.

"If you were me, would you tell your story?" I asked him once. "When you tell your story the hearer owns a little part of you. They have a thread, and they never let it go. Whenever they want to, they can pull that thread, and you start to unravel."

It was the end of the season. In the marina only the last few boats were tarped and knotted into their slips. The great orange lifter the Pamajongs used to move the boats was grinding and rolling back and forth from water to aluminum hangars. Its long metal tongue slid underneath each hull, then cranked upward lifting the boat as in the palm of a hand. When the giant wheels turned, the machine rolled forward, carrying its prize across the gravel parking lot. Armless and legless, the boats out of water looked as useless as old bathtubs.

A slim boy jumped down from the cab. "Morning, Miss Ditchburn. Morning, Tyke," he said. He strode across the lot toward the marina store. It was one of Marge's grand-kids. Cory couldn't trace them anymore. Generations of Pamajongs had maintained Safe Harbour, cutting the dead trees, replacing the dock after it had been damaged by ice. One of them called when the hurricane went through and blew the roof off the cabin in 1963. Again in 1974, when it was struck by lightning. The fire had smouldered in the juniper roots that snaked through the cracks between the rocks for two days in the heat, and then burst up in flames. One of Jimmie's sons, that time, had been driving by and by sheer chance spotted the smoke rising.

Their guests stood idly by, unable to think what they should do to help. Tyke got out the plaid car rug on his last trip from car to boat. Cory scowled when he tucked it around her, but lapsed immediately into a smile as he guided the boat slowly between the red and green buoys that marked the marina entrance. By the time they'd reached the lighthouse she was beaming.

"It's the light, you see," she said, to Maida, grudgingly acknowledging the watery light of the huge Bay, not dark-ened by shore, the light of the open.

Tyke watched her lips move; he could only hear her in spurts over the motor. It made him happy to care for her. He had always wanted to.

"You see the autumn light takes the colours right down to platinum and grey but then — you get this deep rust of old juniper in spring — and this time of year the greens are so deep..."

Cory hugged herself under the blanket. The raised bow of their boat sliced through a light chop that tossed up the odd whitecap in the channel. Every spring she was soft, weak in the arms, uncertain on her feet. But by this time, fall, she'd be lean and tough, maybe gouged on a shin or forearm, sore in the shoulder and leg muscles from chopping wood or canoeing. Maybe even next year too, if her eyes held out.

Was the body one of the pleasures you had to give up, when you got old? Albert thought so: Even when he was twenty-five years younger than she was now he referred to his body as "a memory." She'd fought losing hers, she still fought. She used to get brown up here too, to get a tan line across her chest, against the white straps over her shoulders, a fish-like white torso where her bathing suit covered. But now she came swaddled, and pale, unable to bend her knees to sit in a canoe. Maybe Tyke could fix her a seat. What luck in a son, she thought, resting her eyes on him, to have a man who was good in a boat.

His look was steady, blue and sunny, unclouded, trustworthy. He was *there*; his presence had a fullness, a quality in it which was like no other she could think of. His attention was rapt; he took up whatever he took up with such energy. He gave himself away, she supposed, instead of saving that. Yet he had something for himself.

His lovers, who she never met. His mushrooms.

At Safe Harbour he installed her in the porch while he carried up the groceries. The martins were gone, as were the barnswallows that had whirled over the martin condominium Tyke had mounted on a pole. But the American goldfinches were here. They were eager, showing off, glib in their flights, darting and plunging in the air as if drunk, which perhaps they were, on the cranberries, and the tiny pin cherries which grew on the black cherry bushes. Playing. Like children. All careless, though she could see, suspended in the air above them, the hawks that followed the little birds on their migration south. The Cooper's and the sharp-shinned hawk circled above, white-bellied, waiting for an unguarded moment.

She watched and forgot the time. Maida and Joel, the young man from New York, disappeared into the kitchen — it was hardly more than a corner — there to hinder as much as help Tyke. At length he arrived beside her, and silently handed her a glass of wine.

"You know, I never played as a child," said Cory. She was aware that as she began to talk the guests closed in to listen, as if she were going to say something tremendously meaningful. "And now I have spent my adult life in play, really, taking pictures. That was what it was, a child's game. I hardly ever wanted to go to bed at night, that's how compelled I was."

She wanted to say this to Tyke, but she could not get him alone, not this trip, not ever, these days. Instead she shot him a look that cut the others out. "And I tried to give you a childhood so you could play, because then, when I came home from the war, I thought you needed to be a child."

He hadn't taken to it. "That's what the rich kids do, Mum," he said. The children of cottagers, he meant. He settled himself with the locals, the natives and the Métis, the working kids who manned the gas docks, the gift shop, and the hotel dining room. They were Cory's people too: She herself was a local, but one who had been away.

It had all changed, massively. Now the dock at the Manitou was buzzing with people any summer day by ten o'clock, with their Tilley hats and their T-shirts with a collar, their carefully battered shorts and water-stained topsiders. Making plans for cocktails, attending aerobics class, picking up their children from tennis, gassing up their big powerboats. Cory's book of Bay photographs was on sale in the gift store. She was part of the local colour.

Everyone had become self-conscious, Cory and Tyke along with the rest. For the benefit of their guests they showed their intimacy with this place. See the Prince Charlie, Charlie Turgeon's fishing boat, pulling back in from the open islands? The Prince Charlie was a sight; you could follow Charlie and his attendant cloud of screaming gulls out to the Umbrellas, the Minks, the Limestones, any of the wave-scrubbed shoals out there and it would be the same as it had been thirty, fifty and hundreds of years before.

Oh yes, they saw it, seagulls wheeling and screaming over it, a home-made wooden boat shaped like a paper hat, painted white, with blue trim. Maida and the New

Yorker listened politely to Tyke's rant. Charlie Turgeon was the last commercial fisherman on the Bay. Because he was not native, but Métis, he had a licence, and as the government was trying to shut him down, they wouldn't let him sell it. He couldn't even pass it down to his son or daughter. All this in favour of the sport fishermen from Michigan and Toronto, who swung up here in season and trolled the bays with oafish determination, coming in so close against the dock that you could read the labels on their beer bottles.

At length, Tyke offered to put Maida's bag down in the studio. She'd get the view at least. It was another addition: a shed with a slanted roof and large window, tables, a sink, and a bed. Cory frowned. She didn't like anyone using her workspace, although she couldn't use it now. The others rose from the corner where they'd been drinking. Only Cory sat, without moving. But she could catch them and hold them back.

"That Kodak," she muttered, as if to herself. "He was the smart one. A suicide at 77. You know what he said? 'Why wait? My work is done.'"

Maida and the young man stopped in alarm.

"Shall I stay? You go —"

"No, wait. Perhaps she'd like to move inside."

Cory felt Tyke's cool glance and was shamed. Shamed and delighted. He knew her, he did. The immense pleasure to be caught out in a trick: That too was something she had almost outlived. She raised her voice and gave them all a wide smile.

"My work is done," she repeated. "But that implied some measurable achievement, and how could I measure my own? What could one say about a lifetime of moments?"

Tyke stepped off a rock to examine a mushroom. It had a rough, red-streaked cap, a heavy yellow sponged underside, and a bulbous stem. A Painted Suilus. Edible. If you were hungry. And they had been sometimes, he and his mother. He put his fingers around the volva, that swelling at the base before the stem divided into its thread-like roots, and pulled it out of the debris of decaying wood and moss where it grew.

Always it was his temptation: to pick the mushroom. There was no real reason to, other than that collector's zeal, the secret greed of those who pretended to nobler, scientific aims. Now that I've disturbed it, he said to himself, I might as well take it inside.

But what for? To show his mother. Hadn't that always been the reason? She had loved to examine his findings, to sometimes photograph them. But he classified them. And he had been the cook. At ten or eleven years old he found out how to soak them in milk to get the tiny worms out, how to batter them in flour, and then fry them in butter. After he'd combed the small forest floor on Safe Harbour he'd gone farther afield, discovering amazing boletes on Dog Island, and the puffballs, oh, the baby puffballs at the back of Nightingale Bay. He'd picked more than he needed, like Cory perhaps, stunned by the wealth, taking more images than she could use.

Tyke was hiding from their guests, at the moment, hoping that Maida in the studio and Joel, the nervous New Yorker in his room, could look after themselves for an hour until dinner. He'd been ambivalent about bringing them up here, but they'd insisted: They needed to see the place, to understand his mother's work. But Safe Harbour was not really his mother's work. It might look like as much: She'd spent most of her life here, after the war, only leaving for side-trips, until he left home and she bought her place in Toronto and began to winter there. She photographed the islands and the water and the rocks in all their moods. But Safe Harbour was, truly, more than a Ditchburn image. It was them, him and her, it was how they were together, it was their life. It was what had been knitted by mother and son, with the absence of father, the absence too of mother for those years. It was what they had made, and what they had left.

How paltry this life had seemed once, how barely enough; how lean and uncertain; how unforgiving. Yet now, as they showed it off — and they did, both of them, the mother and the son, show it off: "See how brave we were, how before our time, how independent, how inventive. Even, how poor. See what style our poverty and isolation bred?" — Now, as they let others in, they betrayed themselves a little. They gave up the past, tore it from their breasts, exhibited it as if it were the scene of some mythic sacrifice. He'd seen visitors look at it that way. But now he too had fallen for the trick of seeing Safe Harbour as a site, an ancient ground where gods and mortals intermingled.

And willingly he did this. What was it Albert said? *We're all for sale in the end.* It was frightening how this man he had never known had entered his life through sayings. *You know what your father would say...* Cory had begun to repeat, years ago.

Tyke walked along the path with a set of yellow magnifying glasses strapped around his face. The glasses were a gift from the last young man, an earnest, horn-rimmed fellow who was working his way up through the bureaucracy of the Department of Heritage. The young man was gone, but the glasses brought the earth, the crumbling logs, the slippery decomposing leaves, pine needles, rocks and lichen closer to him. In an October like this, dry and warm, the mushrooms were plentiful, although not particularly good.

The boletes, for instance, under the large pines, with their spongy bottoms, their full umbrella shape, were still standing, plump and erect and usually in rather distant, standoffish groups. But they were old. The yellow flesh inside the cap, full of holes like the seafoam candy his grandmother used to get for him in Parry Sound so many years ago, was cut through by little worms.

The chanterelles and false chanterelles were just coming out, their beautiful Roman orange like a flare on the mossy hillside on the north side of the island. Not far away were two small pear-shaped puffballs, white with tiny hairlike brown warts. Those he could have for dinner, frighten the guests no end, couldn't he?

They were unbelievably sexual, mushrooms: It must

have been what attracted him to them as a boy. Their parts were like organs, they *were* organs, bloodless but strikingly human. The veil of youth, which grew underneath the cap, to be torn away as the mushroom head swelled upward. The ring. The tiny pleats of gills, which dropped the spores. They were otherworldly things, which appeared, swollen, impudent, and unbidden, and soon dried, crumbled and vanished again. Their vulgarity, their slime and sometimes elegance, their humour, even, delighted him.

He saw, under the little scrub oaks on the hillside, the unnatural white like a signal in the dirt and moss. He squatted. The greenish-white cap glowed peculiarly in the rubble of plant matter from which it poked its head. About ten centimetres in diameter, the fungus was flat-topped, with faint radiating black lines, free gills, and a bulbous base with a white, torn bag as volva. It was a deathcap, *amanita phalloides*, a destroying angel. It was very fresh, the white veil still attached. A button, a young, developing fungus, was nearby. He'd never seen one here before, though he'd found its near relation, the bright orange, white spotted *amanita muscaria*, the toadstool of storybook appearance.

The deadly mushroom was beautiful in its ghastly way.

He stood for a long time, looking at the silent inhabitant of the forest floor, one of the most poisonous growing things known to man. Even the spores were toxic: If you ate the mushroom itself you would vomit, have convulsions, fall into a coma, and likely die. He could either leave the mushroom growing, leave it to blush unseen as the poet said, though it was a very pale blush, or take it. He decided to leave it, but after a few steps, he turned back.

Try though he might, he could not leave the deathcap. Telling himself that he would make spore prints, that he could take some research notes, he picked it up and put it in his bag to carry back to the house, along with the button. Even the greatest poisoner of all had its life, its young, its cycle.

For years he had blamed his mother for the fact that he could not love a woman. He hadn't chosen men so deliberately as he had avoided women, after a while, as too serious a proposition. With men the sex was rougher, more playful, also more dangerous, and he always knew that nothing permanent would come of it. Some men had accused him of being a tourist, of not really being gay, of secret desires to find a woman to marry. This accusation, though correct from time to time, had become more wrong as the years went by. It was unthinkable now that he should become other than what he was, singular. It was a sensible and satisfying state. But it still left room for the Maidas of the world.

Why did he want her, and for what? Taboo, almost: They had become like siblings as she composed the catalogue for the Retrospective. She carried his mother away, named her, classified her. Tyke wanted to take into himself all of what she knew. And more than that. To enjoy the comfort of someone who understood how life had been, for him, with Cory.

He supposed he had spent as many shattered nights in

Marge's cottage behind the Manitou sobbing into the hard mattress as she had on the killing fields of Italy and France. If she was a hero, so was he. And when she had come home, although she loved him, there had been something unbidden in it; it was excessive, proprietary. He understood he was to make up for deaths of various kinds: death of friends, death of faith.

And yet, he had been no less happy than other children, the Pamajongs, even the children of the rich cottagers. He lived in a beautiful place, and he had been privileged to grow up in proximity to an extraordinary woman. "Mother" had not been her greatest role, that was all. There were women like this, as, God knew, there are men for whom to be a father is of little interest.

And anyway, the young woman who had hurt him was gone. In her place was someone else, someone fragile. His girlfriends used to get angry with him because he protected her. He could hurt her now, he knew that; he could explode her precious serenity by revealing his wounds, by venting the pain, teasing her with tales of his perverse habits. But there seemed to be no point.

For dinner Tyke made fish kebabs with zucchini and red pepper. Cory made the rice. When they put their forks in the large cube of salmon it split into firm, flat pink pieces, sweet and rich and moist.

"We used to eat pickerel," said Cory.

"When we were hungry, I'd just go and sit in the boat till I caught something."

"It wasn't so bad in summer. But in winter I worried about you in that little hut on the ice with the men."

"I didn't mind catching it. It was coming home and having to cook it too."

"That's nonsense. I cooked."

All these remarks were thrown as scraps to a dog. Cory ate methodically, lost in the process; she had little small talk at the best of times, but eating took her into herself. Tyke's fingers, blunt and sensitive, lifted slightly from the metal of his fork and knife, as if he were sensing, testing the air like an insect with antennae. At the end of the meal he removed the plates and she looked up. His was the face of a man fully himself, ripe with wit and subterfuge, enjoying what was his in the life that had been theirs. Dutiful son was the mask he wore, and not an unpleasant one, as masks went.

After dinner Cory wanted to sit in the dark and watch the night.

"Don't turn the lights on. Don't you see what they do? They lock you in. They make the windows into mirrors. You can't see the moon or the stars. Turn it off!"

Maida, Tyke and Joel were thus turned out into the studio sleeping porch, to play cards. Three tatty wicker chairs, which looked as if a cat had been sharpening her nails on them, faced the dark lake in the general direction of the vortex of light and cloud left where the sun had been. To their right, out of the line of vision, the dark bulk of the cabin rested. The crickets chirped. The wind from the open tore at the tops of the trees, then abandoned them, and then tore at them again. Water chucked against a rock, withdrew, then rushed back invisibly, to give its throaty, frog-like sounds.

Then another sound came in on a trajectory, direct, fast. A boat that you could not see.

"Someone's in a hurry."

"How can they see?"

Around through the gap came a blue light, steadily beating its way across their place of vision.

"Oh, it's Jimmy, " said Tyke. "Jimmy knows what he's doing."

Then they heard the boat draw up to the dock. No questions were asked.

Cory didn't get down the dock to help Jimmie tie up as she used to do. She would greet him casually, in full view of anyone who might be passing, anyone who might be curious about Jimmy and his old friend, Cory Ditchburn, about what had become of them since he'd married and had all those kids and grandkids.

He came into the porch where he knew he'd find her.

"Got up here one more time before winter, did you?"

He kissed her. The pressure sent a message of pleasure down through her gullet, and she thought of the salmon Tyke had left on the kitchen counter, entrails removed, and that heart-shaped cage of bones inside it.

They sat like that, lips together, moving, their ears and eyes tuned to the night.

"Seems a shame not to take advantage of the setting," he murmured.

His body was hard, the skin dry and roughened, and he was careful, of himself and of her. A man of eighty-five — and her last lover. There was no one more dignified than Jimmy. His chest was like the chest of a boy, smooth and almost without hair. She put her face to where his heart must be. The taste of his sweat was sweet to her lips. And she remembered what Albert used to say all those years ago, that every time he made love he knew it might be his last.

"You see now," Cory repeated at breakfast.

"See what?" said Joel. He had terrific bags under his eyes, as if he hadn't slept at all.

"See how the walls close me in down in the city? What is there of significance? A line of cars on Church Street — what do I care? I don't know who is in them or where they are going. But here — every boat, I know. I see Hypolyte Trudeau go by every morning on his way to the Bertons to work. And I will see him come back again at the same time tonight. If I don't, then I can start thinking about why he's late."

"Terrible wind, wasn't that?" he said.

"Was it?" said Cory absently. "I suppose."

"And there was some animal running on the roof."

"Red squirrel."

They looked out the window. There was Maida, her plump form balanced on little wedge sandals, ascending the large mound of rock and moss on which stood the flagpole, with Tyke in front of her, reaching out his hand to help her up. Chris, as he preferred to be called. And why not? He was a man of fifty-five. Handing up a woman onto a rock. Helping out, being there to assist, his quickness and cleverness all in attendance — how useful he'd been, how she had depended on him. He'd never gone away.

While his mother watched, Tyke caught Maida's forearm — the hand not being enough to balance her — and swung her onto the top of the rock. They teetered side by side. He was showing her the writing at the foot of the flagpole.

It had been going to say Home from Away or perhaps it was Home for Good, but they got tired of scratching and the rock was not large enough and finally — because Cory hated redundancy — Home seemed to say it all. Lichen had encroached on it, and one particularly rainy summer a patch of grass had taken root.

On this island
Cory Ditchburn and Chris Ditchburn,
September, 1945.
Home.

Chapter Thirty-Five

Her son has photographed the photographer at eighty-five with a camera held up to her right eye, the left eye narrowed like a marksman's. The camera acts as an eye-patch or a masking, effectively removing one side of her face; the visible, right side is impassive, unsmiling. Her thick white hair springs upward in a shot wave, leaving a shadow on the wall behind her. The light is merciless and unromantic, as if the man who took this photograph has refused to shield his mother in her old age, but wishes her to be exposed to the same objective scrutiny under which all her subjects fell.

⁊ᴥ

THEY ENTERED IN THE DAZZLE OF THE CAMERA LIGHTS. MAIDA moved forward, offering her hand. The way his mother looked at her he knew what she was thinking, "The

Flounder approaches." Cory was in a dangerous mood. Tyke knew it from the moment he picked her up. His mother was dressed in the pencil-thin black pants that had become her signature, with an antique lace blouse and a black blazer. Her hair was washed and still damp, its white curls standing at the crown, and clipped tight to her nape. She looked sixty-five, not eighty-five.

"Congratulations! It's your night," Maida said to Cory.

Tyke stood between them, holding one hand of each. It was done, he thought. Cory had not made it easy for them. She had held on to her treasures, taunting, teasing, wanting and not wanting to be understood, to be found out, to be followed. She had exiled herself, first across an ocean, and then by living on an island. One of the privileges of exile was to invent one's story, as she did, plant it, deny it, conceal and finally reveal it, in the form of one's choice.

Yes, self-invention was the privilege, and perhaps the purpose of exile. You go away, and you cut the traces; you leave people in one country, take up with people in another; you see your life, as Cory did, as a series of shouts and salvaged moments. Then you can't be checked, and you can't be captured. In this way she had maintained control.

Tyke saw their Retrospective, mounted, consecutive, resplendent, and wondered: Had they told a true story? Yes. It was a true story, but not the only one: A thousand others might have been similarly composed.

Room One: early work — first London photographs, Albert, Tyke as a baby in Parry Sound, the munitions factory. Room Two: war — courtesy the *Express*, and Orestes Hrudy. Room Three: everything since — rock, water, tree, clouds. Final antechamber: the self-portraits. Including the new one: Corinne Ditchburn at eighty-five.

Cory felt the trace of the cameras on her. In the crowded room she was suddenly in empty space, distanced from the others; she was out in the open again. To be faced with her photographs, all at once, was too much like dying. There was the silence, the whiteness, and the stillness; a sense of completion. An absence of desire.

No, Cory chided herself: Now she sounded like Albert. It was not like dying, exactly. It was more like being set down in that train car so many times prefigured, on that train which never arrived, where one came face to face with all the important visions one had while living, each in its frame.

Here they were, each frozen gesture representing a fraction of a second, totalling less than a minute, out of eighty-five years. Cory's eyes were not up to it. She saw, in what must have been the war room, great blocks of light and shade, falling bodies, and rising clouds. Soldiers at play, with a desperate larkiness in their faces. Then the clamour of memory unnerved her and she moved on: In the later rooms were serenity, granite's heave, and the delicacy of lichen. The real people of her life.

"Miss Ditchburn, come this way, please." The technician handed her a wire to put up her shirt and clip the tiny microphone to her collar. The interviewer was called Jill.

She was coloured like a peacock, with sleek red hair, a turquoise suit and purple lipstick. Regarding herself momentarily on the monitor she grimaced, attempting to scrub the sticky colour off her teeth. Then she faced Cory, a smile pasted on. She held the microphone, a black egg on a stick, in front of Cory's mouth, licked her lips and took a signal from a cameraman. Go. Her first question was about being a recluse. Jill wondered how Cory felt, bringing her personal imagery forward.

"Mortified," said Cory decisively. "It's as if the work has suddenly become dirty. Maybe it's not good enough. I want to keep it for myself."

Jill's alert face sprang to a smile. "I'd have thought you'd be over that by now. In your long career —"

Cory hated the word career. She grimaced. "Absolutely not. I never got over it. It was like lifting my skirt and taking money for a glimpse at private parts of me."

JILL: (look of consternation) Not really!
CORY: Yes, really. I did it all for myself, you know. I hated to give up any of them.
JILL: Even though you could make another.
CORY: That's a fallacy. Every print is unique. I couldn't repeat a single one.
JILL: (working harder) I suppose for you as well as for us, this retrospective is an opportunity to see your work in perspective, to reflect on your youth...
CORY: But what is a retrospective? You can't know when you're thirty-five what you will know at eighty-five. You

can no more easily know at eighty what you were at thirty-five. If you try to present all this in the light of hindsight, it's distorted. My mother used to quote Alexander Pope: "In vain the Sage with Retrospective Eye, would from the apparent What conclude the Why." Do you understand?

JILL: (looking doubtful) Could you explain that?

CORY: We see better at the split second when the light flashes. Everything is let loose then, it floats before our eyes and we understand the world. Time will only blur and confuse us, don't you see? The instant gives us the flash of insight into the heart of life.

JILL: Still, you must look at some of the old photographs, I mean the photographs you took when you were very young and —

CORY: There's no chronology to them. None of them are "old" or "young." There are simply objects. They have no history for me. I can be as surprised when I look at my early work as much as I can by anyone else's images.

JILL: But we cannot look at this magnificent array ... without thinking about your life.

CORY: As for my life, there was war and there was Albert. People know that. Nothing else is of interest.

JILL: Of course, it wouldn't seem so to you, having lived it, but don't you see your life is a model, perhaps, for women in that era —

CORY: God, no. I did what I had to. Why would anyone else want to live like that?

JILL: You were the first, you did a lot for women —

CORY: Perhaps. I never thought about it. I'm sorry. I won't be very helpful if you take this line of inquiry.

JILL: You mentioned the painter, Albert Bloom. He was your mentor?

CORY: He was my lover. I would call him an anti-mentor. He showed me how not to be.

JILL: What do you mean?

CORY: I wanted to be an artist. I grafted myself onto him. Then I outgrew him, and the battle was bloody. I don't think this kind of thing goes out of fashion.

JILL: Why an anti-mentor?

CORY: He was dangerous. Also, he became everything I disliked. I only had to look at him to see. It's very important, you know, to have these bad examples in our life. It took me a while before I learned to follow some of his advice and reject other parts of it. When I learned to see with my own eyes, I had enough.

It's like the poison we take to put light in our lives.

And besides, I loved him. Do you understand? It's not what should be, is it? I should have followed someone who wanted nothing but the best for me. But that's too easy. I'm afraid we don't work that way.

JILL: How much did Albert mean to you?

CORY: I talked to him all my life and then he died and I talked to the silence he left.

JILL: There are a number of other famous faces here amongst your photographs — Lord Beaverbrook, for one.

CORY: Famous faces are not interesting! It's only the photograph that's interesting. If I made anything of my work, it was because I was an outsider. I was born in a log cabin at Pointe au Baril —

JILL: The island is certainly part of the mythology. But in England you played with the rich and famous. Some people say you owe your chances to powerful men.

CORY: Who says?

JILL: I suppose the feminists.

CORY: Are you asking, was I a man's woman? Yes. I was very much in favour of men at the time. Everyone was. Men were fighting the war and getting themselves killed. We needed them to be brave.

JILL: What was war like?

CORY: War is a mistake. Within it, there are many more mistakes, but they don't matter. You can't have a mistake within a mistake.

JILL: (persisting) Can you say what it did to you?

CORY: What it did to me? No, I can't say. Some people loved war. It opened their eyes. A blind man can't see a candle but he might know a bonfire is near. But they were never the same after, either; peace was just a blur. I wasn't one of them. I survived because of my camera. It protected me. I believed that.

JILL: And do you still believe it?

CORY: Yes. I do. I needed that camera. In the black arts, you know, the dilemma is to stay outside the action. It's like the television reporter who stands beside the earthquake victim to give his reportage. The victim is half-naked and covered in slime. All we notice is that the reporter's trench-coat is unwrinkled. That's inhuman. But he has to be, to practise the black arts. Compassion has to be for the general, not the specific. No, I don't mean with a capital G. I hated the capital G Generals!

JILL: Did you hope your work would help stop the war?

CORY: I did at the time. "A powerful force for the public good," and all that. But no. War makes an excellent subject. It's "a strong life." Did my photographs do anything to discourage more war? I doubt it. Now I agree with what William James said eighty years ago. "Showing war's irrationality is of no effect." We grow accustomed to this, too.

JILL: Perhaps the most moving part of the exhibition is the final room, your series of self-portraits, each very different: you in pregnancy, in uniform with your camera, and now, in your eighties. How does it feel to see them now?

CORY: They're like people I knew once. But I don't know them any more. They're dead.

JILL: Miss Ditchburn, your career, after the war, more or less levelled off. You disappeared to your island. Since then you've rarely travelled. Can you explain?

CORY: You know I fucked up, in the war? Don't you? I was thrown out, with Reg Morris. I never got to Dachau. I did not feel I'd been useful. I had a son to raise. After the war there was no place for me in the world we'd made. And I'd seen too much of people. Rocks and water, patterns and lines, that was what I wanted. I'd finished with Europe. I wanted a new art in a new place. As it turned out it was my country.

JILL: Has it been a good life?

CORY: It's been the right life. I loved my work. And a few people, too. I even managed that, which was, you know, a triumph. It's just that when I came out from behind my camera and let myself be known, it was pretty well always a mistake.

JILL: (gratified smile) Thank you, Corinne Ditchburn. For giving us a little of your story —

Jill signalled to her camera: That was a wrap.

Cory began again. "At the end of the day —"

Jill waved frantically. The retreating camera began to roll again toward Cory, and on the screen of the little monitor, her face grew large. "There's only one story. And it's my story too. A light goes out, the moment someone dies."

Tyke's eyes pricked with tears. What story ends, there, in that eclipse of the bright, electric energy that is one person and only that person? What long trail of chances and trials and decisions and strokes of luck and evil that make up a lifetime?

The television crew were congratulating each other. They were through with Cory. But she was still talking. She turned to Tyke, her only real audience.

"The light goes out," she said. "I saw the light around his body when Albert died. I swear it came to me over the Atlantic. I felt the light of my mother go out, too, and I felt her balm settle over me. I know this to be true."

The camera stopped. That spotlight, which had been blinding, was now gone. Things appeared to be as they were before, but they weren't, because something had been taken away. There was silence, a kind of standing back. There would be questions but Cory was gone. She was on Georgian Bay. It was a windy day in late July.

The sky is what Tyke calls topless blue. The wind has ripped away the veils, and the colours are so vivid they seem to spring from another dimension, from imagination. But it is not the light of the Mediterranean, not European light at all. It is not that Greek light, which floods everything without discrimination, cradle-of-civilization light, a searchlight, a beam that lays down its shadows in blocks and turns blue electric and blinds a sailor striking out to sea.

No, and it is not Italian light, diffused, powdered gold, which licks all colours up to their most lavish, like a cat's tongue on velvet. Not the light of old masters, sepia and subtle and flattering. Not, especially not, English light, that watery embracing softness, or the orange that filtered over London, dear beloved London, at dusk.

It is none of these lights. It is northern light, new-world light, all the more beautiful for its coolness and distance. There is nothing sentimental in this light, nothing to flatter. Its shadows are definite. It makes nothing beautiful that is not already so. It shows a tree or a face to be what it is. I said unsentimental but sometimes, just occasionally, like now, it has that touch of rue.

In the afternoon, when the shadows lengthen, this light becomes piercing, almost unbearably so. Ordinary objects seem to jump out of the landscape at you, and nothing is left to lie. This is the light that I tried to catch. It makes the water transparent to such a depth that you put your hands in front of your head when you dive, though the bottom is twelve feet down.

I so fear you there, on that fucking primeval photogenic island —

"Miss Ditchburn, Miss Ditchburn —"

But Cory was gone. She was out there in the open, in her canoe, writing to Albert.

Dear Albert —

That sound, the fullness, "roar" as it is most often called, of water, is not a roar. It is a huge soft sound made of a million smaller sounds, most like the noise of an expectant crowd, soft, unceasing, swelling. Over it, the high whirr of some nearby insect penetrates my ear, the peep of some nesting bird, the breath of a errant wind over the bulge of the rock bringing the odour of baked cedar to my nostrils.

Out there, riff after riff of rock, a small deep blue-green channel of water between each, and the hard yellow broom-like weed, the pink, crushable wild rose. That's all.

I am lying on granite; it's hot against my stomach. The landscape looks so empty from even six feet above but here at water level it is full, chock-full. There is no room even for my observations which is why I consign them to you this way. This is more 'scape than land, less land than a surfeit of energy beating against shores.

Did you know you must head directly into the wind when paddling alone? On my way out here in the canoe, I nearly lost it. I let the bow turn a few degrees and then the wind and the water caught me and turned me broadside. I would have done a full circle, losing precious hundreds of feet too, had I not managed to get into the lee of a small island, by leaning desperately into the paddle, and clattering ignominiously over the rocks.

A couple of fishermen, facing each other silently in their red plaid shirts, were anchored not far away. I could hear what they were thinking. *Crazy woman. Alone. There she goes in that hat. What's she trying to prove?*

I'm out of their sight now. I lie in a stone gully, my face close to a crevice, somehow a bit of soil has collected here, caught out of the way of the wind and the water. A dead cedar grows upright like a tortured menorah, stripped and bleached. Around me rocks are piled, scattered, strewn, a rubble of them, a poor man's field.

I walk, leaping the cracks, the potholes, out along the miles of flat rock that now tend to the north-west, following their pink and charcoal stripe. Here is the giant pine, its roots gone in through the cracks. I take a broken-off chip of rock and dig *down, but they give no way. They are thin roots, divided, no one of them is worth anything on its own, but the loss of any one would destroy this tree.*

A Monarch butterfly, savage orange and black, is here and then like a leaf turns sideways to disappear. Walking with a stick in case of rattlesnakes, I look straight down at the rock in bright sun. Coral. Pearl. Silver. Garnet. The stripe of milky quartz that sometimes glitters.

Albert, remember at the end when I said, for two cents I'd throw this ticket away and never get on the boat at all. And you said, for one cent I'd go after you... And then we went ahead and followed our plans, like dumb animals down the ramp to loading, and left each other. It is going to be awful. It is going to be very very bad.

I do not know the where of you, even the when. It seems an unnecessary insult that it is not even the same time of day in England as it is here, you've gone way past tea-time now and may even be lying down to bed, your eyes all tired out, your pants lying rumpled across the chair.

Now I hear the choking explosion of the motor-boat starting. The fishermen are gone. I lie flat on my back in the indentation where my canoe has fit. I look at the clouds. And all I can think of is why aren't you here, how can you exist, halfway across this continent and then the ocean too, how can you be there and not here. I want you to see what I'm seeing—

Acknowledgments

WHEN I BEGAN TO WRITE THIS NOVEL, LITTLE DID I REALIZE how many fine accounts of Britain in the late thirties, and especially in the years of the Second World War, existed. To understand civilian life I read widely, and forgot almost as widely, hoping to leave myself with an impression of that time that might approximate the memory of one who had lived through it. I gained an overview of military action through reading *The History of the Second World War* by B. H. Liddell Hart. Among the war books whose facts fed my imagination are Mary Lee Settle's *All the Brave Promises*, Martha Gellhorn's *The Face of War* and Margaret Bourke-White's *The Taste of War*. Two individual Canadian experiences of the Second World War are brilliantly conveyed in *Journal of a War* by Donald Pearce, and *My Father's Son* and *And No Birds Sang* by Farley Mowat.

I made use of many institutions, whose collections were opened to me by helpful individuals. The knowledgeable Hugh Halliday, at the National War Museum in Ottawa, walked me through many war artists' paintings, which hang cheek to jowl in back rooms. I must also thank Peter Robertson, at the National Archives in Ottawa, whose expertise in military photography was of great use; similarly, Theresa MacIntosh shared her research for Carleton

University's Institute of Canadian Studies on women war artists. Sonya Noble, at the *Toronto Star* library, helped me through the microfiche jungle to discover the reportage of two great *Star* war correspondents, Frederick Griffin and Matthew Halton. I spent a week in the stacks of the London Library as well as several days in the McLaughlin Gallery in Oshawa, Ontario.

Many private individuals also were of great help as I wrote this novel. I would like to thank the late veteran Charles Magee, who joined me for lunch at Swiss Chalet, loaned me his books, and told me his stories. Mrs. Edwina Vardey of Leatherhead, Surrey, was helpful to the point of joining me in an unsanctioned prowl around Cherkley Court. Michael Hall, the architectural editor of *Country Life*, Rod Currie, Sandra Gwyn, and others helped me capture some particular facets of history that I needed.

I would like to especially acknowledge the help of local historians John Macfie, of Parry Sound, and John L. Armstrong, of Nepean, who saw the drama in their part of Canada long before I did. The title "Angel Walk" was suggested to me by Mr. Armstrong's *History*. Mr. Armstrong and Mr. Macfie were part of the trail that led me to W. M. (Bill) McDonald, who was a welder at the Defence Industries Plant in Nobel. Mr. McDonald explained to me, not once but twice, how he designed a machine to defuse the landmines. As well, Marian McIsaacs spent an afternoon with me reminiscing about her job at the Defence Industries Limited factory in Nobel.

Finally, I was privileged to spend a couple of hours with

the novelist and former war correspondent Martha Gellhorn, whose succinct and powerful ideas swept away many of the assertions of official war historians. My friend Barbara Nettleton made a wonderful reader for the manuscript, Greg Ioannou and Marjan Farahbaksh were invaluable editors, and Kim McArthur's faith and boundless enthusiasm have come to feel essential.